Val McDermid is an international number one bestselling author whose books have been translated into more than forty languages and sold over eighteen milli... multi-award-w... novels have bee... and radio, most notably th... *in the Blood* series featuring clinical psychologist Dr Tony Hill and DCI Carol Jordan, and ITV's *Karen Pirie* series.

Val was chair of the Wellcome Book Prize in 2017 and has served as a judge for both the Women's Prize for Fiction and the 2018 Man Booker Prize. She is the recipient of six honorary doctorates and is an Honorary Fellow of St Hilda's College, Oxford. She is a visiting professor in the Centre of Irish and Scottish Studies at the University of Otago in New Zealand. Among her many awards are the CWA Diamond Dagger recognising life-time achievement and the Theakston's Old Peculier award for Outstanding Contribution to Crime Writing. Val is also an experienced broadcaster and much-sought-after columnist and commentator across print media.

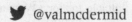 valmcdermid

@valmcdermid

THE
SKELETON ROAD

VAL McDERMID

SPHERE

SPHERE

First published in Great Britain in 2014 by Little, Brown
This paperback edition published in 2015 by Sphere

21 23 25 27 29 31 30 28 26 24 22

A CIP catalogue record for this book is
available from the British Library.

ISBN 978-0-7515-5128-0

Typeset in Meridien by M Rules
Printed and bound in Great Britain by
Clays Ltd, Elcograf S.p.A.

Papers used by Sphere are from well-managed forests
and other responsible sources.

Sphere
An imprint of
Little, Brown Book Group
Carmelite House
50 Victoria Embankment
London EC4Y 0DZ

An Hachette UK Company
www.hachette.co.uk

www.littlebrown.co.uk

For my Jo:

'But this dedication is for others to read:
These are private words addressed to you in public.'

Geography is about power. Although often assumed to be innocent, the geography of the world is not a product of nature but a product of histories of struggle between competing authorities over the power to organise, occupy and administer space.

Critical Geopolitics
Gearóid Ó Tuathail

Prologue

Sunset is often a glamorous business in the Cretan holiday harbour of Chania. Reflections of gold and red and pink splash along the hulls of the day-tripper boats, the mid-price yachts and the cabin cruisers. The historic walls of the outer harbour loom solid against the fragile sky like shadows projected on a screen, and the quaysides are languid with tourists making their leisurely way from pavement artist to jewellery stall, from restaurant to souvenir shop.

Around the harbour, buildings crowd higgledy-piggledy back into the town, some staggering up the hillside, some crammed together like Roman tenements. Holiday flats and retirement homes look down on the swarm of boats and people, streaked with the sun's last lazy rays.

At one of the outside tables, a man sits watching the tourists, his face expressionless, the remains of a large seven-star Metaxa in front of him. In his early sixties, by the looks of him. Broad-shouldered and a few kilos overweight. He's wearing dark navy shorts and a bottle green polo shirt that shows off muscular forearms tanned the colour of his drink. He's wearing tinted glasses that are noticeably more fashionable than the rest of his outfit. His silver hair is cropped close to his head and he has a heavy moustache which he wipes with the back of his hand from time to time. It's a gesture he completes more often than his drinking requires; as if perhaps the moustache is something he's self-conscious about. It's the only thing about him that betrays the appearance of absolute self-possession.

He is completely unaware that he is being watched, which is surprising because he has the air of a watchful man.

He finishes his drink, wipes his mouth one last time then gets to his feet. He walks along the quayside with a firm step. People move out of his way, but not fearfully. With respect, it looks like. Only a couple of metres behind him there's another presence. A shadow, taking advantage of the crowds to stay close on his heels.

A few streets back from the harbour, the man turns into a narrow side road. He casts a swift look around, then heads into a modern apartment building. Not too smart, not too cheap. Just the sort of place a retired history teacher would buy to enjoy the Cretan way of life. And that's exactly what his neighbours think he is.

The watcher slips into the building behind him and silently climbs the stairs in his wake. Stealth is second nature in this line of work and tonight is no exception. A blade slides from its sheath without a sound. Sits balanced in the hand, waiting. So sharp it could split a sheet of paper.

The man stops in front of the door to his apartment, key already in hand, prepared for a quick entry. He slots the key into the lock and turns it, pushing the door open. He's about to step across the threshold when a voice indecently close to him says a name he hasn't heard in years. Shocked, he begins to turn around, moving into his flat as he goes.

But he's too late. Without hesitation, the blade moves in a gleaming arc and slices the man's throat from ear to ear. Blood gushes and spurts, splashing a different red over the door and the walls and the floor.

By the time he's finished dying, his assassin is back among the tourists, heading for a bar and a well-deserved drink. A seven-star Metaxa, perhaps. And a toast to the single death that doesn't begin to atone for all those other deaths.

1

Fraser Jardine wanted to die. His stomach was knotted tight, his bowels in the twisted grip of panic. A teardrop of sweat trickled down his left temple. The voice in his head sneered at his weakness, just as it had since boyhood. Biting his lip in shame, Fraser forced open the skylight and pushed it outwards. He climbed up the last three steps on the ladder one at a time and gingerly emerged on the pitched roof.

Never mind that tourists would have paid for this sensational view of a city classified as a World Heritage Site. All Fraser cared about was how far he was from the ground.

He'd never liked heights. As a child, he'd done his best to avoid the tall slide in the park. The vertiginous stairs that clanged like some ominous tolling bell with every step. The cold rail clammy under his sweating palm. The smell of sweat and metal that made him feel he was going to throw up. (And how terrible that would have been, projecting a rain of multicoloured vomit over the kids and parents below.) But sometimes there had been no escape. He'd stood on the tiny metal platform at the top, a melting sensation in his bladder, the knowledge that wetting his pants was too close for comfort. Then he'd shut his eyes, drop on to his backside and hurtle down, refusing to look again till he shuttled off the end of the shiny metal strip into the hard-packed sand beyond. Skinning his knees felt like a blessing; it meant he was back in touch with solid ground.

That lifelong terror of high places had been his only reservation when he'd been considering his choice of career. Surely a demolition quantity surveyor couldn't avoid going out on roofs from time to time? You couldn't ignore the fact that some structures might pose dangers for the crew itself or add extra costs to the job. He wasn't stupid; he'd asked about it specifically at the careers fair. The man representing the building trade had made light of it, claiming it was a rare occurrence. Fraser had been three months into his training period before he'd understood the careers advisor hadn't had a clue what he was talking about. But the job market was crap, especially if you were a young man with a moderate degree from an indifferent university. So he'd bitten the bullet and stayed put.

Over the past six years he'd become adept at figuring out which upcoming jobs would present the worst prospects, then neatly managing to sidestep them. Too busy with another assessment; a dental appointment for a troublesome molar; a training course he needed to attend. He'd turned avoidance into a fine art and, as far as he was aware, nobody had noticed.

But that morning – and a Saturday morning too, just to add insult to injury – his boss had sprung this on him. A rush job for a new client they wanted to impress. And everybody else already committed elsewhere. The job of checking out the Victorian Gothic battlements, turrets and pinnacles of the John Drummond School had dropped on Fraser's steel-capped toes.

Dry-mouthed, hands slippery with sweat inside his work gloves, he crab-walked cautiously down the steep pitch of the slates. 'It could be worse,' he said aloud as he automatically checked out the state of the roof, noting gaps where slates had slipped from their moorings or disappeared altogether. 'It could be much worse. It could be raining. It could be like a bloody fucking ice rink.' The fake cheer wouldn't have fooled his two-year-old daughter. It certainly didn't fool Fraser.

The trick was to keep breathing, slow and steady. That, and not to look down. Never to look down.

He gained the relative safety of the shallow lead-lined gutter behind the crenellated perimeter wall and concentrated on the task before him. 'It's only a wall. It's only a wall,' he muttered. 'A pretty fucking crappy wall,' he added as he noted the crumbling mortar. The pressure on his bladder increased as he contemplated how weather-weakened

7

the structure had become. There was no way of detecting that damage from below. What else was lying in wait for him on this decaying bloody roof?

Fraser had driven past the John Drummond countless times, marvelling at the fact that from a distance it still looked as impressive as ever, even after standing empty for the best part of twenty years. It was an Edinburgh land-mark, its elaborate facade impressively dominating what amounted to a small park beside one of the southbound arterial roads. For years, the sheer scale of any redevelop-ment of the abandoned private school had daunted developers. But the exponential expansion of the city's student population had created more pressure on accom-modation and more profits for developers with the nerve to go for major projects.

And so Fraser was stuck on this decaying roof on a cold Saturday morning. He began making his tentative way round the perimeter, dividing his attention between the parapet and the roof, dictating occasional notes into the voice-activated recorder clipped to his hi-vis tabard. When he came to the first of the tall mock-Gothic pinnacles that stood at each corner of the roof, he paused, assessing it care-fully. It was about four metres high, not much more than a metre in diameter at its base, rising in a steep cone to its apex. The exterior was decorated with extravagant stone carvings. Why would you do that, Fraser wondered. Even the Victorians must have had better ways to spend their money. So why would you choose that? All that over-the-top detail where nobody was ever going to see it up close, balls and curlicues stark against the sky. Some had fallen off over the years. Luckily nobody had been standing underneath when that had happened. At roof level, there was a small arch in the stonework, presumably to provide access to the interior of the pinnacle. Access for the youngest and smallest of the mason's apprentices, Fraser reckoned. He doubted he could even get his shoulders through the widest span of the arch. Still, he really should take a look.

He lay down in the gutter, switched on the head torch on his hard hat and edged forward. Once his head was inside, he was able to make a surprisingly good assessment of the interior. The floor was covered with herringbone brick; the interior walls were brick, sagging slightly in places where the mortar had crumbled away, but held in place by the weight pressing down from above. A bundle of feathers in one corner marked where a pigeon had lost the battle with its own stupidity. The air was tainted with an acrid whiff that Fraser attributed to whatever vermin had visited the building. Rats, bats, mice. Whatever.

Satisfied that there was nothing else of note, Fraser backed out and eased himself to his feet. He tugged his tabard straight and continued his inspection. Second side. Second turret. Don't look down. Third side. A section of crenellated parapet so decayed it appeared to be held together by faith alone. Happy that there was nobody there to see the drips of sweat falling from the back of his hair, Fraser got down on his hands and knees and crawled past the danger zone. That wall would have to be taken down first before it came down on its own. Down. Christ, even the word made him feel faint this far up.

The third pinnacle loomed like a place of safety. Still on his hands and knees, Fraser switched on the head torch again and thrust his head inside the access arch. This time, what he saw made him rear up so abruptly that he smacked his head on the back of the arch, sending his hard hat tumbling across the floor, the beam of light careering around madly before it finally rocked itself still.

Fraser whimpered. At last he'd found something on a roof that was scarier than the height. Grinning at him across the brickwork was a skull, lying on a scatter of bones that had clearly once been a human being.

2

'You're joking me, right?' Detective Chief Inspector Karen Pirie craned her head back and stared up at the corner pinnacle high above. 'They're not seriously expecting me to go foutering around on the roof of a building that's technically condemned? All for the sake of a skeleton?'

Detective Constable Jason 'the Mint' Murray looked dubiously at the roofline, then back at his boss. She could see the wheels going round. *Too fat, too stechie, too much of a liability.* But thick as he undoubtedly was, the Mint had learned some sense under Karen's wing. Though he'd have struggled to spell the words, over the years he'd acquired the rudiments of discretion. 'I don't understand how this is ours anyway,' was what he said. 'I mean, how is it a cold case when they only found him this morning?'

'Just for the record, we don't know for sure that it's a him.

Not till somebody who knows about bones takes a look. For another thing . . . Jason, who do you work for?'

The Mint looked puzzled. It was his default expression. 'Police Scotland,' he said, his tone that of a man stating the obvious but who knows that nevertheless he's going to get stiffed.

'More specifically, Jason.' Karen was happily building up to the stiffing.

'I work for you, boss.' He looked momentarily pleased with himself.

'And what do I do?'

There were many possible answers, but none of them seemed appropriate to the Mint. 'You're the boss, boss.'

'And what am I the boss of?'

'Cold cases.' He was confident now.

Karen sighed. 'But what's the actual name of our unit?'

Light dawned. 'HCU. Historic Cases Unit.'

'And that's why it's ours. If it's been up there long enough to be a skeleton, we get the short straw.' Stiffing completed, Karen turned her attention back to the man in the hard hat and hi-vis tabard hovering next to her. 'I take it we're talking about a confined space up there?'

Fraser Jardine's head bobbed up and down like a nodding donkey on fast forward. 'Totally. You'd struggle to get two of you in there.'

'And the approach to it? Is that pretty restricted as well?'

Fraser frowned. 'What? You mean narrow?'

Karen nodded. 'That, yeah. But also, like, how many approaches are there? Is it just one obvious way in and out?'

'Well, it's on a corner, so I suppose theoretically you could come at it from either side. When you climb out from the skylight on to the roof, if you go left, it would be the second wee tower you come to. I'd started off going to the right so it was the third one I got to.'

'And these approaches,' said Karen, 'I take it they're open to the elements? The wind and the rain?'

'It's a roof. That kind of goes with the territory.' He gave a sharp sigh. 'Sorry, I don't mean to be a smartarse. I'm just a bit shaken up. And my boss, he's like, "Is this going to hold you up doing your estimates?" So I'm kind of under pressure, you know?'

Karen patted his upper arm. Even through his overalls, she could feel hard muscle. A man like Fraser, he'd have no trouble carting a body up to a roof pinnacle. It could narrow the suspect field down a fair bit, a crime scene like this. If the victim had died somewhere else. 'I appreciate that. What's the building like inside? Did you see any signs that someone else had been there before you?'

Fraser shook his head. 'Not that I could see. But I don't know how easy it would be to tell. It's pretty messed up inside there. It's been a long time since they sealed the place up and the weather's got in. So you've got damp and mould and plants growing out the walls. I don't know how long it

13

takes to turn into a skeleton, but I'm guessing it would be a few years?'

'Pretty much.' She spoke with more confidence than she felt.

'So if a whole team of guys had been through there years ago, you'd never know. Nature takes over and rubs out the traces we leave behind. Sometimes it only takes a few months and you'd hardly know it was a place where people lived or worked.' He shrugged. 'So it's no surprise I didn't see any footprints or bloodstains or anything.'

'But you did see a hole in the skull?' Move them around, don't let them get comfortable with the narrative. Karen was good at keeping interviews shifting away from solid ground.

Fraser swallowed hard and did the head bobbing again, his momentary confidence chased away. 'Right about here,' he said, pointing to his forehead above the middle of his right eyebrow. 'Not a huge hole, not much bigger than a shirt button really.'

Karen gave an encouraging nod. 'Not very dramatic, I know. But it's enough. What about clothes? Did you notice if there were any clothes on the body or on the ground?'

Fraser shook his head. 'To be honest, I wasn't really look-ing at anything else, just the skull.' He shivered. 'That's going to give me fucking nightmares.' He glanced at her, guilty. 'Sorry. Excuse the French.'

Karen smiled. 'I've heard a lot worse.' She reckoned Fraser Jardine had nothing useful to add to his dramatic discovery. There were more important conversations for her to have now. She turned back to the Mint. There wasn't much damage he could do with a witness whose contribution to the inquiry was so limited. 'Jason, sit Mr Jardine down in the car and take a full statement.'

As soon as the Mint had led Fraser out of earshot, Karen was on the phone to the duty Crime Scene Manager. Karen had worked often with Gerry McKinlay and knew she wouldn't have to spell out every detail that she wanted covered. These days, it felt like chasing villains came second to balancing the books. Some of the CSMs demanded requisitions in triplicate for every task they undertook. Karen understood the reasoning but the delay to the investigation was always infuriating. 'What's your problem?' one CSM had challenged her. 'The bodies you deal with, they're a long time dead. A few days here or there isn't going to make any difference.'

'You tell that to the grieving,' Karen had snapped back. 'Every day is a long time for them. Now get off your arse and do your job like you give a shit.' Her mother would be appalled at her language. But Karen had learned the hard way that nobody paid attention to prissiness at the sharp end of policing.

'This your skeleton, Karen?' Gerry asked, the nasal intonation of Northern Ireland obvious in the elision of her name to a single syllable.

'The same, Gerry. According to the witness, it's in a confined space, difficult to access. The routes in and out are along a roof. They've had years of attrition from the weather. So what I think we need is a homicide-trained CSI to do the pix and the fingertip search inside the crime scene. Now it's up to you whether you want the same person to do the eyeball on the roof or if you think it needs another body. Me, I'd just use the poor sod who's got to climb up there anyway. I've got a uniform restricting access to the skylight that leads up to the roof, so it's not like there's any other foot traffic to contend with.'

'What about the route to the skylight?'

Karen puffed her cheeks and blew out a stream of air. 'I don't know what evidential value you'd place on anything you found. The building has been standing empty for twenty years or so. It's not been vandalised or squatted, but it's pretty much rack and ruin inside, according to our witness. Sounds like those photos I keep seeing of Detroit. I'm going inside in a minute to take a look for myself. Why don't you get somebody over here? If they think it's worth more than an eyeball, we'll talk again.'

'OK. Will you get it bagged and tagged while we're still around? So we can see if there's anything lurking underneath?'

'I'll do my best, Gerry. But you know what it's like on a Saturday in the football season. Amazing how many phones seem to lose their signal.'

Gerry chuckled. 'Good luck with that one. Catch you later, Karen.'

One more call to make. She summoned a number from

her contacts and waited for it to connect. She could have called out the duty pathologist. But old bones meant one thing to Karen. Dr River Wilde, forensic anthropologist and the nearest thing Karen had to a best friend. Cursed by her hippy parents with a name nobody could take seriously, River had worked harder and smarter than any of her colleagues to earn respect beyond dispute. The women had worked together on several key cases but for Karen the friendship was almost as important as the professional impact of knowing River. When you were a cop, the job got between you and other women. It was hard to build a connection that was more than superficial with anyone who wasn't in the same line of work. Too much trust could be dangerous. And besides, outsiders just didn't get what was involved. So you were stuck with other women cops around the same rank as you were yourself. There weren't that many as senior as Karen, and she'd never really clicked with any of them. She'd often wondered if it had something to do with them being graduates and her having worked her way up through the ranks. Whatever the reason, until Karen had met River, she'd never found anyone connected with law enforcement that she truly enjoyed hanging out with.

River answered on the third ring. She sounded half asleep. 'Karen? Tell me you're in town and you want to meet for brunch.'

'I'm not in town and it's too late for brunch.'

River groaned. Karen thought she heard bed noises.

17

'Damn it, I told Ewan to wake me before he went out. I just got back from Montreal yesterday, my body doesn't know what bloody day it is.'

There would be time for conversation later. Karen knew there would be no offence taken if she cut to the chase. 'It's Saturday lunchtime here in Edinburgh. I've got a skeleton with a hole in its head. Are you interested?'

River yawned. 'Of course I'm bloody interested. Three hours? I can probably do it in three hours, can't I? An hour to Carlisle, two hours to Edinburgh?'

'You're forgetting the shower and the coffee.'

River chuckled. 'True. Make it three and a quarter. Text me the postcode, I'll see you there.' And the line went dead.

Karen smiled. Having friends who took the job as seriously as she did was a bonus. She hitched her bag higher up on her shoulder and headed for the side door of the John Drummond School, where a uniformed officer stared glumly across the gravel path at a thicket of rhododendrons. She'd barely gone three steps when she heard the Mint calling her name. Stifling a sigh, she turned to find him lumbering towards her. It never ceased to amaze her that someone so skinny managed to move with all the grace of a grizzly.

'What is it, Jason?' Would it be a famous first? Would he have discovered something worth listening to? 'Has he told us anything interesting?'

'Mr Jardine, he heard something about this place. Ages ago, like.' He paused, expectant, eyes shining, living up to the origin of his nickname, the advert that proclaimed, 'Murray Mints, Murray Mints, too good to hurry mints.'

'Are you planning on telling me? Or are we going to play Twenty Questions?'

Unabashed, the Mint continued. 'What reminded him . . . When he was driving over here, he rang one of his pals to say he wouldn't make it to the pub for the early kick-off game.' He looked momentarily wistful. 'It's Liverpool v Man City, too.'

'You should all be supporting local teams, for God's sake. What's Liverpool ever done for you, Jason?' Karen tutted. 'And now you've got me at it, stoating all round the houses instead of getting to the point. Which is?'

'When Mr Jardine said he was surveying the roof of the John Drummond, his pal asked if he was going up from the outside or the inside. Which reminded him that he'd heard something about the John Drummond before, from some other guy he hangs about with. It turns out that there's a thing that climbers do with buildings like this. Apparently they go up the outside without ropes or anything.'

'Free climbing?'

'Is that what they call it? Well, apparently the John Drummond's well known among climbers as a building that's fun to climb, plus there's no security to chase you. So our dead guy might not have gone up through the skylight at all. He might have climbed up under his own steam.'

3

Professor Maggie Blake swept her gaze around the seminar room, trying to make eye contact with everyone. She was gratified to see that they were all paying attention. Well, all except the geek girl in the far corner who never raised her head from her tablet, not even when she was expressing her opinions. There was always one who defeated her best efforts to draw them in. Even at a special conference like this, where they'd actively chosen to attend a series of lectures and seminars over a weekend. 'So, to sum up, what we've focused on today is the notion that the very act of describing a geopolitical relationship can bring it into being,' she said, her warm voice animating a conclusion that might otherwise have seemed an anti-climax to the vigorous discussion that had preceded it. Teaching was a kind of theatre, she'd always thought. And her role as the lead actor was always a carefully considered performance. She was convinced it was one of the reasons she'd earned her chair at Oxford by her mid-forties.

'We've seen that when the media polarises a conflict as a battle between the good guys and the bad guys, it shapes the way we understand the participants. The language actually creates the geopolitics. We can watch it happening right now with the Ukraine conflict. Because the West needs to demonise Putin, a regime that is in many respects no better than Russia is turned into the victim and thus, the good guy. The reality is that there is always a disconnect between the push towards a binary between good and evil, and the actuality.'

A hand shot up and without waiting to be invited to speak, its owner butted in. 'I don't see how you can be so dogmatic about that,' he said belligerently.

It would be Jonah Peterson, Maggie thought. Jonah with his carefully confected hair, his low-slung jeans that revealed the brand of his underwear, his designer spectacle frames and his Elvis sneer. She loved students who disputed ideas, who thought about what they were reading and hearing and found logical contradictions that they wanted to explore. But Jonah just liked contradiction for its own sake. He'd been doing it since the beginning of the course and it was wearisome and disruptive. But these days students were also consumers and she was supposed to engage with irritants like Jonah rather than slap them down the way her tutors and lecturers had been wont to do in the face of wanton stupidity. 'The evidence of history supports this interpretation,' she said, determined not to show how much he got under her skin.

Jonah clearly thought he had her on the run. He wasn't giving up. 'But sometimes it's obvious that one side are the bad guys. Take the Balkan conflict. How can you not characterise the Serbs as the bad guys when they perpetrated the overwhelming majority of the massacres and atrocities?'

Maggie's seminars and lectures were always meticulously planned; a cogent construction that built a solid foundation, brick on brick, rising to a clear and supported conclusion. But Jonah's words jolted her, like a train jumping the tracks. She didn't want to think about the Balkans. Not today, of all days. Accustomed to guarding her feelings, Maggie's face revealed nothing. The ice was all in her voice. 'And how do you know that, Jonah? Everything you know about the Balkan conflicts has been facilitated by the media or by historians with a particular geopolitical axis. You have no direct knowledge that contradicts the theory we've discussed this afternoon. You can't know the nuances of the reality. You weren't there.'

Jonah stuck his jaw out stubbornly. 'I was still in nappies, Professor. So no, I wasn't there. But how do you know there were any nuances? Maybe the media and the historians were right. Maybe sometimes the media story gets it right. You can't know either. My view is just as valid as your theory.'

Pulling rank wasn't something Maggie generally did. But today was different. Today her reactions were skewed. Today she wasn't in the mood for playing games. 'No, Jonah, it's not. I can know and I do know. Because I *was* there.'

Maggie had been aware of the stunned silence as she gathered her notes, her class register and her iPad in one sweep of her arm and walked out. She'd been halfway down the corridor when a fragmented buzz of conversation had broken out and followed her to the front door of the Chapter House, a Victorian copy of an octagonal medieval monastic building now used for seminars and tutorials. She let the heavy oak door click shut behind her and cut down to the river bank that formed the easterly border of St Scholastica's College. Even in early spring, there was colour and texture in the flower beds that lined the path, although Maggie had no eyes for them that afternoon. She breathed deeply as she walked, trying to calm herself. How could she have let Jonah's crass comments breach her personal defences?

The answer was simple. Today she turned fifty. A half-century, the traditional point for taking stock. A day when she couldn't ignore the events that had shaped her. She might have consigned a chunk of her life to history, but today it seemed destined to emerge from the shadows of the past. It would be churlish to pretend she didn't have plenty to celebrate. But thanks to Jonah, her attempts to focus on the good stuff had failed. As she walked back up the path to

23

Magnusson Hall, all Maggie felt was the pain of what was lost.

She'd feared it would be like this. So she'd brushed aside the various suggestions from friends who had wanted to push the boat out with her. No party. No dinner. No presents. Just a day like any other, as far as the rest of the world was concerned. And come tomorrow, there would be nothing to commemorate and she could stuff the history back in its box and consign it to the dark again.

Maggie made for the Senior Common Room. At this time of day, it would be more or less empty. Nobody would be expecting conversation. As she generally did after a seminar, she'd extract a cappuccino from the machine there then retreat to her set of rooms and get on with some work. Take her mind off her memories with something rather more demanding than a student seminar. She pushed open the door and did a double take. Instead of a peaceful, empty space, a crowd of familiar faces formed a loose arc around the door. She barely had time to register music and balloons when someone shouted, 'Happy birthday,' and a cheer went up.

Her first thought was to turn on her heel and walk out. She couldn't have been clearer about the kind of birthday she wanted. And this emphatically wasn't it. But a second look reminded her that these were her friends. Her colleagues. People she liked, people she respected and even some she admired. However distressed she felt, they didn't deserve to be slapped down for something they'd done out of love and kindness. And so Maggie nailed on a smile and walked in.

The afternoon wore on and Maggie smiled until her face hurt. To an outsider, the party would have appeared the perfect celebration, honouring a woman who was clearly a much loved friend as well as a distinguished academic, prolific author, beloved tutor and efficient snapper-up of research grants. Only Maggie knew that her apparent enjoyment was a lie. She wished she could relax and enjoy herself as much as the other guests were obviously doing. But she couldn't shake off the sadness that was the constant counterpoint to the party atmosphere.

The music changed from Dexy's Midnight Runners to Madness. Someone had compiled a playlist solely from her undergraduate years, which was a blessing. Nothing there to provoke a fresh onslaught of unwelcome memories. Welcome to the house of fun, indeed. As if on cue, the latest arrival made an entrance through the French windows that led on to the back lawn and the river. Raven-black hair with strands of silver that caught the light as if they'd been strategically placed for effect. Pale skin, high cheekbones and eyes set too deep to discern the colour until they were inches away. Tessa Minogue strode in with her usual self-assurance, nodding and smiling her way through the knot of people lurking on the fringes of the party where they could enjoy the fresh evening air. Tessa, who knew more about the dark places than anyone else. Tessa, who had been her best friend, then something more than that, and now was her best friend again.

Maggie moved further into the room, not taking her eyes off Tessa. A casual observer would have thought she was drifting through the party, scattering smiles and greetings as she passed. Maggie knew better. Tessa would be by her side in a matter of moments, her lips brushing the soft place beneath Maggie's right ear, her breath warm, her cheek resting fractionally too long against Maggie's.

And she was right. Before she could count to fifty, Tessa was there, soft words in her ear. 'You look lovely.' Made all the more charming by the remains of a Dublin accent that had been buffed to softness by time and distance.

'You knew about this.' There was no quarter in Maggie's voice.

'It wasn't my idea. And I thought if I told you, you wouldn't come and then everybody would feel like idiots. And then you wouldn't forgive yourself,' Tessa said, linking one arm in Maggie's and reaching for a glass of Prosecco with her free hand.

Maggie felt the bones in Tessa's arm press against her own plump flesh. Christ, any thinner and a hug would break her. 'I wouldn't count on that. And you didn't have the nerve to be here from the get-go.'

'Ach, I was stuck in a meeting at the Foreign Office.

International criminal tribunal stuff. How many times have our plans crashed and burned because of long-winded lawyers?'

'You're a lawyer, remember?'

'But not one of the long-winded ones.' Tessa had a point. One of the reasons Maggie enjoyed her company so much was her uncomplicated nature, surprising in a lawyer who dealt in the thorny moral dilemmas of human rights. Now Tessa waved her glass expansively at the room full of people. 'Anyhow, I'm here now and that's what matters. I know you could make a patchwork quilt of your history from all the different recollections in this room right now, but I'm the only one who could make a coverlet out of the whole cloth.'

'There's one missing, Tessa.' And the person who wasn't there was the only one that mattered. His image had been clouding her mind's eye since the moment Jonah had derailed her. Nobody had been insensitive enough to mention his name, but Maggie had felt it hanging unsaid more than once. Obviously, he hadn't been invited. Because he hadn't left a forwarding address. Not when he'd walked out without a final farewell eight years before, nor any time since. Dimitar Petrovic had left without a backward glance. Maggie had told herself a million times that he'd been trying to protect her. But she'd always wondered whether it was more about protecting himself from the complications of an emotional life.

Tessa's mouth twisted into something between a smile and a sneer. 'He could have sent flowers.'

'Mitja never bought me flowers.' Maggie tilted her chin up and faced her party, lying smile firmly in place. 'He never had a talent for cliché, Tessa. You know that.'

'He does, however, have a tendency to repeat himself,' Tessa said briskly.

Maggie half-turned and gave her friend a sharp look. 'Meaning what?'

'He's up to his old tricks.' Tessa disengaged her arm. 'One of the prosecution team told me about it last night. Miroslav Simunovic this time. You remember him?'

'One of Radovan Karadzic's henchmen. Up to his armpits in the dead of Srebenica? That Simunovic?'

'That's the one. He'd escaped the tribunal, you know. They're not taking any more new cases. Simunovic must have thought he was free and clear. He had reinvented himself as a retired history teacher. Living on Crete, in a flat with a nice view of the harbour in Chania. His neighbour across the landing found him three days ago. Lying in the doorway with his throat cut ear to ear.'

Maggie closed her eyes tightly. When she opened them, her dark blue eyes were like flints. 'You don't know that it's anything to do with Mitja,' she said, tight-lipped.

Tessa shifted one shoulder in a faint shrug. 'Same MO as all the others. Look at the timeline, Maggie. Milosevic dies before the International Criminal Tribunal for the Former Yugoslavia can find him guilty. Mitja gets drunk for three days and rages against the likes of me for failing his people.

28

The first killing happens six weeks after he walks out on you, all fired up with his mission to put right what we couldn't manage in The Hague. If it's not Mitja, it's somebody else with the same list of names to blame.'

'That doesn't narrow it down. It's not like those names are a secret, Tessa.'

'Three or four of them come into the realm of specialist knowledge. If he's not out there showrunning his own theatre of vengeance, what exactly is he doing that's kept him out of your bed for the past eight years, Maggie?' The words were harsh, but Tessa's eyes were full of pity.

The music segued into David Bowie's 'Let's Dance'. A middle-aged man who should have known better than the drainpipe jeans he'd squeezed into bussed Maggie on the cheek, oblivious to the tension between the two women. 'Come on, Maggie,' he urged. 'Like the man says, let's dance.'

'Later, Lucas,' she said, managing a distracted smile in his direction. Pouting, he shimmied back into the crowd on the dance floor, waggling his fingers at them as he went. Maggie took a deep breath and ran a hand through the shock of thick brown hair that she refused to allow to reveal the hints of grey that lurked in secret. 'You make me sound irresistible. And we both know that's not true.'

Tessa laid a hand on the other woman's shoulder and leaned into her. 'I wouldn't mind giving it another try.'

Maggie snorted with bitter laughter. 'Your enthusiasm is

overwhelming.' She patted Tessa's hand. 'We're better off as friends. We only fell into bed together because we were both missing Mitja so much. I lost the man I loved and you lost your best friend.'

'What have I told you about talking yourself down? You were never second-best to Mitja. You and me, we were friends while he was elbowing his way into your life, and you're still my best friend.' Tessa gave a dry little bark of sardonic laughter. 'I sometimes think you're my only friend. The point is, really, that Mitja loved you. Nothing short of a one-man crusade against war criminals could have kept him from you.'

Maggie shook her head, still smiling politely at the room. 'You know what I think.'

'You're wrong.'

'And you're stubborn. Look, Tess, Mitja wasn't a boy when we met. He was a very grown-up thirty-two when we ran into each other in Dubrovnik in '91. I'm not stupid. I knew he must have had a past. A history. A life. But we both agreed that we weren't going to be defined by what went before.'

Tessa made a derisive noise. 'Convenient for him.'

'Convenient for both of us. I wasn't exactly lacking a past myself. But it's not me we're talking about here, it's Mitja. I always assumed there was a woman tucked away in some Croatian backwater. Maybe even kids. I just didn't want to know what he'd left behind to be with me.'

Tessa knocked back the remains of her drink. 'So why would he go back to that? When he had you? He'd already left her for you. He wouldn't have left you for her, he'd only ever have left you because he had a mission that was irresistible. Overwhelming.'

Maggie took a step away from Tessa, letting her friend's hand fall from her shoulder. 'I love that you think so much of me you have to come up with some noble theory to explain why my lover walked out on me.' She looked around the room, taking in the dancers, the talkers, the drinkers. The vista of the people who loved and respected had no hope of chasing the sorrow away. 'Whatever I was to him, Tessa, it wasn't home. That's why he left. Mitja just went home.'

4

Alan Macanespie had once confided to a friend that he was not a man given to introspection. His pal had guffawed, almost choking on his beer. When his coughing fit subsided, he said, 'Christ, if I looked like you, I'd take introspection over the view in the mirror every time.' It was a point of view that had been reinforced when Macanespie had split up with his long-term girlfriend a couple of years later.

'Next time I want to live with a ginger pig, I'll buy a Tamworth,' had been her parting shot. Increasingly, when he looked in his shaving mirror, he found it hard to disagree. His ginger hair had grown paler and more sparse, his stubble coarser. His eyes seemed smaller because his face had become fatter. He didn't want to think about what his body looked like; these days, there were no full-length mirrors anywhere in his flat. When she left, she told him he'd given up on himself. He had a sneaking suspicion she'd been right about that too.

Macanespie didn't like the way that made him feel. He realised that his career had stalled, but that didn't mean he'd shirked his job at the International Criminal Tribunal for the former Yugoslavia. OK, investigating war criminals and helping to track them down wasn't where he'd imagined his law degree would take him, but it was preferable to writing wills and conveyancing in some scummy wee town in the central belt of his native Scotland. He'd carved out a nice little niche in one of the grey areas between the Foreign Office and the Department of Justice and it suited him just fine. The worst thing about it was having to share an office with that miserable Welsh git Proctor.

But all that might pale into insignificance if today went tits up. His previous boss, Selina Bryson, had what a more charitable man than Macanespie might have called a laissez-faire attitude to her ICTFY operators. Macanespie described it more pithily: 'She couldn't give a flying fuck what we do as long as we deliver results she can take credit for and we don't fart at the ambassador's cocktail receptions.' But Selina was history and today the new boy was coming to wave a big stick at him and Proctor. Making them come into the office on a Saturday, just because he could.

He might be lazy but Macanespie wasn't stupid and he knew forewarned was forearmed. So he'd called one of his London drinking buddies and sought the low-down on the new boss. Jerry had been happy to oblige on the promise of a bottle of Dutch genever the next time Macanespie left The Hague for London.

'Wilson Cagney,' Macanespie said. 'Tell me about him.'

'What have you heard so far?'

Macanespie made a sardonic face. 'Too young, too well dressed, too black.'

Jerry laughed. 'He's older than he looks. He's nearer forty than thirty. He's got enough miles on the clock to dish out plenty of bother. He dresses Savile Row but the word is that he lives in a one-bedroomed shed in Acton and doesn't drive. Spends all his readies on good suits and all his spare time in the office gym. Sad careerist bastard, basically.'

'How did he climb the greasy pole? Merit? Backstabbing? Or trading on being black?'

Jerry breathed in sharply. 'I hope this is a secure line, mate, saying things like that. HR are bloody everywhere these days. He's got the qualifications – law degree at Manchester, then a Masters in security and international law, according to our star-struck IT assistant. But he's the only black face at his grade, so make of that what you will. Put it this way, Alan. He's not one of us. You'll never find him down the Bay Horse on a Friday night.'

'So he's not coming over to give us a pat on the back and say, "As you were, chaps."'

'Word is he's looking for so-called austerity cuts. Which is spelled c-u-l-l. Watch your back, Alan.'

And so Macanespie, card marked, had determined that he wasn't going to be the lamb to the slaughter. Welsh lamb, that was a much better option. He'd be the ginger pig, tusks flashing danger signs at anyone who thought he was a pushover. He'd arrived in good time and to Theo Proctor's astonishment, he set about clearing his desk and tidying his end of the office.

'You trying to be teacher's pet, then?' Proctor demanded.

'I just looked at this place through somebody else's eyes and decided it didn't need to be a pigsty,' he said, grabbing three dirty mugs and popping them into his bottom drawer. Proctor, clearly uneasy, began straightening files and papers on his desk.

Before he'd made much impression, one of the canteen staff came in with a Thermos jug and a single cup. She consulted a piece of paper. 'Which one of you is Wilson Cagney?'

'He's not here yet, love. And you need two more cups.' Proctor always managed to sound an officious prick, Macanespie thought.

'No, I don't.' She waved the paper at him. 'Look: "Order for Wilson Cagney. Black coffee for one." Can one of you sign for it?'

'I don't see why I should sign for it if I'm not getting to drink it,' Proctor grumbled.

'Give it here,' Macanespie said, scribbling his signature on the bottom of the sheet. 'We'll not drink it, I promise.' When she left, he unscrewed the top and inhaled. 'Aye, that's the good stuff,' he said.

'For crying out loud, Alan, close it up. He'll smell it.' Proctor looked panicked, but Macanespie just curled his lip in a sneer as he closed the jug.

Five minutes later, a tall black man in an immaculate charcoal pinstripe suit walked in without knocking. His hair was cut close, emphasising his narrow head and surprisingly delicate features. 'Good morning, gentlemen,' he said, then poured himself a coffee from the Thermos jug. He glanced briefly at them both then gestured with his cup at Proctor. 'You must be Proctor.' Theo nodded. Cagney looked pleased with himself. 'Which makes you Macanespie.' This time there was a faint note of distaste in his voice.

Cagney sat down and hitched his trousers at the knee before he crossed his legs. 'I imagine you know why I'm here?'

'You're Selina Bryson's replacement,' Macanespie said. 'Making a tour of the front-line staff.' He smiled, instantly worrying that he was showing too many teeth in a display of nerves.

Cagney inclined his head. 'Right. And also wrong. It's true that I've taken over from Selina. But I'm not here to press the flesh and tell you all what a sterling job you're doing. Because in the case of you two, you're not.'

Proctor flushed, a dark plum stain spreading upwards from his bright white shirt collar. 'We're one small part of a big operation here. You can't blame us for everything that's gone wrong.'

Cagney sipped his coffee, clearly savouring it. 'The UK government is committed to the concept of international law. That's the main reason we supported the UN in the formation of the International Criminal Tribunal for the former Yugoslavia. It's why we seconded people like you to work with the tribunal. Everybody knows it's going to wind up at the end of this year, so we're all drinking in the last-chance saloon. And some people aren't happy about that. Would you say that was a fair assessment of the situation?'

Macanespie hung back, waiting to see which way his colleague would jump. Proctor stuck his chin out, his expression belligerent. 'A tribunal like this is never going to manage to satisfy people's demands for justice. Stands to reason. After all this time, you can't expect to develop the kind of evidence that will always stand up to challenge in court.'

Cagney set his cup down. 'I appreciate that. What worries me is the cases that have never made it to court. The ones where a dossier was put together and a raid was planned to arrest the alleged war criminal. Only, the arrests were never carried out because, by pure chance, the target of the operation was assassinated before we swung into action.'

So that was the way the wind was blowing. Someone was getting cold feet about someone else's black ops. Macanespie shrugged. 'Rough justice. You'll not see many tears shed over the likes of them. But that's the way the cookie crumbles sometimes.'

Cagney smacked a hand down hard on the table, making the crockery rattle and the teaspoons jingle. 'Don't give me that. There was nothing serendipitous about these deaths. At least ten of them. The last one, Miroslav Simunovic, just last week.'

'There's still a lot of murdering bastards in the Balkans,' Proctor said.

Cagney glared at him. 'Remind me not to recommend you for a diplomatic post. The point I'm making is that, while my predecessor may have been willing to turn a blind eye to whatever programme of DIY justice was going on here, I'm not.'

'Like you said, it's all going to be over and done with by the end of the year,' Macanespie said, his voice surly.

'So, what? You think I should just let sleeping dogs lie?' Cagney paused dramatically. The other two exchanged a look. It was apparently enough to create a consensus that the question was rhetorical. They stared at Cagney with expressions of stubborn mulishness. He shook his head, clearly impatient. 'You just don't get it, do you? This is the end of the tribunal. This is where we draw the line in the sand. This is where we say to Bosnia and Croatia and Montenegro and Kosovo and the rest of them, "It's done. Settle down and try to behave like you're inhabiting the twenty-first century, not the twelfth." It's where we tell them that we've done our best to mete out justice to the bad men. And now they have to move on. Let the past bury its dead.'

Proctor made a noise halfway between a cough and a dry, bitter laugh. 'I don't mean to sound rude, but it's obvious you're new to that part of the world. They're still fighting those ancient battles. They talk about it like it was yesterday. We might think it's over and done, but nobody on the ground over there thinks like that.'

'Well, they're going to have to learn. If they want to be part of modern Europe, they're going to have to learn to live like modern Europeans, not like the private armies of medieval warlords.'

Macanespie shifted his bulk in the chair and reached for the coffee jug. 'It's not that simple. It's all bound up in ethnicity and religion and tribal factions. It's like Northern Ireland multiplied by ten. Rangers and Celtic to the power of mad.' He took a mug out of his drawer and poured. Cagney looked momentarily furious, then mildly amused. But it wasn't enough to divert him from his course.

'And how else is it going to change if we don't impose a higher expectation on them? You think there isn't a new generation of young people in the Balkans who want things to be different? Who look at the world through the prism of Facebook and Twitter and see another way of living? Who are fed up with the old way of doing geopolitics in their back yard?'

Another look exchanged. Macanespie's shoulders slumped, confronted yet again by the ignorance of a suit from London who didn't have a clue how this world worked. 'Maybe. But I don't see what that's got to do with us.'

Cagney compressed his lips into a thin exasperated line. 'The killing has to stop. These assassinations – because that's what they are, let's not glorify them with words like "rough justice" – they've got to be history.'

'I take your point,' Macanespie said. 'But why is that our problem? We didn't do the killing or commission it. Not even behind our hands.'

'Because what they all have in common is that every one of those assassinations was a case where we had a key front-line involvement. We, us, this office. We're the common denominator. Either somebody on our team thinks they're channelling Charles Bronson or there's a mole leaking the product of our investigations to a third party who's got his own programme of Balkan cleansing going on.'

Proctor was visibly shaken and Macanespie suspected he was too. He'd never put it together quite like that. They exchanged another look, this time aghast. 'Fuck's sake,' Macanespie hissed under his breath.

'Like he said. We're not killers,' Proctor said, indignant.

Cagney allowed a smile to twitch one corner of his mouth. 'Now that I've met you, I'd have to agree. But some-body is. And I'm making it your job to find who.' He pushed back from the table and stood up.

'We're lawyers, not detectives,' Macanespie said.

'You might have been lawyers once. But these past few years, you've been hunting dogs, triangulating the whereabouts of a bunch of butchers. This is your last assignment. Find the avenger. You can make a start first thing tomorrow.'

'Tomorrow's Sunday,' Macanespie protested.

'You sound like a shopkeeper.' Cagney's contempt was obvious. 'The sooner you get started, the sooner you can deliver. Then maybe you'll have a career to come home to.'

5

Maggie Blake went to pull the heavy drapes across the
window of her sitting room. Catching sight of the full
moon, she paused, looking out over the silvered rooftops
towards the dreaming spires of central Oxford. St
Scholastica's College was far enough out to feel a little aloof
from the hurly-burly of the tourist-trap heart of the city, but
from her suite of rooms on the third floor of Magnusson Hall
she looked over gleaming slates punctuated by chimney
pots, across the blank space of the University Parks towards
Keble, the Pitt Rivers Museum, and beyond that, slivers of
the crenellations, towers and stone facades of a variety of
college and university buildings. She was one of the few
remaining fellows of the college who lived within its walls
and she was grateful for the privilege. It freed up more of her
income to travel for pleasure, not purely at the dictates of
her research grants. And she loved the view from this room,

where she read and wrote and met the handful of postgraduate students she supervised.

Because this had been a day shot through with memories, she recalled the first time she had brought Mitja to her rooms. They'd both been war-weary, sleep-deprived and aching from two days in the back of a truck that had dropped them off on the Banbury Road in the small hours. The college had been still, only a couple of lights burning in student rooms. The bathetic quacking of a mallard duck had disturbed the peace as Maggie had fumbled her key into the front-door lock of Magnusson Hall, and Mitja had chuckled. 'Dinner,' he said softly.

They'd climbed the stairs slowly. Maggie remembered the straps of her rucksack biting into the tender places on her shoulders and the tremble in her quads as she'd headed up the final flight.

And then they were in her sitting room, and the moonlight bathed the panoramic skyline. Mitja dropped his bag like a sack of stones and made for the windows as if drawn by a tractor beam. He leaned his forehead against the glass and groaned. 'Do you remember when Dubrovnik was as beautiful as this?'

She wriggled out of her rucksack straps and crossed the room, wrapping her arms around him, leaning round his shoulder to see a little of the view she'd missed. 'I remember. The first time I saw the city at night, I thought it was like something from a fairy tale. The city walls. The grid of streets. The bulk of the cathedral like a treasure chest. The harbour glittering in the moonlight. The floodlights at Fort St Ivan reflected like columns in the water.'

'And now it's rubble. It's ruins.' He straightened up and pulled her round to his side, drawing her close with an arm tight across her back. 'I don't understand why my people never grow up. You English—'

She dug an elbow in his ribs. 'Scottish, remember?'

He shook his head, impatient. 'You see, you may be as bad as we are.' There was indulgence in his tone, but weariness too. 'OK, then. *Those* English had a civil war. But they got over it. You don't have cavaliers and Cromwell's men still hating each other and killing each other. They had their wars of roses as well, those English, but people from Yorkshire and Lancashire don't fight in the streets.'

'Only over football, I believe.' Maggie couldn't help being facetious; being back in Oxford was filling her with deep joy, like a reservoir recovering from a long drought.

'I am serious.'

'I know you are. But it's late and I am beyond tired. I have whisky. Shall we take a glass to bed?'

This time, he laughed. 'You know exactly how to make things better.'

They had taken the bottle to bed, but hadn't got past that first glass. The unfamiliar combination of warmth, comfort and the absence of fear made them easy prey for sleep, and not even the desire that sprang constantly between them could keep it at bay.

That night had been the start of a new phase in their relationship. Like every other phase, it had been complicated, tumultuous and glorious. No life plan Maggie had ever concocted had included anyone like Mitja. But then, it hadn't included underground universities or civil wars either.

Leaving the curtains open, Maggie sat down at her desk, deliberately angled at forty-five degrees to the window so she had to turn her head to get the full benefit of the view. She should be heading for bed. It had been a long and stressful day, the unwelcome party shading into an unwanted dinner for twenty, and she was physically tired. And yet her mind was still busy, jumping restlessly from one encounter to another, and always coming back to the one who wasn't there.

Without thinking about it, she ran her fingers over the touch pad and wakened her Mac. Maybe it was just the wine talking, but what if it was time to give in to the nagging voice at the back of her mind that kept suggesting she needed to write about her time in the Balkans? She'd addressed it professionally, of course. *Balkan Geopolitics: An Archaeological Approach* had become the standard textbook on the region. And the reader she'd edited that had dissected the media responses to the conflict had attracted mainstream attention on radio and TV as well as print. Maggie had written about the consequences of the siege of Dubrovnik. But she'd never written about what it had been like to live through it. She'd never told the story of how she came to be there, nor of the convoluted journey that had led her to Kosovo with its massacres and rape camps.

At first she'd shied away from telling that story because it was too fresh. Maggie wanted more distance from those traumatic events so she could set them in context. Then she'd held back because she couldn't write a narrative without placing Mitja front and centre, and she was living with him in Oxford by then. She knew he wouldn't approve of or agree with everything she had to say about those years shuttling back and forth between her life in Oxford and her life in a war zone. And she didn't want to sow discord between them.

And finally, she'd kept her silence because he was gone and she couldn't let go the hope that he'd come back. To make public things he'd be unhappy to read felt like too big a risk.

But the years had drifted past and there had been no word from Mitja. Not so much as a birthday greeting or a Christmas card. Nothing to acknowledge what they had been to each other. Just silence. A silence more profound than she'd ever known in the Balkans. 'There's nothing silent here,' he'd once said to her. 'Everything speaks, if you only know how to listen.' Well, this silence wasn't speaking, that was for sure. And there was no valid reason now for Maggie to hold her tongue. Even if she decided not to publish, there would be a satisfaction in setting things down. A chance to revisit her history and perhaps find a different angle, a new truth.

Even if she didn't know how the story ended.

6

Karen drove slowly down the late-night back street, not wanting to disturb the neighbours. The houses here were homes to the kind of families that didn't have wild weekend parties. Steady, middle-class lives behind solid respectable facades. More often than not, there was barely a light showing if she came home after eleven. Her job had made her sceptical about what really went on behind those smartly painted front doors, but as far as she was aware, none of their neighbours had so much as an outstanding parking ticket. It was entirely different from the rackety street where she'd grown up, with its loud evenings and shouting matches on the pavement, the drunken midnight fights and singing. Loving Phil Parhatka had altered her life in more ways than she could have imagined.

For years they'd worked together in the former Cold Case Unit in Fife, adapting to new technologies, learning how to read between the lines of old case reports, winkling the truth out of its defensive shell. She'd always been one step above him on the ladder of rank, but they'd never let that stand in the way of being mates. They had each other's back, and there had been times when she'd felt he was the only one on her side. They'd been a team and their success rate proved the value of that.

For her part, she'd known early on she was fighting against feelings that ran much deeper than friendship. She fancied him, she fantasised about him and she hated herself for risking their working relationship with her schoolgirl longings. When he was kind, she told herself he'd treat the Mint – or even a pet dog – with the same consideration.

And then it had all changed. Right in the thick of their toughest case, she'd discovered he felt the same way. Within weeks she'd moved out of her identikit box on a soulless modern development and into Phil's late Victorian villa, a house that had been restored to within an inch of its life by his sister-in-law, an ardent architectural historian who had watched too many TV makeover shows. Karen still couldn't quite believe she'd escaped into so much respectability.

Sometimes she was tempted not to turn into the gravel drive between the voluptuous herbaceous borders, to keep on driving to the end of the street and beyond, back to where she wouldn't be found out for the fraud she feared she might be.

But not tonight. Tonight, she led the way into the

stone-built semi like a woman who belonged. The house was silent and dark, save for a dim glow from the rear. 'Phil home?' River asked, her boot heels clattering on the encaustic Victorian tiling. 'Or is it just cop instinct always to leave a light on?'

'He's away on a course this weekend. Something about developing collateral offences.' Karen switched on lights as they went through to the kitchen at the back of the house. It was the only room where Phil had managed to stem the tide of his sister-in-law's fantasy. When Karen had moved in, it had been a seventies relic. Now it was all stainless steel and wood, surfaces littered with appliances and general clutter; a proper kitchen where meals were made and people sat around talking to each other.

'What does that mean?' River collapsed into a kitchen chair, looking grateful for the break. Her dark hair was uncharacteristically loose and wild, forming a chaotic halo round her head, and her big grey eyes had blue shadows underneath them. She'd always been slim; now she was tending towards skinny, her veteran waxed jacket taking on new vertical creases where there was no longer flesh to fill it. Her jeans were unusually loose on her, the denim pooling at her knees and inner thighs.

'I know I was dubious about him leaving cold cases just because we're together, but he's really got stuck in to this Murder Prevention Team. Apparently, there's been some research that indicates that men who are violent abusers tend towards petty criminality in other areas of their lives. Like, they don't pay their TV licence, they drive their cars without insurance, they run red lights, they shoplift. The kind of shit people do to prove to themselves they're not just another brick in the wall.' Karen pulled a bottle of Aussie red out of the wine rack and unscrewed the cap. 'So Phil's team is developing this strategy where they try to take the abusive partners out of reach of the victims by putting them under the microscope and hitting them with every little infringement. Sometimes they get enough to put the bastard behind bars. Other times, they just harass the bastards to the point where it's easier to walk away and go and live somewhere else.'

'Isn't that simply shifting the problem somewhere else?' River picked up the glass that Karen had poured for her. She sniffed it, sipped it then nodded once. 'Nice.'

'Yeah. But hopefully somewhere that also has the same policies in place. The idea is that they eventually get the message that abusing their partners means they'll be abused themselves in a slightly different but very uncomfortable way. Plus sometimes the team gets enough to put them behind bars, which means they're right out of the equation in a way that spares the victim having to give evidence about what he did to her.'

'And does it work?'

Karen shrugged. 'Phil thinks it saves lives.' She took a large bag of salty-and-sweet popcorn out of the cupboard and tipped it into a bowl. 'But more to the point: tell me about my skeleton.' Once they'd bagged and tagged the remains, River had taken them to the mortuary. Karen had left her to it. In her experience, people got on better with the things they were best at if you left them to it. Looking over their shoulders never improved the quality of the work. While the forensic scientist had examined the body, Karen had focused on the recent history of the John Drummond, trying to establish who had had access and when. It would have been a thankless task at any time, she suspected, but on a Saturday afternoon and evening, it was damn close to impossible. All she'd been able to establish were denials. Nobody had made regular use of any part of the building for a dozen years, not since a charity involved in organising outdoor adventure training for deprived inner-city teenagers had moved out. Nobody had squatted the building. Nobody from the security company nominally charged with its preservation from harm would admit to having ever climbed the stairs. Nobody associated with the school back in the mists of time had been reported missing. Most importantly, her quest to find anyone who knew anything about freeclimbing the John Drummond had gone cold. Fraser Jardine's pal had his phone turned off and until he got back to them, that tantalising line of inquiry was going nowhere. All those negatives. Now she was gagging for something positive.

River crunched a mouthful of popcorn to annihilation.

'It's a male. And he died from a small-calibre gunshot wound to his forehead. Beyond that, much of what I can tell you is best-guess at this point. I'd guess he was murdered because of the site of the entry wound.' She pointed to a spot above her right eyebrow. 'I've never seen a suicide shoot himself there. The temple. The roof of the mouth. Once, right between the eyes. But never way off centre like this.'

Karen nodded, stuffing popcorn in her mouth. 'Mmm. Thought as much.'

'Plus there's no sign of a bullet. But that doesn't necessarily mean someone removed it. There are signs of rodent and bird activity on the bones and around the body.'

'So a squirrel or a magpie could have carried off a bullet and dropped it elsewhere?'

'Easily. As far as ID is concerned, I'd say he was somewhere between forty and fifty when he was killed. His dental work is interesting. There's a couple of crowns, pretty expensive gold and porcelain work, probably done in the two or three years before he died. And probably in this country. But there's other stuff, older stuff. I've seen work like that in bodies from the west end of the old Eastern bloc. Ukraine, Albania, Bulgaria, Bosnia, that neck of the woods.'

'So you think he'd come from there but he was living here?'

'Looks that way. Unless he was some sort of deep undercover agent. That's not the sort of place you'd choose to have your teeth fixed if you had a choice. Not back then.'

'Back when?'

River considered, swirling the wine in her glass. 'I'd say he's been dead between five and ten years. It's hard to be precise, there's too many variables. His clothing has decomposed, which means natural fabrics. We did find a few fibres under his body. I'd say he was probably wearing cotton underwear, cotton chinos rather than jeans – no rivets – and a shirt that was a mix of cotton and linen. Woollen socks and what looks like some kind of grippy climbing shoe. Most of the material has rotted or been scavenged by rodents or birds for nesting, but the rubber trim and soles are pretty much intact. There are a few bits of wool still between the sole and the bones of the foot.'

'The shoes make sense. We've got a witness who says there are mad bastards who free-climb the outside of buildings like the John Drummond. That offers an explanation of how he got up there without having to come through the building and reach the skylight without a ladder. Because there's no sign of a ladder anywhere.'

River took another handful of popcorn. 'People never cease to amaze me. Why would you want to climb up a building when there's a perfectly good staircase inside? I get the point of going up a mountain. The challenge, the relationship to nature. The views, for God's sake. But buildings? That's just weird.'

'Aye, well, I don't care how weird it is if it gives me a way in to this case. Because what you're telling me's painfully short on detail. No clothes colours, no style, nothing we can compare with descriptions of what a misper might have been wearing . . . ' Karen sighed.

'Sorry. I can't even tell you what colour his socks were. But I'm sure there'll be other things about him that'll stand more chance of matching one of your missing persons.' River pulled out her mobile and summoned a gallery of photographs. 'Look.' Karen hitched her chair round till she could share the screen. 'This must have been in his back pocket.' The phone showed a dark red card with a magnetic strip, the size of a credit card. 'Do you recognise it?'

'Should I?'

'I don't know. It looks like a hotel room key to me, but there's no printing on it to suggest where it came from.'

Karen shook her head. 'There's hundreds of hotels and guest houses in the city. Maybe forensics can get some detail off the magnetic strip. But before I let them loose on it, I'll see if the fingerprint bureau can get anything off it. Was that the only ID on him?'

'That's it. From where it was positioned, I'd guess it was in a back pocket. Whoever killed him probably took his wallet and anything else he was carrying that might identify him. I'm guessing once they had that, they stopped searching.'

'You have to have a pretty strong stomach to search a corpse. I'll just have to hope we get something off the keycard.' Karen refilled their glasses and yawned. 'Still, it makes a change from the usual cold-case scenario. No ploughing through somebody else's crappy notes and getting depressed at the poverty of their skills.'

'You never know, you might end up getting a foreign trip out of it if your victim turns out to have a past somewhere else.'

Karen gave a dark chuckle. 'Aye, right. Knowing my luck, he'll be an Albanian people trafficker. So when will you have some more for me?'

'DNA by Monday morning. I'll get the bone analysis under way first thing tomorrow. There's always facial reconstruction to consider if you're not getting anywhere with the hotel key and the hardcore forensics,' River added thoughtfully.

Karen pulled a face. 'I know. And they've got much better at it these days, with the 3D computer imaging. But it's expensive and if our guy is from overseas, chances are slim we'll pick up enough hits for a definite ID. I don't know if I can justify it in terms of budget. But I'll bear it in mind.'

'That's the joy of modern forensics, Karen. ID used to be the hardest thing to establish when you came across human remains. But these days, there's no hiding place. We all carry our history under the skin. That glass of wine you're drinking now? It's just another contribution to the sum total of Karen Pirie.'

Karen laughed and chinked her tumbler against River's. 'Another hundred and twenty calories to the sum total of Karen Pirie. And speaking of which, you've lost weight you didn't have to spare.'

River's eyes slid away from her friend. 'I'm fine,' she said. 'I've just been busy. You know how it is.'

'I know when I'm busy I put weight on. Eating rubbish on the run.'

'I'm the opposite. I forget to eat.'

Karen shook her head, a wry smile on her lips. 'See, that's a sentence that makes no sense to me. How can you "forget" to eat?'

River pulled herself together and forced joviality into her voice. 'Same way you "forget" to sleep when you're hot on the heels of an answer to something nobody else has been able to figure out.'

'You know me so well. But I'm not hot on anybody's heels tonight.' She yawned again. 'And tomorrow is another day. Shall we hit the hay?'

River glanced at her watch. 'In a bit. I need to call Ewan. He'll still be up. I'm in the usual place, right?'

Karen stood up, draining her glass. 'Yeah. And tomorrow we can get cracking on the mystery man's ID. The sooner we know that, the sooner we can find the person who put a bullet in his brain. There's a killer out there who's had too many undisturbed nights. It's time to give him nightmares.'

In the Balkans, the shortest distance between two points is never a straight line. History and geography have constantly collided with the human capacity for cruelty in those disputed territories. It's the place where I discovered my own vulnerabilities with depressing repetitiousness. But it's also a place where I discovered love and hope and the possibility of redemption.

Nothing has ever made me feel more mortal than the crash bang wallop of an artillery barrage. The scatter of light bursting across the sky, the shaking of the building around me, the terrible echo of the booming explosions filled me with terror. It's not how I expected my working life to turn out when I signed up for a geography degree thirty-two years ago. I had no idea that being a geographer would include being shot at by snipers or driving an ambulance crammed with medical supplies

halfway across Europe or hiding from secret policemen in
rat-infested basements.

I wasn't raised for this sort of adventure. I grew up in
the Howe of Fife, an island of conservatism and
agriculture at the heart of a radical region with a history
of mining, shipbuilding and fishing. My father was what's
politely called an agricultural labourer but would more
accurately be described as a serf. My mother worked part-
time in the farm dairy and she was the driving force
behind my reaching escape velocity.

I was lucky enough to arrive at University College,
London just as the human geography aspect of the
discipline was forging new areas of interest. Geography
departments had traditionally been overwhelmingly male,
but a new wave of feminist academics was infiltrating
everywhere. The human geographies of women's lives
were laying claim to our attention, with headline-grabbing
movements such as Greenham Common providing fruitful
sources of research and published papers. I know this is a
statement that may provoke some incredulity, but it was
the most exciting time to be a baby geographer.

My PhD supervisor was one of those radical
groundbreakers. Melissa Armstrong had returned to
London after five years of postgraduate and post-doctoral
work in the US, fired up with Marxist and feminist
ideology. She hit UCL with all the disruptive energy of a
tornado, uprooting existing power structures and shifting

the tectonic plates of physical geography to make way for something completely different. Melissa spent as much time with philosophers and social scientists as she did with her departmental colleagues and her energy left her colleagues reeling.

I was one of only two female geography postgrads and we became her wingmen, her disciples and her proselytisers. Our admiration bordered on adulation, especially when she put her politics into practice. In the late 1980s, the dissident philosophical community in Prague issued a clandestine invitation to Western academics they suspected might be sympathetic to their cause. Come and help us subvert the regime by conducting underground seminars, they said.

Melissa became a fellow of St Scholastica's College, Oxford just in time to join that first wave of collaborationist libertarian academics. She became one of a group who taught in crowded flats and rooms above bars, bringing the same liveliness and imagination to those seminars as she delivered to us back in Oxford. (For I had followed her to Oxford, earning a Junior Research Fellow post at Schollies.) Even though the people they were teaching and inspiring were working long hours as scaffolders and shop assistants, street sweepers and lavatory attendants, they somehow found the energy and passion to respond more enthusiastically than I suspect we ever did.

Melissa made the risky and unnerving journey many times. She smuggled books in her luggage – feminist texts disguised as airport novels – and smuggled out *samizdat* papers from the people she increasingly came to see as colleagues in Prague and beyond. Eventually the authorities grew suspicious of her repeated visits and after some harrowing encounters with the security police, the Czechoslovakian authorities told her she would be granted no more visas. Melissa was furious and frustrated, but her determination to fight for freedom of speech and of learning burned just as bright in her heart. I remember the evening she found out that she would never be allowed back to work with her unofficial students in Prague again. We were in her office at St Scholastica's and she opened a bottle of wine with such force that she bent the corkscrew.

'I'm not giving up,' she declared, sloshing Soave into a pair of tumblers. 'They think they can shut us up, but it's not going to work.'

'But what can you do if they won't let you back in?'

Melissa took a long swig from her glass, then let her dark hair fall forward so I couldn't see her face properly. 'Some of the others are setting up a foundation to raise money to support the dissident community. They want to try to smuggle people out and support them till they can find university jobs here.' Then she tossed her hair back, defiance on her face. 'I don't think that's how you change the world.'

61

'So what will you do?'

'I'll find somewhere else to do what we've been doing in Prague. It's not the only place where people are denied the freedom to talk and think. This is too important to walk away from, Maggie. These people need us.'

It wasn't long before Melissa found a solution that went some way towards satisfying her desire to spread the word of the new discipline that was being carved from the marriage of feminism, philosophy and geopolitics. The answer lay in Dubrovnik. Although it was part of the wider Soviet bloc, Yugoslavia had more freedom to connect with the West. And at the Inter-University Centre there, it was possible for academics from both sides of the ideological divide to meet. Those oppressed and constrained by the regimes they lived under could hide their dissident tendencies and disguise the nature of the encounters that made their time at the IUC so fruitful. They could engage in seminars and discussions of the latest theories, then take those subversive ideas back to their own campuses and spread them via the handfuls of students they could trust. Melissa was in her element, enthusiasm and intelligence transmitting themselves to everyone she encountered.

Just as she did in Oxford, Melissa made learning fun. Seminars segued seamlessly into social occasions, late-night drinking sessions filled with discussion and disputation. She started a journal for dissident feminist philosophers and geographers, persuading a small German academic publishing house to fund the anonymous contributions. I remember sitting up into the night typing the handwritten articles, trying to make sense of the sometimes fractured English. But I was happy to be part of the adventure. Everybody loved Melissa; everybody wanted more of her.

Unfortunately for Melissa, the fellows of Schollies were among that number. Instead of being proud of what she was achieving in the wider world, most of the governing body suffered from the tunnel vision that outsiders suspect all academics of. They were more interested in their own convenience than in the human rights of a bunch of wannabe philosophers they'd never heard of. Melissa was being paid by Schollies to teach and to shoulder her share of administrative duties. In her absence during the summer term of 1991, when it looked as if Croatia would be engulfed in civil war any day, the college Governing Body had appointed her Dean and were insisting she honour her teaching commitments.

Melissa was livid. Although from my present perspective as a senior member of college I can see that the Governing Body had a difficult balancing act to fulfil, at the time, I was wholeheartedly in Melissa's corner. Following the fall of the Berlin Wall and the imminent collapse of the Soviet Union, the role of Western academics was even more crucial for the future, she argued. Much more crucial than teaching undergraduates whose education had been infinitely more privileged. In my eyes, she had sole occupancy of the moral high ground. But in spite of her impassioned arguments to anyone who would listen, the college remained impassive. Come the autumn term, Melissa's wings would be clipped. She wouldn't be running seminars for dissidents in Dubrovnik. She'd be teaching Malthus and the history of population development in first-year tutorials.

And that's how I ended up in Dubrovnik on 1 October 1991, when the bombs started falling that cut off the water and the electricity to the city.

7

Alan Macanespie scratched his belly through the gap in his shirt buttons and slurped milky coffee from a cardboard carton. Theo Proctor's lip curled in disgust as his colleague belched sour breath across the table. 'You are disgusting, you know that?' The Welshman waved a hand in front of his face and reached for his bottle of mineral water.

'Just because you've no idea what a Saturday night's for doesn't mean the rest of us have to behave like we're a bunch of choirboys.' Macanespie shifted in his chair, his stomach following his movement like a sine wave of fat. 'After listening to that twat Cagney yesterday, I needed to wash the bad taste out of my mouth. I've got better things to do with my Sunday morning than deal with this pile of crap.' He scowled at a stack of folders piled on the table by Proctor's hand. The loser's hand that Cagney had dealt them had left him feeling bitter and insecure; unless he could see some light at the end of the tunnel that wasn't an oncoming train, he felt he was staring at an undistinguished and premature end to a pretty low-key career.

Proctor laid a slim hand on top of the pile. 'No, you haven't. Not if you want to keep your pension. Cagney's got it in for the likes of us. He's got a chip on his shoulder and he thinks the only thing us hard-working grunts are any use for is to make him look good.'

Macanespie snorted. 'He's got his bloody Savile Row suits for that.'

'And he wants the bosses to think those bloody Savile Row suits are where he belongs. So he needs results and if he doesn't get them, he'll have to hang somebody out to dry – and I sure as hell don't want it to be me.' Proctor flicked his laptop open and tapped it into life. 'After WikiLeaks and Edward Snowden, the one thing they're all paranoid about is leaks. And let's be honest, you can't look at what's been happening on our watch and not think somebody's been taking the law into their own hands.'

Macanespie burped again, glaring at the coffee carton as if it were somehow responsible for his own lack of finesse. He ran a hand over his ginger stubble and sighed. 'And nobody gave a shit. Getting rid of that human sewage was doing the world a favour.'

'You'd better not let Wilson Cagney hear you say that.' Proctor frowned as he summoned up a spreadsheet. The fine black hairs on the backs of his bony fingers made them look like magnified insect legs as they scuttled across the keys. 'You're single, Alan. You've no kids. You might have nothing ahead of you but drinking yourself into an early grave, but I've got to think about Lorna and the girls.'

There was a stony silence. Macanespie was motionless, his face revealing nothing of what was going on inside. Proctor had gone too far. For years, he and Macanespie had worked well together because they'd maintained a studied indifference to each other's faults. It was like a marriage in a Catholic country before divorce had become legalised. They were stuck with each other and so they'd made the best of a bad job, pretending their mutual contempt didn't exist, avoiding comment on the personal habits they despised. Proctor had never criticised Macanespie's drinking or his disgusting departures from what the Welshman considered obligate personal hygiene. For his part, Macanespie had tolerated finicky behaviour that he reckoned was borderline OCD and never complained about Proctor's perpetual displays of family photographs and endless tedious narratives about the brilliant, beautiful, erudite, talented paragons that were his daughters. That effective concordat had been blown out of the water by Wilson Cagney's display of gunboat diplomacy. Now it seemed Proctor was happy to throw him under the bus, his sole justification the failure of Macanespie's last relationship to go the distance. Probably, the Scotsman thought, he'd always been jealous because the fact that Macanespie hadn't been married meant she hadn't been able to take him to the cleaners after the split. Served her right. Macanespie had asked her to marry him more than once, but she'd always sidestepped the offer. So she walked out the door with no more than she walked in with. But Proctor, he was stuck with the prim and proper Lorna till death. Served him right, frankly.

Macanespie cleared his throat. 'Remind me. What are we looking at?'

'Over the past eight years, there have been eleven instances of an ICTFY target being assassinated within days of when they were due to be arrested.' Proctor called up another screen and frowned at it. 'The paperwork had been processed, the operation had been ordered. But in the gap between set-up and execution—' He flushed as he realised the inappropriateness of his choice of words.

'—there was an execution,' Macanespie blurted, only too predictably. Sometimes he couldn't help himself. That Scottish black humour just wouldn't sit quietly in the corner. 'And how many of those cases were ours?'

'Eight had Brits leading the investigation. The other three had Brits on the team.'

'The same Brits?'

Proctor ran his finger down the screen. 'Doesn't look like it. Alexandra Reid was second string on two cases then led one. Will Pringle led three, Derek Green led two and helped out on a third, and Patterson Tait headed up the other two. So we can probably rule them out as our vigilante. But we'll have to work our way down the totem pole in every case to find the common factor. The mole.'

Macanespie grunted. 'You're kidding, right? You're not seriously talking about embarking on the biggest waste of time this side of the 1987 Labour Party election campaign? We all know what this has been about. It's been a kind of ethnic cleansing of scumbags. Scrubbing the Balkans clean of the gobshites that made it hell on earth in the nineties. You know and I know the top name in the frame for all of these assassinations.'

Proctor breathed heavily through his nose. He pursed his lips and scowled at his computer, stabbing the keys as if they were Macanespie's eyes. 'We don't know that,' he growled.

'"We don't know that,"' Macanespie mimicked in a mimsy voice. 'It's been common knowledge round here for years, Theo. Don't start pretending you don't know what I'm talking about.'

'It's just rumour and gossip.'

'Rumour and gossip that nobody's ever contradicted in my hearing. The Balkan boys, they all give a nod and a wink whenever people start going on about what a funny coincidence it is that another sadistic fucker with a war crimes record as long as your arm gets the wooden overcoat before we can get him into custody.'

Proctor shook his head. 'Doesn't make it the truth. It's just a good story.'

'It's a story that fits the facts. That's why it keeps coming up again and again.' Macanespie began ticking off the points on his fat fingers. 'Who knows all the key players from way back when? Who's the kind of great big fucking hero that half the bloody Balkans would lie their slivovitz-guzzling heads off to protect? Who shouted his mouth off to every news organisation that would listen about how useless ICTFY was before he went underground just a matter of weeks before the first assassination?'

Proctor realigned the edges of his pile of files. They didn't need it. 'You're talking about Dimitar Petrovic.'

'Exactly.' Macanespie stuck two thumbs up and grinned triumphantly. 'You always get there in the end, Theo. Takes some pushing, but you always get to the top of the hill.'

'As usual, Alan, you're completely missing the point. Even if you're right about Petrovic – and I'm not conceding that you are – even if you're right, it still doesn't get us off the hook. Wilson Cagney probably knows all about Petrovic already. Petrovic isn't the issue here. The issue is where Petrovic is getting his information from. Somebody's pointing him in the right direction, Alan. And from where Cagney's sitting, it looks like one of us or else somebody very bloody close.'

VAL MCDERMID

8

There was good news and bad news. Annoyingly for Karen, the good news came first. Although that got the day off to the right sort of start, it made the bad news all the more of a disappointment.

The plus side of the ledger came from the fingerprint officer who had picked up the card from the CSI assigned to the skeleton. Karen had left the house before River was awake, taking a travel mug of strong coffee to kickstart her synapses. She could have checked out the forensic progress by phone, but she liked to eyeball the techies whenever she could. She'd always had the knack of flattering them into going the extra mile for her. And when you were working cold cases on the smallest of budgets, that extra mile could make all the difference.

So early on a Sunday morning, there wasn't much traffic and she made record time to the brand new Scottish Police

Authority's Serious Crime Campus. It sat in what Karen liked to think of as Scotland's answer to the Bermuda Triangle – the godforsaken area that lay between the M80, the M73 and the M8. It had been christened the Gartcosh Business Interchange to make it sound exciting and dynamic. It would, she thought, take more than rebranding to wipe the local population's memory of the massive strip mill and steelworks that had employed getting on for a thousand men whose working lives had effectively ended when British Steel closed the plant in 1986. A generation later, the scars remained.

The new building was a dramatic addition to the view. Its white concrete and tinted glass exterior looked like giant barcodes embedded in the landscape at odd angles to each other. The first time she'd seen it, Karen had been baffled, tempted to dismiss it as a piece of self-indulgence on the part of the architects. But Phil, who'd been reading about it online, had explained that it was in the shape of a human chromosome and that the barcode effect was meant to represent DNA. 'It's a metaphor,' he'd said. Grudgingly, she'd accepted that since part of the building would be housing the forensic science arm of Police Scotland, there was a point to the design. She was just glad that nobody was suggesting she should work inside a bloody metaphor.

One good thing about Sunday was the parking. The government wanted everyone to be green and use public transport to commute to work. So when new buildings went up, it was policy to create far fewer parking spaces than there were employees. According to one of Karen's former colleagues, Gartcosh had two hundred and fifty spaces for twelve hundred employees. But those employees had mostly been relocated to Gartcosh from somewhere else in the Central Belt. And very few of those somewhere elses had public transport links to Gartcosh. 'Some folk get to their work before seven o'clock, just to get a parking space,' he'd told her. Others swore a lot and churned up the grass verges of the surrounding roads. It wasn't going to change government policy, but it did make them feel better.

Inside the building, everything was shiny and new except for the people. They were as dishevelled, nerdy and grumpy as ever. Fingerprint expert Trevor Dingwall still looked like he'd been reluctantly rousted out of a pub football game. St Johnstone FC away shirt, baggy sweat pants and oversize trainers might have looked passable on a student. On a paunchy balding beardie in his forties, they just looked depressing. Karen found him in a corner carrel in an almost deserted open-plan office, hunched over an array of tenprints.

'See this job? It never ceases to amaze me,' was how he began the conversation.

'Good to see you too, Trevor. What's on the amazement agenda today, then?'

He pushed his glasses up his nose and peered at her. 'How long do you reckon that body's been up on the roof?'

Karen rolled her eyes. Why could nobody get to the point these days? Everybody seemed determined to turn the most straightforward of conversations into performance art. 'As things stand, the best estimate I've got is between five and ten years.'

Trevor nodded sagely. 'Like I said, amazing. The CSI said it probably started out inside a pocket, but when the fabric rotted away, it ended up leaning against the wall, at an angle. So one side was kind of protected, if you see what I mean?'

Karen saw what he meant. In her mind's eye, she could imagine the dark red plastic card propped against the wall, left stranded as the material of a hip pocket decayed around it. 'Uh huh. So, what have we got?'

'Two fingermarks. Probably index and middle finger.'

OK, Karen thought. Fairly amazing. 'What's the quality like?'

'Actually, surprisingly good. Flat surface, not handled too much. It didn't take much processing to get them either. To be honest, I thought it would be more of a challenge.' He looked disappointed.

'Next time I'll try and come up with something a bit more worthy of your skills.'

Oblivious to her irony, Trevor pressed on. 'If I had to guess, I'd say he was handed a room key at the hotel check-in. Maybe used it once then stuck it in his pocket. There's traces of what might be a mark on the other side, possibly a thumbprint, but it's too degraded to get anything from it.'

'So, the prints you did get – have you run them?'

'I input them before I went home, had them running overnight. And they came up clean on the IDENT1. So your body has no criminal record here in the UK. And that's it, I'm afraid.'

Good news, bad news. Karen sighed. 'OK. Thanks anyway. Can you pass the card on to the digital forensics team? I need them to look at the magnetic strip, see if we can get any details on that.'

'Already done it. I dropped it in after I'd lifted the prints.'

'I'll pop in and see what they've got to say for themselves. Thanks, Trevor.'

'No bother.'

Karen was halfway to the door when she stopped, struck by a thought. 'Trevor, do the military keep fingerprint records at all?'

He frowned. 'What, you mean of serving soldiers? No. They print insurgents when they're somewhere like Afghanistan, so they can check out likely lads that they pick up at checkpoints or in raids afterwards. But that's about it.'

'What about the security services? Do they print people they have working for them? I'm thinking foreign nationals.'

Trevor's bushy eyebrows jerked upwards. 'Now you're asking. I've never come up against anything like that. Any reason why you think your skeleton might be one of them?'

'The anthro thinks his early dental work happened in the

75

old Eastern bloc. I just wondered if he'd been working for us.'

Trevor sniggered. 'More likely a Polish plumber than a spook.'

Karen sighed. 'You're probably right. Except why would a Polish plumber have a bullet in his brain at the top of the John Drummond?'

An unconcerned shrug. 'They've got gangsters, just like us.'

'Great. That's all I need – an excursion into East European gang-bangers,' she groaned. 'As if we don't have enough home-grown hard men.' But she made a mental note to talk to the squad who dealt with organised crime among the immigrant communities of the central belt.

Walking through the building to the digital forensics department, Karen was struck by a dramatic view of the distant Campsie Fells. That was one of the things she loved about living in Scotland. The landscape was always butting in, showing its face in the most unexpected of places. Really, it wasn't surprising that so many foreigners came here intending it to be a way station on their journey, only to find that they wanted to stay. Was that what had happened with the John Drummond skeleton? Had he come here for whatever transient reason then been sucked in to a different kind of life? Or had it been a life on the wrong side of the tracks that had brought him into her orbit?

Karen pushed open the door into the reception area of the

digital forensics lab. There was nobody behind the desk, but a sign instructed her to ring a bell on the wall. She'd almost given up hope when a door opened to reveal a broad-shouldered young woman in a muscle vest and magenta jeans with a pimped-up shock of platinum blonde hair and a nose stud. Karen immediately felt dumpy, unfit and uncool under her fierce scrutiny. 'I'm DCI Pirie,' she said, determined to seize what initiative she could. 'Historic Cases Unit. I'd like to talk to someone about a piece of evidence we submitted to you yesterday.'

The woman shifted a wad of chewing gum from one side of her mouth to the other. 'I'm Tamsin Martineau and I'm the one you need to talk to,' she said, an Australian accent evident even in those few words. 'Come on through.'

Karen followed her into a room dimly illuminated by computer screens. 'I know it's early days, but I was in the building.'

'No worries,' Tamsin said, settling into an ergonomic chair in front of a work station that featured three monitors and various black and silver boxes whose function was a mystery to Karen. 'Drag up a chair.'

Karen brought over the nearest simple chair and sat down. 'Is there anything you can tell me?'

The words were barely out of her mouth when she regretted them. Tamsin smiled like a woman who's just been handed the keys to somebody else's sports car. 'Well,' she said, drawing the word out tantalisingly. 'Let me see.' And she was off. 'Your CSI said he thought it was a hotel key-card, and I'd put money on that myself. Theoretically, the card could still hold some data. But that data isn't going to be much use to us. It's not going to say, "No-Tell Motel room three hundred and two for the night of June twentieth in the name of Mr Bojangles". No such luck. Truth is, it's unlikely to contain much except a random string which matches the access key for the relevant hotel door at the time in question. If we got really lucky, it could also have markers that would indicate the nature of the booking.'

'The nature of the booking? What, you mean how it was booked? Like, phone or Internet?'

Tamsin gave Karen an impatient look, as if she were a small and stupid child. 'No, I mean like, was it room only, or bed and breakfast, that sort of thing. Whether they're allowed to charge to their room. Which would indicate that the hotel's done a pre-authorisation on a credit card. Whether or not they have access to any additional facilities like a gym, a pool, an executive lounge. That in turn would help you narrow down which hotel the key-card is for.'

'Right.' Karen felt on safer ground here. 'Like, if he had access to the gym and the pool, it's not likely he was staying in a guest house in Leith.'

'Got it in one. There might even be an expiry date and time, which'd give you a window on when he checked in. The only problem would be that the data held on these cards is almost always encrypted. They use a master encryption key which is unique to the property and set when the key system is installed. On the plus side, the encryption key is usually pretty short by modern standards. And because there aren't too many manufacturers of these key-entry systems, there's not so many algorithms to factor into the equation. So somebody like me can bust the encryption wide open in a couple of weeks or so.'

'A couple of weeks?' Karen couldn't hide her disappointment.

'Come on, Detective. You know that's no time at all in my world. Hardcore decryption can take bloody months. But anyway, all of this is aca-fucking-demic. Because your key-card's been sitting out in the open and most of the magnetic strip has flaked off like dandruff on a jacket collar.'

Dismayed, Karen said, 'Bugger.'

'Well, yes and no. There's a bit of data that I've been able to pull off it. And it turns out to be worth a lot more than whether or not Mr Bojangles had access to the executive lounge ... ' Tamsin paused expectantly.

Karen knew what was expected of her. 'Really? That's amazing. What did you manage to find out?'

'Here's the thing. If you jam a couple of cards together in your pocket, sometimes the data from one magnetic strip gets picked up by another. And that's what happened here. Mr Bojangles obviously had his bank debit card snuggled up to his hotel room key. And some of the info rubbed off. It's your lucky day, Detective.'

'Have you got a name?'

Tamsin shifted her chewing gum again, taking her time. 'As good as. Just call me your fairy godmother, Detective. I've got a sort code and the first five digits of the account number. I don't think you'll need an expert code breaker to sort that one out for you when the banks open in the morning.'

9

Even Karen's talent for bending the world to her will wasn't enough to dig out bank details on a Sunday. She might be able to roust out a cooperative sheriff to sign a warrant, but that wouldn't really speed anything up and she didn't want to waste any favours owing on a pointless exercise. She knew River would be in the lab, interrogating the skeleton for information about its origins, but there was nothing she could usefully do there, and besides, River would let her know as soon as she came across anything that would provide a lead. Fraser Jardine's free-climbing pal hadn't returned her call. Maybe it was time to give him a wee kick up the bahookey, remind him that ignoring police officers wasn't such a brilliant idea.

She leaned against the bonnet of the sensible, inconspicuous Ford Focus she had chosen for its anonymity and called Ian Laurie. Just when it seemed the phone was about to go to voicemail, a husky grunt replaced the ring tone.

'This is Detective Chief Inspector Karen Pirie. Who am I speaking to?' Karen didn't have to pretend to sternness.

Throat-clearing, rattle of phlegm. Phil had his faults, she thought. But at least he never made a noise like that in the morning. 'Is this a wind-up?' A deep, dark voice. Clearly Fraser Jardine had taken her seriously when Karen had told him to keep his mouth shut about his grisly discovery.

'This is the police, sir. Are you Ian Laurie?'

'Aye. But I've done nothing wrong.'

'Nobody's accusing you, sir. I left a message on your voicemail yesterday asking you to contact me as a matter of urgency.'

A throaty gurgle of laughter. 'You're for real. Fuck. I thought you were one of my pals taking the mince. I'm sorry, officer. I'm not normally this much of a fuckwit. It's just that I'm getting married in a week and my pals are ripping the piss out of me every chance they get.'

Life in the fast lane, right enough, Karen thought. 'I am for real, sir. And I do need to talk to you about a serious matter. I'm just down the road. If you'd like to give me your address, I can be with you in about half an hour. I won't detain you long, but this is most definitely not a taking of the mickey.' Her tone had an edge of 'don't mess with me' that usually did the trick, particularly with the innocent.

It worked. An hour later, she was toiling up an apparently endless flight of tenement stairs in Gorgie. Why did they always live on the top floor, she wondered, heart rate rising along with the altitude. At least this close was clean; she'd lost count of the number of times she'd tried to climb stairs while holding her breath because of the noxious brew of piss, decaying takeaway food and other things she didn't want to think too closely about.

The Mint waited by Laurie's front door for her to catch him up and get her breath back. He looked as happy to have had his Sunday disrupted as she was to have him there. But although there was talk of changing the law, the Scottish system still demanded corroboration at every stage of an inquiry. If Karen walked into Ian Laurie's flat alone and he confessed to an entire string of murders, it wouldn't be admissible evidence. In the eyes of the court, she could have simply made it all up. And so she was stuck with sharing her Sunday with the Mint.

Ian Laurie's living room had a view of chimney pots and sky. Looking out of the window was preferable to the interior. Laurie was wearing baggy sweat shorts and a grey T-shirt advertising a city-centre gym. He had the stringy muscles and skinny build of a distance runner or a climber, but today it was mismatched with yellow-tinged eyes and skin, scrubby black stubble and breath that would have stripped the Forth Bridge back to the bare metal. Karen didn't envy his wife-to-be.

83

He waved them towards a baggy leather sofa that looked as if it had originally been expensive but had been serially maltreated. Laurie himself slumped into a matching arm-chair that faced a vast plasma TV where a fireplace had once stood. 'So,' he said. 'What's this serious matter?' He didn't look or sound convinced.

'I'll get to that in due course,' Karen said. 'I wanted to talk to you about something you said to Fraser Jardine.'

Laurie scratched his armpit and yawned. 'Fraser? What did I say to Fraser?'

'When he said he was going to the John Drummond School building, one of your mutual pals asked if he was going up from the inside or the outside. And that jogged his memory and he came up with something you'd said about climbing the John Drummond.'

Laurie straightened up and looked wary. 'Never happened. A wee joke, that's all.'

'Mr Laurie, I'm not looking to nick anybody for trespassing. But I am looking for some help. There's no catch here. I'm just trying to fill in a bit of background.'

'I've never been in the John Drummond,' he said, quickly and firmly. 'There's absolutely nothing I can tell you about the place. Nothing.'

'What is it you do for a living, Mr Laurie?' Karen asked casually. The framed monochrome photographs of black jazz musicians that lined the walls were not, she suspected, a clue. More of a style statement.

'I work for RBS.' Seeing her lip curl, he added hastily, 'I'm not a banker. I'm a buildings services executive.'

Karen smiled. 'What? You count the chairs? Not so many of them as there used to be, I guess. So, like most people you don't have anything to do with the police on a daily basis. I just want to explain that it's nothing like the telly. I'm a lot smarter than most of those dozy detectives you see on the box. And I'm a lot less patient. I'm trying to do this the polite and quick way. But we can do it down the police station in a way that'll make you very late for your work tomorrow.' She gave him a smile that her colleagues had learned the hard way not to trust.

Laurie looked at the Mint as if he was expecting some male solidarity. The Mint looked stolidly at his feet.

'I've not done anything,' he said plaintively.

'Free climbing,' Karen said. 'What do you know about free-climbing buildings, Mr Laurie?'

'I've seen videos on YouTube. That kind of thing.'

'I think you can do better than that. I don't know why you're being so cagey, Mr Laurie. I couldn't give a toss about what you do in your spare time. All I'm trying to do is find out how a murder victim might have got on to the roof of the John Drummond School without any trace of a break-in.'

'Murder?' Laurie's voice was a squeak. 'You never said it was a murder.'

'I was trying to spare your feelings. Now, are you going to tell me about the John Drummond or not?'

'I want a lawyer,' Laurie stammered.

The Mint looked up. 'Like the boss said, we're not accusing you of anything. We're just looking for information. You get a lawyer, you start to look like a man who's done something wrong.'

Karen looked at the Mint with new respect. Twice in two days he'd said something that wasn't stupid. Was there some new drug going the rounds that she hadn't heard about? 'So, the John Drummond?' she said.

Laurie hunched his shoulders and folded his arms. 'It's not like we do anybody any harm, right? It's the challenge.'

Karen wanted to give him a verbal slap but she held back. A bunch of well-heeled boys desperate for a cheap thrill. Not content with bringing the global economy to its knees, they had to go about the place like daft wee boys showing off. 'Right,' she said. 'Who's the "we"?'

'Me and a couple of guys I was at uni with. We did a bit of climbing back then. Winter climbing in the Highlands, a bit of Alpine stuff. Then we got hooked on free-climbing rock. It's an amazing feeling. Anyway, about three years ago, there was this BBC series, *Climbing Great Buildings*. Which basically did what it says on the tin. And we started tracking down online vids of people free climbing big buildings.' His voice tailed off.

'And then you started doing it?'

Laurie looked sheepish. 'We weren't hurting anybody. We did it at night, always out of the way, so we wouldn't freak anybody out.'

Karen shook her head, despairing at the jackass stupidity

of young men. 'So tell me what you know about the John Drummond.'

He sighed. 'You get to know people who do the same thing. A lot of them I just know from online. But we share info. Routes to get up difficult buildings, tips for getting past particular obstacles. Somebody from down south was talking about the John Drummond, about how there was pretty much no security and you could get up and down without any fear of getting caught. And how it was really challenging as a climb because there's a lot of overhangs on the way up. And a guy I know from Glasgow, he chipped in and said he'd done it solo on Midsummer's Eve when it didn't even get properly dark and how amazing it had been and the view was great.' He sighed again. 'So we did it. And that's all I know. I don't know anything about a murder, I swear to God.'

'So you did go up the John Drummond?'

He nodded. 'September. Friday the thirteenth. We thought it would be funny to go up when it was supposed to be unlucky.'

'Did you go on the roof?'

'Aye, that's the whole point. You've not really climbed it unless you go right the way up.'

The Mint leaned forward, raising a finger for permission to speak. He knew better than to interrupt Karen directly in mid-flow. She nodded. 'Does that mean you climbed up the wee turrets in the corners?'

'The pinnacles? Aye, we each did one of them.'

'Did you go inside any of them?' Karen was back in the driving seat.

'Dougie stuck his head in one for a look. But he said there was nothing to see and it was too wee to get inside. So we left it at that and went back down again. Was that where he was, the dead guy? In one of the pinnacles?' The yellow complexion took on a greenish tinge.

'Did you ever come across a free climber from the old Eastern bloc?' Wrong-foot them with the question they don't expect. That was Karen's MO.

Laurie looked confused. 'What? You mean a Russian or something?'

'Maybe more like the Baltic states. Or the Balkans?' It dawned on Karen that he didn't know what she was talking about. He'd barely have been at primary school when the Balkan conflict had shaken Europe's postwar consensus. 'Latvia. Lithuania. Estonia. Croatia. Serbia. Bosnia. Poland, even.'

His face cleared. 'Right. No, I don't think I ever have. I've messaged with a couple of Americans and New Zealanders, but that's about it for foreigners.' He smirked. 'Unless you count the English.'

That was a record for 2014, Karen reckoned. Almost lunchtime before somebody had given a nod to the upcoming independence referendum. 'You're going to have to give us a list of all your free-climbing contacts. DC Murray here will sort that out with you.'

'How did he die?'

It was the question they always asked. How had the victim's life been stripped from them. 'He was shot,' Karen said. 'Somebody stood in front of him and pointed a gun at his head and pulled the trigger.'

The Mint made a gun shape with the first two fingers of his right hand. 'Boom,' he said. 'Just like that. He'll no' be doing any more free climbing.'

All that summer, there had been talk of war. At the beginning of June Croatia had seceded from Yugoslavia, determined to escape the domination of the Serbs. But there were enough ethnic Serbs within the borders of the new country to create a groundswell of support for the idea of creating a new Serbian state inside Croatia. It was an idea that had the wholehearted backing of Serbia and of the Yugoslavian armed forces, egged on by Slobodan Milosevic with his strong-arm, strong-man tactics. The clash of aspirations was a recipe for disaster, but I was too young and Melissa was too optimistic to believe the disaster would really happen.

And so when Schollie's Governing Body put a stop to Melissa's latest Balkan mission, we saw this as merely a temporary hiccup. In Melissa's head, her absence would be short-lived and the gap could easily be plugged by a bright post-doctoral research fellow groomed to think in the same way as her mentor. I would lead some seminars, work with the writers of papers, and help to set up courses at the new institutions that would rise from the ashes of the old Communist state. What could possibly go wrong?

For the first few weeks, it seemed as if Melissa might have been right. That all the sabre-rattling would come to nothing. That there was no real appetite for a fight. Yes, there was fighting going on in Vukovar, but that was a long way away and nobody in Dubrovnik seemed to be panicking over it. Dubrovnik didn't feel scary at all. Not like the trip to Prague I'd taken with Melissa a few years before, when the secret police had come knocking at the door of a house where we'd been leading a clandestine seminar. The hosts had opened a concealed trapdoor in the kitchen floor and bundled us into a damp cellar where the only sound apart from our panicked breathing was the scrabble of rats' claws on stone and the overhead thuds as they jumped over the joists in the floor above our heads. That had been scary, all right. But by the time I travelled to Dubrovnik, the stranglehold of the Communist state had been broken. We were all Europeans now.

I embraced my new life with open eyes, open arms and open heart. I'd discovered when I escaped Fife and arrived in London that immersing myself completely was the way to make the most of every new experience and I was happy to have the chance to do that again. I was renting a room from Varya, a primary school teacher. Melissa had worked with her on a research project and knew the hard currency I'd be paying for my garret under the eaves would make a difference to her family. I was, I think, the only person who had a room to herself – even Varya's elderly mother had to share with the ten-year-old daughter of the house.

My room was spartan – a single iron bedstead with a wafer-thin mattress, a plain pine cupboard with shelves and hanging space for three shirts and a jacket, a table barely big enough for an open A4 notebook, and a rickety wooden chair. A crucifix hung above the bed with an emaciated Jesus gazing down mournfully, reflected in the small mirror on the opposite wall so I could see him from my bed. But the view across the city made up for everything. Varya's house was outside the walled city itself, at the foot of Srdj, the steep ridge above Dubrovnik. At the back of the house, a narrow garden ran to where the pine trees and scrubby undergrowth began. But from my window at the front of the house, I had a panoramic view of the ancient walled city.

Until I saw Dubrovnik, I had no notion of what a walled city really meant. I'd seen a fragment of the wall the Romans had built around London. Six metres high, two and a half metres thick. I thought that was impressive. The walls of Dubrovnik are twenty-five metres high and eight metres thick – between three and four times the scale of London's defences. Looking down across the patchwork of terracotta roofs and the white hulls of boats in the harbour was an inspirational start to those September days when I was first finding my feet in the city. Some mornings, the sky was a deep unbroken blue, a colour we never see in the UK. On other days, because the summer was drawing to a close, wispy skeins of cloud created a tigerskin sky.

The seminars I was leading had a real sense of liberation about them too. There was an exhilaration in the air after all those years of oppression, but also a kind of disorientation. We take so many of our freedoms for granted; in those early days in Dubrovnik, I saw at first-hand how it was unsettling as well as liberating to have permission to think, write and speak openly. And of course there were plenty of academics around from the Communist era who were clinging grimly to their old jobs and their old ways. Still, what we were doing felt like continuing a revolution.

The sparkle of intellectual independence seemed to light up our social interactions too. Although people's resources were limited, everyone was eager to find any excuse to get together and have some kind of party. From sedate afternoon teas graced with pastries laden with honey and nuts to raucous drinks parties fuelled by slivovitz and rakija, I had invitations galore.

I was young and eager enough to show up to most of them. I knew this period in Dubrovnik would open up professional possibilities for me – contacts to be made, papers to be written, maybe even a book – and so I wanted to meet as many people as I could. I was surprised at how many knew about the underground university movement, and I was touched by their pleasure in our continued involvement. And so most of my evenings were occupied with these social encounters that constantly opened new areas for my intellectual curiosity to explore.

Melissa had prepared me for that. What she hadn't prepared me for was love.

10

By late afternoon, Macanespie and Proctor had worked their way through all eleven files. There were undoubtedly common factors over and above the ones Wilson Cagney had raised, as Macanespie pointed out, reluctantly acknowledging his boss might have had a point.

'Every one of them thought they'd got away with it,' he said. 'They'd seen their cronies getting picked up and dragged up here to face trial. But they were all feeling pretty secure. They'd all changed their names and rewritten their histories. Most of them had cut loose from their families and their friends.'

'Better to be alive than to have a life,' Proctor muttered.

'Oh, I think they mostly had a life. Just a different one from the one they started out with. Look at how they were living, for fuck's sake.' He pulled out one file. They'd numbered them because that was easier than trying to remember names and aliases. 'Number six. Allegedly in charge of a rape camp outside Srebrenica. Estimates say between a hundred and a hundred and thirty women and girls were basically fucked to death by a succession of Serb soldiers. According to witnesses, number six enjoyed watching. And taking part himself on occasion, if the girls were young enough. He ordered the village elders to dig a grave pit ten feet deep. Then when he and his men had done with the women, they dumped them in the pit, put a layer of builders' lime and soil over them, then added a layer of dead dogs and donkeys so that when the cadaver dogs went tonto, we'd dig down and find the dead animals and think that was all there was to it. And what happened to number six?'

Proctor cast his eyes heavenwards, summoning up the content of the file he'd read earlier that day. 'Is he the one who ended up in Tenerife?'

'No. He's the one we tracked down working as a fitness instructor in Calgary. With the new young wife and the two daughters.'

Proctor winced. 'Now I remember. Nice house in the suburbs, pillar of the local Serbian community.'

'Who later claimed they had no fucking idea at all that he was one of the evil butchers of Kosovo.' He threw the file down in disgust. Reading them one after the other this way had stirred a response that had sneaked up on him. In spite of himself, Macanespie was beginning to feel he'd like to track down this killer, if only to shake his hand. 'So, as I said, all this lot had new identities. Here's another thing. Not one of them was still in the Balkans, unless you count Greece. And the ones that were in Greece were all on islands well away from anywhere they might bump into anybody who knew what they'd done in their previous lives. Rhodes, Cyprus, Crete – you're not going to find many Kosovar refugees wandering about the beaches there.'

'It also means that whoever has been murdering them is more likely to have a clean run at it. If the guy on the run has chosen a bolthole where he's unlikely to bump into any of his victims, chances are the assassin will be in the clear too.'

Macanespie frowned. 'I'm not sure I agree with you on that one. I think we have to assume that the killer was never on the same team as his targets. So you've got number six hiding in plain sight among the Serbian community in Calgary. I'm betting some of them knew exactly who he was but they didn't have a problem with sheltering him. However if the assassin is somebody who was around during the war years, they could be the very people who would recognise him.'

Proctor thought about it. 'Good point. Of course, we can't assume that our assassin was around then. It could be he was too young to have been involved. But he's gone on this journey of revenge because of the damage the war did to his life. To his family, maybe. Or to his people, if you want to make a big patriotic thing of it.'

'"Journey of revenge",' Macanespie said sarcastically. 'You Welsh are the poets, right enough. So, we've got the new life. We've got living in exile. And we've also got the MO. They all had their throats cut from behind.'

'That's really up close and personal,' Proctor said. 'You'd need some nerve to do that.'

'Which points us right back at General Dimitar Petrovic. Military training – hell, we trained him ourselves. And nerves of steel, by all accounts. He's got an impressive record for an intelligence officer. Mostly they stay well out of the line of fire, but he was right in the thick of it more than once. He took "nobody left behind" very bloody seriously.'

Both men sat in silence for a moment, contemplating the files. 'There's only one thing that I struggle with,' Proctor said at last, clicking his mouse and pulling up a set of personnel records.

'What's that?'

'I'm looking at Dimitar Petrovic's details here. He's over six feet and he's not a whiplash. The thing I have to ask myself is how he got close enough to these guys to slit their throats from behind.'

Macanespie shook his head. 'Doesnae bother me. Just because he's a big man doesnae mean he's not light on his feet. My dad was twenty stone but he had fairy feet on a dance floor. He could sneak up on my mother when she was washing the dishes and nearly give her a heart attack. And look at the locations. He's taken them all down at a time and place where he had them to himself. I think he's staked them out over a period of time and worked out the vulnerable point where he could make his move with the best chance of success.' He prodded the files, knocking them out of alignment again. 'Look – a jogging trail. An underground parking garage. On the doorstep in a block of flats, twice. Inside the rear entrance to a dry cleaners. In a back alley, putting out the rubbish. In the guy's own pool hut. Et cetera. He didn't just leap out of the bushes like a fucking ninja. He planned this, every inch of the way.'

'Petrovic, then? Are we agreed on that, at least?'

Macanespie sighed. 'He's the obvious choice. He disappeared off the radar just before the killing spree started. And every one of the victims was involved in atrocities that he had direct knowledge of. Either during the Croatian war, where he was directly involved as an active participant, running intelligence for the Croatian Army. Or during the Kosovo conflict when he was seconded to NATO. He was close to the international observers then – he saw a lot of shit first-hand, or else he heard about it from the poor bastards that survived. And his intel pinpointed some of the units directly involved in the atrocities.'

Macanespie tried to sound matter-of-fact, to hide from Proctor that this task was getting to him. His job had brought him into uncomfortable proximity with a wide range of the worst things human beings could do to one another. Over the years he'd learned to build a wall between the knowledge and the rest of his life. But occasionally an incident found a chink in his armour and inveigled its way into his nightmares. One of those had risen from those files to haunt him again.

A hill village in Kosovo. A group of Serbian soldiers with the red mist of conquest in their eyes. A round-up of all the males in the village. Supposedly you weren't considered qualified to bear arms till you were fourteen, but the Serbs liked to err on the side of caution, so any boy who looked more than twelve was forced into the big barn on the edge of the village along with the others. Harsh commands backed up with rifle butts smashed into faces and bayonet slashes to arms and legs, and within half an hour, all the men were herded into the barn without even the respect paid to livestock. Because livestock were useful, after all.

Forty-six of them were pushed right back against the far wall, crowded into a small space, nostrils filled with the smell of other men's fear. They knew what was coming but they tried to convince themselves this would be different from the horrors they'd heard about. Maybe what had filtered back to them had just been rumour, grown fat on people's terror. Maybe their panic would be enough to send the Serbs on their way, laughing in derision at the pitiful Kosovars who couldn't even control their bladders.

Seven soldiers filed into the barn, Kalashnikovs casually slung across their bodies. Then, on a word from their commander, a stocky shaven-headed man, they raised their guns and emptied their magazines into the bodies of the forty-six. A couple of the soldiers kicked the bodies aside when they had done, to make sure they were all dead. When they left, they set fire to the barn.

The only reason Alan Macanespie's nights were disturbed by what had happened that afternoon was that there had been an unintended witness. One of the boys was not in fact dead. He'd been squeezed into the far corner of the barn. When the shooting started, he'd been flattened under the weight of bodies, briefly passing out in the crush. And so he'd appeared dead when the soldier's boot crashed into his ribs. He'd come to as the flames were taking hold of the barn.

Somehow, in the smoke and the heat, he'd managed to crawl to a loading-bay door at the side of the barn and push it open far enough to tumble to the ground below, out of sight of the soldiers, who were laughing and drinking outside the barn. Dazed and wounded, the boy nevertheless managed to make it into the thick woodland behind the village. He lived to tell the tale. And he told it vividly, making it come alive as no official report could do. His words had lodged in Macanespie's head. If he had shared Dimitar Petrovic's visceral involvement with the Balkans, he'd have wanted to take the most primitive revenge possible on the evil thugs who had raped and murdered their way across his country.

Now, he forced the memory back in its box. 'I can't say I entirely blame him,' he said.

'They're probably planning a hero's welcome for him back home,' Proctor said.

'Even so, that's not going to cut the mustard with Cagney. What we need to do now is draw up a list of everybody that had access to those files. From investigators down to the operational planners. We have to find some common denominators here.' Macanespie looked glum. 'That's going to be a fucking nightmare shitstorm of trawling though files.'

'Or we could take a short cut.'

'How? We can't farm it out. Nobody with that level of clearance is going to be daft enough to take it off our plates.'

Proctor shook his head. 'That's not what I meant, not at all. What does Cagney really want?'

'The mole.'

'That's just a smokescreen. If we find the mole, that's enough to earn Cagney a pat on the back. But the real glory? That's not exposing some file clerk in ICTFY. The real glory is bringing Dimitar Petrovic to justice. That's what'll turn Cagney into a hero. The man who put justice first.'

Macanespie snorted. 'Maybe so, Theo. But Petrovic is like the Scarlet fucking Pimpernel. How exactly do you think a pair of Foreign Office lawyers are going to bring him in?'

Proctor tapped the side of his nose. 'Trust me, Alan. I've got one or two ideas on that score. Watch and learn, boyo. Watch and learn.'

11

You did this job for long enough, you learned the idiosyncrasies of the various sheriffs who were responsible for signing the warrants you needed to get the job done. In theory, Karen should have presented her case to a sheriff in Edinburgh. But that was still on the outer edges of her comfort zone. Much better to turn her charm on a Kirkcaldy sheriff that she already had a good working relationship with. And besides, if she pitched up at the local court first thing on Monday morning, she wouldn't have to hang around the way she would in the capital. Even more importantly, she'd get an extra hour and a half in bed.

Karen had spent most of her working life in her native Fife but the creation of Police Scotland in 2013 had changed everything for her. The Cold Case Unit she'd been happily running from her office in Glenrothes had been amalgamated with those of other forces in a mash-up that skinned jobs down to the bone and shifted her workplace across the Forth Bridge to Edinburgh. Theoretically, she had more status – now she was in charge of a unit with national responsibilities. In reality, she was running a much bigger operation with almost the same amount of resources. The bosses called it 'economies of scale'. But from where Karen sat, it meant doing a lot more with a lot less.

She'd lobbied to keep the job based in Fife, arguing that it was important to show people that the new national force wasn't all about Edinburgh and Glasgow. She'd hastily backpedalled when her boss had suggested she might like to base herself at Gartcosh. That would have been a near-impossible commute. It was bad enough shuttling back and forth from Edinburgh in the rush hour. When she died and went to hell, it would be the approach road to the Forth Bridge in the rain and the dark of a cold December morning. The new, second crossing was billed as the magic panacea for commuters but she suspected it was going to be about as much use as the over-hyped, over-budget Edinburgh trams.

Karen had broached the subject of a move to Edinburgh. Or at least across the bridge. DC Jason Murray had already done just that, sharing a flat with three students, leading Karen to comment that it would take a gross of Mints to equal the joint IQ of his flatmates. But Phil, usually reasonable and willing to compromise, had dug his heels in. Living in Kirkcaldy was handy for his new job in Dunfermline; they'd only just finished doing up the house; Edinburgh house prices were outrageous; and he liked being able to walk to Raith Rovers home games so he could have a beer with his pals. It was the nearest they'd come to a serious falling-out, and it pissed Karen off that her priorities were so low down their collective totem pole. She loved Phil, but this nerve-shredding daily journey was doing her head in.

There was an obvious solution. She still owned her own house on the edge of the town. After she'd moved in with Phil, she'd rented it out, but she could easily serve notice to quit on her tenants. She'd have no trouble selling it and with the proceeds she could put down a decent deposit on a wee flat within walking distance of work. The only thing holding Karen back from that decision was the fear that it might mean the end of the road for her and Phil. He was the only man she'd ever lived with and part of her was afraid that if they split up, that would remain true. Besides, she loved him.

But that was in the future. Right now, she had to negotiate her way to a warrant that would force a bank to hand over information on one of its customers. She met the Mint off the Edinburgh train and together they walked through the Memorial Gardens and down to the familiar Scottish baronial-style turreted building that housed Kirkcaldy Sheriff Court. Karen sought out her favourite usher and checked who was on that morning's bench. Relieved that the court seemed curmudgeon-free, Karen plumped for John Grieve. He always leaned towards the little guy, which didn't always work to her advantage. But these days, getting one over on a bank definitely outranked putting the cops' noses out of joint.

They were ushered into Sheriff Grieve's room, a square box in the modern extension to the court. He looked up from his desk, peering over his half-moon glasses. With his bushy grey sideburns and wing collar, he resembled a man auditioning for a role in a Dickens TV adaptation. 'DCI Pirie. And DC Murray. I thought you'd relocated to Edinburgh?'

'Ach, we're all one nation now, hadn't you heard?'

His thin smile reminded her of a lipless lizard. 'But which nation, Chief Inspector? That's the question.'

'We'll all know the answer after the referendum, my lord.' She laid the paperwork on the desk in front of him. 'Right now, I'd settle for a warrant.'

He gave the application a quick once-over. 'You're looking for information from FCB?' He chuckled. 'Braver men than you have tried and failed.'

'It's not like I'm asking for anything that could compromise their business. Just a wee bit of minor inconvenience to help me with a murder inquiry.' Karen stressed the word 'murder'. Even with sheriffs who dealt in serious crime as a matter of course, it never hurt to remind them what was at stake.

Grieve smiled. 'A day I can cause inconvenience to a banker is a day not wasted. After all, every one of us has to live constantly with the consequences of their cavalier attitude to our money. It's really rather pleasant to have the chance to punch them in the metaphorical nose.' A line appeared between his eyebrows as he read the warrant more carefully. She wasn't worried. She'd made her case. Two minutes online had established which bank the sort code belonged to, and the specific branch. It was clear this was the primary lead on a murder. 'And besides, this does seem to be an eminently plausible reason to seek their assistance. We do owe the dead a debt, I think.' He uncapped an old-fashioned fountain pen and signed with a flourish. 'There you go. Good luck with that, Chief Inspector. Any problems with the execution, don't hesitate to come back to me.'

And she was off. 'I have no problem with executing this lot,' Karen muttered under her breath as she drove off towards the head office of the Forth and Clyde Bank. The bank occupied a quartet of black glass pyramids that slouched ominously by the point where the road from the Forth Bridge divided into two dual carriageways, one heading for Glasgow, the other for Edinburgh. When the grand new complex had been unveiled in 2007, just before the banks drove capitalism to the brink of collapse, the chief executive of the FCB had said, 'This site is a metaphor for the new dynamism of Scotland. We are based in neither of our great cities, but we look towards both. We are about synergy and energy. We are the future.'

Unfortunately, the future hadn't worked out quite as he'd imagined. When the banks hit the buffers following the collapse of Lehman Brothers in 2008, it soon became clear that FCB had abandoned the canny fiscal conservatism of its founding fathers. Along with many other apparently sound institutions, FCB had turned its solid foundations into Swiss cheese by inventing increasingly Byzantine ways to chase an illusory dime. And like many of those other institutions, it was deemed too big to fail.

Since the UK's taxpayers now owned 69 per cent of FCB, Karen thought she and Phil should have the right to set up their portable Hibachi on one of the billiard table lawns or Italian marble courtyards and enjoy a picnic with the bank's enviable views of the Pentland Hills to the south and the Ochils to the north. She snorted with sardonic laughter at the notion. For a start, they'd have to get past guards and gates that wouldn't have been out of place in a medium-security prison. If she hadn't phoned ahead to discover the name of the appropriate executive and then insisted on an appointment that morning, she'd have had no chance at penetrating the complex. Not even her police ID would have got her past the hard-faced behemoths in the gatehouse.

As it was, their photo ID was scrutinised and copied. Karen's car registration plate was photographed, her appointment checked by phone and then finally they were allowed to enter.

The smoked glass that separated FCB's offices from the outside world gave the interior a strange ambience. It was like being in a Hollywood movie where the colour register was slightly off. The effect was not so much futuristic as disconcerting. Gordon Fitzgerald, who rejoiced in the title of Head of External Compliance, was waiting for her as she arrived at the black granite reception desk. She'd expected the sort of tailoring that looked like it had cost as much as Phil's entire wardrobe, including his exhaustive collection of Raith Rovers shirts. But what she got was high street off-the-peg that wasn't any more of a statement than the Mint usually managed.

He thrust a hand out towards her. 'DCI Pirie, lovely to meet.' He gave the Mint a cursory nod. 'Constable. Call me Fitz, everybody does.' Dream on, she thought. 'Hope you were impressed with our security.'

'Anybody would think you had something worth robbing,' she said, deadpan, taking his practised hand in hers. Warm, dry, firm but not challenging. Karen would have bet he'd learned it on a training course.

He laughed, a high nervy whinny. 'Well, we are a bank.'

'Aye, even if you don't have any real money on the premises.'

'It's not about protecting money, the security. It's because of the personal threats against individuals here at the bank after the financial crisis. Feelings ran high, as I'm sure you'll remember. We do have your colleagues to thank for protecting us so effectively.'

Karen sometimes wondered heretically why they'd bothered. It didn't happen often, but every now and again, it felt like mob rule maybe had a bit more decency at its root than what the ranters were reacting against. But she was a polis; she had a duty of care to members of the public. Bankers and wankers, junkies and jakies, the theory of policing said they were all equal before the thin blue line.

As if.

'And now you have the chance to reciprocate. Can we go some place a wee bit less public?' Karen gestured at the foyer. It was hardly a bustling hub of activity, but she wanted to assert herself from the word go. 'Ideally somewhere with a computer terminal so you can access account information.'

He looked affronted, as if she had suggested inappropriate sexual contact. 'I'm not sure about that,' he stalled. 'But for now, we'll use one of our meeting rooms.' He led the way across the atrium and opened a door into a small but elegantly furnished room.

Interesting, Karen thought. She wasn't being allowed inside the bank itself. This was little more than an anteroom to the real heart of business at FCB. Still, it would do for a start. She moved straight into one of the executive leather chairs that surrounded the round table at the centre of the room. The Mint hovered by the door and Karen didn't wait for Gordon Fitzgerald to settle himself before she launched into her spiel. 'I'm investigating a murder,' she said. 'I have a significant lead which consists of a sort code and the first five digits of an account number. I need you to match them up for me with a customer.'

Fitzgerald gave her his thin smile again. 'We do have a duty of confidentiality, Detective. We can't just hand over the details of hundreds of customers on your say-so.'

Karen smiled. 'Come on now, Fitz. We both know we're not talking hundreds of customers. It's not like a particular branch has a block of account numbers that they hand out in order. Account numbers are assigned centrally, non-sequentially. So of the nine hundred and ninety-nine possible customers with the same first five digits, the chances are that only a very few will share the same branch sort code. I'm right about that, am I not?'

'You are. But that doesn't change the basic position. Client confidentiality, Detective. That's paramount here.'

Karen opened her bag. 'Very commendable. But I have something here that trumps your client confidentiality. Did you really think I'd come here asking for personal details of a bank account without a warrant?' She placed the signed warrant on the table.

He picked it up as if it were toxic. 'I'm going to have to run this past our legal eagles.'

'It's a warrant, Fitz. If you don't cooperate, you'll be in front of a sheriff this afternoon for contempt. In Kirkcaldy, to add insult to injury. Look, I'm not asking for the moon here. I can even narrow it down further for you. The man whose murder I'm investigating has been dead for at least five years. So I'm guessing that account hasn't seen much action lately.'

He got to his feet. 'I need to go and talk to somebody,' he said.

Karen made a show of taking out her phone and setting the timer. She held it up to face Fitzgerald. 'You've got half an hour. Then I'm phoning the sheriff's officer.'

The glossy surface of his composure slipped for a moment, then he gathered himself. 'I'll be as quick as I can.' He left the room faster than he'd entered it.

The Mint sat down opposite her. 'You enjoyed that, didn't you, boss?'

She grinned. 'Was it that obvious?'

'I think he got the message. So, will they come across?'

'We'll see. Now, do your maths homework or play Candy Crush or something useful while I check my email.'

The timer on Karen's phone told her that twenty-seven minutes had elapsed when the door opened again. It wasn't Gordon Fitzgerald who came in. It was a woman in her mid-forties dressed in an anonymous black suit and discreetly striped shirt. She carried a slim manila folder and introduced herself as she made for the chair between Karen and the Mint. 'I'm Gemma Mackay,' she said briskly. 'I work for the bank's legal department. I've read through your warrant and it all seems to be in order. We've taken a look at accounts held at that branch and there is only one that fits the partial number you supplied us with.'

'Which makes everybody's job easier,' Karen said.

'Indeed. However, you told my colleague that you

anticipated the account in question would be dormant. Is that right?'

'We think the account holder may be a murder victim. So yes, that's what we anticipated.'

Gemma nodded. 'Well, in a sense, you're right. But in another sense, you couldn't be more wrong.'

12

heo Proctor fussily double-checked the preparations for the Skype call. 'I still think you should talk to her,' he said. 'You know her better than I do.'

Macanespie pulled a face. 'She's not going to give anything up to the likes of me. Tessa Minogue has too good a conceit of herself for that.'

'But you worked alongside her for a couple of years. You've got common ground.'

'The key word in that sentence is "common". Tessa thinks she's a cut above the likes of me. She thinks I'm a pig. And it's not like we always saw eye to eye. She's a human rights lawyer, not a criminal advocate. So she was forever shouting her mouth off about the rights of the accused versus the rights of the victims, whereas we had to stick within the parameters of the law. She was all about what was right, and there were times when I thought she was completely off the wall. I was all about what was achievable. She once told me that legalistic bastards like me were the last hiding place of men like Radovan Karadzic.'

Proctor winced. 'That's a bit harsh.'

'Aye. Especially since Karadzic's lawyer was in the middle of arguing that he wasn't getting his human rights. Just like all the bleeding heart human rights lawyers. Black and white. But able to change sides in a heartbeat.' He looked at his watch. 'Ten minutes. Anything you're not sure about?'

Proctor ran through everything in his head. Tessa Minogue had been his idea, but he'd expected Macanespie to do the actual talking. He knew quite a lot about Minogue, but he couldn't have said how he knew all of it. Over the years in a tight community like that surrounding the ICTFY, knowledge percolated through, apparently by osmosis.

So, he knew that Minogue had first been in the Balkans during the Croatian war. She'd been a postgraduate researcher in international law at the time and, although her research had to do with the rule of law in the midst of a wider conflict, she'd been co-opted by Maggie Blake in the campaign to restore the shattered Old Town of Dubrovnik. Presumably that had been when she first met Petrovic, who had been running the Croatian Army's intelligence operation in the area.

But the end of the siege of Dubrovnik was only the end of the beginning of the long conflict in the region, a conflict whose heart Petrovic was somehow always close to. When the fighting spilled over into Bosnia-Hercegovina, with Karadzic and Milosevic forming an unholy alliance against the Croats and the Muslims, Petrovic was the man who always appeared to have his finger on the pulse of the action. He seemingly had contacts everywhere; sometimes in the least likely places. His intelligence background made him useful not only to the Croatians but also to a wider coalition of concerned parties. Before long, Sarajevo was under siege, experiencing constant bombardments and terrible privations that made Dubrovnik look like a tech rehearsal. Sarajevo endured almost four years of hell, provoking despair in everyone who had anything to with its defence and survival. And through it all, like a thread in a tapestry, was Dimitar Petrovic. He moved apparently seamlessly between the Croats and the international observers, offering intelligence to NATO commanders and his own generals alike.

Somewhere in the middle of all this, Tessa Minogue was doing service as an international observer and a provider of legal advice to the EU and NATO forces who were trying to damp down the appalling rise of barbarism in the region. The more stories emerged of atrocities, massacres and gang-rapes, the more vital it became that there should be some record of what was happening. Tessa and her colleagues made it their mission to provide witness, to gather testimony and to work towards some kind of long-term legal recourse.

Also in the middle of it all was Maggie Blake. She'd some-how managed to turn the conflict into a rich seam of academic product – research papers, conference lectures, individual chapters and then whole books on the geopolitics of the Balkan wars. Whenever she could be away from Oxford, she was somewhere in that battleground, interviewing anyone who would talk to her, watching and listening to every detail of what was going on around her, apparently unafraid of the bombs and the snipers and the marauding soldiers of all sides.

At first, Macanespie and his colleagues had thought the places where Maggie turned up were pretty random. And then Tessa Minogue had let slip that it was more than academic kudos that drew Maggie to the Balkans. Macanespie had seen the note on the file, scribbled on a yellowing page from a Banja Luka hotel notepad:

Manjaca concentration camp reckoned to be holding about seven hundred Croats and Bosniaks. Conditions appalling, beatings everyday occurrence, deaths reported. Two more mosques demolished this week. Tess Minogue says Dr Maggie Blake is here because she's Col. Petrovic's lover. Has been since Dubrovnik '91. They've kept that very quiet. Dagovic has been called back to Belgrade, nobody saying why.

On a couple of occasions, Petrovic had turned up in the UK, always with solid military or diplomatic reasons. Both times he'd vanished off the official radar for a few days; both times Tessa had mentioned in passing to colleagues that he was staying with Maggie Blake in Oxford. Then after the Dayton Agreement in 1995, Petrovic had surfaced in Oxford. He'd spent six months living with Maggie, but when the Kosovo Liberation Army organised itself and started fighting back against Milosevic's campaign of violence and property sequestration in Kosovo, he'd returned to the war zone, this time as an accredited NATO observer.

Frankly, Proctor thought, it was hard to imagine anything worse than being one of the impartial witnesses to the brutality and barbarism of those dying years of the twentieth century in that corner of the Balkans. The Second World War was supposed to have put an end to that sort of savagery in Europe; Kosovo had been the worst kind of wake-up call to remind everyone how thin was the skin of civilised behaviour.

Preparing the witness statements for the court hearings was bad enough for Macanespie and his colleagues. He couldn't begin to imagine what it would do to a man's soul to experience these situations at first-hand. Petrovic had done all that, and more. As a colonel in the Croatian Army, he must have been involved in some of the strategic planning that had ended so badly. He'd seen so much destruction; so many lives lost, homes destroyed, people stripped of the future they'd planned. Really, it was no wonder that something inside him had snapped.

The team at ICTFY had been committed to delivering

justice, partly so there could be some form of truth and reconciliation in the former Yugoslavia. But inevitably,
bureaucracy and the interminable wrangling of lawyers had
ensnared that purity of purpose and what they'd ended up
with had been a shadow of what they'd hoped for. For men
like Dimitar Petrovic, the frustration must have been beyond
bearing. Macanespie had heard that three of the Balkan
countries – Slovenia, Croatia and Serbia – had suicide rates
that put them in the world's top twenty. Faced with that
level of despair it was little wonder that a man with the
wherewithal to take the law into his own hands should do
so. Left to their own devices, Macanespie knew he and
Proctor wouldn't have found it in their hearts to do anything
about Petrovic's personal crusade.

But they hadn't been left to their own devices. Wilson
Cagney, a man personally untouched and unmoved by what
had happened in the Balkans in the last decade of the twentieth century, had decreed that vengeance outwith the
confines of the law was not going to be tolerated.

Before Macanespie could pursue that thought further, the
laptop trilled, signalling that Tessa Minogue was on the line
and ready for the call. Moving with unexpected speed, he
scooted round the desk so he was in Proctor's line of sight
and able to see the screen but invisible to the laptop's
camera. He readied a pile of paper and a Sharpie so he could
write notes to his colleague if necessary.

Proctor set the recording system running then picked up

the call. As always with Skype, the skin tones were like nothing found in nature and a face he knew to be attractive was distorted like the reflection in a fairground mirror. 'Hello, Tessa,' he said, giving her the closest he could manage to a welcoming smile. 'Thanks for agreeing to talk to me.'

'It's always a pleasure talking to you boys at the tribunal, Theo. We're all after the same things, are we not?'

Already Macanespie felt she'd wrong-footed them. There was often an uncomfortable gap between what the human rights lawyers wanted and what the tribunal officials were willing or able to give. They all had bitter experience of that, and the morally ambivalent horse-trading that went on as a result.

'I don't have to tell you we're in the process of winding things up,' Proctor said.

'Like I could forget. It's a tough call, Theo. There comes a point where so much time has gone by that arguably your witness testimony is tainted by repetition and coloured by reportage. It's an irony that we take such care of the human rights of people who had no regard for the rights of their victims. But I do get where you're coming from and I can't honestly take up arms against you.'

'That's very generous of you, Tessa. But that's not what I wanted to talk to you about. We've got a few cases that we're still proceeding with. Karadzic, Mladic and a couple of others. We're in the last stages of trying to make sure the cases are watertight and I've got the thankless task of tracking down one or two outstanding witnesses that we think can supply us with reliable testimony.'

'Good luck with that one,' she said, her grin arriving on his screen as a pixelated grimace. 'So many ended up scattered to the four winds. And who can blame them?'

'One of the people we're trying to pinpoint is an old friend of yours. General Petrovic of the Croatian Army. Dimitar Petrovic.'

Tessa pushed her long black hair behind one ear. 'Mitja? God, there's a name from the past. I haven't seen Mitja in, what? Eight years? He was living with Maggie Blake in Oxford. Then he walked out on her.'

'What happened to make him go?'

Tessa shrugged. 'Who knows why a man does anything? Why this interest in Mitja now, though?'

Proctor smiled. 'You know how it is. He's always been on our list but there were always more pressing names to talk to. He just slipped through the net. And now, we're struggling, to be honest. Do you know where he went after he left Professor Blake?'

'Ah, you know she's got a chair now. Obviously somebody's keeping closer tabs on Maggie than on Mitja.'

Proctor's eyes widened, then Macanespie held up a sheet of paper with 'Publications' scrawled across it. 'I wouldn't say that,' Proctor said. 'It's more to do with the fact that she keeps writing about the Balkans and we see her publications.'

'If you say so, Theo.'

'So, going back to my question … Have you been in touch with General Petrovic since he left Maggie Blake? And do you know where he is?'

'That's two questions, Theo. To which the answers are, "no", and "not exactly".'

Macanespie's head popped up, his expression eager. He gave Proctor a thumbs-up. Proctor seemed unconvinced that it was justified. '"Not exactly"? How inexactly are we talking here?'

'I don't know anything for sure. But I always thought Mitja would go back to Croatia. He loved his country, Theo. He really missed it.' She sighed. 'He never talked much about his life before the war, which made me wonder what it was he'd left behind. Wife, probably. Kids, maybe. Extended family for sure. He grew up in the east. He once said Vukovar had been his nearest decent-sized town growing up.' She spread her hands in a gesture of futility. 'That's all I know. He was always very good at deflecting questions about his past. But then, none of us was talking much about our history during the war. We were all too busy making sure we had a future. When there are bombs falling all around you, you're completely focused on the here and now.'

'So you think he went home?'

'Don't you? Back to the arms of his family. Back to the people who would heal him. I often wondered whether he was nursing a case of PTSD, you know. There were times when he seemed to absent himself from the company. He'd just shut down. He was in the room, he was at the table, but he wasn't present, if you know what I mean?'

'I've seen what you're talking about. And that's why he left Maggie? Because he was homesick? After six or seven years living quite happily with her in Oxford, he just upped sticks and went back to Croatia?' Proctor couldn't help sounding incredulous.

Tessa sighed. 'It's not so fanciful a notion, Theo. He didn't have much of an identity over here. He did a bit of lecturing – war and peace studies, that sort of thing. The occasional bit of security consultancy when one of his old NATO mates tossed him a bone. But Maggie had become the star. Ironic for him, a man who was right at the heart of that whole series of wars, that the person with the opinions that counted was his girlfriend. Who was only there in the first place because she *was* his girlfriend. I can see how that would be hard to accommodate in the long term, can't you?'

'But back in Croatia, he'd still be the big man, is that what you're saying?'

She gave a rueful smile. 'I'd have thought so, wouldn't you? He was one of their unequivocal war heroes.'

'It's a reasonable assumption. But if that's the case, it's hard to believe he hasn't shown up on our radar. Ever since the tribunal was set up, we've had teams on the ground, looking for leads into the whereabouts of alleged war criminals. And witnesses, obviously. But not once have we had a whisper that Petrovic is on the patch.'

Tessa pushed her hair behind her ear again. Was that a tell? Was it her involuntary reaction to a question that made her uneasy? Or just a play for time? 'I don't know what to say to that, Theo. It's possible people are shielding him? You know how clannish they can be over there. If he's made it clear that he's done with all that, I could imagine a little village in the mountains closing ranks and keeping him under wraps. Karadzic was living in Belgrade for years when he was one of the most wanted men in the world. Supposedly going to Serie A football matches over in Italy, for heaven's sake. If they can protect a monster like him, they're not going to think twice about helping a hero like Mitja to live under the radar.'

'I suppose. And you've not heard from him at all?'

She shook her head, looking regretful. 'Not so much as an anonymous email. And neither has Maggie. I tell you, Theo, it was a bit of a blow to the old self-esteem. I thought we were pals, me and Mitja. It was one thing to leave Maggie. That kind of crap happens all the time. Fifty ways, and all that. But I was his friend. And he cut me off with no word of farewell. Still, I hope he's happy. I thought he was happy here for a long time, but obviously I was wrong. Can't the Croats help you with his background details? Surely they must have something on file? The Communists were top of the pops when it came to bureaucracy, after all.'

Proctor shook his head. 'Like so much in that part of the world, a chunk of military records didn't make it through the war. An incendiary bomb, apparently. We're knackered on that score.'

An expression Macanespie couldn't identify flickered across her face. 'Bad luck, Theo. Look, I'm sorry I can't be more help. But I need to crack on. If anything else occurs to me, I'll be sure and let you know.'

'Thanks, Tessa. Take care now.'

She cut the call off without another word. Macanespie popped up like a jack-in-the-box. 'What do you think?' he demanded.

Proctor shrugged. 'I think she's lying. But I'm not sure what she's lying about.' He chewed his thumbnail, a worried look on his face.

Macanespie lumbered across to his own desk. 'Looks like Plan B, then.'

Proctor glanced up. Already Macanespie's chubby fingers were prodding his keyboard, calling up the KLM website. 'Plan B it is,' he said heavily. 'But just for the record, I'm not happy about this.'

It wasn't love at first sight. But something sparked between us the first time we met. I was hosting a seminar about feminism's engagement with anti-nuclear protest one September afternoon. Towards the end of the session, one of the university administrators who had offered us a lot of practical help at the IUC slipped into the room accompanied by a man in olive green army fatigues. Fabijan Jokic made a hand gesture to indicate I should continue my winding up of the afternoon's proceedings, so I carried on talking, uncomfortably conscious of the stranger at the back of the room.

He looked surprisingly relaxed. The top button of his shirt was undone and his thumbs were tucked into his belt, one hand resting casually on the butt of his handgun. I still felt uneasy in the presence of men with guns, but I tried telling myself there was nothing to worry about. Besides, he was the best-looking man I'd seen since I'd arrived in Croatia.

A shade over six feet, he was lean and his rolled up shirtsleeves revealed muscular forearms. He had black hair, a lock of which hung over his forehead. He pushed it back at regular intervals but it would gradually spring back and curl across his brow. The cynic in me reckoned it was a carefully calculated look. Later, I was forced to reconsider that judgement. He was, I discovered, a man almost entirely without personal vanity.

I kept talking, but I was running on automatic pilot. I couldn't escape the distraction of his presence. The more I glanced across at him, the more reasons I discovered to find him attractive. His face was composed of familiar Balkan features: slightly hooded dark eyes, Slavic cheekbones, slim nose, full lips. In him, the combination was particularly striking. If you're familiar with the graceful and languid Tottenham and Manchester United centre forward Dimitar Berbatov, you will have a good idea of how the unfamiliar soldier looked. There was a stylish elegance to his movements, a cast to his features that could be translated as pride or arrogance, depending on your vantage point.

When I finally reached the end of my summary of the discussion I'd been leading, a couple of students wanted my attention. Fabijan and the soldier approached slowly, heads close in conversation. I probably gave the students less detailed responses than normal, for I was curious about my visitors.

Once the room had emptied out, Fabijan finally introduced me to the soldier. 'Maggie, this is Colonel Dimitar Petrovic of the Croatian Army.'

I tried not to simper. After all, I'd just delivered a scathing analysis of the destructive effects of the degree of influence that the NATO powers cravenly handed to their military commanders. Up to that point, I'd never had a conversation with a member of the military that hadn't been rooted in hostility. The last soldier I had in fact addressed had been a US guard at the Menwith Hill base. I think the actual words had been, 'Why don't you and your war-mongering pals fuck off back to America?' So it seemed improbable that I was going to find common ground with Colonel Petrovic, no matter how bloody handsome he was. 'Nice to meet you,' I said, simpering.

He graciously inclined his head. 'The pleasure is all mine. I apologise for intruding on your seminar, but I'd heard you had some interesting things to say and I wanted to hear them for myself.'

God help me, I blushed. 'Your English is very good,' I said. What can I say? I'm Scottish. We have no idea how to accept a compliment graciously.

He gave a crooked smile. 'I spent six months at Chicksands with your Military Intelligence people. It was sink or swim. I chose to swim.'

'I have no idea why a colonel in Croatian military intelligence might be interested in the ramifications of feminism and protest and their relationship to geography.' Sometimes I astound myself with my own pomposity. But he seemed not to notice.

'We're trying to build a different kind of society here in Croatia,' he said. 'That means thinking differently about everything. Communism is dead, so everything from those bad old days is also presumed dead. We have to find living organisms to replace the things that have died.' He gave an elegant shrug. 'We in the military too. Under the old regime, there were no protests. So we never learned how to deal with protest in a reasonable way. I read a paper you co-authored with Melissa Armstrong about the feminisation of the protest at Greenham Common, and I was intrigued. I tried to arrange a meeting with her when she was here in the spring but I was called away.' He nodded towards Fabijan, who was looking bored. 'Then he told me you were coming instead of Professor Armstrong and I hoped you would agree to talk to me.'

'I'm not an expert,' I said.

I was worldly enough to recognise the practised charm of his smile. That didn't stop me from being captivated by it. 'Compared to me, you are.' He glanced at his watch. 'I have an appointment with the mayor now, but can we meet soon?'

129

I tried not to look too eager. 'I've got a pretty full diary, but I can generally be flexible.'

'Tomorrow evening?'

I nodded. 'Any time after seven.'

'Do you know Proto? On the corner of Siroka Street and Vara?'

I didn't, but Fabijan's expression of startled incredulity coupled with the Old Town location told me all I needed to know. For whatever reason, Colonel Petrovic wanted to impress. 'I'm sure I can find it.'

He pushed back the errant lock of hair and nodded. 'I'll book a table for eight.' That charming smile reappeared. 'I look forward to it.'

'Me too,' I said as he gave a formal little bow and turned away. Fabijan gave me another exaggerated look of surprise then followed him. I wasn't entirely sure what had just happened, but I wasn't about to question it. The most handsome man in Croatia had asked me out to dinner. There might be clouds on the horizon, but that was sunshine enough for one day.

13

Maggie hadn't been expecting Tessa, but that didn't mean she wasn't happy to see her, particularly since she came bearing a carrier bag from the local Thai restaurant. 'I hoped I'd catch you before you went down to dinner,' Tessa said, spare hand on Maggie's shoulder, lips to her cheek.

'Perfect timing. I even have some Singha beer in the fridge.' Maggie led the way through to her tiny dining-room-cum-kitchen and while Tessa unpacked the cartons of food, she fixed them up with beers and glasses. Tessa kept up a running commentary on the food and the eccentric couple who ran the takeaway so there was no room for conversation till they were sitting down and tucking into larb ghai and spicy fishcakes.

'So what's the occasion?' Maggie said, dipping a fishcake into the sweet chilli sauce.

'Does there need to be an occasion?'

'No, but there's generally something going on when you turn up out of the blue with food. Either that or something you need to apologise for.' Maggie's tone was warm, amused. The women had been friends for long enough to be direct with each other.

Tessa gave a short, sharp sigh. 'You know me too well.'

Maggie felt a shiver of anxiety. Ever since Mitja had left, she'd become unreasonably apprehensive about losing her close friends. And Tessa had the sort of skills and profile that made her attractive to employers all over the world. 'So, what's going on? Don't tell me. You've been offered another UN job and you're thinking about taking it?'

Tessa put down her chopsticks and squeezed Maggie's hand. 'I'm not going to leave you,' she said. 'I promised you that and I meant it. We might not be lovers any more, but I still keep my promises.'

Maggie looked past Tessa, through the window to the college gardens beyond. If she focused on the familiar trees, she might avoid tearing up. Tessa had saved her from despair after Mitja had walked out; later they'd found a different kind of solace, but they both knew in their hearts it was need and not love that had brought them together. They'd drifted back to friendship without rancour, but sometimes the fierceness of Tessa's loyalty moved Maggie more than she was entirely comfortable with.

'OK. So if it's not some sensational job offer, what is it?' Maggie managed to produce a jocular tone.

'I had a very odd Skype meeting today,' Tessa said, turning her attention back to her food. 'One of the British guys attached to the ICTFY asked for a chat. I had no idea what he was after. I assumed it was something to do with the way the tribunal is being wound up. Some sort of negotiation about the victims whose cases remain unresolved, that kind of thing.'

'But . . . ? I mean, obviously there's a "but" lurking in the undergrowth.'

Tessa nodded, chewing and swallowing. 'A bloody great big but. I was talking to this guy, Theo Proctor? You ever come across him?'

Maggie dredged her memory. Her Balkans contacts extended well into three figures, but Proctor's name rang no bells. 'I'm pretty sure I haven't.'

'You'd remember him. A little Welsh creep with eyes that never stay still. One of that cohort of ambiguous faces whose role is never entirely clear and who slip and slide from under your finger when you try to find out exactly what it is they do and who they serve. I'd heard on the grapevine that there's a new face further up the totem pole who likes things done differently – a high-flyer called Wilson Cagney. And now we're seeing the evidence of the new broom.'

'So far, so gossipy. But what's all that got to do with you?'

'Not me, darling. You.'

Startled, Maggie let a piece of chicken slip from her chopsticks. 'Me? Why me? I made all my notes available to the

ICTFY investigators years ago. Anything I've written since, I've sent a copy to the team at Scheveningen.'

'It's not your notes they're interested in. It's Mitja.'

That jolt at the sound of his name hadn't diminished over the years. It still shook Maggie when other people said it. It was as if speaking it aloud could somehow summon him. Stupid, she knew, but even now it affected her. 'I don't understand.'

'Proctor spun me a line about looking for witnesses to tie up some of the final details in the outstanding trials and appeals. He said Mitja had been on the potential witness list for ages but he'd somehow slipped through the net. And did I know where he was.'

Maggie struggled to make sense of what Tessa was saying. 'Mitja gave statements right at the beginning of ICTFY. That's part of the reason he was so angry when cases started falling apart. He thought all the evidence was there to be drawn on but that the lawyers hadn't done their jobs properly. And my God, it sounds like he was right on the money if they're only just coming back to him now. How many other lost witnesses are there out there, Tessa? How many of them are still out there because of incompetence? Or is it corruption?' She pushed her plate away, all appetite gone.

Tessa sighed and fiddled with her beer glass. 'Whatever it is, it's too late to change anything now. Which is why that call today was bullshit. Pure and utter bullshit, Maggie.'

'What do you mean?'

'It was a pretext. They're not looking for Mitja because they want a witness statement. They're looking for him because Wilson Cagney is a new broom who wants to sweep the Augean stables clean.'

Maggie's face tightened. 'Stop talking like a bloody lawyer, Tess. That's not like you. Speak plainly. What are you saying?'

Tessa ran a finger through the condensation on her glass. 'They suspect – no, actually, it's more than that. I think they think they know what he's been up to. And they've decided it's time to flex a bit of muscle and say, "Enough. The murders have to stop and the killer has to pay."'

Maggie slammed her hand down on the table, making the plates and glasses jump. 'Oh, for fuck's sake. Not this again. I told you at the party what I think. Mitja went home.'

'And I'll tell you again. Look at the timeline. The tribunal screws up some cases that should have been open and shut. Mitja bends our ears till they're just about bleeding with what an outrage this is. He rants about corrupt lawyers and witnesses being bought or terrorised. He storms and rages about the failure of justice and the message that sends to the victims and the next lot of butchers—'

'All of which is perfectly bloody reasonable,' Maggie interrupted, her blood up now. 'You agreed with him. I agreed with him. We were all outraged. And then we moved on. Because all that bile, all that anger, all that shame was taking us nowhere. Just another emotional dead end. I talked about it with him. I saw his despair but I also saw his acceptance. It hurt him, Tessa. It pierced him to the heart. But he understood the futility of obsessing about it. He let go of it.'

Tessa shook her head stubbornly. 'I think you want to believe that, Maggie. Because you don't want to think he left you behind so he could be free to be a vigilante. The kind of hero you'd disapprove of.'

'Hero? You think the person who did all these murders is a *hero*? Jesus Christ, Tess. Sometimes you scare the shit out of me.'

'QED. He knew what your reaction would be. He knew he couldn't have both. He couldn't have his vengeance and still have you. And hard though it is for you to accept, he chose what he saw as the righteous thing to do.'

Maggie ran both hands through her hair in despair. 'Don't you dare impose your bloody Irish gesture politics on Mitja. How can you entertain such an idea about him? He was your friend. How can you think that the man we both knew could turn into a cold-blooded killing machine? How can you, Tess?' Maggie's raised voice bounced off the walls of the little room, resonant with disillusionment and dismay.

Tessa rubbed her eyes with the knuckles of one hand. 'Because it's the only thing that makes sense, Maggie. How else can you explain him just walking out like that?'

Maggie shook her head, despairing. 'It's easy, Tess. The rage reawakened his love for Croatia. He'd been damping down the fires ever since we came back here after the war was over. He tried to convince himself that us loving each other was enough to compensate for leaving his home. But he couldn't manage it. And the rage brought the pain of his loss to the surface.' She gave a shuddering sigh. 'He didn't run away because he wanted to become a killer, Tess. He ran away because I wasn't enough for him. Do you have any idea how shit that makes me feel? But I'll tell you one thing. It does not make me feel so shit that I have to reinvent Mitja as a serial killer to make myself feel better.' She began to pick up the barely touched containers of food and threw them in the bin. 'I think you should go.' She turned her back on her friend and leaned on the edge of the sink.

'What I believe doesn't matter, Maggie.' Tessa stood up and slowly moved to the door. 'I didn't come here tonight to fight with you. In your heart, you know that. What you need to be aware of is that there are other people out there who are convinced Mitja's a mad dog who should be taken out of circulation. If you have any idea at all where he is, you need to let him know that.'

137

14

Not for the first time, River found herself wondering about the possibilities of long-distance relationships and commuting. Working with Karen Pirie previously had meant she'd had to 'borrow' the facilities at Dundee University, where the old entity, Fife Police, had handed off much of its forensic work. Presuming on that relationship again had left her in a state of envy for the facilities a campaigning head of department had acquired to service the teaching and practice of anatomy and forensic anthropology. Nobody here had to feel, as River did, that her discipline was the poor relation, the budgetary afterthought in the University of North England's reckoning. In career terms, a move to Dundee would offer so many more possibilities.

But there was Ewan. DCI Ewan Rigston of Cumbria Police, as attached to his territory as a Herdwick sheep hefted to its fell. Her feelings for him had tethered her finally to one place. Cut her travelling to the bone, turned her from a nomad to someone with roots. Transformed her from a hunter-gatherer to a cultivator of a particular pasture. She'd never stayed in one place for so long, and it still surprised her that she didn't resent that.

However, River had been wondering lately whether her academic career had stalled. There was little prospect of promotion at UNE; her path was blocked by complacent men who had alighted on the university as a convenient place to see out the rest of their working lives. They could live in some of the most glorious countryside in the country and spend their days in an institution that had no intention of ever punching above its weight. That might have been bearable if they'd been ancient dinosaurs with a few years to go before retirement. But they were only half a dozen years older than her and they were clinging to their professorial chairs with the grim determination of a politician to a safe seat.

As she waited for the stable isotope analysis to finish, she wondered how feasible it would be to work somewhere else. Somewhere like Dundee. She could probably do a four-day week teaching and processing her lab work, one day working from home writing up her results and preparing publications. So she'd only be away three nights a week. And realistically, there were at least a couple of nights in any given week where work or its social obligations kept Ewan from home. It probably wouldn't be so different. Plus she'd be so much happier at work, it would rub off at home. And the travelling wouldn't be too horrendous. Train from Carlisle. Change at Edinburgh. She could make good use of the time; experience had taught her she could work anywhere.

The mass spectrometer beeped softly to signal that it had completed its cycle. River downloaded the results to her laptop then uploaded them into a program that would identify the geographical location indicated by the bone sample from the femur of the skeleton. She had one further test to run before she could put together a profile for Karen and it was the newest of her magic box of tricks.

The night before, she had taken a sample from the bone that anchors the key components of the human hearing system. The petrous section of the temporal bone is one of the hardest bones in the body; part of it houses the membranes that provide us with a sense of equilibrium, and allow us to receive sound waves. Where the two connect is one of the earliest parts of the skeleton to take shape. And so an analysis of that bone will reveal where in the world an individual's mother was living when he was still in the womb. 'I love this,' River said under her breath as she loaded the prepared piece of bone. Within half an hour, she would know the soil where their skeleton's roots had flourished.

While she was waiting for the mass spectrometer to do its thing, she turned her attention to the tooth she'd been working on late into the night. Like rings on a tree, teeth have layers that reveal the age of their owner. Every year, our bodies lay down two microscopic layers of cement – one light, one dark. Whatever we do to look youthful on the outside, after we die, our bodies reveal the hidden truth.

River had started on the tooth first thing the previous morning, cleaning it off with a slurry of pumice, then she'd left it under running tap water for eight hours. Next she'd cleaned it with alcohol before slicing it into sections with a diamond-edged cutter. Finally, she'd dehydrated the slices with more alcohol, cleaned them with xylene and mounted them on microscope slides. Already, she'd asked two anatomy students to study the slides under the microscope and count the rings. Always better to have as many eyes as possible on a detailed job like this. Besides, the students would improve their skills.

River focused the microscope and started counting. Her first pass came out at forty-six. Next time, forty-seven. Third time lucky repeated the second result. Only then did she compare it with the students' results. One said forty-seven; the other, forty-eight. So, they were all in the same ball park. It looked like Karen's skeleton was in his late forties. Maybe a bit old to be clambering around on the outside of buildings, but some people just never knew when to give up. River sat back, flexing her shoulders. Time for a cup of coffee, then she'd have all her ducks in a row for Karen. She'd give her a written report, of course. But she knew Karen too well. Her friend would want as much detail as fast as possible. It always amused River that the woman in charge of cold cases was probably the least patient person she'd ever come across.

Fortified with caffeine, River made the call. Karen's voice had the hollow sound and background noise that signalled she was in a car. 'You driving?' River asked.

'No, I'm letting Jason have a wee shot behind the wheel. We're on our way to Oxford.'

'Oxford? As in, England?'

'Aye. Not the one in Northumberland, either.'

'Why are you going to Oxford?'

'To talk to a professor about a bank account.'

River chuckled. There was nobody better than Karen at making you drag a story out of her. 'You care to expand on that?'

'We got the imprint of some partial bank details on that room key you found at the crime scene,' Karen said. 'Turns out it was an FCB account. So I toddled off to the pyramids this morning in the hope of finding out who it belonged to. I tell you, even with a sheriff's warrant those bastards did not want to talk to me.'

'Hard to believe.'

'Turns out the reluctance was due to the fact that the account isn't entirely dormant.' Karen paused, waiting for River to play her part.

'How can it not be dormant if the guy's dead?'

'Because it's a joint account. It was opened in 2001. Every

month since then, one of the account holders has paid in four hundred pounds. Up until September 2007, the other account holder paid in irregular amounts, ranging from a hundred pounds to seven hundred and fifty pounds.'

'Interesting. What about money going out of the account?'

'Until September 2006 cash got taken out at ATMs. Mostly in Oxford, but some in London, some in Edinburgh, and some in Venice and Ravenna. And there were payments to a credit card as well. Nothing big. Modest grocery bill levels. But since then – nothing.'

'That's weird. If one person's still paying in, you'd think they'd be taking it out as well.'

'You would, wouldn't you?'

River was intrigued. Knowing Karen, she suspected there was more to come. 'So who are these people?'

'The one who stopped paying in is a man called Dimitar Petrovic. The address he gave when they opened the account was St Scholastica's College, Oxford. Does anything about that strike you as weird?'

River dredged her memory. 'Wasn't that the last college to go mixed? Was it still a women's college back then?'

'Give the girl a coconut. You are spot on. This guy with no visible credit history, according to the bank, was apparently living in a women-only establishment. And nobody at FCB noticed. Or if they did notice, they didn't give a toss. Because the other account holder was as respectable as you or me—'

'Hey now,' River protested. 'Don't you be accusing me of respectability.'

'Very funny. Do you want to know about this woman or not?'

'Tell me, tell me. Who is she?'

'At the time the account was opened, she was Dr Margaret Blake, geography fellow of St Scholastica's College. She's now Professor Blake. And every month she's paying four hundred quid into a bank account she never touches. Tell me why you'd do that.'

'Hmm. I'd say she hopes he might be coming home.'

'Either that or she thinks he might have needed the money, wherever he was going. Whichever it is, it's interesting, don't you think?'

'Definitely. I'm guessing you haven't phoned to say you're coming?'

'Got it in one. I don't want to give her time to come up with some clever academic doublespeak to bamboozle me with, the way you smart buggers do.'

River laughed. 'Like you're such a pushover. Well, it's term time, she should be in her lovely study looking out over the dreaming spires, enjoying the luxury of a light teaching load and high-table dinners.'

'So, given that it looks like Dimitar Petrovic might be our man, what can you tell me about him?'

River woke up her screen and went through the key points. 'The skeleton is definitely a male. He was somewhere between forty-six and forty-eight when he died and around six feet tall. I already told you about his dental work. When his mother was carrying him, she was living in an area that's now eastern Croatia or north-western Serbia. He was in the same area when he was around six or seven years old, when his adult teeth were formed. The analysis of his femur tells us a different story, and it's a bit confused. Based on my experience, I'd say he'd spent the last seven or eight years of his life between the Balkans and the UK. He could have been in Kosovo or Montenegro. It's impossible to be more precise than that, I'm sorry.'

'That's still pretty amazing,' Karen said. 'Now I know that, it's maybe worth googling him.'

'There's a bit more. He's got a small metal plate on his left femur. He'll have had a bad break there at some point, but it was a long time ago. The bone's healed round the plate and there's nothing on the metal or on the screws to identify a manufacturer. And that says Eastern Bloc to me, given the age of the injury. They were slow to start marking up orthopaedic implants. So it only has value as presumptive ID.'

'Interesting. What about DNA? Did you get any?'

'I did. I've sent it over, you'll have to get someone to run it on the database.'

'Brilliant. Good job, River.'

'I enjoyed it,' she admitted. 'I do like a good puzzle. But it looks as though you've sorted it all out without me.'

'You're my belt and braces. You make it impossible to argue with what I've found out. And since Margaret Blake seems to be kidding herself on a massive scale, I'm going to need all the help I can get on that score.'

15

Glasgow was a changed city from the one where Maggie had passed a miserable January week the year before she'd gone to Dubrovnik. She'd spent New Year partying with family and old school friends in Fife, then travelled across the country for the Institute of British Geographers' annual conference where she felt like a very small fish in a very big pond. The grim concrete student residence was more depressing than anywhere she'd lived in London or Oxford, and every time she walked out of the front door, she was greeted by a different form of rain.

It had been 1990, the launch week of the city's year as European City of Culture. Maggie couldn't help cleaving to that oldest of jokes, that she'd seen more culture in a tub of yoghurt. The city felt grey and grim, and every modern building spoke of architects who didn't give a shit about the people who had either to occupy or to look at their work. It was bewildering to her. All around were old buildings that spoke of an aesthetic that had got lost along the way – imposing sandstone tenements, the stunning Victorian Gothic of the university quadrangle buildings, the slender white church tower that rose above the elegant Park District, the towers of Trinity College. How had people turned their back on that and produced glass-and-concrete boxes that took no account of how people lived their lives? She'd come away feeling that it was about time geographers started looking at the impact of ugliness on urban living.

But a revolution had happened to the city since then. Maggie had been reluctant to accept the invitation to give a seminar at the university because her previous visit had simply reconfirmed her conviction that Edinburgh was the only Scottish city fit for living. However, the prospect of turning fifty had persuaded her it was time to take stock of her life and tunnel her way out of the ruts and habits that trammelled her life and her thinking.

And so she had accepted. And now she was glad. Everywhere, the city was being tarted up for the impending Commonwealth Games. Even the white lines on the roads were being repainted. Her hotel was right on the banks of the Clyde, opposite the striking contemporary buildings housing the non-identical media twins of BBC Scotland and STV. After dinner, since it wasn't raining and there were few things she enjoyed more than walking in cities at night, she set off along the river. The brown water moved sluggishly with the tide, distorting the reflections of a series of dramatic apartment and office blocks on both sides of the river. There were new bridges too, one known locally as the Squinty Bridge because it crossed a bend in the Clyde at an angle, another a footbridge thrown across the water to celebrate the millennium. If she hadn't seen it for herself, Maggie wouldn't have believed this glittering riverside panorama was in Glasgow.

The hum of the constant flow of traffic on the motorway over the Kingston Bridge formed a counterpoint to her thoughts. After so many years, she could go for days without consciously thinking about Mitja, but the milestone birthday and the party gathering of the people she cared most about had thrust him into the front of her mind, even without Tessa's unwelcome intervention at the weekend.

Maggie understood intellectually why he'd left the way he had. He knew her – and himself – well enough to under-stand that she would use every weapon at her disposal to keep him and that part of him would want to be kept. She would have been a ball and chain around his leg, making him drag her behind him every step of the way till finally friction wore through the bonds and freed him. It would have been a horrible, destructive process for both of them. Kinder, really, to walk away as he had done.

And yet ... She could not quite understand or forgive the silence that had echoed down the years. By not spelling out to her that he truly was gone for good, he had condemned

149

her to hope. That was what felt cruel to her, and Mitja was not a cruel man. So it made no sense.

After he'd gone, some of her friends had urged Maggie to go looking for him. To return to Croatia, to use her connections to track him down as if he were a war criminal like Milosevic or Karadzic. She'd thought about it. She'd even imagined a showdown in some tiny mountain village, confronting him with his desertion in the face of his wife and a brood of raven-haired children with his eyes and mouth. But in the end, she had too much pride for that. He'd wounded her self-esteem, no doubting that. But her self-respect was not holed below the waterline. There was enough to keep her dignity afloat. Just.

She'd half-expected him to surface in Croatian politics, or on a wider stage. Every few months, she'd google him to see whether he'd shown up. But always, she drew a blank. Perhaps the years in Oxford with her had taught him that he could live a quiet life; reading and thinking, working their allotment, rock climbing with friends. Perhaps he'd settled for precisely that sort of life, but instead of living it with her, he'd wanted to be surrounded by his family and the people he'd grown up with.

Sometimes the pull of home was irresistible. She'd never felt it herself. Maggie had lived too long away from Scotland to want to return. But she'd seen it in so many others. This, the year of the independence referendum, had also been branded the year of homecoming and she knew several academics who had upped sticks and gone back north of the border, unable to bear the thought of their country choosing a destiny without their input.

What she couldn't believe was that he'd fallen out of love with her. She couldn't believe he was running from her, only that he was running to something he needed more. And tonight, as happened so often when she was walking by water, she wished he was by her side. In Dubrovnik, they'd often walk by the sea, the rhythm of their steps matching the rhythm of the waves. Then later, in Kosovo, they'd always tried to find a river or a lake to walk beside as a respite from the fear and the fighting. And in Oxford, of course, there had always been the Cherwell and the Isis. He would have enjoyed this Glasgow riverbank walk, she thought as she approached the dark underbelly of the Jamaica Street bridge.

Some lights would have been a good idea, Maggie thought as the dimness swallowed her. The light pollution of the city produced enough of a glow to walk by, but someone less schooled in night city walking might easily have been unnerved.

As if to reinforce her thought, the bulk of a man's body suddenly appeared at the far end of the arch, blocking out light and looming large. Feeling no sense of disquiet, Maggie veered slightly to one side, leaving plenty of room for him to pass.

But he veered too, and into her path rather than away

from her. Within a couple of steps they were almost face to face. She tried to sidestep him but he spread his arms, blocking her passage.

Now she felt disquiet. 'Excuse me,' she said in her most imperious voice.

'Well, well, well. If it isn't Professor Blake. How's it going, Professor?' he said. The accent was local but it sounded exaggerated; coarse and threatening.

'Who are you? What do you want?' Maggie was no stranger to danger but this was all the more unnerving for being hundreds of miles from a war zone, in a city centre where street crime was at an all-time low.

'Just a wee bit of information and nobody gets hurt.'

'Are you sure you've got the right person? I'm just a geography professor.'

He moved closer. She could smell rank sweat and garlic breath. 'I've got the right person. Where's Dimitar Petrovic?'

Her heart lurched in her chest. 'I don't know what you're talking about,' she said, sounding more panicky than she wanted to. She took a step backwards, then another. A third step and she'd be far enough away to turn and run. Her assailant didn't look like he had much of a turn of speed.

She raised her foot for that crucial third step and nearly fell over as a hand pushed her firmly in the small of the back. 'Not so fast,' a voice behind her growled. 'Answer the question.'

Maggie swivelled round. The man behind her was smaller

but he too had his arms spread wide, obstructing her escape route. 'Let me past,' she demanded, anger rising in her and overwhelming the fear.

'Not till you answer the bloody question,' the fat man behind her said, close up and menacing.

'I told you, I don't know what you're talking about. Now let me pass or I swear, I'll start screaming.'

'You can scream all you like. This is Glasgow. Nobody cares.' Now his hand was on her shoulder, heavy and threatening.

And then salvation. The slap of running shoes, the sound of urgent breath, and all at once a third man was among them. He skidded to a stop. 'You all right, hen? These guys bothering you?'

'Fuck,' the fat man said, turning on his heel and lumbering back the way he'd come. The other man pushed past Maggie, making her stagger, running to catch up with his partner.

Left alone with the runner, Maggie felt a wave of physical weakness. The man's voice brought her back to the moment. 'Are you all right? Did they guys hurt you?' The genuine concern in his voice touched her.

'They didn't touch me. They just scared me, that's all.'

'Where are you heading? I'll walk you back.' He was jogging on the spot now, as if he too was experiencing a reaction from the brief drama.

'I'm staying in a hotel along the Broomielaw, near the

exhibition centre. Thanks for the offer but I think I'll just get a taxi back. In case those two are still hanging around.'

'OK. But let me walk you up to Central Station. You'll be able to pick a cab up at the rank there.'

'I'll be fine,' she said, almost believing it. She'd been shelled and shot at. She'd seen the aftermath of massacres and gang rapes. Surely she was capable of dealing with threats from two middle-aged men in suits under a Glasgow bridge?

'No way,' the runner said. 'My mammy brought me up right. I'm not letting you out my sight till you're safe on board a black cab. And that's that.'

And so it was. Sitting on the edge of her seat in the back of the taxi she stared out into the night. What the hell was going on? First Tessa, now these thugs. Why was Mitja suddenly on people's agenda? And why did everyone think she knew where he was?

When I asked Varya what the dress code was for Proto, she looked as startled as Fabijan had. 'Proto?' Her bark of laughter was harsh. 'At Proto, you're swimming with the big fishes, not just eating them. I don't think I know anybody who ever had dinner at Proto.'

That would be best bib and tucker, then, I deduced. Only, I didn't have any bib and tucker with me, never mind my best. A trawl through my limited wardrobe produced a sleeveless black jersey dress with a scoop neck. It hadn't flattered me in Oxford, but I'd lost a crucial few pounds since my arrival in Dubrovnik, thanks to my system adjusting to the unfamiliar diet. I'd get away with it if I could find a pretty wrap or a scarf to drape across my shoulders and knot above my cleavage.

Next morning, I took a detour to the morning market in Gundulićeva Poljana, only a few streets away from the

cramped rooms where I was teaching. As usual, the Old
Town was bustling; half of Dubrovnik was heading to or
from the market to stock up on fresh groceries, honey and
wine. I knew there were a couple of stalls that sold
embroidered tablecloths and shawls and I reckoned I
might find something cheap and cheerful – the opposite
of what Proto sounded like.

I was surprised by how sparse the stock was, but I
assumed people shopped early at the market, and that
the early birds had stripped the stalls of their best
produce. I managed to find a simple gauzy scarlet cotton
wrap with tassels and a pattern of painted gold scrolls,
which looked classier than it cost.

If I wanted to know what I taught that day, I'd have to
track down one of the class and ask them. I felt like a
teenager, stomach hollow and head adrift. I knew at the
time how ridiculous it was to feel this way about a man –
a soldier, for God's sake – that I'd barely met. And yet my
attempts to scold myself into attentiveness were fruitless.

From the outside, Proto didn't look much different
from many of the Old Town restaurants. An old stone
building on a corner with tables hugging the walls, well-
dressed couples leaning towards each other over cold
Dalmatian wine, glasses misted with condensation. I
walked in and as soon as I said I was with Colonel
Petrovic, the maître d' bowed deeply and ushered me up
a flight of marble stairs to a leafy outdoor terrace. It was a

warm September evening, the light just beginning to fade
from the sky, and he was standing at the edge of the
terrace in a dazzling white shirt and tight black dress
trousers with a red stripe down the seam.

I may have moaned.

He met me halfway across the room, taking my hands
in his and kissing them both. Then, a hand in the small
of my sweating back, he escorted me to our table. 'Thank
you for coming, Doctor,' he said as the waiter placed the
menus in front of us.

'Thank you for inviting me, Colonel.'

He shook his head. 'Please. My friends call me Mitja.'
He gave me that killer smile. 'I hope we're going to be
friends.'

'I hope so too, Mitja.' I struck back with my own finest
smile. 'My friends call me Maggie, by the way.'

And so it began. Over seafood soup rich with tomatoes
and mussels, grilled squid and rožata, we talked and
talked and talked. From focality to Foucault, from the
fault lines of the landscape to the fault lines in Balkan
politics, we covered the kind of ground that generally
requires longer and deeper acquaintance than we could
lay claim to. We laughed too, ambushed by humour in
unlikely places. And all the while, I watched his face,
learning its planes and contours. We were both startled
when the waiters started clearing the tables around us in
that pointed way that says unequivocally it's time to go

home. I felt dazed and dazzled by the conversation. I didn't want it to end.

We emerged into the dimly lit street, ours the only footsteps as we headed towards the Pile Gate. 'I have a car,' he said, steering us past the taxi rank.

'It's not far, I'll walk,' I said. 'I like the night air.'

'In that case, I'll walk with you,' he insisted. 'Wait a moment.' He jogged across the street to a big Mercedes. The driver's window descended, Mitja spoke briefly then came back to me. 'My driver is never happy when I go off on my own,' he said ruefully, falling into step beside me, a careful few inches between us. 'He's convinced some crazy Serb will try to kill me.' He gave a soft chuckle. 'He has an inflated idea of my importance.'

And so we came to the subject we'd both managed to dodge all evening. 'Is there going to be all-out war?' I asked.

He thrust his hands deep into his trouser pockets. 'It's hard to see how we can avoid it. Vukovar is under siege. They come under fire daily from the JNA. People are dying in the streets and we can't stop it happening. The Serbs want to crush the city and take over the territory. I know it's on the other side of the country, but it's foolish to think what's going on will end there. Milosevic wants a Greater Serbia that will swallow us all and make us his slaves.'

'So, shouldn't you be off doing military things, not

taking geographers for fancy dinners?' I wasn't teasing. I genuinely wondered what the answer would be.

He danced a few steps ahead of me and turned to face me, arms extended, moving backwards so the distance between us stayed constant. 'You think I'm ... what? Fiddling like the Emperor Nero while Rome burns around me? Maggie, all day I am doing "military things". We go over and over the same things. The same plans, the same dispositions.' His voice rose, the passion obvious. 'We try to wave a magic wand and generate more troops, more weapons, more ordnance. Every day, we analyse the latest intelligence, and what it tells us is that we are probably fucked. But still we prepare ourselves. We are as ready as we can be. Now we just have to wait.'

'Can't you do something? Can't you take the fight to them?' I suspected this was probably a stupid question but I didn't know what else to ask.

'They have overwhelming superiority in numbers, in strength. In reserve. Our only chance is to keep the moral high ground. To be the good guys. So when the time comes to call for help, people like your government will go, "Those Croatians, they deserve our help."' He pressed his palms together in an attitude of prayer. 'Meanwhile, I convince myself there will be a future that we need to prepare for. So I try to find people who will help me understand how to do that.' He gave a sweeping bow, then swung back to walk alongside me. 'Of course, it helps if they are beautiful as well as clever.'

'Cheesy,' I said. 'I expected better.'

'Ah, I am just a simple soldier,' he said, hamming up his accent.

'I don't think so.' I was trying to sound cynical and hard-bitten but my stomach was churning. I longed for him to reach out and touch me, to take me in his arms so we could move beyond the cerebral to learn something more feral about each other.

He fell silent, hands back in his pockets. We walked through the night city, the silence unbroken except for the stray barking of tethered dogs and the occasional mutter of TVs through open windows. 'I'm afraid of what will happen to my country,' he said eventually, his voice low and serious. 'We are a little cog in the big wheel of somebody else's politics. What we thought we knew is gone. We don't know how the future is going to be for us. All I know is that there are going to be some bad times ahead.'

It wasn't the time for anodyne words. I reached out and tucked my arm in his. We carried on in silence to the threshold of Varya's house, a few minutes away. 'This is me,' I said. I didn't want to say goodbye, but there wasn't any other option. I slid my arm out of his and turned to face him. For a moment, I thought he was going to kiss me.

But no. He simply inclined his head towards me and

said, 'Thank you for a beautiful evening. I enjoyed our conversation.'

'Me too. And that wonderful meal.'

He took a step backwards. 'Life was supposed to get easier after communism,' he said. 'This doesn't feel easy.' His face was in shadow; I had no idea what those expressive eyes were saying.

'Maybe we can do this again?'

'It would be a pity not to. But now, I have to go and do what you called "military things". Goodnight, Maggie.' He turned away, moving quickly down the street and disappearing round the corner. I leaned against the crumbling stucco of Varya's house, all of a sudden too weak in the knees to stand upright. For the first time since I'd arrived in Dubrovnik, I wondered about the wisdom of being here.

16

Arriving in Oxford from the north, you could make it to St Scholastica's College without so much as a hint of the dreaming spires. There were bits of the city that Karen was sure she'd seen on reruns of *Inspector Morse* but those were the bits that could have been pretty much anywhere south of the Pennines. There was something about the between-the-wars semis and the Victorian redbrick that was definitively English and, to Karen's eye, definitively alien.

The college itself was nothing like she'd expected. No venerable Cotswold stone quadrangles with manicured lawns and staircases worn by generations of undergraduate feet. There were more gothic pinnacles on top of the John Drummond school roof than there were here. Even the entrance was mundane – plain wrought-iron gates firmly closed against the world, a porter's lodge built from dirty yellow brick that looked more like a sentry box than the way in to a world of learning. Even the Adam Smith College in Kirkcaldy presented a more enticing prospect.

'Looks closed for business,' the Mint said.

'These places never close, they just keep the rest of us at arm's length.'

He checked the time on his phone. 'Will she not have gone home by now?'

'She lives here. Drive back the way we came, we'll park on the street. I don't want us to draw attention to ourselves.'

'She lives here? What, like a student?'

'Kind of. But they get a wee flat, the fellows do. They call it a set.'

'Fellows? I thought this was a women's college? How can they be fellows?'

'It's what they call the teachers here. I suppose it goes back to when there weren't any women.' Karen shrugged. 'Which I'm guessing wasn't that long ago, relatively speaking.'

'OK. I get that. It would be like me calling you "sir", like they do with Starbuck in *Battlestar Galactica*. Which is pretty stupid, but I kind of get it. But how come they call a flat a set?'

'You've got me there, Jason. I just know they do.'

'How come?'

Karen sighed. Educating Jason was an uphill struggle. 'How come I know? Because I read books, Jason. Because I watch things on the telly that aren't boy comics doing panel games.'

They found a parking space a couple of streets away and walked back to the lodge. A middle-aged black man sat behind the counter, resplendent in gleaming white shirt and perfectly knotted dark blue tie. He smiled and stood up. 'Good evening. How can I help you?'

Karen matched his smile. 'I'm looking for Professor Blake.'

The porter shook his head regretfully. 'I'm afraid she's not in college this evening.'

'Will she be back later?'

'Would you like to leave a message? You can put it in her pigeonhole.' He pointed over Karen's shoulder to a honeycomb of wooden compartments that lined the wall. Names were painted neatly beneath the top two rows; the lower levels were larger and were simply alphabetised. 'She'll pick it up as soon as she returns.'

'Will she be back this evening?' Karen persisted.

Now the porter's smile had faded, replaced with a stubborn set to his jaw. 'I couldn't say.'

So much for low key, she thought, fishing out her ID. 'I'm DCI Pirie from Police Scotland,' she said. Her tone was still pleasant but there was steel lurking in it. 'I've come a long way to speak to Professor Blake. I'd appreciate it if you could give me some idea of when she'll be here.'

The porter looked disconcerted. 'You've come from Scotland?'

'That's right.'

164

'It's a long way,' the Mint reiterated, in case there was any doubt.

'Is everything all right? Is it her parents?'

'Obviously I can't discuss the matter with anyone other than Professor Blake,' Karen said repressively.

The porter gave a little laugh. 'I suppose so. But it's ironic, you coming all the way from Scotland to talk to her. Because Professor Blake's gone to Glasgow.'

'You're kidding. Glasgow?'

'She left this morning. She told me she's giving a seminar at the university.'

Karen groaned. 'I don't believe it. Do you know when she'll be back?'

He nodded. 'As it happens, I do. She said that, with it being term time, it would be a quick trip. She'll be back tomorrow evening.'

Karen thanked him and walked out into the muggy evening air, Jason at her heels.

'Are we going to go to Glasgow, boss?'

'No point,' Karen said slowly, thinking aloud. 'It's already too late to head north tonight. Plus we don't have a Scooby where she's staying. By the time we track her down, she could be on her way back ...' Her voice tailed off and she pulled out her notebook. 'Plus we've got another address, remember?'

'Where they were staying when they opened the account.' Jason looked pleased with himself.

'Aye. Let's go and shake the tree and see what falls out.'

The original address for the joint bank account of Dimitar Petrovic and Margaret Blake was a squat Victorian villa in a side street that ran between the Woodstock and the Banbury roads, about a mile from St Scholastica's College. The two detectives sat in the car and contemplated it. 'The form said 21A,' Karen said. 'I'm not seeing a 21A. Just a 21.'

'Looks like there's a basement, boss. You can see the tops of the windows from here. Do you want me to go and take a wee stroll up the drive and see what I can see?'

'What? And have some respectable citizen call the locals to say there's a prowler? Do you fancy explaining yourself to a woolly suit looking for an easy boost to his arrest record? No, we'll go and knock on the door. The way things are going on this inquiry, chances are it'll be somebody that moved in six months ago,' she added gloomily, getting out of the car.

The bay window that fronted on to the street divulged a wall of books, a chintz-covered sofa and heavy curtains held back with generous swags. It was too dim to see anything more, but the frosted glass panel in the front door revealed a distant glow of yellow light. Somebody was home. Or else trying to convince burglars that was the case. Karen pressed the bell; they heard it ring in the recesses of the hall. Long seconds passed, then the quality of light changed, as if a door had opened. A brighter light snapped on. More time passed, then a vague darkness began to take approximate human shape. They heard a tapping sound, then the door opened and stopped abruptly, held in place by a chain. Half a face, framed in short white hair, peered at them through one large varifocal lens. 'I don't want to change my gas supplier, and I have no need of Jesus,' a sharp, precise voice said firmly.

'You and me both,' Karen said, fishing out her ID and holding it close to the single magnified eye. 'DCI Karen Pirie, Police Scotland. I'm looking for 21A. Can you help me?'

The single visible eyebrow rose. 'No such place. It doesn't exist. And besides, this isn't Scotland.'

'We know that,' Jason muttered from behind Karen.

'It used to exist,' Karen said.

'In a manner of speaking.'

Already, Karen hated Oxford. 'What does that mean, exactly?'

'It existed in effect but not in reality.'

'I'm sorry, I'm just a simple police officer. You're going to have to explain that in words of one syllable. Could we come in while you do that?'

The eye studied her steadily. 'Why don't you tell me what this is about?'

'I have a professional interest in someone who used to live at 21A.' This was precisely the kind of idiotic exchange that had made Karen stop watching *Inspector Morse* some years before.

'That narrows it down to Professor Blake or General Petrovic, then.'

'Is that because they're the only two people who ever lived there?'

Half a smile carved a series of wrinkles into a cheek. 'Well done, Detective Chief Inspector.' The door closed and the chain rattled.

'Is she letting us in?' Jason demanded.

The door opened. 'She is,' the old woman said. 'Shut the door behind you.' She had the imperious tone of someone accustomed to being deferred to. And obeyed. She set off down the hallway, listing to one side, NHS-issue metal walking stick supporting her. Karen and Jason exchanged a look and followed the woman into the living room they'd seen from the street. The switch by the door turned on three floor lamps that bathed the comfortable room with light. Now they could see her clearly, Karen estimated her to be in her late seventies or more. She could see the signature traces of pain and stubbornness in her face. The woman settled in a high armchair beside a plain, elegant wooden fireplace and waved her stick towards the sofa. 'Sit down.'

'What's your name, ma'am?' Karen asked, nudging Jason, who was looking around him as if he'd never seen bookshelves before. 'Notebook, Constable.'

'I am Dr Dorothea Simpson,' the woman said. 'Not a doctor of medicine, but a doctor of philosophy. Although I am an historian rather than a philosopher. Until my retirement, I was, like Maggie Blake, a fellow of St Scholastica's College.'

'Is that how you know Professor Blake?'

Dr Simpson inclined her head, 'Indeed. Would you care to tell me the nature of your interest in my former tenants?'

'We're trying to trace Dimitar Petrovic,' Karen said.

The woman gave a cynical snort of laughter. 'Better women than you have failed in that particular quest, Chief Inspector. I don't know of anyone who has seen hide nor hair of the general since he walked out on Maggie ... let me see, it must be at least seven years ago. Or was it eight? I confess, I was taken aback by his desertion. Mitja and Maggie seemed so well matched, both as intellectual combatants and lovers.'

'How did you come to know the general?'

'Maggie brought him back as her trophy from the wars,' Dr Simpson said. Her smile was warm, but the look she gave Karen was mischievous. She paused, cocking her head to one side, waiting for Karen to pick up the baton.

'I'm not sure I follow you,' Karen said.

'Maggie's a Balkans specialist. She spent a lot of time there during the various conflicts in the nineties.'

'And they met there?' A nod. 'So he was a general in which army?' Karen knew next to nothing about the Balkan wars, but she knew enough to know that some factions were definitely considered to be worse than others.

This time, the nod came with an approving smile. Karen

felt like a student who was surviving a particularly tricky tutorial; she hoped Jason would continue to keep his mouth shut. 'He started out in the Croatian Army. The side of right, you might say. But later he was attached to NATO forces as a special advisor. He was an intelligence specialist, I believe,' Dr Simpson said.

'So he met Professor Blake when she was, what? Researching the war?'

'She was teaching a fledgling version of feminist geopolitics at the Inter-University Centre in Dubrovnik when the war caught her out. They met there, in Dubrovnik, and when the war in Kosovo was finally over some years later, he joined her here in Oxford. But the college was still a single-sex institution. They needed somewhere to live and they didn't have a lot of money. I was about to retire and I loved to travel until this damned hip shackled me.' She whacked her leg with the cane without wincing. Extra-strong painkillers, Karen thought. 'So we were the answer to each other's needs. Mitja has a panoply of practical skills and he transformed my basement into a self-contained flat. In return, I had resident house-sitters while I went gallivanting.'

'How long did they live here, in your basement?'

Dr Simpson studied a corner of the ceiling while she considered. 'Between six and seven years,' she said. 'They didn't travel much. I'd have thought they'd have been in and out of the Balkans once things settled down, but even Maggie's scarcely been back in recent years. She has a team of post-graduate researchers of one stripe or another to do the groundwork these days, of course. She produces brilliant research proposals that bring the university pots of cash, then she writes equally brilliant books that add lustre to her reputation. All without leaving the comfort of her fellows' set at Schollie's.'

Karen thought she detected a tinge of bitterness; perhaps Dr Simpson felt she'd deserved the career Maggie was enjoying.

'And when the general left? What provoked that?'

'I have no idea. Nor, I think you'll find, does anyone else. Maggie came back from a three-day conference in Geneva to find he'd gone. No note, no explanation. At first she thought he might have gone climbing. But his equipment was still sitting in the cupboard downstairs. All of it, as far as she could tell.'

'Didn't she report him missing?' Like a kitten who spots a loose piece of string, Jason seized on something he knew he could usefully engage with. Karen, who wanted to travel in a completely different direction, entertained mildly violent thoughts.

'I don't know how you deal with these things north of the border, but the police here took the view that a grown man in good health who walks away from his life is quite within his rights. They could not have been less concerned.'

'I'm afraid it's not a high priority for us, unless there's

good reason to suppose otherwise. And I'm guessing there was no reason for that?' Karen decided to follow this line for the moment.

'Indeed. It was baffling rather than suspicious. Maggie has always believed he went back to Croatia, to a putative family life there. I've never quite managed to convince myself of that, but no alternative ever presented itself. And now here you are, asking about Mitja after all this time. Which suggests to me that an alternative has finally presented itself. Would I be right?'

'I'm afraid I can't disclose the details of our inquiry at this point.' Karen knew it was an unsatisfactory response; she'd just plummeted from an alpha student to a borderline fail.

'You are planning to talk to Maggie, though?'

'As soon as we can. She's out of town at the moment. I really appreciate your help. But I wonder, could we just backtrack a wee bit? You mentioned rock climbing. Was General Petrovic a keen climber?'

Dr Simpson smiled. 'It was a passion rather than a hobby. He and his friends spent many weekends in the Scottish Highlands. Bagging Munros, I believe it's called.'

'Where we come from, that's generally thought of as hill-walking rather than climbing,' Karen said. 'Did he do the serious rock stuff as well?'

'Oh yes. There's a cupboard downstairs that's still full of his equipment.'

Karen tucked that away for future reference. If Maggie

Blake didn't have any obvious source of Petrovic's DNA, there might be something in Dr Simpson's basement that would do the trick. 'What about buildings? Did he ever talk about free-climbing buildings? I bet you've got some real challenges here in Oxford.'

Dr Simpson pursed her lips. 'That would be against the law, Chief Inspector.'

Karen shrugged. 'A man who came through the Balkan wars wouldn't be put off by a wee bit of civil disobedience, I suspect.'

But the shutters had come down. Whatever Dorothea Simpson knew about Dimitar Petrovic's transgressions on university property, she wasn't about to share it. 'I have no idea what you're talking about, Chief Inspector.' She struggled to her feet. 'And now I need to be left in peace. I'm an old woman and I tire easily.' She looked expectantly at the door. Karen took the hint and shooed Jason down the hall. On the way out, she thanked Dr Simpson. She considered asking the old woman not to warn Maggie Blake of their interest. But that, she reckoned, would be pointless. Tough old birds like Dr Simpson did what they were going to do regardless of interdictions from lassies like Karen.

As they walked back to the car, Jason said, 'So. Looks as if we've got a war hero on our hands.'

Karen raised her eyebrows. 'He might be a general, Jason. That doesn't make him a hero.'

17

Alan Macanespie stared out of the window at the empty green landscape the train was hurtling through. He'd never have admitted it, but in spite of the fact that he was racing towards a meeting with Wilson Cagney, all he felt was relief.

He wasn't by inclination a man of action. His strength lay in interrogating the intel that passed across his desk and making sense of it and in building bridges with those who kept the wheels going round, not in terrorising middle-aged women. He'd hated having to do it and hated even more being possessed by this anxiety that it was going to have terrible unforeseen consequences for him, his continued employment and his pension. He should never have allowed himself to be seduced by Proctor's hare-brained plan, as if he was one of a pair of James Bonds. Even Proctor was acting now like the idea had been nothing to do with him.

But at least he was out of the front line, and for that he was grateful. Only an hour earlier, he'd been hunched over his phone in a hotel lobby, wishing he looked more nondescript. He was pretty sure there hadn't been enough light under the Jamaica Street Bridge for Maggie Blake to have seen any identifying features. And he had been wearing a beanie hat pulled down low over his ears, hiding his tell-tale ginger hair. But still. She'd seen him outlined against the city's glow and she must have been traumatised by the encounter. What if his silhouette was carved on her mind's eye, clear as day? What if she stepped out of the lift and instead of walking into the breakfast room, she turned towards reception and saw him lurking there like a great fat toad? She might not have called the police the night before, but she'd sure as hell call them this morning if she saw one of her attackers hanging around her hotel lobby.

He'd tapped his phone and sent an instant message to Proctor, who was outside the hotel in a hired car. They had no idea whether Maggie Blake would be on foot, in a taxi or in a car driven by herself or someone from the university, so they'd tried to cover all the bases. Macanespie wasn't even sure why they were still following Maggie Blake. Proctor had been adamant they should stay on her tail, though. 'She might run to him,' he'd said.

'No way,' Macanespie had grumbled. 'If she knows where he is, she'll know how to get in touch with him without putting him in the wind.'

'She's a middle-aged geography professor, not an asset.'

'And he was a general in intelligence. You think he won't have drilled her in the basic business of covering his back? For fuck's sake, Theo, you could take misplaced optimism as your specialist subject on *Mastermind*.'

But still, Proctor had won the argument. So Macanespie had been stuck in the hotel lobby since the crack of sparrowfart, just in case Maggie Blake decided she needed to leave the hotel at dawn for a ten o'clock seminar less than a mile away.

And then everything had changed. His phone had rung, jerking him out of his fugue of monodirectional vigilance. The screen told him it was Wilson Cagney and his heart juddered. He was supposed to be in Scheveningen, not Glasgow. If Cagney was paying attention – and Macanespie reckoned Cagney was always paying attention – he'd realise he wasn't hearing a foreign phone ringtone.

He jerked into action, as if sudden movement would make everything all right. 'Yes, Wilson?' he said as soon as he answered.

'Get on the next flight to London,' Cagney said without preamble. 'You and Proctor. I need you in my office asap. Let me know when you're on the ground at this end.'

That was it. A dictionary definition of peremptory. No room for manoeuvre. But interesting that whatever bee Cagney had in his bonnet, it was buzzing so loudly it had drowned out the sound of the wrong ringtone. Galvanised,

Macanespie had jumped to his feet and practically run out of the hotel.

Proctor had been incredulous and then grumpy. 'We'll be quicker getting the train,' he'd reasoned as they drove back to the hire-car agency along the quayside from the hotel. And so now they were heading south, trapped for the best part of five hours in a cloud of ignorance.

When they announced their arrival in London, Cagney instructed them to meet him in a coffee shop in Covent Garden. 'I'm attending a conference at King's,' he explained. 'I haven't got time to go back to the office.'

They found him in a corner at the rear of the busy café, back to the wall, his intimidating glare keeping other customers at bay. When they arrived clutching their Americanos, he drained his double espresso and turned the glare on them. 'I set you a task. So why is it that I'm the one handing over the information?'

'The trail went cold eight years ago,' Macanespie said. 'That's a lot of ground to cover.'

Cagney rubbed one eye with the tip of his index finger. 'You pair make me so tired. Here's the latest instalment in what you need to know. Obviously, we have a flag on General Dimitar Petrovic. And yesterday that flag started waving. A detective constable from Police Scotland ran his name through criminal records and DVLA. Nothing of interest came up, of course. But I want you two to go to

Edinburgh and talk to DC Jason Murray and his boss, DCI Karen Pirie. Who happens to be in charge of their Historic Cases Unit. I want to know what her interest in Petrovic is and whether she has any information that could help us lay hands on him.'

'Why can't we just phone her?' Macanespie said. 'We're all supposed to be on the same side, aren't we?'

Cagney's look of contempt turned the coffee sour in Macanespie's mouth. 'Because we're not lazy bastards. And because, as you should know by now, you always get more face to face. I want to know what's happened to make Police Scotland care about Petrovic and I want to know the whole story, not some cobbled-together five-second version handed down by a busy DCI over the phone. It's got to be more than a coincidence that they're suddenly interested in Petrovic right when we're moving on him. I want to know how his name has turned up in their inquiries.'

'Could you not just have asked?' Macanespie said. 'You've got the reach, after all.'

'When officers at my rank start asking questions, alarm bells ring. Whereas you—'

'Edinburgh?' Proctor said, trying to deflect Cagney's barely suppressed irritation.

'It's where the Historic Cases Unit is based. Don't phone ahead. Keep the element of surprise.' Cagney ran a hand down his silvery silk tie, smoothing it against his starched white shirt. 'See if you can get this one right, boys.' He stood up and edged out from behind the table, taking care not to brush against anything that might be grubby. 'I'll expect to hear from you very soon.'

Macanespie watched his perfectly tailored back zigzag through the coffee addicts till he disappeared from sight. 'Patronising wee twat,' he said. All the same he couldn't help recognising that something was stirring in him in response to Cagney's dismissiveness. Macanespie wasn't ready to be written off yet.

'I can't believe we've got to go back to Scotland. Why couldn't he have told us that over the phone? We'd have been in Edinburgh by now, whether we'd been coming from Scheveningen or Glasgow,' Proctor complained.

'He thinks he can drive us out through the petty exercise of power.' Macanespie grimaced at the acidic tang of his coffee and stood up. 'Well, fuck him, say I. He's going to have to try a lot harder. Come on, Theo, let's away back to Scotland and see if we can get a decent cup of coffee from DCI Pirie.'

18

While Jason had still been deciding between a full English or kippers, Karen had already been researching the next phase of her inquiry into the death of the man she was now presuming was Dimitar Petrovic.

Her day had begun even earlier, with a Skype conversation with Phil Parhatka. Whenever she worked with River, she found herself thinking more fondly of her lover. They'd finally got together in the middle of the same high-profile cold-case investigation where she'd first met River. Karen had been in her early thirties then, resigned to living alone, self-reliant and stoic. She had plenty of pals; she was known as good company. Sociable and reliable but ultimately a loner. But in the space of a few weeks, her life had turned upside down. Love and friendship had kicked down the protective barriers she'd spent years constructing, and now she recognised that she was a different woman from the one who had always put her job front and centre because there wasn't anything else big enough to occupy her.

Now not a day went by without her talking to Phil. There was no sense of obligation on either side; when work forced them apart they spoke because they wanted to, because a day without communication felt incomplete. It had practical advantages too. Even though they were no longer in the same unit, their shared occupation meant each could offer the other meaningful advice. And the distance between her work on cold cases and his on the Murder Prevention Team – unhelpfully known as the Muppet Squad – added a useful layer of detachment.

And so her first act on waking had been to Skype him. She'd caught him at the kitchen table, supping a mug of tea and working his way through a bacon-and-egg roll. 'I turn my back for five minutes and bang goes the fruit,' Karen teased.

'River ate it all,' he said. 'She thinks five a day is her starter for ten.'

'You don't mind her staying?'

'Not at all. We went out for a curry and a couple of beers last night, that's how I missed your call.'

'On a school night? She's a bad influence.'

'No, it was me. I felt like a wee celebration. We had a bit of a result yesterday.'

Karen gave a grim smile. She loved when Phil's team nailed one of their targets. It meant one more woman safe in her home, at least for a while. 'Tell me about it.'

'You remember that big-time property developer I told you about? The one who's behind that new shopping mall just off the motorway by Rosyth?'

She did. And she wished that was one piece of knowledge that wasn't embedded in her head. 'The one who raped his wife in front of one of his investors then let him have a go too? That the one? Told her best pal and the pal came to us?'

Phil nodded. 'And we couldn't persuade the wife to make a complaint because she was so scared of what he would do to her. Well, we started putting him through the grinder and we were struggling. The usual stuff – vehicle excise duty, car insurance, TV licence – wasn't giving us any leverage because all that gets sorted out by his very efficient PA. So, we heard a whisper that he was taking cash backhanders. But we couldn't get anybody to talk to us and we couldn't see any of the usual signs of flashing unaccountable cash. Then Tommy had a brainwave.'

'Really? I didn't think he had enough brains to cause a wave.'

Phil pulled a face at her. 'You think anybody who supports Rangers is brainless.'

'And your point would be ... ?'

'That for once, he was able to draw on his recent understanding of lower league football to come up with an interesting idea.'

Karen pretended to swoon. 'I'm all ears.'

'Among our target's other interests is a major shareholding in a First Division football team. Last season, the average attendance at a home game was just over fifteen hundred. But this season they've been reporting home gates of nearly three thousand. And let me tell you, it's not the quality of the football. Not to mention the fact that the photos we've tracked down online show roughly the same number of bodies in the stands.'

'I'm not sure I follow you.'

'Ghost punters, Karen. A lot of the spectators hand over hard cash going through the turnstiles on the day. Fifteen quid a time. If you're adding an extra thousand fake bodies to your tally, you've laundered fifteen grand, just like that. You've successfully legitimised dirty money. Multiply that by twenty home games and you're looking at a cool three hundred K over a season.'

Karen gave a low whistle. 'That's fabulous. Bribery and corruption, defrauding the taxman and the VAT ... Oh, that's beautiful, Phil. But how do you stand it up?'

'Tommy managed to get a crew together on Saturday. Woolly suits keen to have a shot at doing something in plain clothes. So every turnstile had one of our boys watching it with a wee clicker in his pocket, head-counting everybody who paid in to see the game. Now, we might be a bit out either way, but Tommy's lads clocked the crowd at fourteen hundred and sixty-seven. The official gate for the match was three thousand and forty-three.'

Karen laughed with delight. 'I can see why you felt like a celebration.'

'Aye. He's a nasty, violent bully, this bastard. And it'll give us great pleasure to nick him. But what about you? How's it going?'

She brought him up to speed with her investigation. 'So we've got to hang around here all day waiting for Maggie Blake to come back from Glasgow. How frustrating is that?'

'But at least you know a bit more about Petrovic than you did before.'

'That's true. I googled him last night and his name comes up in passing in a couple of long articles about Bosnia and Kosovo. But it's not very informative. If it really is him, I'll need to track down somebody who knows what they're talking about in terms of the Balkan wars.'

'But in the meantime, you can pursue the angle of who might have been up the John Drummond with him.'

Karen frowned. 'You reckon?'

'Isn't climbing supposed to be one of those close-knit communities? Where everybody knows everybody else? If he had climbing buddies in Oxford, chances are they might still be around. Maybe there's a club or something?'

'Round here? I've not seen a gradient since we got here. There's nothing to climb.'

'Except buildings.' He looked annoyingly smug.

'They'll not have a club for that, it's against the law.'

'Aye, but I bet they'll have a proper climbing club that

goes off on trips and excursions. I bet a few of them are into the extreme building stuff.'

Karen pouted. 'I hate it when you're right. I'll get on to it as soon as I've had a shower.'

'Minger. Fancy Skyping before you're clean and dressed.' He grinned at her.

'I've got a T-shirt on. And besides, you can barely tell I'm human on Skype, never mind whether I've done my hair and cleaned my teeth.'

'Are you coming home tonight?'

'I hope so. It kind of depends on when Maggie Blake gets back.'

'OK. Well, text me when you know what your plans are. I miss you, Karen.'

'Me too. Later, babe.' They blew kisses at each other and then it was over. As always, Karen felt her spirits lifted by talking to Phil. And now she had something concrete to chase down.

Fifteen minutes later, she was absorbed in her screen. There was a university climbing club, but she reckoned that would be a waste of time. Anyone who had been a student when Petrovic had been in Oxford would be long gone. There was a climbing wall at Oxford Brookes University where there might be staff who were plugged into a wider climbing network. Karen imagined that training on a climbing wall might be a decent apprenticeship for going up the outside of buildings. Her third option was a local climbing club that claimed to cater for everybody from casual hikers to serious rock geeks. That, she thought, would be her first target.

By the time she made it to the dining room, Jason was munching his way through a sticky pile of pastries. 'Morning,' he mumbled. 'You have a good lie-in?'

'I've been working, Jason,' Karen said, trying not to let him irritate her so early in a day when they would be spending most of it together. She helped herself to fruit salad, yoghurt and a large latte from a machine. What she really wanted was what was on Jason's plate, but she was gradually winning her lifelong battle with bad eating habits. If she was going to fall off the wagon of sensible choices, then she was determined it would be for something more luxurious than Coco Pops and a mass-produced Danish. 'We're going to talk to someone who knows about climbing,' she said, enjoying the sense of virtue even more than the fruit.

'Round here? There's nothing to climb. I don't think we saw a hill since Sheffield,' he said, unconsciously echoing her.

'There's buildings, though. And these mad bastards have to learn their techniques somewhere. I've already tracked down the secretary of the local climbing club and he's arranging for a couple of their lads to meet us in East Oxford later this morning.' She couldn't help feeling pleased with herself. Between Phil's brainwave and her people skills, it looked like the day wouldn't be wasted after all.

*

It wasn't hard to identify the two men Karen had arranged to meet in the vegetarian café in the Cowley Road. One was in Lycra cycling leggings and a clingy neon-green T-shirt that she suspected was made from some fabric that had had more scientific input than the entire contents of her wardrobe. His hair was cropped close to his head and his bony face was scraped clean of any hint of facial hair. The other wore the kind of trousers that unzip at the knees to take advantage of the three days of British summer, topped with a lightweight plaid shirt covered in zips and pockets. His hair was badly shaped and shaggy and he had one of those full-on beards that hasn't seen a razor or trimmer in years. Each had a small day pack at his feet, a water bottle in the side pocket.

Karen walked up to the table in the window, Jason trailing behind her. 'John Thwaite and Robbie Smith?' She gave them her standard warm greeting smile. They looked about the same age as her; old enough to have been around when Dimitar Petrovic had been alive and climbing.

The cyclist nodded. 'I'm John, he's Robbie. And you're the police, right?' He had the sort of northern accent that wouldn't have been out of place in *Coronation Street*.

Karen made the introductions, ordered chai for herself and tea for a slightly baffled Jason. 'Thanks for taking the time to meet me,' she said.

'Not a problem. We both work the evening shift in the labs at the hospital. I just cut my bike run a bit short. No big deal,' John said. He was displaying an eagerness that Karen was familiar with. For some people, the chance to be involved in something as edgy as a murder investigation is more thrilling than almost anything else they can imagine. Even when the victim is disturbingly close to home. That always made her feel slightly queasy.

Robbie looked less keen, studying them from under heavy eyebrows. 'I can't stay long,' he said in an accent that Karen couldn't narrow down any further than 'southern'. 'I've got a dental appointment at noon.'

'Thanks for coming. I understand you've both been active members of the climbing club for about ten years?'

'I joined eleven years ago,' John said. 'And Robbie came along that winter. We're both serious rock climbers, so we've done quite a few expeditions together. The Torridon range, the Cuillins, the Assynt peaks in your country. Do you know them at all?'

Patronising prick. 'I'm more of a walker,' Karen said. 'The West Highland Way, the John Muir Way, the Cape Wrath Trail.' It was a lie, but she didn't care. She wasn't going to be condescended to by some geek who probably shaved his legs more often and more thoroughly than she did.

'Some great walking there,' Robbie said. 'I did Cape Wrath a few years ago. Spectacular, I thought.'

'But you didn't ask to meet us so we could swap walking routes,' John cut in. 'How can we help you, Chief Inspector?'

'We're trying to make contact with a man called Dimitar

188

Petrovic. I wondered if you knew him?' Both men looked doubtful but Karen persisted. 'He was a general in the Croatian Army who came here at the end of the Balkans War and I'm told he was a keen climber. About six feet tall, black hair. His friends called him Mitja.'

Robbie's face cleared. 'You mean Tito. She means Tito, Johnno.' He smiled and his face was transformed. He looked ten years younger and 100 per cent happier. 'We don't bother with proper names when we're out on the hill. I only know this one's name because we work together. I know it sounds a bit mad, but when you're climbing you want to lose yourself in what you're doing. So your guy, he was always just Tito to us after he let on that he was from Yugoslavia.'

'So how well did you know him?'

'Tito? I haven't thought about him in donkey's. He was a good rock monkey,' John said, admiration in his voice. 'He was already climbing with club members when I joined, though I was never clear whether he was actually a member.'

'One thing I noticed – because it was odd, with him being a foreigner – he never did any of the foreign trips,' Robbie said. 'We did expeditions to the Alps, the Dolomites and the Pyrenees the first few years I was in the club, but Tito only ever did the home nations climbs.'

'You know, I'd never thought about that,' John said. 'But you're right.'

'Was there anyone in particular he always climbed with?' Karen asked.

They looked at each other, shaking their heads. 'He'd climb with anyone. It wasn't something that bothered him. He was more patient than I am with people who are a lot less skilled.'

So, no particular partner. Damn. 'When you all went on your trips to Scotland and the like, I presume you stayed in bothies and climbing huts?'

Robbie nodded. 'Mostly. But sometimes we'd just sleep out in bivvie bags if the weather was OK.'

'When you were sitting around in the evening, eating and drinking and talking, what did Tito have to say for himself?'

This time, their shared look was genuinely nonplussed. 'Nowt, really,' John said. 'Not personal stuff. He had a girl-friend that he lived with, but that's all I know about his life outside the rock.'

Robbie tugged at his beard. 'He didn't join in much. It felt like he was only there for the climbing. The rest of it – the rest of us, really – he could do without. When he stopped coming, I think it was a while before I noticed. He didn't contribute much to the conversation, only the climbing. And other people were just as good as him at figuring out routes and holds.'

'That's right. It was a bit of a jolt when it dawned on me we hadn't seen him for over a year,' John added.

'Did he ever fall out with anybody, that you know of?'

They looked at each other, puzzled. 'Not that I ever heard,' John said.

'No disagreements on climbs, no arguments?'

Robbie scratched his armpit while he considered. 'He wasn't that kind of bloke. He never got into it with anybody. Some people, it's like they're always looking for a chance to get stuck in. But Tito wasn't like that. He was pretty much live and let live. Maybe he got all his fighting done when he was in the army.'

Now for the tricky part. 'I'm going to ask you about something that some people think is illegal. Hand on heart, I'm not interested in minor infringements of the law here. I'm more concerned about making sense of some puzzling information.'

John began to bounce in his chair. 'Is this about that body they found on a roof in Scotland?' He prodded Robbie in the ribs. 'Remember? I showed you in the canteen yesterday. A skeleton up on a high roof, somewhere that's been shut up for twenty years.' He grinned at Karen. 'You think it's him? You think it's Tito?'

'I'll be honest, guys. Right now, I don't know. But his name has come up. So what about climbing up buildings then? We know it goes on. We know it's a bit of a dark secret because people get into all sorts of trouble. But was Tito into it when he was in Oxford? Because, frankly, there's nothing else to climb around here.'

Robbie stared at the floor. John looked panicky, then

shrugged. 'Oh, what the hell. Yes, buildering goes on. And yes, Tito was into it. We were talking about it one time on a trip to the Peak District and he said he'd done it a few times.'

'Did he do it by himself? Or with other people from the club?' Karen tried not to show how eager she was to hear the answer.

Robbie raised his eyes. 'He wouldn't tell us who he went out with. Just that it was somebody he used to know back in Yugoslavia.'

I refused to allow myself to have any expectations of Mitja. All day after our dinner at Proto I kept teetering on the edge of teenage mooning over the handsome colonel, but I scolded myself back to sense. After all, I was twenty-six years old and far too worldly to fall for the obvious charms of a clever, handsome man who could doubtless take his pick when it came to wanting more from an evening than a discussion of neocolonialism, feminism and deconstructing the Cold War. No, we'd had a fascinating evening and that would be an end to it.

And so I was genuinely surprised to emerge from a day's lectures at the Inter-University Centre to find a Mercedes parked on the road beyond the slender palm trees. The rear door swung open and Mitja unfolded himself out of the back seat in full dress uniform. 'I have an hour to spare,' he said. 'I thought we could walk up to the old town and have a drink, if you're not too busy?'

Of course I wasn't too busy. Even if I did feel a little uncomfortable to be walking alongside a senior officer in full regalia. We headed up between the two forts towards the Pile Gate, picking up our conversation where we'd left it the night before. 'Is there any news from Vukovar today?' I asked.

'Nothing new,' he sighed. 'But I am more concerned with what's happening in Montenegro.'

That was the first time Mitja had mentioned Montenegro to me. Only a few miles to the east, events there were likely to have more effect on me here in Dubrovnik than whatever was going on in Vukovar on the eastern borders of the country. 'What's happening?' I asked.

'Any day now, we are going to hear the JNA and the puppets who are running Montenegro saying that Dubrovnik is a threat to their territorial integrity. They want to "neutralise" us to avoid ethnic clashes – that's their way of saying they want to destroy us. They have this crazy claim that we should be part of their country anyway, that this narrow strip of coast only belongs to Croatia because some stupid Bolshevik cartographers made a mistake drawing up the maps.' He made an explosive noise with his lips. 'As if we have anything in common with those bloody butchering Montenegrin Serbs.'

'That sounds ominous,' I said.

'It's just propaganda. They're spreading rumours that we've got an army of Kurdish mercenaries ready to attack the Bay of Kotor and invade them.' He gave a sardonic grin. 'Even stupid Montenegrin Serbs know better than that. Who would rely on Kurdish mercenaries, for God's sake? If I was planning to invade Montenegro, I'd have a Croatian army at my back.'

'And are you planning to invade Montenegro?' I tried to make my voice sound light.

He laughed, his brown eyes sparkling with mischief. 'No, Maggie. There are things I would much rather do this evening than invade Montenegro.'

We were drawing close to the Pile Gate, the massive stone bastion that guards Dubrovnik to the west. He pointed up at the eroded statue of St Blaise in its niche above the gate. 'You see underneath the saint, there is a relief of three heads close together? The man flanked by the two women?'

'What about them?'

'You know the story?'

I shook my head. I'd barely got to grips with the major landmarks of the Old Town, never mind the details of the statuary. 'No, who are they?'

'Legend has it that they're two nuns and a priest who fell in love with each other. Forbidden love in every way. Apparently they were more interested in having sex together than in their holy offices. So their images were carved into the gate to mortify them.'

I laughed in delight. 'An early version of the tabloid press. We name and shame the guilty.'

'Maybe. But I like to think that we're a people who understand and celebrate love in all its different forms.'

I felt a little shiver run up the back of my neck. 'What? Croatia is the embodiment of Foucauldian fluidity?'

'Why not? We don't have to become bourgeois in every respect just because we're no longer Communist.' He reached out and took my hand. I know it's the worst kind of cliché but truly, it did feel like an electric shock. 'There are other ways of being, wouldn't you say? As a feminist?'

Everyone thinks themselves unique when they fall in love. The truth is, we all lose ourselves in the same way. Whether it takes hours or days or weeks, we all find ourselves in a place of wonder and urgency, where we believe nobody has ever been before to quite the same degree. If everyone felt like this, our script goes, the world would come to a grinding, grinning halt.

And that's how it was with Mitja and me. I couldn't have told you the morning after how we got from the Pile Gate to the tangle of sheets in the hotel room in the Old Town; at this distance, it's even more of a blur. All I remember is the door closing and the terrible hunger for each other's bodies. The brief grip of panic when I wondered whether seeing me naked would kill his desire, whether we'd fit together or be awkward and uncomfortable, whether this was just a mad response to the threat of war. Then the tumult of desire answering desire.

One thing I do know for certain. From the very first time, the sex was sensational. I wasn't short of experience when I met Mitja. I enjoyed sex and I'd been lucky with my lovers. But all that good stuff faded to grey beside the love we made. And the quality of our physical relationship cemented everything else. Maybe it was the meeting of our minds, the sharing of a common sense of humour, the delight we both took in challenging the other's position that gave the sex an extra helping hand. However the biofeedback went, it worked.

And it never stopped working. From those first weeks when we fell into each other's arms every time like starving wolves to the night before he walked out of my life for ever, making love was always what pulled us straight into each other's orbit and healed whatever else was wrong in our world. I believe that continuity of tenderness, that perpetual passion was one of the principal reasons he left the way he did. If he'd tried to talk it through, explain why he had to go, I'd have dragged him into bed and that would have been another night, another day when he'd have stayed because he wanted to.

But I'm getting ahead of myself now.

That night reconfigured everything for both of us. In truth, we couldn't have picked a worse combination of time and place to fall in love. The morning after that first night, on 16 September 1991, the JNA mobilised the 2nd Titograd Corps in Montenegro, supposedly because of the threat posed by Croatia. I heard the news at work; I'd been in a daze all day, but that popped the bubble of my happiness. Everybody knew where this was heading now. Nobody could bury their head in the sand any longer.

Leaving on the next bus would have been the rational thing to do. It's what most people with any sense did. I might even have done it myself if the mobilisation had been announced a few days earlier. But going was no longer an option. To leave Dubrovnik then would have been to turn my back on my best-ever chance of happiness.

I look back at that choice now and all that stemmed from it. I saw horror and hardship, courage and catastrophe, devastation and daring. I experienced things I still can't talk about with equanimity. But even with the benefit of hindsight, I know I would have stayed. And I'm glad that I did.

19

All day, Maggie had been twitchy. She felt eyes on her back when she stopped for coffee on her way to the squat concrete block where she was due to give her seminar. She heard footsteps behind her as she cut up the steps from Ashton Lane. She'd never scrutinised a seminar audience so closely, checking every man in the room to gauge whether he could have been one of the pair under the bridge.

The first thing she'd done when she'd got back to her hotel after last night's incident was to instruct the front desk to deny she was there if anyone phoned or asked in person. If her hosts called to check she'd arrived safely, that would be too bad. She hung the Do Not Disturb sign outside, slid the chain in place and double-locked the door. And just because she could, she shoved the chair under the door handle. Maggie wasn't sure how effective it would prove, but that was what people did in books and films. It couldn't hurt.

Once she was certain she was as secure as she could be, she opened up her laptop and tried to concentrate on her notes for the morning's seminar. She needed to take her mind off what had happened. She knew from years of experience under fire in the Balkans that there was no point in brooding after the fact. You had to turn your back on what had terrified you and move on to the next thing, otherwise you'd go crazy. She'd seen that happen to journalists more than once. Raw kids, swaggering into a war zone, determined to make their name. No fallback internal resources to sustain them when they looked death or worse in the face. Next thing, they were running for the first transport out, rapidly deciding that maybe they could be a music critic after all.

The best way to draw a line was to hang out with people who'd walked the same beat. She'd been lucky. She'd had Mitja. But even if he wasn't around, as often as not she had Tessa. Failing that, there were always colleagues or NATO personnel that she could sit in a bar with. She'd never felt alone with her demons. But that encounter under the bridge had been different. It had come out of the blue and she had no idea what lay behind it. Except that Tessa had told her Mitja was showing up on someone's radar.

So her attempts to divert her attention to the morning's work were only partly successful. She ended up in bed, still wearing her underwear and a T-shirt, watching junk TV till exhaustion finally swamped her in the small hours. When she woke up, the BBC breakfast show was interviewing some classical composer about a collaboration with a crime writer. It was almost as dreamlike as the memory of the men under the bridge.

By the time she'd showered and dressed, she'd managed to distance herself from the episode. But that didn't mean she'd forgotten it and she remained vigilant all through breakfast and on the short taxi ride to the university precincts.

After the seminar, lunch. Maggie knew she was distracted to the point of rudeness, but she couldn't help herself. She excused herself as soon as basic manners would allow and practically ran out into the street, gulping at the fresh air as if it could protect her. She hailed a passing taxi then abruptly changed her mind, stepping back on to the pavement and letting the tide of lunchtime shoppers swallow her up. A hundred yards down the street, when she was as sure as she could be that nobody was on her trail, she flagged down another cab to take her to the station.

As her train slipped south across the river, on the bridge next to the one that had sheltered her attackers, her anxiety levels fell to manageable levels. She was sitting in the last seat, able to see the length of the carriage, a turn of the head away from anyone who entered from behind. Even so, she couldn't quite relax. Every time the train stopped, she was alert.

When her taxi deposited her at last at the gates of St

Scholastica's, Maggie finally felt on safe ground. She longed to be back in her own rooms, but habit carried her into the lodge. She greeted the porter over her shoulder as she went to check her pigeonhole. As well as the usual assortment of post, there was a blue envelope with her name in familiar flowing script, clearly delivered by hand. A note from Dorothea, in the context of recent events, obviously wouldn't keep.

She shoved her thumb under the flap and tore it open. But before she could pull out the contents, a voice close to her shoulder said, 'Professor Blake? Could I have a word, please?'

Maggie whirled round, even as her brain processed the information; a woman's voice, an East Coast accent, another bloody stranger. She took in a stocky woman of middle height with a shrewd gaze, a messy haircut and a slightly crumpled business suit. Behind her loomed a much younger man with a worried look and an equally wrinkled suit. 'Who are you?' she blurted out, sounding guilty even to her own ears.

'I'm sorry, Professor, I was just about to tell you they were looking for you,' the porter said.

'Who?' Maggie repeated.

'I'm Detective Chief Inspector Karen Pirie from Police Scotland. And this is Detective Constable Murray. We'd like to speak to you.' The woman glanced at the porter. 'In private.'

'Police Scotland? Is this about my parents?' Maggie didn't believe that. If something had happened to them, it would be a local bobby delivering the news. But it was a good holding question. She wasn't mollified by the identity of the strangers. She remembered what Tessa had told her: the people she'd heard were interested in Mitja were on the official payroll too. And she couldn't think of any other reason why the police would be looking for her.

'I don't know anything about your parents, Professor. That's not why I'm here.'

'So what is this about?'

Karen Pirie smiled. It was a bit too uncertain to be reassuring, Maggie thought. 'I'd rather explain somewhere more private. Do you have an office we could go to?'

Maggie considered her options. She could dig her heels in and insist on information here and now, but the porters were as leaky as they were loyal. Besides, this woman didn't seem the sort who'd back down easily. She could take them to the Senior Common Room, but at this time of the evening, there would be no privacy there either. That left her with two choices: tell these cops to piss off, or invite them to her set.

'Why would I want to talk to you?' she hedged.

Karen's mouth tightened momentarily. 'Why would you not? Professor, I've been hanging around here for the past twenty-four hours because I need your help. That's the top and bottom of it. I don't understand why you would see that as a problem. I really don't.' She spread her hands in a gesture of openness.

'What if I refuse?'

Karen dropped her hands. 'Then we will go away. I'll get the answers to my questions somewhere else. It won't be as straightforward, but I will get the answers. And if they're the answers I expect, it's going to be a lot harder on you than talking to me now. I'm not saying that as a threat. I'm trying to say it as a kindness.' This time, it was sympathy Maggie saw in the other woman's eyes.

Unsure whether she was doing the right thing, Maggie gave in. 'Come up to my rooms,' she sighed.

'Shall I tell the Principal?' the porter asked as they moved towards the door that led into the college.

Maggie half turned and gave him a withering look. 'Not until I'm arrested, Steve.'

In silence, they followed her down the driveway till they came to Magnusson Hall, a daunting Victorian sprawl of red and yellow brick that had started life as an insane asylum. 'It's the top floor,' Maggie said, leading the way to an ornate wooden staircase. 'No lift, I'm afraid.' It was a lie; to comply with legislation on disabled access, the college had installed a lift at the rear of the building. But Maggie was feeling petty. She generally took the stairs. If they wanted to talk to her, they could visit on her terms.

By the time they reached her front door, Karen was pink and breathing hard. Maggie felt a moment's schadenfreude;

her heart rate was barely elevated. She unlocked the door and led them down the hall to the room where she conducted her supervisions, gesturing at a pair of armchairs opposite the small sofa where she preferred to sit. She dropped her backpack by her seat and perched on the edge, elbows on knees, leaning forward. 'Now tell me,' she said.

'I'd like you to cast your mind back thirteen years,' Karen said. 'You opened a bank account at the Forth and Clyde Bank. It was a joint account with a man called Dimitar Petrovic.'

Maggie felt a cold sensation in her chest, as if part of her body had been put in a blast chiller. 'What if I did?' To her surprise, her voice came out cramped and breathy.

Karen sighed. 'We know you did. It's a matter of record. Can you tell me why that was? Were you in a relationship with Dimitar Petrovic?'

Maggie jumped to her feet. 'Jesus. I might have known. You lot are all in bed together.' She pulled her phone out of the pocket of her jeans and stabbed at the screen. 'I'm saying nothing to you without a lawyer.' Even in her agitation, she could see Karen looked stunned. 'Don't act the innocent with me. I'm calling my lawyer and until she gets here, this conversation is over.'

20

If you couldn't deal with being wrong-footed, you'd never cut it as a cop. Karen knew that. But that didn't mean she'd learned to be sanguine about it. She always felt that she should be better prepared. Forewarned, forearmed. All that sort of thing. So when Maggie Blake started ranting about lawyers, she was almost affronted by her failure to anticipate such a move. They'd come, in effect, to do a death knock. Usually the greatest call on her experience was to find a way to be sympathetic while extracting the necessary information. There had been one occasion when it had all gone off like a box of cheap fireworks, but that had been when she was delivering the bad news to the mother of a notorious drug-dealing villain, who seemed to think her son's death was the fault of the police rather than her son's lifestyle choices. A nice middle-class woman with nothing to hide shouldn't be kicking off and demanding a lawyer.

Unless, of course, she didn't have nothing to hide.

Karen sat still while Maggie Blake made her phone call. Somebody called Tessa, apparently.

'I've got the cops here,' Maggie said. Her shoulders were hunched defensively round her phone. 'Yes, here. In my study ... They're being very cagey but it's something to do with Mitja ... No ...' She ran a hand through her hair and paced towards the window, turning her back on them. As she passed her desk, she reached out and grabbed a silver photo frame, flipping it face down without breaking step. 'Can you get here right away? I'm not answering any questions without a witness. And advice ...'

Karen watched Maggie's shoulders relax. It sounded like this Tessa was a friend as well as a lawyer. If Karen was right about the identity of the John Drummond skeleton, it would be better for Maggie to have a friend at her side. Even if the friend was a lawyer.

'Great. Thanks.' Maggie drew a deep breath then swung round to face them. 'My lawyer's on her way. So if you don't mind, we'll put this on hold till then. Would you like a drink? Tea, coffee? Something stronger?'

Karen shook her head. She didn't want Maggie to leave the room. There wasn't exactly rapport between them. But there wasn't quite hostility either. 'You sound like you're from my neck of the woods?' she said. It was a cheat of a question; she'd checked out the professor on the web and discovered she'd attended Bell Baxter school in the heart of

Fife, less than twenty miles from where Karen lived. 'I'm from Kirkcaldy,' she added.

Maggie looked sceptical. 'Is that what they teach you to do? Stoke up the fellow feeling to break down the barriers?'

Karen sighed. 'I was only making conversation while we wait for your pal Tessa to turn up. If you'd rather sit here in silence, please yourself. Me and DC Murray'll get our phones out and play Angry Birds to pass the time if you'd rather?'

Maggie closed her eyes briefly. 'I'm sorry. I don't mean to be rude. I'm just not very comfortable right now.'

'I understand that.' Karen gave her the smile that Phil insisted transformed her from ogre to sweetheart. 'I'm not trying to trip you up or catch you out. Just doing a wee bit of Fife lassies' bonding. Because I'm a long way from home too.' Face it, she thought. She'd have to rely on the geographic bonding because on the surface they didn't have much else in common. Maggie was immaculately groomed and stylish, her neat brown hair shaped like a bell, her make-up understated but effective, her outfit well-chosen to emphasise a figure that was slim and shapely. She reminded Karen of one of those faintly glamorous executives who turned up on BBC4 dramas. What saved her from homogeneity was her eyes: hyacinth blue, direct and nested with laughter lines. They made Karen think that, in other circumstances, they might have enjoyed a drink together.

Now Maggie nodded wearily. 'I grew up in the Howe of Fife. Just outside Ceres.'

Farming, then. Range Rovers and green wellies. 'A bit different from down my way.'

As if she'd read Karen's mind, Maggie expanded: 'My dad was a farm labourer.'

Ouch. Very wrong, Karen. More like you than you thought. 'Mine worked at Nairns. Linoleum then vinyl flooring.'

'Funny how linoleum's come back into fashion.'

'Aye. It's environmentally friendly. Unless you live downwind of the factory or you've a fondness for the smell of linseed oil.'

The two women chuckled. *Ice broken. Job done.* 'You're a long way from the Howe of Fife here,' Karen said.

'In more ways than one. When I was younger, all the interesting work in my field was being done down south, so I didn't have any choice in the matter.'

'You ever think about coming back to Scotland? Especially now. The year of Homecoming. The referendum. All that?'

'This is my home now. I only go back a couple of times a year to see my parents. My friends are here, my colleagues are here.'

'You don't feel like you're living in exile, then?' Karen, who hadn't yet decided which way to vote, was nevertheless convinced she'd feel like a foreigner if she had to live in England.

Maggie shrugged. 'I try to live like I'm a citizen of the world. I've seen the damage narrow nationalism can do and I don't want any part of that.'

'Fair enough. I take it you're talking about the Balkans when you talk about nationalism?'

In a moment, some of Maggie's defensiveness returned. She stuck her hands in the pockets of her jeans and leaned against her desk. 'Why do you say that?'

Karen fell back on the placatory smile. 'I googled you, of course. Your book on the geopolitics of the Balkans is apparently the standard work on the subject.' She gave a self-deprecatory shrug. 'I don't even know what that means, geopolitics. But I'm guessing you've spent a bit of time over there to get a better idea of what you're writing about.'

'I have. It's a part of the world that changes people's perspectives. It certainly changed mine.'

Karen desperately wanted to ask about Petrovic, but she forced herself to stay silent. 'A wee bit different from Fife,' she said.

Maggie gave a wry smile. 'Yes and no. The extreme sectarianism that infects parts of Scottish civil society isn't so very different from the religious hatreds that divide communities in the Balkans.'

'You mean Rangers and Celtic? Protestant against Catholic?'

'Exactly. As in the Balkans, what they have in common is that all sides share the same mix of ethnicity. It's as if they have to be twice as fierce in their hatred of what they perceive as "difference" so they can establish the right of their own position. It's madness. And it's gone on for centuries. But finally, with this generation, there seems to be a sliver of hope for change.'

'In Scotland?'

'I don't know about Scotland. I mean in the Balkans. And it's thanks to the Internet. In the past, each community tried to keep itself quarantined from the people it defined as "other". Each generation was taught to demonise the outsiders. They didn't communicate with them, they didn't have any opportunity to discover how much common ground there was between them.'

'So when it came to the breakdown of Yugoslavia, they could go right back to their old habits?'

'As you say. And when it came to civil war, it was easy to think of the enemy as less than human. That made it OK to rape and torture and massacre, because they were vermin who needed to be put down.' Maggie pushed off from her desk, warming to her subject, moving around and gesturing with her hands as she spoke. Karen could see exactly why she'd be a success in a lecture theatre. Clever, dynamic, lit up by passion.

'And you think it's finally changing?'

'I think there are grounds for cautious optimism. This generation, the post-war kids, the ones who're coming through their teens now, they're growing up in a different world. Twitter and Facebook and all the other social media mean that they're encountering kids from the other communities online and they're discovering that they have much more in common.'

'Really? I'd have thought that online anonymity provided more of an opportunity for bullying and trolling,' Karen said. 'That tends to be what we see most of in our job.'

'I'm not denying some of that goes on. But mostly what they're seeing is that their attitudes are the same as the people they thought were their enemies – none of them wants to spend their lives trapped in the old cycles of violence and revenge.' Maggie waved at her desk, where assorted digital gadgets huddled together. 'They want an economic future where they can have games consoles, and stream music, and buy the latest clothes. Not one where they might end up as refugees with all their possessions tied up in a bedsheet on the back of an ox-cart.'

'Ironic that it's taken twenty-first-century materialism to give them a different set of priorities. Communism didn't manage it, but offer them an X-box and suddenly the past doesn't matter,' Karen said.

'It's a mash-up of those aspirations and their new understanding of how little difference there truly is between them. It might mean that we can lay to rest a thousand years of brutal wars in that region. That, and the fact that they no longer have a valid role as the buffer zone between the Ottoman and the Austro-Hungarian empires.' She stopped abruptly, as if recalling who she was talking to.

'Interesting,' Karen said. 'Maybe we'll get there in Scotland too.'

'Try eradicating educational segregation on religious grounds,' Maggie said. 'It makes it harder to discriminate if you can't figure out someone's religion based purely on the name of their school.'

Karen gave a derisive snort. 'Aye, right. Oddly enough, that's not one of the suggestions that's being put forward by the pro-independence lobby.'

Before they could dive further into the murky waters of sectarianism, a deep buzzing cut across Maggie's reply. 'That'll be Tessa.' She left them for a moment to let the lawyer in.

'Something dodgy going on, eh, boss?' Jason muttered under the low murmur of indecipherable voices from the hallway.

'Aye, but dodgy doesn't always mean illegal.' Karen stood up, ready to face her opponent. However hard she tried, she couldn't think of lawyers in any other terms.

The tall, slender woman who swept in ahead of Maggie had all the self-assurance of the best of the breed. Black hair stranded with silver was pulled back in a loose ponytail; her pale skin and soft features combined to give the impression of collected intelligence and compassion. She was dressed casually, in linen trousers and a dark blue sweater, but it was the kind of casual that cost a lot to achieve. 'I'm Tessa Minogue,' she said. 'I'm a human rights lawyer, strictly speaking. But I am here on Maggie's behalf. If I don't like the way your questions are heading, I will intervene.' She didn't bother smiling. She took the opposite end of the sofa from where Maggie had been sitting, demonstrating a confident familiarity with the room and its occupant.

Karen introduced herself while Maggie perched on the edge of her seat again, hands clasped between her knees. 'We're here looking for help,' Karen concluded. 'That's all.'

'I'm not trying to be obstructive,' Maggie said.

'We all have a right to protect our own interests,' Tessa said.

Bloody smug lawyers. 'So if we could just crack on?' Karen said. The other women nodded. She flipped open her notebook. Time to be very precise. 'You opened a joint bank account thirteen years ago with Dimitar Petrovic. For six years or so, you both used it. You paid a monthly sum into the account, he deposited various amounts at irregular intervals. Most of the withdrawals were cash, and on his card. Then eight years ago, he stopped using the account. You continued to pay in four hundred pounds a month but you don't draw down that money.' She looked up. 'Were you in a relationship with Dimitar Petrovic?'

Maggie glanced at Tessa, who nodded. 'He was my partner, yes.'

'We've had some difficulty finding any official information about Mr Petrovic. Can you explain why that might be?'

'Why are you so interested in General Petrovic?' Tessa interrupted.

'All in good time, Ms Minogue. Professor?'

'There isn't a paper trail because he's not British,' Maggie said wearily. 'He was a general in the Croatian Army. He was an intelligence specialist. Later he worked with NATO during the Bosnian conflict and with the UN during the war in Kosovo.'

'Is that where you met?'

Maggie nodded. 'I was teaching in Dubrovnik when the Croatian war broke out. That's when I met Mitja.' She inclined her head towards the lawyer. 'And Tessa too.'

'We all spent a lot of time together during the siege of Dubrovnik,' Tessa said. 'When you come under fire, it forges close bonds.'

'I imagine it does. So, the three of you were friends?'

'Mitja and I were a couple,' Maggie said. 'And Tessa was friends with both of us.'

'He came to join you here after the war was over?' asked Karen.

'Yes.'

'And what was he doing for a living?'

'He was a security consultant. He also gave occasional lectures. War and Peace Studies, that sort of thing. But I don't understand why you're interested in this. We were tediously law-abiding.' Maggie was regaining her edge, turning Karen's questioning back at her.

Sensing that, Karen sharpened her approach. 'What happened eight years ago?'

'In what respect?'

'He stopped using the bank account. Why?'

Maggie gave Tessa a pleading look. The lawyer crossed her legs and held her left elbow with her right hand. 'General Petrovic moved away.'

'He left you?' Karen addressed herself to Maggie.

'He left,' Tessa said.

'Where did he go?' Karen was still facing Maggie.

'I presume he went back to Croatia.' Every word cost Maggie, Karen could see.

'But you don't know that? Did he not tell you where he was going?'

Maggie wrapped her arms round herself. 'He didn't tell me he was going, never mind where. He just left, all right?' There was a pause. Karen waited. She was good at waiting in interviews. 'I knew he missed Croatia. He talked a lot about the regeneration work that was under way. Sometimes he sounded quite wistful. Nostalgic. But when I suggested making a trip back, he said he didn't want to be a tourist in his own country.' She sighed. 'I assumed the pull towards home was stronger than the pull towards me. I kept putting the money in the account in case he needed it. I know that sounds pathetic, but I knew that things wouldn't be straightforward for him in Croatia. Nothing's ever straightforward in the Balkans,' she added with a bitter laugh. 'And I hoped that my putting the money in the account for him would make him understand he could come back when he was ready.'

'So you haven't heard from him since he left? He's not been in touch?'

Maggie stared at the faded kilim on the floor. 'No. Not a word.'

'And what about you, Tessa? Has he been in touch with you?'

'Of course not. Why would he be in touch with me and not Maggie?'

Karen could think of at least one reason, but this probably wasn't the time to accuse the lawyer of sleeping with her best friend's bloke. 'I just wondered,' she said mildly. 'So, Professor, when he left, did he say he was going out for a while? Or going away for a few days? How did he put it?'

'It wasn't like that. I left on the morning of the third of September eight years ago to go to a conference in Geneva. Mitja said he might go climbing in Scotland while I was away. When I got home, he was gone. He'd taken almost nothing with him, which made me think he'd gone climbing, as he'd said he planned to do. But he didn't come back.'

'The people he usually climbed with hadn't seen him or heard from him,' Tessa chipped in. 'We checked.'

That fitted with what Karen had learned earlier in the day from John Thwaite and Robbie Smith. 'Did he ever say anything about free climbing? Or buildering, I think it's called. Where people climb the outside of buildings?'

'He'd done it a few times,' Maggie said. 'But he didn't tell me much about it because it was illegal and he didn't want me to get into trouble if he got caught.'

'And was there any mention of doing it with an old friend from the Balkans?' Karen asked.

Maggie shook her head. 'All his climbing buddies from Croatia were still there, as far as I know.'

'Apart from us,' Tessa said. 'A bunch of us used to do a bit of hillwalking when we were all in the Balkans at various points during the conflict. There were a few places you could go in safety and get away from it all. And the three of us still did get out in the hills after Mitja moved here. Snowdonia and the Black Mountains, mostly. But we never went with anyone else from those days. What has all of this to do with anything?'

'Was there anybody from his life in the Balkans that he saw much of while he was living here?'

Maggie frowned. 'Occasionally someone would come over on government business. Or some sort of military training. They'd meet up for a drink, or he'd invite them over for dinner. But he didn't go out of his way to seek them out.' She shrugged. 'We had a social life of our own.'

'Mitja wasn't somebody who harked back to the past,' Tessa said. 'He lived in the here and now. But I'm going to ask you again, Chief Inspector: what is all this in aid of?'

They had arrived at the hard place now. 'So neither of you has seen or heard from Dimitar Petrovic since September 2007?'

Both women nodded. 'That's right,' Tessa said.

Karen lowered her voice. 'I'm sorry to have to tell you this, but I think I may have some very bad news. A few days ago, the skeletonised remains of a man were found on the roof of a building in Edinburgh. We have reason to believe that man was Dimitar Petrovic.'

Maggie's mouth fell open and her eyes widened. 'No. There has to be a mistake. I'd know if he was dead. I'd know.' Her voice was firm, filled with denial.

Tessa straightened up, uncrossing her legs and shunting herself along the sofa so she could put an arm round her friend. 'It can't be Mitja. It just can't. How did this man die? Was it a fall?'

'Nothing so straightforward, I'm afraid. He was murdered.'

21

I t was as if Karen's words made sense of an absurdity. Murder was plausible to Maggie Blake in a way that simple death had not been. Tears spilled from her eyes and she began to moan, low and insistent, as if a terrible pain was twisting inside her. Karen, who had broken this news more than her fair share of times because of her gender, held back both sympathy and inquiry. She knew it was always better to let the first storm pass.

Tessa meanwhile attempted to pull herself together. 'He can't be dead. That's not possible. If he's dead, then who—'

'Don't you dare,' Maggie exploded, rounding on her. For a moment, Karen thought she was going to slap her friend. 'I told you. I said he could never—'

Tessa grabbed her arm. 'Not now. We'll do our grieving in private.' She stressed the last two words, giving Karen a swift sideways look.

'I'm really sorry,' Karen said.

Maggie ran her hands up the sides of her head, gripping her hair in bunches, as if trying to tear it out by the roots. 'Are you sure it's him?'

'We can't be a hundred per cent sure at this point,' Karen said. 'He had no ID on him. But he was found with a hotel key-card that had the imprint of some debit-card details on the magnetic strip. When we checked that out, it corresponded to your joint account. Given that General Petrovic hasn't used the account for eight years, and now you're telling me you haven't seen him or heard from him in all that time ... I'm sorry, but it's hard to think of another explanation.'

'Unless he killed the skeleton then went on the run,' Jason said. 'With him being a soldier and all, maybe that's how it went? I mean, anybody could have his hotel key-card, right? He might even have left it himself to confuse things.'

Karen looked at him in disbelief. Sometimes she wondered how Jason had lived this long. Did he seriously think that Maggie Blake would feel better about being deserted by a murderer rather than losing her lover to a killer?

'He's got a point,' Tessa said. 'And Mitja might not have pulled the trigger – he might simply have been there when it happened. But after what he'd been through, there are good reasons why he might have chosen to disappear. If it was his word against a Brit, for example. Or if he was afraid

221

the killer might come after him. Really, Chief Inspector, what you have is very circumstantial. Very thin.'

Maggie slumped against the arm of the sofa. 'I don't understand. Is it him or is it not? That's all that matters.'

'And that's what we need to establish,' Karen said. 'I'm really sorry, Professor Blake. I think you have to prepare yourself for the worst, but we do need to make sure we've made a correct identification. How old was General Petrovic when he left?'

Maggie looked baffled. 'He was forty-seven on the seventeenth of August. Just a few weeks before he left. Why? What does that prove?'

'The remains we found have been aged by our forensic team. They put him between forty-four and forty-seven.'

'But that's meaningless. That doesn't narrow anything down.' Maggie's words were defiant but her eyes told a different story.

Karen didn't need to point out that it failed to exclude the general from the reckoning. 'Can you tell me, had he ever broken any bones that you know about?'

Maggie frowned. 'Not when we were together.'

'He never mentioned any accidents from before?' You wouldn't necessarily tell your partner every detail of your medical past. But River had said it would have been a bad break. An interruption to the dead man's life, presumably.

'He had a scar on his left thigh. He said it was from an accident when he was a student. Some idiot in a delivery

222

van knocked him off his bike. I think he might have broken his leg, but I don't remember the details. Is it important?' Maggie looked close to tears again.

'That might be a useful detail. We do know our victim broke his left femur at some point. It doesn't prove anything, obviously, but it does seem to tie in with what you remember.'

'What about DNA? Isn't that the gold standard of ID these days?' Tessa leaned forward, fixing Karen with her eyes.

'We have managed to extract DNA from the remains, but as yet we've nothing to compare it to. Do you have contact details for any members of General Petrovic's family?'

Maggie shook her head slowly. 'I never met them. So many people lost track of their families during the Balkan wars. People died. People ran to distant relatives in other countries. People were displaced. All I know is that he was an only child. I don't even know the name of his village.' She covered her face with her hands. 'It never seemed important,' she mumbled through her fingers. 'We were about the future, not the past. That's what he always said.'

There was an awkward silence, broken only by Maggie blowing her nose. Tessa reached for her hand and squeezed it tight. Then Jason spoke again. 'What about next of kin? Did he not have to provide the name of a next of kin for official documents and that?'

Maggie gave Tessa a sidelong glance. 'I was his next of kin.'

'Not officially, though,' Tessa said.

'Yes, officially. I'm sorry, Tess. I know I should have told you, but we didn't want to make a big deal out of it. It just made it easier for him to stay.'

Tessa stiffened, her face frozen. 'You married him? When?'

'A few weeks after he came over for good. Do you remember, we rented a cottage in the west of Ireland? We did it then. Somebody he knew in the UN sorted out the paperwork.' She sniffed and fiddled with a heavy silver ring on the third finger of her right hand.

'Bloody hell, Maggie. Why didn't you tell me? I thought we had no secrets.'

'We didn't tell anyone. We didn't want to make a big fuss. We wanted something that was ours, that's all.' She pinched the bridge of her nose and shivered. 'Right now, even that feels like a betrayal. I never got to grieve properly when he went. I had to act like, you know, shit happens. Men leave. But it wasn't just a casual thing. He was my husband. We didn't do it lightly, but when he disappeared, I thought he'd torn up all those vows we made, and that really hurt.'

Tessa put her arms around Maggie again and held her close. 'You poor darling.' She stroked her hair, her face all concern and sorrow.

Everybody has secrets, Karen thought. Secrets and lies. But she reminded herself that she had a job to do. 'We still need to find a way to establish a positive ID,' she said. 'There's no point in speculating what happened on that roof until we know for sure whether we're looking at General Petrovic or somebody else entirely. And if we've not got access to a blood relative, we're going to have to come at this from a different angle. Do you still have anything belonging to the general that might have retained his DNA. A hairbrush? A toothbrush? Something like that?'

Maggie frowned. 'He never used a hairbrush. He just ran his fingers through his hair.' A hint of a smile as a memory ghosted across her mind. 'I threw away his head from the electric toothbrush after a couple of years – it was dusty and disgusting. I thought when he came back, I'd just give him another one.'

'Makes sense,' Karen said. 'Anything else of his that you've still got? Any clothes he'd actually worn, that sort of thing?'

She thought for a long moment then got unsteadily to her feet. 'His electric razor. It's in the bathroom drawer, right where he left it. I've never cleaned it or anything.' She started for the door.

'Jason,' Karen said. 'Bag and tag, please.'

He got to his feet and set off in Maggie's wake, patting his pockets for an evidence bag. Tessa looked Karen straight in the eye and said, 'You're pretty sure it's him, aren't you?'

'I've been in this job a long time and, in my experience, the simplest explanation almost always turns out to be the right one. DC Murray, he still gets carried away with romantic notions about people who run away from their lives so they don't get the blame for something they didn't do. People do run, it's true. But we're social creatures. For most of us, it's unsustainable to butt out of the lives of our nearest and dearest and never go back. We see it all the time in witness protection. They just have to see their old gran on her eightieth birthday. Or their beloved football team in the cup final. Or their granddaughter's first communion. Bear in mind, these are people that can pretty much guarantee that resurfacing anywhere near their old life is going to have serious consequences. But still they do it. Now, from what you've both told us about their relationship, I can't see Dimitar Petrovic abandoning the woman he loves without so much as a Christmas card to say he's all right.'

Tessa shrugged one shoulder. 'He walked away from his life in Croatia – whatever that was before he met Maggie. I was around a lot of the time when the fighting was still going on. I met plenty of his fellow soldiers, guys he was friendly with. But I never met anybody from his life before Dubrovnik. It was as if he'd cut himself loose from his past so he could be with Maggie. If he could do that once, he could do it again, surely?'

'I don't know. I never met the man. But there's no point in speculation. If we can get a sample of his DNA, we'll have the answer in a day or so.' Karen gave her an assessing look. 'What were you going to say when Maggie cut you off?'

Tessa blinked slowly. 'How strange is that? I really can't recall. You know how it is, the shock provokes strange

226

outbursts. And then you forget as quickly as you started to speak what it was you were going to say.' She gave a lazy smile. 'All I was thinking about was how I have to be there for Maggie.'

Aye, right. She was a good liar, Karen thought. But a liar nonetheless. Whatever she was hiding might have nothing to do with Dimitar Petrovic's death. And it might have everything to do with it. Sooner or later, she'd find a way to dig it out. 'We're going to have to go back through his movements around the time he disappeared,' she said.

'Good luck with that one, officer. Can you remember what you were doing on a particular night eight years ago?' Tessa sounded remarkably amused for a woman who'd just learned one of her best friends was dead. Maybe she hadn't been as fond of General Petrovic as she made out. Or maybe she'd been too fond. The kind of fond where you have to cover up.

'I've been in cold cases quite a while now. We've developed techniques for helping people to remember,' Karen said. 'Jogging their memories with what was in the headlines back then. What was in the charts. What was on the telly. You'd be amazed what surfaces. We'll obviously be asking you, since you knew him.'

Before Tessa could reply, Jason and Maggie returned. He held up a sealed plastic bag with details of the shaver inside scribbled on it. 'Got it, boss.'

'Thanks. There's one more thing, Professor. We don't

actually know what General Petrovic looked like. I wonder, could you let us have a photograph of him? It might be helpful when we're interviewing potential witnesses.'

Maggie's hand flew to her mouth. Before she could respond, Tessa said, 'Why don't I email you a selection of photographs? I can do that when I get home.'

Karen stood up. 'That would be perfect, thank you. We'll be back in touch as soon as we have a result one way or another. In the meantime, Professor, it'd be helpful if you could start making some notes about the last week or so before General Petrovic went missing. We'll be taking a full statement from you in due course, but if you write down what you can remember, it'll make things easier when we do that.' She fished a business card out of her jacket pocket. 'This is me. Call me any time if you come up with anything that might help us figure out what happened on that rooftop. And again, I'm very sorry to be the bearer of bad news.'

Maggie looked ten years older than she had when Karen had pounced on her in the porters' lodge. She sighed heavily. 'People say it's better to know, don't they? So you can have closure?'

Karen nodded. 'I believe so.'

Maggie's expression was scornful. 'That's bollocks. Knowledge destroys hope. It's hope that's been keeping me going for the last eight years. How am I going to get through the days now?'

At first, it was almost possible to believe we might yet avoid full-scale war. In the snatched hours Mitja squeezed out of his day to spend with me, I learned that the JNA were having their own problems. Apparently, not all their soldiers were keen on a fight with their next-door neighbours. The JNA generals were threatening dire reprisals against deserters and reservists who were ignoring the call-up. And the federal authorities in Belgrade kept insisting there would be no attack against Dubrovnik.

We'd lie in bed in our hotel room – it had to be hotels because I couldn't take Mitja to Varya's and he couldn't take me to his barracks – and hold each other close while we talked about the probability of war, the possibility of peace. It doesn't sound very romantic, I know. But ideas were what had drawn us together. Being at the heart of what happens when ideology spills over into real life was both terrifying and fascinating for both of us.

The hope that we would somehow escape the conflict died a week after the mobilisation. JNA artillery hammered the villages to the south-east of the city. It was clear that they planned to start with the southernmost tip of Croatia and work their way up. Melissa had sent me a series of increasingly insistent emails, telling me to cut and run. I suspect my bland refusals must have driven her mad with frustration.

That night, Mitja said, 'It's not too late to leave, Maggie. I can make sure you get safely away.' He didn't look happy at the prospect, but I could see he meant what he said.

'I can't,' I said. 'I've made my choice. I can't walk away from you.'

His grip on me tightened. 'I understand that. But once the fighting starts, there won't be many opportunities for us to be together. I'm a soldier, Maggie. In a war, I have to go where they send me. Do what they tell me.'

'I know. But you're in intelligence, right? You're not going to be in the front line. You'll be here, doing your thing. And I'll be here too. Whenever you can manage to get away, I'll be waiting.'

'That's not how your life should be.' For the first time since I'd known him, he sounded angry. 'What happened to your feminism? Suddenly you're going to be some submissive little woman waiting for her man to grace her with his presence?'

I was shocked. 'No, that's not what I meant. Whatever happens, I'll find something useful to do with myself. I'm not going to sit around weaving a bloody tapestry. What I'm saying is that now I've found this, now I've found you, I'm not walking away. I'm not counting the cost, Mitja. I—' I stopped abruptly. It had only been nine days, after all. So far, we'd avoided 'I love you.' I love your body, I love when you do that, I love being here with you – all that we'd said, but we'd never quite nailed our colours to the mast.

'I know,' he said, laying his head on my shoulder. 'I feel the same.'

I could feel his heart beat against my hand. Three words, but I'd only ever said them a couple of times in my life. I don't believe in saying things you don't mean, even if it makes life less awkward. But it was time. 'I love you, Mitja.'

'I love you too, Maggie. And that's why I want you to go. I can't protect you here. We've got less than five hundred troops in Dubrovnik. We can't defend fifty thousand people, it's not possible. I need to be able to do my job without worrying about your safety.'

'Tough,' I said. 'It's not up to you. I'm staying, Mitja, and that's that. You need to get used to the idea of having someone who loves you.' It didn't occur to me then, the chances were that I wasn't the only one who loved him. We hadn't shared much of our emotional histories; we'd been too busy creating our own past. But later, I couldn't help wondering whether he'd severed himself from a life complete with wife, children and home when he chose me. He never said anything to suggest that was the case. Nevertheless, when he left, I thought perhaps I'd indulged in a wilful blindness. It suited me not to think of him having loved anyone completely before me because that was the position I was in.

And so we both pledged our allegiance to each other as the bombs started to fall on southern Croatia. Two days later, the Yugoslav navy began its long blockade of the sea roads leading to Dubrovnik. We were well on the way to being an island. Well on the way to being under siege.

22

It was gone midnight by the time Jason dropped Karen off at home. In spite of having had to drive her all the way back to Kirkcaldy, he'd been remarkably cheerful, seeing the extra miles from his flat in Edinburgh only as an excuse to spend the night at his parents' house and have his mother cook him breakfast. 'That way I can pick you up nice and early in the morning, boss,' he reminded her as she dragged herself out of the car.

Phil and River were still up, slumped in front of the TV picking holes in a rerun of *Se7en*. When she walked in, Phil was holding forth. 'And that's the fatal flaw. We're expected to believe that the killer set all this in motion more than a year ago. But he couldn't have known then that the detective hunting him down would have the deadly sin of anger, could he? He might have ended up with a laid-back lazy sod who wasn't that bothered. Or a jobsworth who only cared about his reputation for clearing cases. So the whole thing falls to— Oh, hello, darling. You guys made good time.' He stretched his arms out to her, looking for a hug, but not quite eager enough to get out of his seat.

Some women might have been irritated by that. Not Karen. She saw it for what it was. Comfortable, relaxed affection. No need to put on a show for her or for River. Nights like this reminded her how lucky she was to have Phil. When she'd just about given up hope, when she'd resigned herself to a life of self-reliance, Phil had wakened up to a complex of emotions that matched hers. He loved her for who she was; he never tried to change her. He was smart enough to know that she was smarter, and secure enough not to mind. But most of all, he was reliable. The idea of coming home to find him gone for good was unimaginable.

Karen shrugged off her coat and perched on the arm of his chair, kneading his shoulders with one hand. In a way, that had been the saddest thing about her encounter with Maggie Blake. Not that she was still waiting, eight years on, for the man she loved to come home. No, what bothered Karen was that she seemed to have taken in her stride the fact that he'd gone without a word. Phil often talked about the women he encountered in the Murder Prevention Team as having a perilously low level of self-esteem; they almost believed they deserved to be treated like shit. It seemed to Karen that Maggie Blake had more in common with those women than she'd ever have allowed herself to believe.

Phil put his arm round her waist. 'Good day?'

'Interesting. Made some progress, but not as much as I'd have liked.' She picked up her bag from where she'd let it fall. 'Before I forget, River, here's something for you to play with.' She took out the bagged shaver and passed it across. 'Sign for it so my chain of custody stays intact. And I've got some pix to forward on to you.'

'Excellent. I can do the Buck Ruxton test and superimpose them on an X-ray of the skull. The quick-and-dirty ID from the pre-DNA days.'

'You had a good day?' Karen asked her.

River grinned. 'Always a joy to be in the Dundee lab. I ran more tests that confirm what we already knew about your skeleton. I did some research on the metal plate and the screws in his femur. It's an alloy that was used for a while in the eighties in Soviet-controlled Central Europe. So, Hungary, Czechoslovakia, Yugoslavia, Romania, Bulgaria. That sort of region. But they made a pretty good job of it, which suggests he was either lucky or important.'

'Or both,' Phil said.

'My guy had a scar on his left thigh from being knocked off his bike when he was a student. He may or may not have broken his leg – the professor can't say for sure.'

River nodded. 'A break so bad it needed a plate could well have broken the skin. And if he was a student, chances are

235

he was treated at a training hospital, which would explain the quality of the work. Some consultant showing off to his students. So he was lucky, your dead man.'

'Aye, well, his luck ran out on top of the John Drummond.' Karen sighed.

The film credits began to roll and River stretched in her chair, yawning. 'I'm off to bed. I'll deal with this first thing, then I'll probably head back down the road. My department is pining for me.'

'Not to mention Ewan,' Karen said.

'Oh, he's too busy coaching the under-twelve rugby team to notice whether I'm there or not,' she said with a laugh. They all knew she didn't mean it.

Left on their own, Karen and Phil snuggled together on the chair for a few minutes longer. Then he gently pushed her away. 'Time for bed. I've got a big day tomorrow. We're fronting up the money-laundering rapist property developer. I'm looking forward to it.' His smile was grim, his eyes cold.

'Good for you. Have I told you how much I love that you're doing this job?'

He pulled her back into his arms. 'You have. How about you show me?'

Walking into her office the next morning, Karen felt distinctly underslept and undercaffeinated. When the receptionist told her she had visitors, it was the last thing she wanted to hear. 'Who is it?' she asked. 'Jason, away and get me an Americano with milk, there's a good lad.'

The receptionist checked her list. 'From the Department of Justice.'

'What? You mean London?'

'That's what their ID said. Alan Macanespie and Theo Proctor.'

It didn't sound like the sort of encounter that would start the day with a zing. 'Never heard of them. Did they say why they were here?'

'Nope. I stuck them in Interview Two down the hall.'

'Nobody ever uses Interview One,' Karen said. 'Why is that?'

'Putting them in Interview Two gives the impression there's more going on than there really is,' the receptionist told her. 'Apparently we like to look busy.'

'Police Scotland,' Karen muttered under her breath. 'OK. I'll just wait for Jason to bring my coffee back, then we'll head in and see what joys the DoJ has for us.'

When Jason returned with the coffees, she steered him down the hall. 'There's two punters from the DoJ in London waiting to see us. Now, you know I'm not a betting woman, but five'll get you ten that this has got something to do with General Petrovic. So what I want you to do, Jason, is to keep your mouth firmly shut. OK? This is about gathering information, not giving it out willy-nilly. We clear on that?'

He nodded solemnly. 'Aye, boss. What do you think they're after?'

'One way to find out.' They had reached the interview room. Without knocking, Karen marched in. 'Good morning, gentlemen,' she said briskly, noting that they'd already annexed the chairs that faced the door. *Boys' games*. As if she needed that sort of petty jockeying for position. She set her coffee down, took out her notebook then dumped her bag on the floor and sat down. 'I'm DCI Pirie, head of the Historic Cases Unit. This is DC Murray. ID please, gentlemen.'

'We signed in at the front desk,' the dark-haired one with the scowl said.

'Yes. You did. And she's a receptionist, not a detective. For all I know, you could have bluffed your way in with a couple of fake IDs you cobbled together in some back-street copy shop. So I'll take a look, if you don't mind?'

The ginger one gave his colleague a rueful shake of the head and produced a leather wallet which he flicked open to reveal he was Alan Macanespie of the Department of Justice. The other half of the wallet showed a pass for the International Criminal Tribunal for the former Yugoslavia. 'You do right, Chief Inspector,' he said.

With a face full of resentment, his colleague did the same. Theo Proctor. Karen made a point of writing both names down. 'Now, why are we all here?'

Macanespie leaned his elbows on the table, spreading his

hands in a conciliatory gesture. 'It's very simple,' he said. 'You instigated a CRO search that flagged up an individual of interest to us. All we want to know is the nature of your interest.'

'We instigate a lot of CRO searches in Historic Cases. Who is it that you're interested in?'

Macanespie dipped his head, acknowledging that he understood she wasn't a pushover. 'Dimitar Petrovic.'

'And can I ask why General Petrovic is an individual of interest to you?'

Proctor glowered at her. 'The clue is in the names. International Criminal Tribunal for the former Yugoslavia. Petrovic.'

'Are you telling me that Dimitar Petrovic is wanted for war crimes?' Karen tried not to sound as if this was a complete surprise.

'We're not telling you anything,' Proctor said. 'We're here to establish what you know about Petrovic and his whereabouts.'

Karen bristled. There were few things she hated more than petty bureaucrats throwing their weight around. She shook her head. 'That's not how it works. For a start, I don't think you have any jurisdiction here. Under the terms of the Scotland Act, we're responsible for our own justice system north of the border. And while we're happy to cooperate, we don't take orders from your ministry or its functionaries.' She had no idea whether she was right, but she enjoyed saying it and it sounded good. She smiled. 'So once you've told me why you're interested in Petrovic, maybe I'll consider telling you what I know. Why don't we give you a few minutes to have a wee think about that?' She got to her feet, ostentatiously collecting coffee, bag and notebook.

In the corridor outside, Jason gave her his standard look of puzzlement. 'How come you don't want to tell them about the skeleton? I mean, once Dr Wilde gives us the thumbs-up on the ID, it'll be on the Internet, right?'

'Aye, but they don't know that. Because they don't know what we know. And likewise, I don't know what they know, but as soon as I tell them what we know, there's no incentive for them to tell us what they know and they'll just disappear back over Hadrian's Wall and leave us none the wiser. Does that make sense?'

Jason looked dubious. 'I suppose. But what if they won't tell us?'

'Then we'll call their bluff and send them on their merry way. And they won't like that because then their boss will have to talk to our boss and he'll not be a happy bunny.'

'Then our boss'll give you a hard time.'

Karen gave the kind of smile that makes small children cry. 'I don't think so. Not for maintaining the integrity of our investigation, he won't.'

Five minutes later, she walked back into the interview room. Macanespie and Proctor looked glum. 'We'll show you ours if you show us yours,' Macanespie said.

'I'm glad to hear it. You first, you're the guests.' Karen won a wry smile from Macanespie and another glare from Proctor.

'We've been seconded to the war crimes tribunal in The Hague. To be honest, it's had mixed success. Part of that has been because a string of significant players never made it to the courtroom. They were, in effect, assassinated before they could be arrested. They were all Serbs. And the prime suspect is General Dimitar Petrovic, who disappeared from our radar just before the killing started.' He leaned back and folded his hands over his generous stomach.

'Why? What made him a suspect?'

Proctor sighed. 'He'd been making a lot of noise about what a poor job the tribunal was doing. That what was needed was a proper truth and reconciliation forum like they had in South Africa. We decided to check him out after the first murder, because he'd been complaining about that particular individual enjoying his freedom on the backs of massacred Croats. He had actually given information to the tribunal about where this individual was living, and his new identity. But he thought we were dragging our heels, that we weren't doing anything about it, when in fact we were building a strong case against him. Anyway, when we went to take a look at what Petrovic was up to, we discovered he'd vanished. Nobody seemed to know where he was or what he was doing.'

Macanespie nodded. 'And after the second murder, a wee

bird whispered that Petrovic had decided to take the law into his own hands. He has a little list, apparently. So far, we think he's executed eleven suspected war criminals.'

Karen almost felt sorry for him. 'No, he hasn't.'

Macanespie looked startled. 'What do you mean?'

'What do you know about it?' Proctor demanded.

'I'll know for certain within twenty-four hours, but I'm pretty sure that Dimitar Petrovic isn't the Lone Ranger of the Balkans. Mostly because he's been dead for eight years.'

'Dead?' Macanespie echoed.

'It must have crossed your mind, surely? It's often the reason people disappear without a trace. Plus, you had a load of other murders in the frame.' Karen couldn't quite believe they hadn't already considered that option. But both men looked discomfited.

'You said "other murders",' Macanespie said. 'He was definitely murdered, your dead man?'

Karen nodded. 'Shot in the head.'

'See, now. Right away, that doesn't fit. The murders we're looking at, none of the victims was shot. They all had their throats cut. And they were Serbs. All the other victims were Serbs. And Petrovic is a Croat. Not to mention that he isn't a notorious war criminal,' Proctor said sarcastically. 'Why would we think he was a victim in the same series?'

'Beats me,' Karen said. 'But if you're looking for Petrovic, I reckon you'll find what's left of him in our mortuary. I don't suppose you can come up with anybody who might have wanted him dead? The first one of your victims, for example?'

Macanespie frowned then shook his head. 'No. Petrovic was potentially a useful witness in several trials, but he wasn't crucial to any of them. He had enemies, like everybody who played a part in those conflicts, but I never heard that he was the top of anybody's shit list.'

'So you can't actually help my investigation?'

'No,' Proctor said firmly.

Macanespie pushed a business card across the table towards Karen. 'But if you come across anything that might help ours...'

Karen scraped her chair back. 'My pleasure,' she said, her tone indicating the opposite. 'Jason will see you out, gentlemen. I've got a murder to solve.'

23

Macanespie and Proctor toiled up the hill to their hotel. Edinburgh was full of unexpected hills, leaving Macanespie breathless and bad-tempered. 'What the fuck do we do now?' he demanded for the third time since they'd left Karen Pirie.

The answer was the same. 'It's Cagney's problem, not ours.'

It wasn't a helpful response. Macanespie was already pretty sure that Wilson Cagney was a man accomplished in always taking the credit and never accepting the blame. Somehow, Petrovic dead was going to end up on their plate just as surely as he had while still putatively alive. And right now, Proctor was about as helpful as a concrete lifebelt.

Back at the hotel, they huddled round Proctor's laptop and Skyped their boss. Cagney seemed flustered, but Macanespie put that down to being dragged out of a meeting with people who could do his career more favours than a pair of down-table lawyers. 'So what's the story?' Cagney leaned towards the camera, looming large and ill-shaped in the middle of the screen. 'Why are the Scottish police interested in our man?'

'Because they've found what they think is his corpse,' Macanespie said.

Momentarily, Cagney's eyes widened and his face relaxed. 'Extraordinary. Where?'

'Where's not the point. What affects us is the "when".'

Cagney frowned. 'What do you mean?'

'What they found is a skeleton,' Proctor said wearily. 'On an Edinburgh rooftop. They reckon he's been dead for eight years. He didn't disappear to become an avenger. He disappeared because he was murdered.'

'Murdered? Are they sure about that? If it's a skeleton, how can they be so certain?' Now Cagney looked pissed off.

'The bullet wound to the head is a bit of a giveaway,' Macanespie said.

'Which doesn't fit the MO of the assassinations. Our string of victims weren't lured to their deaths, they were killed during routine stuff they did every day. And Petrovic was a Croat, not a Serb,' Proctor added.

Cagney sat back, his brow furled in thought. 'So somebody killed Petrovic before the other killings started, which means his death might have nothing to do with theirs. It might be nothing more than a bizarre coincidence.'

'There's an outside chance that the skeleton isn't his. They're waiting for DNA,' Macanespie added.

Cagney sat up straight, flicking imaginary fluff from his lapel. 'In a way, though, it's academic. We should leave the Scots to worry about Petrovic. He's no longer our concern. All this means is that we were wrong about the prime suspect.' A tight grim smile compressed his lips. 'Your job just got a little bit harder.'

'Where are we supposed to start looking now?' Proctor sounded plaintive. It was, Macanespie thought, a fatal show of weakness to a man like Cagney.

'Do I have to spell everything out to you? There are still two avenues of investigation. The first one is internal. You have to work out where the leak is. Someone had sufficient access to all those investigations to finger the victims. Find the data trail and see where it leads. There can't be that many people who have that level of clearance.'

'It's not quite that simple,' Macanespie said. 'Most of the lawyers who work at Scheveningen would be privy to what moves were being planned next. If you're trusted enough to be part of the process, you have access to pretty much all of it.'

'So make a list. And work your way through it.'

Proctor started to speak but Cagney cut across him. 'And then there's the external investigation. You need to go back and talk to the local police who dealt with the murders on the ground. There will be CCTV coverage on some of the cases, surely. Did nobody sit on the local cops at the time?'

'Nobody was very bothered at the time.' Macanespie spoke clearly and firmly. 'The human rights brigade made all the right shocked and horrified noises, but you could tell they weren't exactly crying themselves to sleep over it. The animals this guy was targeting, nobody doubted they were guilty. Not for a minute. There were a few questions over the strength of the prosecution material. Some doubts that it might not be quite rigorous enough for the court. But the investigators, they were rock-solid certain. So when those bastards turned up dead, the general feeling was, good riddance to bad rubbish.'

Cagney muttered something under his breath. 'And this was seen as the delivery of justice, was it?'

'The court did its best. It's still doing its best. But it's hamstrung by procedure on occasion,' Proctor said wearily. 'You ask the people on the ground and they'll tell you, too many of these bastards have walked free. Too many war criminals never got charged in the first place. Some of their victims have to live day to day walking the same streets as the men who butchered their husbands or raped their daughters. You'll not find many who'll say that what they got was justice.'

Cagney sighed. 'Be that as it may. The ending of the tribunal marks a new start for the Balkans. It's time to draw a line and move forward. As I said before, these killings have to stop and we have to be seen to be dealing with those who have apparently meted out rough justice with impunity. I want this boil lanced. So you'd better get back to Holland and draw up a plan of action.'

Cagney's image froze for a moment before disappearing. The call was over.

Macanespie looked at Proctor and gave a resigned shrug. 'Looks like we're fucked.'

Karen had never had an entirely easy relationship with her senior officers, even before she had been responsible for one of them serving life for murder. She'd been happy to leave her old boss from Fife behind when she'd been chosen to head up the Historic Cases Unit. But within weeks, her new boss had been felled by a heart attack and his shoes filled by the man she thought she'd left behind. Assistant Chief Constable Simon Lees, known without affection as the Macaroon, believed that if only his officers would simply obey the rules, there would be far fewer problems in his life. That was a conviction that had set him on a collision course with Karen from Day One.

It wasn't that she'd set out to annoy him. When he'd arrived from Glasgow apparently believing he'd been sent as a punishment to live and work among a people barely one generation away from living in caves, she had been far from the only one he had patronised and dismissed. It had acted as a goad to a bull. Karen knew how good her colleagues were. Just because they weren't flash city blowhards didn't mean they weren't on top of their jobs. So when it came to knocking Simon Lees off his high horse she'd been happy to oblige. She'd found interesting ways to undermine him, not least by coming up with a nickname that tied him to an item of confectionary whose main claim to fame was a historic series of adverts that would be viewed now as eyewateringly racist.

He'd tried to extract payback by sidelining her. But her reputation for intelligent and effective work in the Fife Cold Case Unit had spread beyond the walls of force HQ and she'd been picked out to lead a high-profile investigation whose success had caught the imagination of the public. Karen, a woman with no pretensions to being a police poster girl, found herself a media darling. Simon Lees had fumed for weeks, terrorising his wife and kids with the bad temper he couldn't take out on Karen.

Finding her under his command again was the least appealing aspect of his new posting. But this time he was determined she wouldn't get the better of him. He'd keep her on a tight rein, making sure she had just enough rope to hang herself but not so much that she could stray from his oversight. At least once a week, he randomly summoned her to his office to demand a full briefing on her current cases.

That afternoon, she'd wandered in half an hour after he'd sent for her. As usual, her thick mop of dark hair looked as if she'd shared a stylist with Dennis the Menace. Her make-up was minimal, her suit slightly rumpled, the trousers a shade too tight over the generous hips. He'd always assumed she was a lesbian, which was absolutely fine in today's police service, but he'd recently discovered she was living with her old sergeant, Phil Parhatka. Probably had had to order him into bed, Lees thought sourly.

'I expected you earlier,' he said, straightening the papers on his desk.

'I was doing some research and I lost track of the time.' She gave an indifferent shrug. 'You know how it is when something interesting turns up.' She perched on the edge of an elegant sideboard he'd brought from his grandmother's house. His secretary kept it buffed to within an inch of its life. Lees felt sure Pirie knew that.

'And what would that be, exactly? That "something interesting"?' He made the quotation marks sign with his fingers.

'The Balkan conflicts at the end of the last century,' she said, with aplomb. 'Croatia. Bosnia. Kosovo.'

'What on earth has that to do with us? Don't you have enough work to do?'

'This is work. We've got a skeleton on the roof of the John Drummond School. Dr Wilde – you remember Dr Wilde?'

Lees tried not to shudder. Another one of those bloody annoying women. She'd turned up in muddy construction boots and a waxed jacket that looked as if it had small animals lodging in its pockets, and helped Karen Pirie ride roughshod over proper procedure. Between the pair of them, they'd made his life far more complicated than it needed to be. It didn't improve matters that Pirie had managed to solve the case on an unbelievably tight budget; until that pair had stuck their noses in, there hadn't been a case to solve. 'I remember,' he said, his tone admonitory.

'She says he's been there for between five and ten years. We've got other forensics that indicate he's a retired Croatian general who was a NATO security advisor in Bosnia and a UN monitor in Kosovo. Went off the grid eight years ago.'

'What the hell's he doing on a roof in Edinburgh?' Lees couldn't help feeling outraged. Why would someone come all the way from Croatia to get murdered in Edinburgh?

'Not sure yet. He was living in Oxford when he went missing. With a geography professor. She thought he'd buggered off to Croatia to the family she never knew he had.'

'All the same, why Edinburgh?'

'We think he was into buildering. That maybe he came up to Edinburgh specifically to climb the John Drummond.'

'Climb the John Drummond? It's not a bloody mountain, Chief Inspector. What do you mean, climb the John Drummond?'

Karen raised her eyebrows. 'Buildering, like I said. Free climbing. Up the outside of challenging buildings like the John Drummond.'

'What? You mean, they treat buildings like a giant climbing frame?' Lees looked as if he suspected her of making it up as she went along.

'That's about the size of it.' Before she could say more, her phone rang. As if she'd never heard him insist that phones were switched off in his presence, she answered it, saying, 'Gotta take this one.' She pushed off the sideboard and turned her back to him. 'You got something for me?' A long pause. 'And there's no room for doubt?' Another pause. 'Brilliant. Thanks for that. I'll call you later.' She pocketed her phone and swivelled to face Lees. 'That's confirmation, sir. The skeleton on the roof is definitely General Dimitar Petrovic. Did I mention he's got a bullet hole in the middle of his skull?'

'No, you didn't.'

'So that makes him mine. I need to go and break the news to his bidie-in. Well, wife, actually. She married him. Let's just hope for her sake he didn't already have a wife back in Croatia.' She half-turned towards the door. 'Obviously I might have to go to Croatia. That's likely where his enemies'll be.'

'Croatia? How can we afford that?'

'If I have to go, I'll get a cheap flight. I don't think Jason has to come too. But in the meantime, I need to find me an expert on the Balkans. That'll be London, I expect.' She held up a hand to still the protest he hadn't uttered yet. 'Don't worry, I'll wait till the cheap tickets come on stream.'

And she was gone, before he could say anything more, leaving him feeling frustrated and outwitted. He was supposed to be her boss. He was supposed to command respect. How could she keep on getting the better of him? Sooner or later, he was going to have to show her who was boss.

He'd look forward to that.

24

Tessa didn't recognise the number but she took the call anyway. You never knew when someone would turn up out of nowhere with key information that could lift the lid on something that some government somewhere wanted to stay well hidden. The voice, however, was not unfamiliar. She recognised Karen Pirie right away. 'Have you any news?' she asked.

'I'm afraid so. We've got the DNA results back and there's no doubt that the man on the John Drummond School roof is General Petrovic. I'm sorry. I know you were close.'

'Oh, God.' Tessa's voice was a groan.

'I'd rather have told Professor Blake face to face, obviously. But I thought it would be better coming from you? If you don't want to be the one to break the news, I'm perfectly willing to phone her myself, but maybe you could be with her? Nobody should be alone for news like this.'

'Of course I'll tell her.' Tessa wasn't sure how she felt. She'd been expecting this news ever since she'd heard what Karen had to say, but having it confirmed was a different matter. In her heart, she'd known that Mitja would turn up at some point. What she hadn't foreseen was that his return would be heralded by an overweight Scotswoman with bad hair and an attitude. Mitja would have expected better.

'We'll need a statement from her in due course, but we can have that taken by local Thames Valley officers. If there's anything she wants to know, she can call me any time.'

'Will there be a murder investigation? Will you be in charge of that?'

'Yes. But because it's a historic case and the evidence trail is limited, it will be on a smaller scale. Which doesn't mean we won't pursue every lead and follow every avenue. Speaking of that, I need to ask you something that's going to seem really inappropriate right now.'

Tessa made a wry noise. 'You want to know if I was sleeping with him? That's what you want to know, isn't it?' She could hear Karen breathing on the other end of the phone and imagined her pulling faces in her awkwardness.

'And were you?'

Tessa gave a low laugh from the back of her throat. 'You couldn't be more off the mark, Chief Inspector. Mitja Petrovic was the opposite of attractive to me. Look, I'm a lesbian. You can ask anybody who knows me. It's not a secret. I had no sexual interest in him whatsoever. I liked him a lot, and the fact that he made my friend happy gave him a shed-load of Brownie points in my eyes. But me and Mitja? That was never going to happen.'

'Fair enough. But I had to ask. You're a lawyer, you appreciate that.'

'I'm not offended. And thanks for not asking me in front of Maggie. But I'll tell you one thing for nothing. Mitja didn't run away because he was shagging somebody else. He fell for her like a ton of bricks all those years ago in Dubrovnik and he was as much in love with her when he disappeared. I know people say that all the time after some-body walks out, but he really was devoted. That's why I never bought into Maggie's notion that he'd upped sticks and abandoned her to go back to the life he left behind him.'

'So what did you think had happened?'

Tessa had lain awake into the small hours debating what to say when this inevitable question arose. Should she admit to the dark theories she'd aired with Maggie? Or, since they'd been blown out of the water, should she just avoid muddying the waters? At last, she'd made her decision. 'I didn't know what to think. At first I thought he might have been pressed back into service, carrying out undercover intelligence work. But when so much time went by ... Well, I assumed that whatever he'd been recalled for had gone horribly wrong. That he was either dead or a prisoner in some hell-hole jail.'

'But you're a human rights lawyer, right? Have you not got contacts that know about stuff like that?'

'What? Who's banged up in the Taliban's jail? Or doing solitary in some Gulf state without access to counsel? There are limits to my reach, Chief Inspector. I'm mostly just a humble part of the international court machinery. Sure, I've put feelers out whenever I had the chance. Obviously, I drew a blank every time. But that didn't mean I wasn't right. I kept on asking because I didn't know he was lying dead on a rooftop in Edinburgh.' Tessa stared bleakly out of her office window, seeing nothing of the street below or the houses opposite.

'Did you ever raise your theory with Professor Blake?'

'Of course I did. And she didn't buy it. She was determined to believe he'd gone home. Turns out we were both wrong. And now, if there's nothing else you have to ask me, I'm going to go and pour myself a stiff drink and tell my best friend her husband's never coming home.'

Maggie always liked to show her DPhil students to the door after their supervisions. It was the kind of thing you did with friends; she thought it made the encounter seem less formal. When she opened the door to usher out the bright Canadian who was writing about the post-mall geography of shopping, she wasn't expecting to find Tessa sitting in the corridor outside her rooms. But she knew at once that the news would not be good.

Maggie was oblivious to the final remarks of her student as he reiterated his bullet points for the next chapter. She only had eyes for Tessa, getting to her feet, still enviably lithe and graceful in spite of the passage of years. Silent, Maggie stepped back and gestured to her friend to enter. She closed the door with infinite care, as if preventing it from making a noise would somehow ward off bad news. Then she leaned against it, waiting.

Tessa turned to face her, sombre and drawn. 'It's him,' she said. 'No room for doubt.'

Maggie closed her eyes and clenched her fists. It didn't matter how much you anticipated something like this, you could never be prepared. She felt suddenly cold, as if she'd walked into an unexpected blast of chilly air-conditioning. A shudder ran through her, snapping her back into the moment. She opened her eyes and saw Tessa, lips parted, eyes troubled, arms held out from her sides as if on the verge of stepping forward to hug Maggie but unsure whether that was what was wanted.

So Maggie pushed off from the door and closed the distance between them, allowing Tessa to wrap her in her arms. 'I'm so, so sorry,' Tessa said. 'Sorry for everything. All the things I thought, all the things I said that hurt you so much. I'm sorry.'

'I know,' Maggie mumbled. 'I know.'

They stood in each other's arms and Maggie had no sense of how much time had gone by. Dimly she thought she ought to be crying or screaming or rending her garments in some Biblical excess of grief. But all she felt was that cold numbness cutting her off from the mechanics of grief. At length, Tessa said, 'Can I get you a drink?'

Maggie drew away from her and sighed. 'I don't know what I want. I don't know how I feel. I always believed he'd walk through that door one day.'

'Maybe if you'd told me you'd married him, I wouldn't have been so sceptical.' Tessa walked over to the window and gazed across the rooftops.

'Should I have told you before or after I slept with you?' Maggie's voice was harsh, like a slap.

'Oh Christ, that's not fair,' Tessa protested. She swung back to face her friend. 'We took comfort in each other. That shouldn't be an occasion of guilt. You were in so much pain, Maggie. And I missed him too. We gave each other love and support when we needed it.'

Maggie made a dismissive sound. 'And then I hurt you all over again when I didn't need it any more.'

Tessa shrugged. 'It doesn't matter now. What matters is we still have each other.'

'But we don't have Mitja.' Maggie's voice sounded almost as bleak as she felt. 'I told you he wasn't a killer. So many times, I told you he didn't have it in him.'

Tessa's face twisted in a wry grimace. 'At the time, it made sense to me in the same way that it made sense to you to believe that he'd gone back to some mystery family like something out of *The Railway Children*.'

Maggie sighed. 'I wish he had. I wish he was alive, even if it meant I couldn't have him. All those years, lying dead in a strange place when he should have been with people who loved him.' She made a choking sound. 'I'd give anything for you to have been right, that all this time he'd been going round killing those evil bastards who destroyed his country. Just as long as he was in the world. Feeling the sun and the wind and the rain. He was always so alive, Tess. Even when things were hard, he had that spirit, that energy that made everything possible.'

'I know. I can't take it in.'

'Who would kill him, Tess?'

'Somebody from his past. He made plenty of enemies during the wars.'

Maggie shook her head. 'No, that makes no sense. If it was somebody from his past they wouldn't do it like that. He knew his enemies. They'd never get close enough to him to do it like that. Who would climb a building with him and then shoot him in the head? If you wanted to kill him, why not just walk up to him in the street and shoot him? Why go all the way to a strange city, do something as intimate as a free climb together and then shoot him?'

'So you think it must have been somebody he trusted? Somebody from home?'

'Nothing else makes sense. You have to trust somebody to go free climbing with them, don't you?'

'Yes, you do.' Tessa frowned. 'If it was somebody from the

Balkans, the spooks should know they were in the country. I could ask Theo Proctor – you remember, the one who called me the other day when they were still treating Mitja like a suspect? He might be able to take a look and see whether there's any record of who was around that weekend from the Balkans.'

'Could you? Do you think they'd tell you?'

Tessa shrugged. 'I can try. We're all supposed to be on the same team.'

A tiny spark of hope ignited in Maggie's eyes. 'I have to know, Tess. I have to know who did this to him.'

'I know.' Tessa headed towards the kitchen. 'I need a drink,' she said over her shoulder. 'Do you want one?'

'Lagavulin,' Maggie said. 'I want something that tastes like medicine. I want something that'll make me better.' All at once, her legs felt too weak to hold her and she staggered to her familiar sofa. When Tessa came back with the drinks, she settled beside her friend, their bodies touching in a complicit moment of shared pain.

'Maybe we'll never know the answer,' Tessa said. 'Maybe there's no point in hoping.'

Maggie took a belt of whisky and winced as the heavy peat flavour hit her tastebuds. 'Somebody killed him. Somebody he trusted. They must have had a reason. I'm not giving up on Mitja. I'm going to find out who did this, Tess. I'm going to find out who took his life from him.'

It was clear right from the start that Dubrovnik was
hopelessly under-defended. The only regular military unit
in the city was a light infantry platoon stationed in the
Napoleonic fort on Srdj hill, near Varya's house.
According to Mitja, that would be a target for enemy
forces. 'You need to move out,' he insisted.

'How can I just turn my back on them? They've been
really kind to me since I got here.'

'Anyone who can leave the city is getting out. You think
they'll take you with them if they decide to make a run for
it? Trust me, Maggie, you'll go home one day and find the
house empty and the cupboards bare. At a time like this,
people look to their own first. And that's what I'm doing
here. If you insist on staying, I want you to be somewhere
safe.'

And so I caved in. He was right about Varya's family,

261

though. They were gone by the end of the week, throwing themselves on the charity of relatives in Slovenia. Ironically, their house remained untouched in the subsequent artillery attacks, while Mitja's idea of safety turned out to be the opposite of safe. Because he was proud of his country and its heritage, it was inconceivable to him that the Serbs would bomb the hell out of a UNESCO World Heritage Site. So he moved us into an apartment in the very heart of the Old Town, a stone's throw from the cathedral, with a view of a slice of the harbour from the bedroom window. It had been the home of a friend of his, a UNESCO bureaucrat, who had fled the city as soon as hostilities had broken out in Vukovar. I've often wondered whether he feels guilt or shame at abandoning his friends and neighbours when he thinks about Dubrovnik. Probably not; that's the kind of emotional response that makes it hard to continue with a fulfilled life.

The apartment was spacious and comfortably furnished. Rado's idea of a kitchen store cupboard was packets of instant noodles and bottles of Scotch. When we moved in, I laughed at that. It wasn't long before I changed my tune and regularly sent up a prayer of thanks for his prescience. In a city under siege, having any kind of food staple is a powerful bargaining chip. And a glass of whisky at the end of the day becomes one of the true glories of life. Having Mitja there some of the time was the icing on my personal cake, the MSG in my instant noodles.

Even though I was buoyed up by love, life soon became pretty grim. The major offensive against Dubrovnik began on the first day of October. The army came at us from the south-east, from the north and from the west. The artillery attacked Srdj hill; the booming echo of the guns vibrated through the city at irregular intervals. I still can't hear unexpected fireworks without my chest constricting. And the air force's MiG-21s pounded Komolac to the west of us, destroying our access to electricity and fresh water.

We were without either from then until the end of December.

We take the staples of modern life so much for granted until we're deprived of them. People do live quite well without what we consider to be basics, but they manage because they've never been de-skilled by their presence. To lose them when you've lived all your life with power at the touch of a switch and water at the turn of a tap is shocking, then unsettling, then grindingly depressing.

There were a few generators in the city, but fuel was at a premium and they were only used sparingly. Most people had a small stock of candles, but they soon ran out. The city fell into the habit of going to bed when it grew dark. It was unusually cold that year, and being under the covers was one way to stay warm. Besides, within days, there was a blackout rule and a curfew. Those of us who'd been trying to meet up in the evenings to maintain a vague pretence of intellectual life as normal were soon stymied.

Mitja was seldom home. It's hard to imagine in this world of instant communication, but in the whole city under siege there was one single satellite phone and fax machine which was moved almost on a daily basis to protect it from the bombardment, and more often than not Mitja was with the phone. The enemy helicopters buzzed the city constantly, trying to spot the satellite dish. Whenever they did, the MiGs would follow, attempting to shoot it out of commission.

Even worse than the strafing fire of the MiGs was the constant shelling. First they attacked the fort on Srdj hill. Then the Belvedere Hotel. Then the Argentina Hotel. And so on. I remember standing in the Inter-University Centre with a bunch of refugees from the surrounding countryside, watching the pines of Srdj hill burst into spikes of flame as they were firebombed. It felt completely unreal, to see the bright orange and yellow flame along the whole ridge, then darker gouts of flame feeling their way down the hill towards the city. And suddenly, clouds of butterflies were all around us, escaping from the inferno that their habitat had become. It was a surreal moment.

I couldn't understand why the Serbs wanted to destroy

Dubrovnik. It had no value as a strategic target. Its walls made it almost impossible to capture; destruction was the only tactic that could be used against it. But why destroy a place if your goal is to absorb it into your wider empire? One evening when Mitja had returned late with a box of scented candles someone had 'liberated' from a gift shop, we sat in the flickering light and I asked him that question. 'It feels like any building that's tagged as a heritage site, or a hotel, or a hospital is fair game. Every bloody church and monastery except the Serb Orthodox church. There'll be nothing left but rubble. Why are they doing this to the city?'

'Precisely because it's a tourist honey-pot,' he said. 'They want to make a point. To say we can't hide behind our history. To show the world they can't be intimidated by what outsiders think is important. And they also thought we're a soft target that would surrender at the first sound of gunfire. They miscalculated badly. They didn't understand how much we love our history. Our heritage. Our country.'

I sighed. 'You'd think that's one thing they would understand. You've been fighting for a thousand years in the Balkans over the same ground.'

He filled up our glasses with more whisky, his expression both grim and weary. 'And we'll probably be fighting for the next thousand over the same things. In a strange way, it's almost appropriate that this should be

265

happening in Dubrovnik. It's a medieval war in a medieval city.'

He was wrong, of course. It was a thoroughly modern war because Dubrovnik was also a modern city. We relied on our home-grown criminals – men who had been smugglers, with their fast, silent boats, men who knew every channel on the Dalmatian coast, men who raced between the Serb ships and the rocky shorelines to bring in weapons and water, medicines and milk. They kept us alive.

The Serbs hated to be outwitted. And so one day they firebombed the old harbour. Late that night, after the all-clear, after the curfew was set, a few of us sneaked down to the harbour to take a look. It was a bright moonlit night; I remember thinking we were taking a hell of a chance because the MiGs would be able to see their targets clearly, if they'd chosen to do a night run. The streets were silent and sinister with shadows. But from the harbour, we could see the bright flares of a dozen or more burning boats being carried out to sea by wind and tide. Burning, then sinking. The Irishwoman standing next to me muttered, 'A terrible beauty is born.'

That was the first time I'd ever spoken to Tessa Minogue. I knew who she was; the IUC was too small for anonymity. But our paths had somehow never crossed properly before. We walked back up from the harbour and it turned out she was living just round the corner from our flat. I invited her in for a drink that night and a friendship was born, a friendship that persists. To this day, Tess is the first person I turn to in times of trouble, perhaps because our relationship was forged under fire.

It makes me slightly uncomfortable to say this but the two relationships that mean most to me in this world came out of the Croatian war. Mitja probably wouldn't have been in Dubrovnik when I was there had it not been for the imminent threat of war. And I might never have bonded with Tess but for that moment by the harbour.

Don't get me wrong. I'm not so egocentric as to think that war isn't a bad thing if such positive outcomes can result from it. Rather, what I feel is a kind of shame, that out of the hell that was the Balkans at the end of the twentieth century, I gained so rich a reward.

25

Karen was surprised to find Phil chopping vegetables in the kitchen when she arrived home in the middle of the afternoon. At her rank, there was no such thing as overtime. But she worked long hours and weekends with few complaints, so she reckoned she was entitled to head out early when there was nothing urgent on her desk. Besides, she always thought better outside the office. 'What are you doing home at this hour?' she asked, hugging him from behind and planting a kiss on the back of his neck.

He shivered pleasurably. 'Careful, these knives are sharp. Everything went tits-up this morning. We had him staked out at home from yesterday teatime. But when we went in mob-handed this morning, the bird had flown.'

'How come?' Karen took off her jacket and slung it over the nearest chair.

'Nobody's taking responsibility, but I think it's pretty

obvious that the late-night stake-out lads decided he was in for the night so they nipped off at some point for a coffee or a curry or a kip. And either our boy dropped lucky and happened to leave for the airport at the right moment by chance, or else he was staking out the stake-out.'

'The airport?'

'Aye. According to his wife, he's away to Liechtenstein for a few days. Presumably to say hello to his money.'

'Bummer.'

'Indeed. Mind you, it's partly our own fault. I should have checked his schedule with the wife.'

'You reckon he knows you're after him?'

Phil shook his head and tipped a pile of chopped shallots and red peppers into a smoking skillet. 'I don't think he did. But I'm worried the wife will tip him off. She swore blind she wouldn't. Although she's refusing to give evidence against him, I'm pretty sure she's not going to stand in the way of us taking him off the streets. But you never know. When she's face to face with him, who knows how it'll go.' A hissing cloud of steam enveloped them both in a rich aroma as he crushed garlic and added it to the pan.

'That's crap. I can't imagine what it must be like to live your life terrorised by the person who's supposed to love you.'

Phil turned and grinned at her. 'Oh, I get the odd inkling.'

'That's not funny,' she said, smiling.

'So what brings you home?' He returned his attention to

the pan, stirring vigorously and adding a chopped head of fennel and a handful of diced chorizo.

'I need to have a think about my next move. Plus I've not stopped since we found the skeleton on Saturday.'

'So where are you up to?' It was how they'd worked best when they'd been on the same team, bouncing ideas off each other. Neither saw any need to stop now they were working on completely different things. Technically, they shouldn't be talking about confidential police matters outside their own group. But Karen had never cared about rules she couldn't see the point of and Phil had caught the habit from her.

Karen brought him up to speed with the day's developments. 'I wish I could have been there to break the news to Maggie Blake myself. I'd like to have seen her reaction. Not that I think she's a suspect. If she was going to bump him off, she would have had plenty of opportunity to do it in a much less complicated way.'

'But it's always good to see how the spouse takes it.' Phil transferred the vegetables to a saucepan and added a tin of chopped tomatoes and a handful of torn basil leaves. 'Did we leave any red wine last night?'

'I think there's half a glass in the bottle.' Karen went to fetch it from the living room. On her way back in to the kitchen, she said, 'If you ask me, whoever did this came from his past. From the Balkan wars. He was there all the way through, you know. In the Croatian Army for the

270

Croatian war, with NATO intelligence for Bosnia and then with the UN for Kosovo. Plenty of chances to make enemies. When he went missing – which is presumably when he was murdered – all the indictments at the war crimes tribunal had been handed down, but obviously the trials were still going on. And a fair few of the accused hadn't been arrested yet. So it wouldn't be surprising to find someone from the old days with powerful reasons to want Petrovic out of the picture.'

Phil tipped the remains of the wine into the pan. 'I'm just going to leave that to simmer,' he said.

'Maybe a wee bit of chilli?' Karen did a big-eyed pleading pose.

'Oh, all right. But only because I love you, right?' Phil took a grinder of dried chilli from the cupboard and gave it a couple of twists over the pan.

'Plus one of the guys from the climbing club said that when Petrovic went buildering, he went with somebody he'd known from back in Yugoslavia.'

'So, somebody based over here, you reckon?'

'Either that or someone who used to come over regularly. But according to Maggie Blake, he didn't see much of anyone from the old days.'

'Which might suggest that he had good reason for avoiding people from the past?'

'That's not such a daft idea. With him being in intelligence, he probably knew all sorts of stuff that certain people

271

didn't want out in the open.' Karen picked a pear out of the fruit bowl and began eating absently. 'Maybe even some of our people,' she added, thinking about Macanespie and Proctor. Maybe their visit had been bullshit. Maybe they'd just been fishing for what she actually knew.

'So how are you going to find out about his mysterious past?' Phil pulled up a chair and sat down opposite her. 'I suppose we must have high-ranking soldiers who knew him from Kosovo?'

'Yeah, but they're not going to tell the likes of me anything useful. Especially if they're in intelligence. And even if they're retired, they still keep their mouths shut. No, I've got a better idea. I went to the bookshop up by the university and checked out the books they've got about the Balkan wars. I was amazed how many there were. There's a lot of people like Maggie Blake making a living from other people's misery. It's like true crime. Anyway, I looked at the indexes, and I found his name in one of them. The author mentions meeting Petrovic after the siege of Dubrovnik when he was just a colonel. Describes him as one of the rising talents, the ones that held out some hope for building a future that wasn't as mental as the past.'

'And that's all he says?'

'It's all he says by name. But this guy clearly knew everybody who was anybody. He's a journalist. He covered the Balkans right through the wars and beyond. Did a lot of stuff for the BBC as well as the print media. I managed to track him down. He's in Brazil now. Apparently they've got some big sporting stuff going on down there later this year?' She paused for effect and Phil poked his tongue out at her. 'So I've arranged to FaceTime him in a couple of hours.' She grinned. 'I have the distinct impression that the Macaroon thinks I'm out of my league on this one. I'm looking forward to proving him wrong.'

Theo Proctor dropped into his desk chair like a stone. 'I'm fucking exhausted,' he complained. 'All that running around, and for what? If we'd just waited instead of chasing Maggie Blake around Glasgow, we'd be exactly where we are now. I should be at home, having a cold beer before dinner.'

Macanespie shrugged and turned on his computer. 'If all you're going to do is whinge, why don't you just bugger off and do that?' He glowered at the screen, fat fingers flying over the keys to bring up the spreadsheet he'd created back when they still thought Dimitar Petrovic was their vigilante assassin.

'What else do you want me to do?' Proctor took off his jacket and threw it on to the desk next to his like a petulant child.

'We've got the best chance of finding some solid evidence in the most recent case. Miroslav Simunovic in Crete. Book us tickets on the first flight out. There must be something in the morning. It's the tourist season. Check the records and find out who the Greek investigating officer is. Then email him and let him know we're coming to review the case.'

Proctor's jaw dropped at this display of decisiveness. 'Have you lost your mind?'

'Did you not understand what Cagney was saying? Failure's not an option here. We're going to be nailed to the wall if we don't deliver what he wants from us. Now, this might just be a ploy to flush you and me down the toilet. But if it is, I'm not going without a fight, all right?' He turned back to his screen and studied it, frowning intensely.

'And you think the Greeks will just cooperate? "Hello, we're coming from The Hague to show up you bumpkins for not doing your job properly." What could possibly go wrong?'

'Well, I'd have thought we could manage a wee bit more subtlety than that. Maybe along the lines of, "We've got one or two suspects in other, similar cases and we want to take a look and see if anything jumps out at us." People they couldn't possibly know were of interest. That sort of thing. How hopeful we are that they might have gathered the crucial piece of evidence that'll make our case. It's called flattery, Theo.'

'And what are you going to be doing while I sort all this out?' The Welshman's scowl was the perfect representation of a man hard done by.

'I'm going through the spreadsheet line by line. We need to narrow down where the bloody inside leak has come from. I'm eliminating everyone who wasn't on the team here at Scheveningen for the whole period of the killings. We've got a definite start-point now. If they weren't on staff when Petrovic disappeared, they're not in the running. And if they'd gone by the time Simunovic was killed, they're also off the list. We didn't work the list hard enough before. Be honest, Theo. We weren't that bothered and we thought we could just busk it.'

'Fair enough. But I think you're overreacting. Cagney can't just fire us, for God's sake. There are procedures.'

Macanespie rolled his eyes. 'Christ. You were the one rabbiting on about not wanting to lose your pension, giving me the bleeding heart stuff about having a wife and kids to support. Bleat, bleat, fucking bleat.'

'Yes, well, that was before I thought things through. Before you dragged me off to Glasgow to play at James Bond. The more I think about that, the more insane it sounds.'

'I didn't drag you into it. It was your idea in the first place, remember? You were perfectly willing when you thought it was a shortcut to Wilson Cagney's good books.' Macanespie gave him a look of utter disgust. 'Now, are you going to get your namby-pamby arse in gear or are you going to fuck off out of my road and let me get on with some proper work? I'm damned if I'm going to be beaten to the draw on this by that wee fat lassie from Police Scotland.'

Muttering under his breath, Proctor turned on his computer and started looking for flights.

26

Karen loved the kitchen in Phil's house, but the wifi signal wasn't powerful enough in there to carry a FaceTime call. So she'd had to set herself up in what they scornfully called 'the library'. Shelves of books – some fake, concealing a plasma TV – overstuffed club chairs, a leather-topped desk and a tartan carpet combined to make Karen feel she'd stumbled into the badly dressed set for some stereotyped sitcom. She adjusted the lighting so the camera wouldn't pick up background detail, set the system to record and called Adam Turner's number.

The ringtone warbled and she thanked her lucky stars again that it had been so easy to track down the journalist. By happy chance, when she'd googled him she'd found a piece he'd filed only a couple of days previously in the *Telegraph*. A quick call to the paper's staffer in Edinburgh had produced a contact number and email address and the rest had been amazingly easy. She'd texted him, he'd replied and they'd set up the call.

And now her own image on the screen was dissolving and morphing into a man's face in the bottom half of the screen, a pock-marked yellow wall behind him. His skin had a jaundiced tint that might have had something to do with the decor or the climate. Or possibly, with him being a journalist, the drink. His eyes were indistinct behind large glasses with fashionable heavy black rims. His untidy brown hair was thinning; under the bright lights of his hotel room, Karen could see pink scalp gleaming through. She hoped she didn't look as unappealing, though you could never be sure with digital communications. 'Hi, Adam. This is Karen Pirie from Police Scotland,' she said, producing her best reassuring smile.

'Hello, Karen. Thanks for accommodating my schedule.' He had a typical broadcaster's voice – rich, dark and warm, with the faintest trace of a northern accent. All the better for delivering horrors into people's living rooms. He seemed alert and eager, which was a welcome plus in Karen's world.

'No, I appreciate you taking the time out to talk to me.'

'You're welcome. I'm always happy to take a walk down memory lane. Even when the memories are as horrific as the Balkans. You wanted to talk about my time in the Balkans? Specifically, about Dimitar Petrovic? Is that right?'

'Spot on.'

He chuckled. 'That's a long time and a lot of miles ago. I

thought everyone had forgotten the Balkans. There's nothing grabs the headlines less than last year's war. So what's your interest? What's General Petrovic been up to?'

'He's not been up to anything for a while. He's been dead for the past eight years.'

Turner's eyebrows rose. 'Really? I didn't know. The last I heard he was living the quiet life in Oxford. But that must be, what? Nine, ten years ago. Why are you so interested in a man who's been dead for eight years?'

'Because we've only just found his remains.'

'I don't understand. Surely somebody must have noticed he wasn't around? Didn't – what's her name? Moira? Maggie? Something like that – didn't she report him missing? Or is she the prime suspect?'

'She thought he'd left her and returned to Croatia. He was a grown man, there were no suspicious circumstances other than his absence. So there was no reason why the police would take an interest. And no, Professor Blake is not the prime suspect,' she added drily, knowing that without that denial Maggie would remain firmly in the media's frame of interest. 'Apart from anything else, I haven't said anything that would indicate the potential existence of any suspect.'

'Come on, Chief Inspector. You and I both know we wouldn't be having this conversation unless there were suspicious circumstances. So where did he turn up? And why did it take so long? I mean, I know disposing of a body's the hardest part of committing a murder, but eight years is a long time.'

'His skeleton was found on the roof of a building that was about to be demolished.'

'Wow.' Turner looked impressed. 'And nobody noticed there was a dead body on the roof? That's weird.'

'Not really. It was hidden from sight. And the building's been empty for the best part of twenty years, so there was no reason for anybody to be poking around up there.'

'Wow. And this was where? London? No, wait, you're Police Scotland. So, Scotland somewhere?'

'Edinburgh.'

'Curiouser and curiouser. What was he doing in Edinburgh?'

'Apparently his hobby was a thing called "buildering". Where you free climb the outside of buildings. For fun.' Karen still couldn't keep the disbelief from her voice. Adam Turner's face froze, his mouth open. 'Oh God,' she groaned. 'Here we bloody go.' She drummed her fingers on the desktop till the blur resolved itself and they re-established a connection.

'So he climbed this building and got killed?'

'That's what we're surmising.'

'And it's a skeleton. I'm guessing he either had his head caved in or he was shot. Anything else would be hard to categorise as murder. How am I doing?'

She had to smile. 'Right on the money. A bullet wound to the head, to be precise.'

'And you think whoever killed him did it because of what he did during the various wars in the nineties?'

Give a little to get a lot. She hoped. 'He was leading an apparently blameless life in Oxford. It seems to me the chances are that whatever happened on that roof was a result of his past life, not his present one. And we have reason to believe he did his buildering with someone he'd known back then.'

Turner chuckled. 'I love that police speak. "Reason to believe". And I'm guessing you're reluctant to talk to the powers that be about General Petrovic's war because they'll spin you a line composed largely of bullshit?' He froze again, his face blurring to resemble a cookie decorated by a toddler. So much for modern technology replacing the face-to-face. Karen wouldn't swap the interview room and the whites of their eyes for a roomful of iPads. It did have its uses, especially when the witness was on the other side of the world. But it was too easy to hide behind the technology. She knew from her own experience that if you wanted to freeze the screen to earn yourself some breathing space, all you had to do was open up more apps or programs that would interfere with your FaceTime demands for bandwidth. Then you could compose yourself and figure out your answer. She didn't think that's what Adam Turner was doing here, but she was glad of a moment to come up with an appropriate answer.

The screen resolved itself and Turner reappeared in sharper definition. 'Did you hear me?'

'The last I heard was "bullshit".'

'What I said after that was that one of the reasons our lot are reluctant to talk about the Balkans is that it's hard to take a black-and-white approach. The Serbs think they get the blame for everything – and there's good reason for that because they mostly started it and they committed the worst atrocities. But nobody has clean hands in those conflicts. Not the Croats, not the Albanians, nobody. They were all capable of appalling things, given half a chance. But the war crimes tribunal focused almost exclusively on the Serbs. So back home, where there's not much of a free press, it's seen totally as a biased tool of NATO and the West, and as a result it hasn't provided any kind of focus for reconciliation. Just more resentment. So our lot want to stay well clear of the after-math. You made the right choice, coming to me rather than the military.'

Nothing like vanity to make a witness open up. And nothing like a bit of flattery to play into that. 'Believe me, I know that. Soon as I dipped into your book, I knew you were the man I needed to talk to. So, what can you tell me about General Petrovic?'

'A very clever boy. He came from nowhere and shot up the ranks at record speed. When Yugoslavia broke up, he was one of the first that we cherry-picked to bring over here and train in our ways and means. He was definitely a rising star when the war started.'

'When you say he came from nowhere, what do you mean?'

'He wasn't one of the ruling elite. He was basically a farm boy. He came from one of those half-a-horse villages up in the hills near the Serbian border. But he got picked up by a school teacher who knew a bright boy when he saw one.'

'Do you know the name of the village?'

'Now you're asking. The nearest town was Lipovac, I seem to remember. What was the name . . . ?' He closed his eyes and pressed his fingertips to his forehead. 'Padrovac. Podruvec. Podruvci . . . I think it was Podruvec,' he said triumphantly, straightening up and looking pleased with himself. 'I've never been there, that's why I don't remember so well.'

'Brilliant. So he came from this wee village and went into the Yugoslavian Army?'

'That's right. The way I heard it, he aced every course they sent him on, so they shunted him into intelligence. Then when the end of the empire struck, he signed on with the Croatian Army. I suspect he never entirely fitted in with the other lot, him being a Croat. Tainted by the Second World War, you see.'

'I'm sorry, I don't know what you mean. You're going to have to treat me like an idiot on this one.' Karen gave a shame-faced smile. This time, it wasn't flattery but a genuine lack of knowledge. She'd given up History before they made it to the Second World War. She was great on the medieval kings of Scotland, but anything more modern was sketchy.

'Right. Well, basically, the Balkans has been conflict

central since time immemorial. And grudges go back a long way. So when the Nazis piled into the area, the Croats saw this as their chance to stick it to the Serbs. They sided with the Germans and got stuck into their own personal genocide. About half a million Serbs were executed, quarter of a million were expelled from their own country and another quarter of a million or so were forcibly converted to Christianity.'

'Jesus. I had no idea it was that bad.'

'So the Serbs feel they had a few scores to settle. All the years Tito held the reins, they nursed their grievances, then when the country fell apart they seized their chance. There's no denying the horror of the atrocities they inflicted, but they think they had just cause. That's rubbish, of course. All you get from an eye for an eye is a lot of people stumbling around in the dark. And there's no virtue in making yourself as repulsive as your enemy.'

'Aye, right. But I can see how you'd get there. And I see how Petrovic would have felt more at home in the Croatian Army. How did you come to meet him?'

'It was just after the siege of Dubrovnik was lifted. I was one of the first journalists in the city once the Sarajevo Agreement was in place. Petrovic had been pinned down in the city during the siege, and I interviewed him for a piece for the *New York Times* about his experiences. I was impressed. Clever came off him like a smell. A couple of months later, he got promoted to general. Round about the

Miljevci Plateau battles, I seem to recall. We ran into each other on a regular basis after that. The Croatians were trying to keep everybody sweet, to play the good guys, so they lent him out to NATO and the UN. But I don't think he ever forgot where his true allegiance lay.'

Karen scribbled some notes as he spoke, wondering where this was going to take her. 'Would you say he had enemies? Personally, I mean. Not just guys on the other side who hated him in principle.'

Turner lit up a cigarette while he thought. He took a deep drag and frowned. 'Not that I ever heard. But then, I wasn't looking. If you want to get an answer to that question, you'd have to talk to people in Croatia who knew him back then.'

'You say both sides were each as bad as the other. Was he ever involved in any of the front-line stuff that people might want to take revenge over?'

Turner shook his head firmly. 'That wasn't really his beat, though he could be pretty proactive when it came to protecting his guys. But he was too far up the totem pole to get his hands literally dirty. And for another thing, he was too valuable to them as an intelligence analyst and a strategist ever to be allowed too near the front line. They lost the benefit of his skills when he got caught up in Dubrovnik and they made bloody sure that never happened again.'

'And yet he walked away from it all at the end of the war to live what looks like a quiet life in Oxford.'

'I think that's the sane option. I only stayed as long as I

did because I knew I could leave whenever I wanted to. The Balkans was a basket case at the end of the nineties. I hear some of the next generation are trying to do things differently, but that's a long time to wait. If you had the brains to stop hating and the chance to get out and make a life that wasn't based around fighting old wars, you'd be crazy not to go for it.'

Karen pondered that for a moment. 'So he took the sensible option. Then somebody took that from him. Why do it? And why wait so long?'

'You're not going to get the answers to those questions talking to the likes of me. If you really want to know, you're going to have to go to Croatia. And then you're going to have to find someone willing to give you the answers.'

Karen gave a thin smile. 'I might just do that.'

Turner shook his head pityingly. 'Good luck with that one. Rather you than me.'

27

Being back in Dubrovnik felt not so much like travelling back in time as moving along a Möbius strip. The city Maggie returned to was not the city she had left, with its bullet holes and bomb damage, its stricken roofs and its battered walls. Rather, it was the city she'd first arrived in, its medieval stone glowing in the sun, its former beauty restored almost without trace. A casual observer would have no sense at all that this had been a city under siege, a harbour that provided no safe haven, an enclave plunged into a past life with no running water or electricity.

She strolled through the Pile Gate, past the Franciscan Friary and down the Stradun towards the old harbour, a route she'd walked practically every day when she'd lived here. Only four months, but it loomed so significant in her memory it felt like a much bigger chunk of her life. She was proud that she'd had some part in the restoration of the city.

The money she'd helped to raise had repaired roofs, replaced windows, paid stonemasons to restore the damage. Now the cafés and bars, the shops and restaurants had reinvented themselves. The tourists were back, appreciating the history and grace of the city, mostly unaware of how close it had come to being lost.

When she reached the harbour, Maggie paused, remembering the night she'd stood shoulder to shoulder with Tessa, watching the burning boats and trying not to think of them as a metaphor for her life. She'd fixed her life to Mitja, believing it was for ever. When she thought he'd left her, it was as if she was cast adrift, her anchor gone, at the mercy of whatever storms blew her way. Now, understanding that he'd been taken from her had restored some of her old certainties. It was a terrible thing to admit, but knowing he was dead was almost easier to bear than believing he'd abandoned her.

She checked her watch then turned and retraced her steps up the Stradun, heading for the familiar red tablecloths of the Café Festival. The last time she'd seen the building with its elegant stone arches, it had been gutted by fire, soot-stained and wrecked. Now, it served as a potent reminder to Maggie of what had been regained.

The tables on the street were full of tourists, people-watching, eating and drinking in equal measure. Maggie walked past and into the long dim interior where a handful of locals took coffee at the bar counter. Now she was less certain of herself. It had been almost twenty years since she'd seen the man she was meeting today, and she had no idea how he would look. He'd assured her he'd googled her and felt confident he'd recognise her from the photograph on the university website. She'd tried to do the same for him, but Radovan Tomic had remained resolutely elusive. Rado, the man whose flat she'd inhabited during the siege, was clearly the kind of UNESCO diplomat who kept a low profile.

She paused, looking around her. Then a paunchy middle-aged man got to his feet and walked towards her, arms outspread. 'Maggie!' he exclaimed. 'It's great to see you.' And before she could avoid it, she was pulled into a hug, his bald sweating head pressed against her cheek, his fat belly hard against her ribs. He held her at arm's length, then hauled her into his embrace once more. 'You look as fabulous as ever,' he said, leading her by the hand to a corner table. He'd perfected his English over the years. Always good, now it was almost without a trace of an accent.

The years had not been kind to Rado, she thought as he fussed with his napkin and the waiter bustled around with glasses of water and menus. Too many years of expense account lunches and business class travel. She remembered a slender, rather glamorous young man, olive-skinned and dark-haired, brown eyes as inquisitive as a blackbird's, chiselled features and high, broad cheekbones. Now the cheekbones were subsumed in plumpness, the eyes sunk in flesh and the close-cropped fringe of hair a salt-and-pepper mixture. 'It's good to see you,' she said after they'd ordered coffee.

'I was counting up when I got your message. I think the last time I saw you was in London in 1996. Mitja was there for some NATO summit and I was at a UNESCO meeting. I can't believe we left it so long.'

'I know. And what's it like, being back in Dubrovnik?'

He pursed his lips in a little moue of dissatisfaction. 'It's not exactly where the action is. Still, I'm only here for six months to cover a colleague who's on maternity leave. It's a bit below my pay grade, but they asked me to do it because I know the patch. But never mind that.' His face grew serious. 'You said when you contacted me that you had news of Mitja. I'm guessing that it's not good news?'

Maggie held back till the waiter had deposited their coffees, then slowly shook her head. 'The worst, I'm afraid.' She stared into her cup, unable to meet Rado's eyes. 'He was murdered, Rado. I thought he'd left me. I thought he'd come back to Croatia, to what he'd left behind. But I couldn't have been more wrong. He did one last climb and when he got to the top, somebody shot him in the head.'

'Oh my God,' he said, aghast. 'Maggie, that's dreadful.' He reached across the table and gripped her hand in his soft plump paws. 'You poor, poor dear.'

'Never mind me. Poor, poor Mitja,' she said, eyes moist.

'Do the police know who did this?'

Maggie sighed. 'No. And it's been so long, frankly I doubt there's much chance of them finding out who killed him.'

'This is terrible news. So why have you come back to Croatia, Maggie? You think the answer is here?'

'I think there are answers here, Rado, but not the ones you mean. I've come back to find out who Mitja was. I need to know his story.' She ran a finger and thumb along her eyelids, wiping the suspicion of tears away. 'I should have done this a long time ago. But at first, there was no need. We were enough for each other in the here and now. We stayed away from each other's history. And then after he went, I was scared to come back here for fear of what I might find. But now there's nothing left to fear. The worst thing that can happen already has. Now all I want is to know the whole story. The bits he never got round to sharing with me. Because I need to know everything there is to know. That's all I have left of him, Rado. A complete history shouldn't be too much to ask.'

A quick flash of panic shot across Rado's eyes. 'Don't you think you should leave sleeping dogs alone? If he didn't tell you, presumably it's because he thought it would be best if you didn't know.'

'That's not the way it works, Rado. You lose those privileges of silence when you die. It's all up for grabs. It's all fair game. I want to see the places where he grew up, talk to people who knew him when he was a kid. Do you know something?'

Rado shook his head. 'What?'

'I don't even know the name of the town where you guys grew up.'

Rado gave a sharp little laugh. 'It wasn't a town, Maggie. It was a bunch of houses and barns. Barely even a village.'

'All the same, it must have had a name, Rado. Tell me the name.'

He looked hunted. 'It doesn't really exist any more. The Serbs . . .' He spread his hands in a gesture of helpless resignation.

'It still had a name. What was it called?'

He swallowed hard. 'Podruvec. You'll struggle to find it on a map, though. The nearest place of any size is Lipovac.' He grimaced. 'That was the big city, bright lights to us.'

Maggie tapped the name into her phone and showed it to Rado. 'Is that right?' He nodded. 'See, here's the funny thing. As well as not knowing where my husband—'

'Husband? You married him?' A look of consternation crossed his face.

'Yes, we got married. We kept it very quiet. It just made life simpler in practical terms. What I was saying, though, is that as well as not knowing where my own husband came from, I never met a single one of his old friends from back home, except you. And your family left the village when you were fourteen and you never went back. So I never knew anyone who could fill in the blanks.' She gave him a watery smile. 'Except you, Rado.'

'But like you said, I left when Mitja and I were only fourteen. You know what it's like at that age. You're self-obsessed. All you remember is your own concerns.'

'I don't believe you. You must have known his family. His parents. You must remember them.'

Rado spooned sugar into his cup and stirred it. 'Sure, I remember them. His mum made the best orahnjaca I ever tasted. His dad kept sheep and goats. He was a bit of a drinker. But he was sharp enough. That's where Mitja got his brains from.' He gave an apologetic shrug. 'That's about all I remember.'

'But you guys met up again later, at university. You must have talked about life back in Podruvec. People you knew. Kids you were at school with. Come on, Rado. There's no point in holding back now.'

Rado's eyes were slithering round the room, coming to rest on nothing. 'I'm not holding back, Maggie. We had other things to talk about. You said yourself, Mitja wasn't somebody who lived in the past.'

'Rado, I spend half my working life with students concocting excuses to explain why they're six months behind with their DPhil. Or they haven't done the revisions to their master's thesis that we discussed at our last supervision. I know when people are being evasive. And right now you're being very bloody evasive. When I said we'd got married, you looked like somebody had dropped you right in the shit. What's the big secret, Rado? I always wondered if he had a wife back home. Kids, even. That's it, isn't it? You can tell me. I'm not going to be angry with you for keeping his secret all those years. Because I know now he walked away from them to be with me. And he stayed with me because he wanted to be with me, not her. Right up to the point where somebody put a gun to his head and pulled the trigger. So I want to know, Rado. I want to know the truth.' Maggie ran out of things to say and stopped abruptly, glaring across the table at the ruined face of Mitja's childhood friend.

Rado got to his feet, pulling out his wallet and dropping an overly generous note on the table. 'Let's walk,' he said.

Maggie followed him out on to the Stradun. He gripped her hand tight and said, 'Give me a minute,' and for the second time that morning she walked down to the harbour. When they reached the quayside, he stood on the edge of the quayside staring out at the pleasure boats bobbing at their moorings. He let her hand go and took out a crocodile cigar case. He extracted a fat cigar and busied himself with lighting it. Once he'd puffed out a cloud of blue smoke, he seemed to relax.

'You're right,' he sighed. 'Jablanka was her name. She was the same age as us, and we competed to take her out when we were thirteen. I used to think she liked me best, but then we moved away and Mitja had her all to himself. And yes, before you ask, she was beautiful. Not brilliant or bold like you. But she was very sweet. Very traditional. And so he married her. By the time he had finished university, he knew he had outgrown her. But they had two sons by then, and he loved his boys so he tried to keep it alive.' He sucked on his cigar and bought himself a few moments.

'So what happened?'

'He met you,' Rado said. 'We went for a drink after he came to your class at the IUC and he was on fire. I never saw him like that before. He couldn't stop talking about this clever, beautiful woman who had inspired him with a passion to understand what the hell she was talking about. And the rest, you know.'

'So, what? He just never went home again?' Maggie's tone was defiant. It was a way to keep the anguish at bay.

'I don't know exactly what happened,' Rado said. 'I know he planned to go back and tell her the marriage was over. But the siege got in the way. And then he made the excuse of waiting till you went back to Oxford.'

'And then he went back?'

Rado sighed, blowing more smoke over the water. 'Like I said. I don't know what happened. He came back from Podruvec in a mess. He was upset and angry. He wouldn't tell me what had happened. I don't know where Jablanka is now, or the boys. My brother went back to Podruvec a couple of years ago – he was working in the area and he thought he'd take a look for old times' sake. But there was almost nothing left of the place. It's one of those villages that got eaten up by the war and never found its feet again.' He took another hit on the cigar, grimaced and threw the unsmoked half of it in the water. 'Whatever happened to Jablanka, she's not in Podruvec any more.'

'But there might still be someone there who can tell me where to find her?'

Rado gave her a look that seemed to offer her pity rather than hope. 'If you're really sure you want answers, that's where you're going to have to go.'

Later, Maggie would remember that curious way of phrasing the reply. But right then, all she could think of was finding Jablanka Petrovic and filling in the blanks in Mitja's past. For the first time in days, she felt she could reach out and touch his hidden life. All she wanted now was the whole picture. And Rado had shown her where she could find the key.

The fall of Vukovar marked a new low in our morale. We'd
had six interminable weeks of our own siege by then, but
in spite of the hardship we were enduring, most of the
damage perpetrated by the Serbian bombs had been to
property, not people. In Vukovar, the human cost was
staggering. Later, we'd learn that somewhere between
two and a half and three thousand people had lost their
lives in the ninety-day battle for the city. And most of the
time we were under siege, hellish massacres were
happening in mountain villages and small towns that we
knew nothing about until weeks had gone past. By
contrast, we lost less than a hundred lives in Dubrovnik.
Not that the numbers diminish the individual loss, the
individual pain.

But on 18 November when Vukovar was taken, we had
no idea what our ultimate fate would be. That day, things

looked incontrovertibly bleak. There was very little food and even less water. Disused wells had been opened up to supplement what the boats brought in, but there was still barely a litre per person per day. I'd been swimming in the freezing November sea, sometimes alone and sometimes with Mitja, just to remember what it felt like to be clean. But Tessa had reported that one of her friends had had a close encounter with a dead body in the little cove below the IUC, which made me lose my appetite for the sea.

By then, the city's hotels were packed with refugees. They were sitting ducks for the Serb guns. The hotels had big picture windows to take in the spectacular views; all the better to be visible to the enemy. The poor bastards who had already fled from attack once were hammered all over again, this time often in a hail of flying glass.

Mitja was growing more haggard and weary with every passing week. But still, amazingly, when he managed to get back to our apartment, his spirits lifted. I made a point of hoarding interesting stories and unusual events to take his mind off the gruelling business of defence and counter-attack that occupied the rest of his time. When he wasn't around, I spent most of my time at the IUC. I was still running seminars and tutorials for anyone who wanted them; since boredom was as much an enemy as the Serbs, a surprising number of people did. That kept me sane, and it also meant I had a stock of conversation to entertain Mitja and force him to think about the world beyond Dubrovnik.

The flipside of our conversations was his desire to share some of the burden of his work with me. I knew there was a lot he couldn't tell me, but he did talk about what was going on in other parts of the city where I hadn't been able to see things for myself. And he opened doors for me to talk to people who gave me valuable interviews that later formed the basis for my best work.

That's how I ended up spending time in the mayor's office. And that in turn made me realise that I had unique channels to access help for the beleaguered city and its inhabitants. I had Oxford, and its web of contacts and influence that spread into the most unlikely corners. Dubrovnik had treated me as one of its own. It was time for me to return the favour.

Although the siege was brutal and unrelenting for the citizens of Dubrovnik, the Serbs hated the fact that the civilised world thought they were pitiless and inhumane. They resented that their own ethnic cleansing at the hands of the Croats and the Nazis during the Second World War appeared to have been erased from our memories. So they allowed the occasional visitor from outside to come and see Dubrovnik for themselves in an attempt to demonstrate that the conflict wasn't simply a one-sided atrocity. For example, Sir Fitzroy Maclean, who was parachuted into Yugoslavia as Churchill's principal liaison with the Tito-led partisans, was allowed through the blockade. But he was an old man by then, his influence drastically curtailed. Back in the UK, nobody paid much attention.

However, these visits gave me – and others such as Tessa and Kathy Wilkes, an Oxford philosopher who was also trapped by the siege – the opportunity to pass information to the outside world. Whenever we knew we were about to be visited by one of these outsiders, we would frantically write letters to anyone we knew with either political or fund-raising connections. I had contacts on national newspapers, and I always included a couple of articles about life under siege. Some of them ended up in the pages of the *Guardian* and the *Independent*; long afterwards, I still encountered people who told me that what I had written had given them their first taste of what was about to happen in the Balkans. More importantly, we had managed to persuade friends and colleagues in the UK to start raising money for the relief and recovery of Dubrovnik.

Although we didn't know it at the time, we'd taken the first steps towards helping the city we loved to heal itself.

28

When Macanespie stepped out of the plane at Chania airport, the warmth wrapped him in its soft embrace and at once he felt ten degrees kinder towards the world. He loved the feel of sunshine on his body and hated that his ginger skin prevented him from basking like a porpoise on the beach. There was no fun in lathering himself with factor fifty. And besides, he always missed a bit on the first day and spent the rest of the holiday hiding under parasols and rubbing aloe vera into pulsating flesh. But for a few brief moments, walking across the tarmac to the bus, he could luxuriate in heat and benevolence.

Proctor trailed at his heels, the perpetual misery-guts. On the no-frills plane, he'd muttered complaints about having to pay for bad food and worse coffee. Then he'd had a good moan about the lack of leg room. 'Anyone would think you spent your life in business class,' Macanespie had said in a vain attempt to jolly his colleague out of his bad mood. That was a triumph of hope over experience, he thought to himself as Proctor's scowl only deepened.

On the flight to Crete, he'd attempted to go through the spreadsheet with Proctor. The longer this investigation went on, the more Macanespie seemed to be rediscovering a sense of professional purpose. It was the first time in years he'd felt energised by work instead of dispirited. Maybe it was time he got out of admin and into something more active. Once this was over, once he'd proved himself in the field, perhaps he could have a word with Wilson Cagney about reassignment. At the very least, he could try to achieve escape velocity from Planet Proctor.

Macanespie was pleased with his revised spreadsheet. The timeline had eliminated a few bodies from the list. As soon as possible, they'd start talking to the individuals who had access to the snatch-squad plans. Shake the tree and see what fell out. Some would be obvious non-starters. There were plenty of people at Scheveningen who saw what they were doing as the embodiment of law in action; they would never subvert what they saw as due process. The ones to focus on would be the ones who viewed it as just another job, who had no investment in the outcomes. There weren't that many of them. And although they were lawyers who drew information from others, they were unaccustomed to being the focus of hard questioning themselves. Macanespie wasn't convinced their mole

301

would be able to withstand him in full aggressive Scotsman mode.

But that was down the line. They had seven hours in Chania for an evidence review. It didn't feel long, but the investigation into Miroslav Simunovic's murder didn't seem to have produced much physical evidence. Their killer had become very good at what he did, apparently.

They emerged landside to find a uniformed woman police officer clutching a clipboard that read 'Makanespy/ Proktor'. She greeted them briskly and whisked them off to a waiting Skoda. 'I take you to our local headquarter in Chania,' she said, driving off before they'd even got their seat belts fastened. They hurtled through a hostile land-scape of rocky red soil and scrubby vegetation that changed as they descended from the high plateau through pine trees and the scrappy start of the town that hugged the hillside. Beyond them, the sea sparkled and the long arms of the harbour extended into the cove where the centre of the town nestled in a higgledy-piggledy array of roofs. 'Very pretty,' Macanespie said over the fast radio chatter spilling into the car.

'Very popular,' the policewoman agreed. The steady build-up of traffic forced her to slow down; the presence of a blue-and-white police car seemed to have no effect on the aggressive driving of everyone else on the road, however. Macanespie was embarrassed to find he'd become the cliché of the passenger clinging to the grab handle above his window as the car swung round a tight corner away from the sea and into the heart of the town.

Within a couple of streets, they'd left the tourist accommodation and tavernas behind. They turned on to a long straight street lined with cars and well-cared-for houses with balconies and gardens. Halfway along, the cop squeezed the car into a space outside a blocky white box with a Greek flag fluttering from the balcony. Only the air conditioning units on the walls and the satellite dishes on the roof distinguished it from its neighbours. A courageous graffiti artist had sprayed his tag along the front of the building. Ironically, it made the cop shop look like the worst-maintained building on the street.

Once they emerged from the car and followed the woman up the side of the building, next to a straggle of olive trees, they could see it went back much further than its neighbours. Still, it didn't look like a police station, Macanespie thought. Inside, however, it was a different story. A short corridor lined with indecipherable but unmistakable wanted posters brought them to an office where three desks huddled together, swamped with paper and the boxy screens of antiquated computer hardware. 'Wait here, please. I will bring my colleague,' the woman said, leaving them standing among the dust motes and the smell of burnt coffee.

'Fuck's sake,' Macanespie said. 'I hope this isn't the sum total of the CID office.'

Proctor sighed. 'I told you this was a waste of time.'

'You didn't have any better ideas.'

As Macanespie spoke, a man in his early thirties bounced in on the balls of his feet. He wore a pale blue shirt, open at the neck, tight enough across the chest and the abdomen to show off his gym bunny muscles. His sleeves were short, revealing ripped biceps and triceps, and his neck was thick with overdevelopment. His trousers strained over muscular thighs. His black hair was gelled in place, a single lock falling over his forehead like Taurus the Bull. He looked as if he plucked his eyebrows, and his forearms were suspiciously hairless. On first impression, Macanespie thought he made Christiano Ronaldo look self-effacing.

'Good morning and welcome to Chania,' he said, his accent strong but comprehensible. 'I am Christos Macropoulos and I am the detective here who speaks English. My colleague will bring us coffee soon, but first we can talk about how we can help each other, yes?'

The two Brits introduced themselves while Christos arranged the three office chairs round one desk. He quickly outlined the circumstances of Simunovic's murder, opening crime-scene photographs on the computer screen as he went. Macanespie hadn't had high hopes for the forensics, which was just as well since there was almost nothing to go on. No footprints. No fingermarks. No blood other than that of the victim. No DNA that any significance could be attached to. No eye witnesses in the building; too many eye witnesses in the streets nearby and no way of tracking most of them down short of advertising on the Internet.

'And we all know that brings out the crazies,' Christos said. The other two nodded sagely, as if they knew exactly what he was talking about.

'Right enough,' Macanespie said. 'And it's hard to get cooperation from your colleagues overseas when it's all kind of tenuous.'

'So, we think the killer came up behind Simunovic when he lets himself into his flat,' Christos concluded. 'He must have been quiet because it looks like the victim didn't turn around. He used a very sharp blade. Maybe something like an open razor. And cut straight across the throat. Too quick for screaming. All the blood would spray outwards, away from the killer. So he wasn't covered with the blood. And so he goes away, into the evening crowds and nobody sees him.'

'How long was it till the body was found?'

'We think about two hours. His neighbour across the stair, he goes out every evening at ten o'clock for a glass of ouzo down by the harbour. He opened his front door and came face to face with this.' He clicked back to the first crime-scene photograph. 'He heard nothing, saw nothing.'

'How did he get into the building?' Proctor asked. 'Is there no security on the outside door?'

Macropoulos shrugged. 'It's a keypad. Not so hard to learn the code, I think. You look over somebody's shoulder or if you're more organised, you put a camera on it for a day or two and get everybody's code.'

'You printed the keypad, right?'

Macropoulos flexed his shoulders. 'Of course this was done. Nothing but smudges and partial prints from official residents.'

And now the sixty-four-thousand-dollar question. 'What about CCTV?' Macanespie asked.

Macropoulos sighed. 'There is nothing on the apartment block or the street. It's far enough away from the harbour to be safe to walk here. Most of the crime we have is street crime. Pickpockets, bag snatchers. Also credit-card fraud. They target tourists. But not in streets like this one.'

'And down by the harbour? You said Simunovic was drinking in his regular bar. Is it in a tourist area? Is it covered by CCTV?'

Macropoulos gave a self-satisfied smile. 'I thought you would ask about that.' He got to his feet. 'There are three cameras that cover the part of the harbour where he walks from his bar towards his apartment. In my office I have the recordings from that night on a flash drive so you can take them with you. But we look at them now, yes?'

'Yes, please,' Macanespie said with a triumphant glance at Proctor. As soon as Macropoulos had left the room, he gave a thumbs-up sign. 'Cooking with gas now, Theo. Cooking with gas.'

'You don't think if there was something to be seen, the Greeks would have spotted it by now?'

Macanespie shook his head pityingly. 'Watch and learn, Theo. Watch and learn.'

When Macropoulos returned, they crowded closer round the screen and concentrated on the images. The first camera was black and white, its images jerky and blurred. A constant flow of pedestrians moved back and forth through the field of vision. Macropoulos pointed with his pen as a big silver-haired man came into shot. 'Simunovic,' he said. They watched as he crossed the screen and disappeared. The video continued for another minute but it was impossible to see whether any individual was following their target.

The second camera was in colour, the register a little off so that everything looked like sixties Kodachrome. It was set a bit lower than the first and they had a much clearer view of people's faces. Again, they watched as Simunovic walked across the screen. This time, Macropoulos picked out half a dozen people who came up behind him, tapping them with a pen. 'We think they are also in the first shot. They are also interesting because they seem to be on their own. Not in a couple or a group.'

The third camera reverted to black and white, almost as fuzzy as the first. This time, Simunovic cut diagonally across the frame. This time, Macropoulos pointed to only two figures. And this time, Macanespie felt a little twitch of excitement. There were two other figures that had definitely been in the previous shot but who hadn't been singled out by Macropoulos. One looked like a teenage boy – baggy board shorts, oversize T-shirt and baseball cap, carrying a skateboard. The other was a woman in a headscarf and big sunglasses, a cotton djellaba disguising her figure. She could, Macanespie thought, be anything from a size eight to a size twenty under that. She could be a he, come to that.

'That's fascinating,' he said. 'Do you have any ID on any of those guys?'

Macropoulos shook his head. 'This happened on a Friday night. Thousands of holidaymakers change over on a Saturday and leave the island. There was nothing we could do to stop that.'

'I wonder ... Do you still have the footage from those cameras for the nights before the actual murder?' Macanespie sounded casual. 'You know how it is. My boss, he's obsessive about detail.'

Macropoulos looked startled. 'You think the killer might be in the earlier footage too?'

'I don't. But my boss is the kind of bastard who would send me all the way back to look, just to make a point. It'd make my life easier if I could take copies of any other footage you've got. Futile, I know. But that's how he is.'

Macropoulos grinned. 'I have bosses like this too. If you wait here, I'll get what we have. I know there is nothing more from the first camera because they reuse the same videotape every day. That's why the quality is so bad. But I think there is more from the other two.'

Macanespie grinned at his retreating back. 'He's got fixed

ideas about how an assassin should look. He doesn't like the teenage boy with the skateboard and he definitely doesn't like the woman in the baggy kaftan. Always supposing it is a woman and not some guy – remember that BBC foreign correspondent who got into Kabul by wearing a burka? So I want to take a look at who turns up earlier in the week. Somebody staked out that door code. This killer doesn't leave things to chance, Theo. But maybe we're the two heads that are better than one.'

29

Her conversation with Adam Turner had left Karen nowhere to turn except her victim's distant past. Nothing in Dimitar Petrovic's Oxford life pointed towards murder. But his history encompassed some of the bloodiest conflicts of the twentieth century. It wasn't much of a reach to think the answer to his death must lie there. Persuading the Macaroon of that would be the hardest part.

So she'd prepared a written pitch, complete with costings. A cheap flight to Venice, train to Zagreb then a hire car to a Croatian village in the middle of nowhere. It was almost as cheap as an overnight in London, she pointed out. She'd worry about the language barrier once she got there. In her experience, there was always a cop with good enough English to help out in an emergency. She'd made it sound as straightforward as a day trip to Glasgow. It was her only chance.

And miraculously it had worked. Phil had been incredulous when she'd told him the night before she flew out. 'You got that past the Macaroon? Karen, you scare me sometimes.'

She laughed. 'It was easy. By making it a written request, it meant he didn't actually have to talk to me. Me talking to him is like in a Tom and Jerry cartoon where Tom sticks his head in a beehive and there's a whole cloud of bees buzzing round driving him totally mental. So if the Macaroon can avoid that ... Easy peasy. I'm off to Croatia in the morning.'

'Take care of yourself. I mean it, Karen.'

'It's not the wild west any more, Phil. They're part of the EU.'

'Aye, but there are still people there who did some seriously bad things not that long ago, and they're not going to be very happy if you poke a stick in their ribs.'

Karen gave an exasperated sigh. 'I won't be going around causing trouble. I'm just trying to get a few answers to some questions about a dead guy.'

'No, you're not. You're looking for a murderer.'

'I'll be fine, Phil. I'm not stupid. I can take care of myself.' She had her stubborn face on now, and he knew enough to leave it.

And so they'd left it. Her flight to Venice had departed Edinburgh on time next morning. Since she'd never been there before, she'd given herself a couple of hours' grace in the city before she had to catch her train for Zagreb. It was just long enough to make her way from Piazzale Roma to St Mark's Square and back again. Karen wasn't as well travelled as she'd have liked, and she'd often found the reality of abroad less scintillating than the anticipation. Not so with Venice. In the end, she had to drag herself back to the station, catching her train with minutes to spare. It had been magical. She'd return with Phil, she promised herself as she emailed him a selection of the snaps she'd taken with her phone.

Nine hours on a train wasn't the worst way Karen could think of to spend a day but it was close. There was only so long you could look at scenery. But she'd had the good sense to download a string of BBC TV dramas on to her iPad and that was enough of a distraction to fill most of the time. She'd stocked up with plenty to eat before she'd left Edinburgh, so she didn't even have to chance the train catering. But by the time the train pulled into Zagreb Glavni kolodvor, she was more than ready to breathe some fresh air and stretch her legs.

Karen shouldered her backpack and walked through the cavernous concourse of the station, looking all around her, trying to work out where the car-hire counters were. It was far too late to set off for Podruvec, but she could pick up the car and head out of the city now while the traffic was quiet. She'd find a cheap hotel on the outskirts and set off properly in the morning.

What she saw next made her misstep and almost clatter to the pale travertine floor. There, standing in the middle of the concourse, oblivious to everyone around her, staring up at the departure boards that flanked the entrance to the platforms, was Maggie Blake. 'What the fuck,' Karen said out loud.

She paused for a moment, watching the professor, then slowly approached. 'Professor Blake?'

Maggie whirled round, her mouth falling open, her expression shocked. Then, seeing who it was, shock gave way to outrage. 'Oh, my God. Are you following me?'

'No. Really. I'm not. Believe me, I'm as surprised as you are.'

'What are you doing here?' Maggie was edging towards anger, Karen could see that.

'I suspect I'm heading for the same place as you. That is, if you're still interested in finding out about Dimitar Petrovic.'

'So where do you think that would take me?'

'Well, I'm heading for a wee place called Podruvec. I was told that's where the general hailed from. I thought I'd start where he started. Is that where you're going?'

Some of the aggression leaked out of Maggie. 'I should have come here years ago. I was never honest with myself about wanting to know Mitja's history. Call him Mitja, by the way. Nobody who knew him ever called him Dimitar.'

'OK. So, are you going to Podruvec too?'

313

Maggie nodded. 'I was trying to figure out whether I could get to Osijek tonight, but I don't think I can.'

'I'm done with trains, me. I was just going to pick up a hire car. I thought I'd look for somewhere on the outskirts to spend the night. You're welcome to join me if you want. I wouldn't mind the company.' The offer was sincere, and not just because Maggie Blake was currently her best source of information. Having a navigator wouldn't hurt on such unfamiliar terrain. It had also occurred to Karen that Maggie probably spoke decent Croatian, given her time in Dubrovnik and the years she'd been with Petrovic.

Maggie looked at her suspiciously. 'Is that allowed, when you're on police business? Taking a civilian along for the ride?'

Karen grinned. 'I won't tell if you don't. Look, we both want the same thing. To find out who killed your general. I think we'll make a better job of that together than either of us will alone.'

'Not to mention that I speak the language. So you won't have to find someone to interpret for you,' Maggie said drily.

'There's that. All I know are the words for please, beer and ice cream, which isn't going to get me far. But I do have a car, and I suspect you're not going to get to Podruvec without one. We're both bringing something to the table.'

Maggie looked Karen up and down, as if measuring her for some unspecified garment. 'All right,' she said at last. 'Just so long as you remember we're not friends. We might not always be on the same side.'

'Fair enough. Now, can you figure out these signs? I'm looking for the rental car agencies.'

Maggie laughed. 'You'll be lucky. We'll have to get a cab to the airport. It's not far. Come on, let's go.' She set off, not waiting to see whether Karen was following. The detective caught up with her as they emerged into the cool night air. 'Oh, and one more thing,' Maggie said as they reached the cab rank.

'What's that?'

'Don't tell them you're a cop. Not if you want them to trust you.'

30

Jason Murray was bright enough to know he wasn't bright enough. He also realised he was lucky to have a boss like Karen Pirie, who was mostly patient and who didn't need to big herself up by putting him down. In another team, he knew he'd be the one at the bottom of the pile, getting whatever crap was going and forever being stuck with the grunt work. So whenever he had the chance to do something that would impress the boss, he grabbed it with both hands.

She was always on at him about using his initiative. Not in a shitty, having-a-dig kind of way, but more like encouraging him. So when she was out of town and he was left behind, it was a perfect opportunity to show her what he could do. The trouble was, once he'd rung Tamsin Martineau and established there was no news on the key-card's digital forensics, he couldn't think of anything useful to pursue except the traditional cop motto. When in doubt, huddle together over food and drink.

Because he'd started the day at his parents' house again, the closest source of these necessities was the canteen at Kirkcaldy police station. Once he was settled at a table with the *Daily Record*, a bacon roll dripping with brown sauce and a mug of industrial-strength tea, Jason felt much less stressed at his inability to think of constructive action.

He was halfway through the sports pages, gloating secretly over the travails of Hibs, when he realised someone was standing over him. He raised his head and took in Detective Inspector Phil Parhatka, dressed down in jeans and a rugby shirt, carrying a fry-up and a mug. 'Mind if I join you?' he said.

Jason nodded, confused by his mixed feelings. He'd liked it when Phil had been his sergeant in the old Cold Case Unit. He was a grafter, Phil, but he always made it look effortless. Easy-going, too. He took everything in his stride and he was good at defusing things when the boss got frustrated and wanted to kick somebody. There was always a good atmosphere in the office when Phil was around. But then he'd got it together with the boss. And that made everything different. It wasn't like he acted differently towards Jason or anything. But it had been a tight wee team, and Jason felt like it had gone from being the three of them united against the bad guys to being two plus one. It had been the first time in his life that Jason had felt like one of the top cats, and that had changed.

That sense of being on the outside had shifted once Phil got promoted and moved to the Murder Protection Team and it was just him and the boss. Then when she got made up to head of the Historic Cases Unit, he'd thought that would be the end of the good life for him. But the boss had taken him with her and although they were a small core team, they had respect because they got results. Still, he wasn't quite as sure of himself around Phil as he'd once been. He had to watch himself; he wasn't daft, he knew Phil would report straight back to Karen anything he thought she should know.

'What're you doing in Kirkcaldy?' Jason asked.

Phil gestured at his plate. 'Cat's away, mouse has a heart attack on a plate. The guy at the top of our target list isn't due back for a couple of days so we're in the fallback place of catching up on checks on the bastards we'll be going after next. I love this berth, Jason. You put these guys away and it's like watching Raith Rovers winning the cup. Every time. They're so bloody sure of themselves, so bloody arrogant. Watching that certainty turn to dust, it's the best feeling I've ever had in this job.'

'Wow, that's saying something.'

'How are you doing? I've had Karen and River bending my ear about this skeleton up the John Drummond. How's it going?'

Jason wrinkled his nose. 'Tell you the truth, I'm a bit dead-ended. The boss was in such a hurry to get away she didn't task me. Maybe because there isn't much to do. The only lead we've got is that hotel key-card, and digital forensics say it could be weeks before they've got anything off it.'

Phil shovelled in a forkful of bacon, beans and fried egg. When he'd finished chewing, he said, 'It's not always the technology that gets results, Jason. Sometimes we get so obsessed by what the scientists can do that we forget the value of what *we* can do.'

'How do you mean?'

'Well, take this key for example. It's got to open a door somewhere, right. If your man came to Edinburgh specifically to climb the John Drummond, chances are he'll have stayed some place nearby. A guest house or a small hotel, I'd guess, given he doesn't seem to have been a rich bastard. So why don't you get Tamsin to send you a pic of the key and go round the guest houses, see if you can get a match.'

'But there might be more than one,' Jason said. 'It's a pretty ordinary-looking key.'

'Yeah, but when you get a match, you ask whether they've still got the details of the guests for that date. These days, with everything on computers, it's not totally unlikely. You might get lucky.' He loaded up another full fork and put it in his mouth. As he chewed, he added, 'You know how she likes it when we bring her a wee present.'

And so Jason had finished his breakfast and set off for Edinburgh. Because Karen had drilled into him the need for preparation, he'd spent an hour on the computer mapping out all the hotels and guest houses within two miles of the John Drummond. Edinburgh being a tourist city, there were a formidable number. Then he had his own bright idea. He could work his way down the list on the phone and eliminate everyone who didn't have red key-cards. That would make the task much more manageable.

The advantage of checking out hotels was that somebody always answered the phone. They might not speak much English beyond what was strictly necessary to take a booking, but Jason was patient and he managed to explain himself to all but one receptionist, who stubbornly refused to believe he was a police officer. He considered turning up at her desk, just to annoy her.

In the end, he had reduced his list to twenty-seven. The first dozen produced six definite noes, two that didn't have computerised records going back eight years and four that had the wrong shade of red. At the ninth address, a small private hotel, he recited his familiar spiel and showed the photograph.

'Yeah, looks like it could be one of ours,' said the friendly receptionist in an unmistakably Glaswegian accent.

'Do you still have your records for September 2007?' He tried his most appealing look, aiming for the supplicant Puss in Boots in the *Shrek* movies. It didn't work on the boss, but it might work on this lassie.

She looked dubious. 'I don't know. Let me go and check with the manager.'

Jason's optimism shrivelled. In his experience, managers generally wanted to cover their arses more than they wanted to help the police. He leaned against the counter, morosely playing Candy Crush while he waited. At least there was something he was good at.

When the receptionist returned, her cheery smile was still in place. 'It's your lucky day,' she said. 'Do you want to come through the office and take a look?'

Jason didn't need to be asked twice. He followed her through to a tiny office that managed to be dingy in spite of eye-poppingly bright lights. A man who looked no older than the receptionist slid out of an office chair and said, 'It's all yours, pal.' It was amazing how the word 'murder' opened doors in some circumstances.

He started with the first of the month, even though he knew at that point Petrovic had still been in Oxford. But it would give him a feel for how the records were laid out. 'What do these codes mean?' he asked, pointing at the screen.

'That tells you how the account was settled. Cash. Cheque. Credit card. Debit card or account,' the manager explained.

There was nothing of interest on the second or the third. But when Jason pulled up the records for the fourth of September, it leapt out at him: D. Petrovic, room 18. Home address in Oxford. 'This one,' he said. 'Tell me about this one.'

The manager leaned over and studied the screen. 'Booked in for two nights. Paid cash in advance. No car.'

'Was he by himself?'

The manager shrugged. 'No way of knowing that. He booked a single room but they've all got double beds.'

'I don't suppose you've got key-card entry and exit records?'

The manager snorted incredulously. 'What do you think we are? MI5? This is it, pal.'

He'd known it was a daft question but he'd known he had to ask it because the boss would ask him. But it didn't matter. Five minutes later, he was walking down Corstorphine Road with a spring in his step and a printout in his pocket that would put him smack dab in the middle of the boss's good books. If Dimitar Petrovic had travelled with his killer to climb the John Drummond, chances were that his name was nestling next to Jason's wallet.

Job done.

The Serb demand that Dubrovnik should surrender was a constant accompaniment to the bombardment of the city. But even our Serb population – who were as consistently stalwart as any other citizen in their commitment to their home town – were adamant that we should not give in. We saw ourselves as a symbol for Croatia. If we caved in, how would the rest of the country find the nerve to stand and fight in the face of such superior numbers?

Around the time of the fall of Vukovar, there was a lull in the attacks because the European Union Monitoring Mission was mediating between the Yugoslav National Army (JNA) and the Croatian authorities in Dubrovnik. But after the JNA attacked members of the mission, that ended. Supposed ceasefires were brokered. Each time, our spirits rose then collapsed again when the gunfire echoed through the broken streets.

Mitja was never home for more than a handful of hours at a time. Humanitarian aid was finally coming in from the sea, thanks to a fleet of civilian vessels. As well as aid, they brought protesters and supporters, and when they left, they carried refugees; people who had lost their homes and who wanted nothing more than a night's sleep without being in fear for their lives. The negotiations and organisation of these arrivals and departures took phenomenal effort; the Yugoslav navy was always teetering on the point of action against anyone delivering medicines and other basic supplies to the beleaguered city. Mitja spent long hours horse-trading and bargaining to keep the aid effort afloat.

When the first convoy was on its way, Mitja tried again to persuade me to leave the city. But again I refused. I was young and idealistic; I was also head over heels in love for the first time in my life. The idea of sailing away without Mitja was intolerable. I wasn't afraid that our love would fail the test of separation. I simply didn't want to be apart from him. I made him promise he would stop asking me to leave and I redoubled my efforts to make myself valuable to Dubrovnik, both at home and abroad.

The November respite had reassured us all, mostly because we had very little idea of how grim things were in other parts of Croatia. We thought because the bombardment against us had eased that the Serbs had come to their senses and realised there are no winners in a war like this. What we had no way of knowing was the degree of savagery being endured by innocent civilians elsewhere. But our innocence was shattered at the beginning of December.

It began with gunfire, peppering the streets of the Old Town. Then the shelling started. Mortars, shells and missiles rained down from dawn for six hours at a time. The air reverberated with the terrible impact of the bombs. The noise was deafening, so loud it seemed to vibrate in my chest. Our flat was close to Stradun, the central promenade of the Old Town, and the constant hammering of the artillery throughout its length terrified me. Tessa Minogue's flat had been hit the day before, and she huddled with me under the heavy oak dining table where we shook with fear.

When Mitja came back that night, he reported that thirteen people had died. It's unforgivable, but at the time we almost felt relieved. I remember thinking so few deaths was a miracle, given the visible devastation left by the attack. Later, we discovered that the IUC library had been destroyed; twenty thousand books shredded. It felt like an assault on the future.

I remember Mitja shaking with rage when he described what had happened at the Libertas Hotel. 'The hotel was one of the first targets, and of course it ended up in flames. And because our people refuse to lie down and die, the city firemen turned out in spite of the bombardment and started putting out the fire. And what did those bastards in the JNA do? They turned their guns on the firemen. It could have been carnage out there if our guys hadn't taken cover. Who would do such a thing? What kind of animals are they?' I had no answers then; I still have none. It has always seemed to me that the Balkans are a seething pit of artificial distinctions between people who can't actually be divided on biological lines. How can ethnic cleansing make any sense when the people you are cleansing are the same as you under the skin?

Though 6 December was the high watermark of the bombing of the city, it wasn't the end of the siege. The JNA soldiers continued their campaign of looting and destruction in the Old Town and in the rest of the city till they were finally driven out in the New Year by the Sarajevo Agreement. But even when the JNA fell back and started to focus on bringing the war to Bosnia and Hercegovina, we still felt insecure. Every time I left the flat, I tried to record what I was seeing, to keep track of what had changed, what had been destroyed, what remained. More than half the buildings in the Old Town were damaged. An overwhelming amount of museum exhibits and privately held art simply disappeared. But that was nothing compared to the human cost. The suffering of the survivors still echoes down the years; the scars persist.

As the siege began to peter out, Mitja was under even greater pressure. In the middle of December, the EU – or rather, the EEC as it was then – agreed to recognise the independence of Croatia in four weeks. I've never been sure what exactly an intelligence officer is responsible for, but in the same way as I was cataloguing the streets, he was cataloguing the crimes of the JNA. Making sure there was a record of the testimony of the hundreds of people – mostly displaced civilians whose homes in the countryside around Dubrovnik had been destroyed – who were thrown into so-called prisoner-of-war camps where they were beaten and brutalised and terrorised, where mock executions were used as a form of psychological warfare, where JNA soldiers played out the role of brutal oppressors without compunction.

By the middle of January, the siege was effectively over. It was possible to communicate with the outside world. There was food, water and electricity again, though such normality felt like a strange counterpoint to the damage I saw everywhere. Melissa, my supervisor, was eager that I should return to Oxford. 'You can do some teaching this term,' she said in one of the first emails I received after the electricity supply was restored. It wasn't a request, it was an instruction. The subtext was that if I didn't come back now, there might no longer be a job for me. 'And you will have so much to write about. I almost envy you the experience.'

Probably the most tactless thing anyone has ever said to me.

I told Mitja about the email late that night as we lay curled round each other in bed. 'I'm going to stay here,' I said.

'No. It's not a good idea, Maggie. There's more and worse to come here. It was different during the siege. I had the perfect excuse to stay here. But I can't sidestep my responsibilities and I can't take you with me.'

I could feel tears pricking my eyes. 'I don't want to be without you,' I blurted out. 'I don't care if we can only snatch little bits of time together, I'm going to stay here.'

'And do what? The IUC is destroyed. There's nowhere to teach. Look, Maggie, Dubrovnik needs things you can do better from Oxford than here. We need people to raise money to rebuild the city. To mend our roofs, to restore our walls. You can't do this here. And you have a voice in England. You can write for newspapers and magazines, you can tell the story of the siege from the inside. You can make people pay attention.'

'You want me to go? You want rid of me? I thought you loved me.'

'Of course I love you,' he protested, tightening his grip. I could feel each finger pressing into my back. 'That's why I want you out of here before it all turns to shit. Maggie, I promise you we'll meet whenever we can. Come back in the vacation time and wherever I am, you can be close by.

And I will be in London or Paris or Berlin sometimes, talking to government people. We can meet then.'

'You've already worked all this out.' It came out like an accusation.

'I've thought a lot about it. The war won't go on for ever and then we get our time. You and me, time and space.'

'I don't want to go.'

'I know. But you have to. Dubrovnik needs you now more than ever. But it needs you somewhere else.'

31

'Jesus Christ, what happened here?' Karen pulled up at the side of a small meadow of mown grass by the single-track road they were driving along. A circle of more than a dozen white wooden crosses surrounded a stone plinth displaying photographs of children.

'A massacre, at a guess,' Maggie said, her voice as bleak as her expression.

'But they're all kids. Little kids.' Karen got out of the car and walked towards the memorial, her throat closing in pity. She counted fourteen crosses. There were no names on them or on the plinth, just the photographs encased in blocks of Perspex sunk into the pale stone. Dark hair, big eyes, gap-toothed smiles, no inkling on those cheerful open faces that death was round the corner. 'Jesus Christ,' she said, a detached part of her brain wondering why atheists like her still invoked a deity in moments of extremis. She stood in silence, wondering at the stages on a journey that brought a man to a place where slaughtering children became a valid response.

Maggie joined her after a couple of minutes, her expression grim, map in hand. 'We're only a few kilometres from Podruvec,' she said, pointing to their position. 'It's the nearest village to here. The children might have come from there.'

'This is terrible,' Karen said.

'A lot of terrible things happened here in the nineties. Seeing media reports doesn't prepare you for the reality. Because we drove down on the motorway, you didn't get a sense of the countryside. I didn't give you the commentary. "This village was shelled, this place lost its menfolk, the women here were gang-raped." That's what a journey through the Balkans can turn into.' She walked round the memorial, studying it as if she was etching it on her mind. 'One of my doctoral students has written about the massacres that happened in all three wars. How those deaths embody the geopolitics of the region. Me, I see them as emblems as well as embodiments. You see something like this and you never forget how easily we lose our humanity.'

Karen looked away. On their long drive, she'd learned much more about Maggie's relationship to this landscape that hid recent horrors beneath its tranquil beauty. 'I don't know how you were able to keep coming back, knowing what you knew, seeing what you'd seen.'

'It was complicated, and not all of it virtuous.' Maggie crouched down to take a photograph on her phone. 'I thought it was important to witness what was happening here. And I was ambitious enough to understand that I was getting the inside track on a historic conflict that would provide me with a career's worth of research material.' She caught the swiftly suppressed look of distaste on Karen's face. 'I told you it wasn't all pretty.' She sighed. 'I also wanted to help. So I got an LGV licence and every time I came back, I came with a truckload of medical supplies. But if I'm totally honest, I might not have done any of it if it hadn't been for Mitja. I loved him, and he had a job to do. Well, a series of jobs, as it turned out. So if I wanted to be with him, I had to steel myself and come back.'

Karen shook her head. 'I love my partner, but I'm not sure I love him that much.'

'Karen, I don't know you very well, but I think I know you well enough to say that you'd probably surprise yourself.'

Karen looked around her, at the green woodland and the rolling hills, the emptiness of the landscape and its beauty. It wasn't that different from parts of Perthshire, she thought. The vegetation was different, but they felt similar. Except she couldn't imagine the people of Tayside rising up against their neighbours in the Highlands in bloody conflict. Even at its ugliest, Scottish sectarianism would stop short at this. Wouldn't it? And if it didn't, could she love a man caught up in the thick of it?

As if reading her thoughts, Maggie said, 'He wasn't a fanatic, you know. He loved his country but he hated what the nationalists on both sides stood for. That's why he ended up working for NATO and the UN. Because he could see there was no future in the fighting. He'd have been pleased to see this next generation of kids talking to each other online, realising there's more that links them than separates them.'

'Whatever he was, it got him killed. And it got him killed on my patch. The first rule of investigation is supposed to be getting to know your victim. So I suppose I should be grateful for seeing the likes of this.' Karen turned away and walked back to the car.

Maggie joined her and they set off in silence. A kilometre up the road, Maggie peered at the map and said, 'It's just ahead, round the shoulder of the hill by the looks of it.'

They rounded the bend and almost immediately a crooked sign by the side of the road said 'Podruvec'. Karen slowed down as they arrived at a cluster of houses and outbuildings that straggled along the narrow road. As they grew closer, they could see many of the houses were deserted, their front doors hanging from broken hinges, their windows smashed, everything covered with grime and stained by weather. The only café was a ruin, one wall entirely missing. A church with a lopsided tower huddled behind an overgrown graveyard.

At the sound of their car, a handful of people materialised in doorways and outside the outbuildings, suspicion outweighing curiosity on their faces. It was, Karen thought, like something out of a post-apocalyptic indie film. 'Eat your heart out, Sam Peckinpah,' she muttered under her breath, falling back on the Scots tradition of black humour as the antidote to fear, distress or upset. She pulled up on a concrete pad next to the ruined café. 'What now?' she said.

'We get out and say hello,' Maggie said. She got out of the car and smiled a greeting, sketching a wave at the watchers.

'In for a penny,' Karen said and followed her.

Maggie was heading for a woman who could have been any age between forty and eighty. Her weathered skin was the colour of an acorn, puckered and scored with lines. A black headscarf covered most of her iron grey hair. A black cardigan and a dark red skirt covered her ample bosom and broad hips. Her arms were folded across her chest and her mouth was a grim inhospitable line. Karen, who had wandered into plenty of Greek hill villages in her time, was surprised not to be greeted more warmly.

Maggie launched into what Karen presumed to be Croatian. It might as well have been Klingon for all the sense it made to her. Hard consonants and soft sibilants, a slur of vowels. On the drive, they'd discussed the line they would take. But Karen had no way of knowing whether Maggie was sticking to the original game plan. Taking a back seat didn't come naturally to her, but here, now, Karen had no choice. She had to trust.

*

Maggie gave Karen one last glance then turned her focus on the stony face in front of her. She reached back into her memory for Mitja's accent and launched herself into speech. 'It's a fine day,' she began. It wasn't just the Brits who used the weather as a way into conversation.

'You're not from round here,' the woman said.

So it was going to be like that. 'No, I'm Scottish. But I spent a lot of time in Croatia in the nineties. I was in Dubrovnik during the siege.' Lay out the credentials alongside the linguistic fluency.

'And what brings you here now?' The woman wasn't giving an inch. One or two of her neighbours were moving slowly closer.

'I'm looking for Mitja Petrovic's family. I've got news of him.'

A spark of recognition but no yielding. 'What news?'

'Like I said, it's for his family.'

'He doesn't have any family round here. Not any more. His parents died before the war.'

'I know that. I'm looking for Jablanka. His wife.'

The woman tried but there was no hiding the shock of hearing that name. 'There's nobody here called Jablanka. You've had a wasted journey.'

'If she's not here any more, where is she?'

'Stop pretending you have any proper business here. If you knew General Petrovic, you would know the answers to these questions. Just leave.' She waved her fingers in a dismissive, shooing gesture as if they were troublesome chickens.

'I'm not leaving till I get some answers.'

The woman laughed and waved her arm to encompass her neighbours, now standing within easy hearing distance. 'You think they're going to talk to you?' she scoffed, then turned away and went back inside her house. Everyone else melted away except for one man. His dark eyes were fixed on Maggie, his scrawny frame tightly held, hands obvious fists in his pockets.

'Did you know Mitja?' Maggie said.

The man nodded. 'I was at school with him.'

Maggie smiled. 'Then you must have known Rado Tomic too.'

'You know Rado?' He looked wary.

'I had coffee with him in Dubrovnik a few days ago. He works for UNESCO now, but I suppose you know that?'

The man shrugged. 'Everybody knew Rado was going places.'

'Mitja too, I'm guessing.'

A quick, shrewd glance. 'Look, what she said? If you really knew him, you'd know about Jablanka. So I'm not talking about him, you understand?'

'He's dead,' Maggie said. It was the last throw of the dice.

The man's eyes widened momentarily in shock. 'Really? I always thought he was a survivor.'

'He was murdered.'

He stared at the ground. 'One more death.'

'Did he have any enemies that you know of?'

A short, sharp bark of laughter and a cynical curl of his lip to match it. 'If you're looking for the general's enemies, you won't find them here. You've wasted your time. There's nobody here will talk to you about him. It's been a very long time since he was one of us.' He uncurled his fists and took a soft pack of cigarettes from his shirt pocket. He tapped one out and lit it with a battered petrol lighter made from a cartridge case. 'You should go.' And he stepped around her and walked away, disappearing into a raddled old barn across the road.

'I'm guessing that didn't go well,' Karen said.

'I don't get it,' Maggie said. 'A place like this, you'd think they'd be proud of their home-grown general. But it's like talking to a brick wall.'

'Did you tell them he was dead?'

'I told the guy. I was holding back with the woman. I thought she'd spill whatever she knew about Jablanka and Mitja's sons.' She gave a dry little laugh. 'I was married to him and I don't even know what his boys were called. Fuck, what kind of a woman am I?'

One who doesn't want to know the truth about her man. Not so very unusual. 'So what now?'

Maggie shook her head. 'I've no idea. I was so sure I'd get some answers here. You know the kind of thing. The village elder who would sit down with me and pass on a fund of stories about Mitja. And maybe the chance to come face to face with his sons and tell them how much good their father did.'

Karen thought about the field of crosses and said nothing. 'I don't want to give up just yet. In a place like this, not everybody toes the party line all the time. Sometimes you just have to open a wee window of opportunity.'

'What do you mean?'

Karen pointed to the church. 'I think we should take the opportunity to have a quiet moment in the church.'

Maggie gave her a derisive glance. 'Tell me you don't believe in all that.'

'Of course I don't. But there's no pub to go to. Plus it might get us some brownie points. Come on, time for a wee bit of prayer and meditation.'

The door of the church was unlocked. Inside it smelled of a mixture of damp and incense. The walls were stained where rainwater had leaked in. The coloured glass windows were cracked and buckled and a spray of what looked like bullet holes arced across the wall in the chancel. But the altar was clean and polished to a high sheen and the chairs were arranged in neat rows. An ornate crucifix hung above the altar, the water stoup by the door was half-full and a box of battery-powered nightlights sat on a table nearby, a couple in holders giving off a flickering light. 'Are they Catholic here, then?' Karen asked.

'Mostly. You get some Orthodox and Muslim, but that's

mostly in Zagreb or Dubrovnik. Outside the cities, it's Roman Catholic. All the faiths clung on to the old religion during the Communist years and they sprang straight back to life afterwards. It might have been better all round if that had never happened,' she added with a note of bitterness.

Karen walked forward and sat down a few rows from the front. Maggie joined her. 'What do we do now?' she asked.

'We sit and wait and hope something happens.'

'Do you do that a lot? Wait and hope something happens?'

Karen's smile was tired. 'More often than we like to admit. The kind of cases I do, people have been sitting on their secrets for a long time. Sometimes they're ready to let them go. You just need to be patient and let them feel like you're what they've been waiting for.'

'Does it often work?'

'Sometimes. Now shut up and act like you're being devout.' Karen leaned on the back of the chair in front of her and stared at the altar.

Maggie closed her eyes and tilted her head back, trying to empty her mind. Ever since she'd stepped off the plane her brain had been like a hamster on a wheel, rerunning all her history with the place. People, places, moments of sweetness and sadness, episodes of fear and delight; it had all been rolling out like a perpetual movie in her head. She had no idea how much time had passed before her thoughts were interrupted by the creak of an opening door. She started to full awareness and swung round in her seat to see an elderly priest making his way towards them, the beat of his stick on the stone flags like the drum announcing the prisoner's walk to the gallows.

'Looks like I was right,' Karen murmured.

32

Maggie said something that sounded to Karen like, 'Pozdrav, svechenitch,' and the priest inclined his head. He had a thick mop of silver hair framing a square face with strong features and incongruously dark eyebrows. Karen put him around seventy. Old enough to know what they'd come to learn.

'They say you are English,' he said. His accent was quite pronounced but Karen could make out what he was saying.

Maggie smiled. 'Scottish, actually. You speak English?' She sounded surprised.

'Where do you think Mitja learned his English?'

Maggie's eyes widened. 'He spent time in England, training at a military college.'

'That made it better, but he learned it first from me.'

'And where did you learn it?' Karen knew that any time spent building a relationship with this man would help them. Showing an interest in him rather than simply pumping him for information was the first step.

He gave her an approving nod, as if he understood what she was doing. 'During the Communist years, there wasn't so much work for a priest. So I became a teacher at the university in Belgrade. A Croat among the Serbs, when we were all supposed to be one Yugoslav people. I taught English literature. It wasn't usual in a Communist state. But here in Yugoslavia, we pretended we were different. We were the good Communists. The ones the West could love. And so I taught Shakespeare and Wordsworth and Robert Burns to bored students who were forced to take my course.'

'That's amazing. You speak really well,' Karen said.

'I have listened to the BBC for years. But you flatter me. I know I don't speak as well as I understand.'

'We should introduce ourselves,' Maggie said. 'I'm Professor Maggie Blake from Oxford University.'

Spoken like a woman who knew exactly how powerful a line it was when it came to opening doors, Karen thought. 'And I'm Karen Pirie. From Edinburgh.' Simpler not to go into too much detail yet.

The priest pulled a chair into the aisle and sank into it with the grateful sigh of the elderly. He placed his hands on the head of his stick and studied them carefully. 'I am Father Uros Begovic. This has been my parish since 1971. Even when it wasn't supposed to be a parish. I have been minister to the people of this village for more than forty years. I used to come home at weekends and holidays and turn from lecturer to priest.' He ran one hand over his black cassock. 'Easier on the outside than on the inside.'

'And that's how you knew Mitja,' Maggie said.

He tipped his head towards her, peering over the rimless glasses perched on the end of his nose. 'I prepared him for his First Communion. But you – why are you interested in him? Why have you come here in search of his past?'

Karen could see the wrestling match going on inside Maggie. She reckoned the priest could too. It was time for the truth. Or at least part of it. She waited, hoping Maggie understood that.

The professor raised her head and stared at the crucifix above the altar. 'I loved him. We were married. I never knew his history.'

'You didn't want to know,' the priest said gently. 'And that's not something you should be ashamed of.'

'But now he's dead. Now I need to fill in the blanks.'

He nodded. 'And you?' He turned to Karen. 'What is your interest?'

'Why can I not just be her friend, along for the ride? Along to support her?'

He smiled. 'You could be her friend, it's true. But I think you are a police officer.'

Karen was taken aback. She was accustomed to the cloak of invisibility granted to wee plump women with uninteresting wardrobes. People who weren't expecting a cop seldom picked up on her profession. 'What makes you say that?'

He pulled a rueful face. 'In this job, in this part of the world, you develop an instinct. You didn't tell me enough when you introduced yourself. And there's something in your eyes. A distance, maybe. And of course Novak told me Professor Blake said Mitja was murdered.' He smiled sadly. 'Besides, you didn't comfort her with a hug.'

Another bloody Sherlock Holmes. Just what the world needed. 'Well, since you've worked it out, you'll know that I need to know about the general because it's my job.'

Begovic laughed, a peal of genuine mirth. 'You came here looking for justice? Here? You think a single death matters to these people? After what happened here?'

Stung, Karen went straight for the jugular. 'Isn't that what your whole faith is based on? One single death among many? You of all people should know it matters. To someone who loved him, nothing matters more.'

The smile disappeared from his face as swiftly as if he'd been slapped. He looked over his shoulder at the crucifix then lowered his eyes. 'You're right.' He took a deep breath and lifted his head to meet Maggie's face, still frozen in shock at the exchange between priest and polis. 'I will tell you what I know. But I warn you, it's a bad, bad story.'

'I don't care,' Maggie said. 'I'm past all that. I've been so wrong already about who he was. All I want now is to know the truth.'

He settled himself in the chair, a solid black block, built to inspire confidence. Karen was still reserving judgement. In her head, all organised religions were elaborate con tricks. Unlike Maggie, she wasn't convinced she could rely on a priest for truth.

'I offered English lessons in the village. Mitja was clever and full of big ideas. So was his friend Rado. A couple of the others started out with them, but they didn't stay long. But those two? Always a competition, to see who was best. But Rado moved away with his family when they were teenagers and Mitja was left without a rival.'

He smiled fondly at the memory. 'It was maybe just as well. Because a new competition had started up between them. The type that spoils friendship. It was a girl, of course. Jablanka Pusic. She was a pretty girl. Very demure and, I think, kind. Not as smart as the boys, but she was the only girl of the same age in the village and they were both in love with her. So when Rado left, Jablanka and Mitja became a couple.'

He sighed. 'He was very clever, very talented. His parents saw that and looked to me to help him. I told him to enrol in the university in Zagreb, not Belgrade. I thought he would be more at home among Croats. And I hoped that he would find a girl who was a match for him.' He looked Maggie in the eye again. 'But if you know him, you know he was someone who struggled to break his word. And he had made promises to Jablanka. They were married the summer after

345

his first year at university and by the time he graduated he was the father of twin sons.'

Karen was impressed by how well Maggie was reacting. Her arms were wrapped around her body, as if they were literally holding her together. But her face was calm and when she spoke, her voice was under control. 'What are their names? His sons?'

The priest appeared momentarily uncomprehending.

'What are his sons called?' Maggie tried another form of words.

He drew in a sharp breath, his shoulders rising. 'I christened them Paskal and Poldo.'

'Where are they now?' Maggie asked.

The priest looked helplessly at Karen. She knew the answer, but she wasn't about to let him off the hook. 'After university, Mitja joined the army,' he said, veering away from the question. 'Jablanka stayed here. It was easier for her to raise the children with her family to support her. Besides, Mitja was never based in one place for long. At first, he came back often. As much as he could, I think. But time went by and his job became more important. He was doing the kind of things he couldn't talk about to anyone, not even me, he came back less often. And then his parents died within a few months of each other, so there was even less reason to be here.' He stared at his hands, knobbly with arthritis, folded over each other on his stick. 'Sometimes couples grow in different directions. But Mitja loved his boys. So when he did come back, he spent his time with them. Out in the hills or playing football or watching American movies that somehow he could always get his hands on.' He blinked hard at the recollection. 'He loved his boys.'

Maggie stared straight ahead, eyes holding images only she could see in a thousand-yard stare. 'He never mentioned them to me. Not once.'

'It was probably the only way he could deal with it,' Karen said. 'Compartmentalise.'

'And then the war came. Mitja was trapped in Dubrovnik and he met you.' He squeezed out a crooked smile. 'He told me about you. The last time he was here. He said he had finally met the woman I had wanted him to find at the university. The woman who was a match for him.'

Maggie looked as if she might burst into tears. 'He said that?'

The priest nodded, but it was clear to Karen he took no pleasure in the moment. 'You went back to Oxford after the siege was over and he made his plans. To come back here, to tell Jablanka it was over between them. That he wanted a divorce.'

'What did she say? How did she react?'

The priest closed his eyes for a moment. It might have been prayer, it might just have been escape. Then he stared dully at the floor. 'Like I said. The war came. It came right here.'

33

Karen could see a slow dawning behind Maggie's eyes. She was finally joining up the dots and it was a terrible reckoning. 'What happened?' Karen was not prepared to give any quarter.

'Mitja was very good at his job,' the priest said. He seemed to be ageing before their eyes. He cleared his throat and swallowed hard. 'The Serbs believed in punishing the places their most dangerous opponents came from. They wanted to make them mad with grief so they were not as good soldiers.' He was turning in on himself, looking inwards, not outwards.

'It was a bitterly cold day,' he said. 'There was a little snow on the ground, on the trees, on the roofs. The light was starting to fade when they arrived. Three Land Rover patrol vehicles. A detachment of JNA soldiers, their faces covered with balaclavas. They drove into the centre of the village and started rounding everyone up.' He paused to gather his words.

'There had been a lot of massacres by then. They didn't all make headlines, but we'd heard about them. Villages, towns, sometimes just a family farm. They thought it would be the men. That they'd be herded into a barn or a field then shot. People were sobbing, the soldiers were dragging everyone out of their houses. Then a truck arrived. The soldiers made everyone climb into the truck then they drove a couple of kilometres down the road. There's a meadow. They drove to the far side and forced all the children out of the truck. The mothers were screaming, the fathers were screaming, the children too. They left the children there with half a dozen soldiers to keep them penned together. Fourteen of them. The oldest were eleven, the youngest was only eighteen months old.

'They drove back across the field and parked the truck in sight of the children. All the adults thought they were going to be shot in front of their own children and grandchildren. But it was worse than that. Much worse.

'The man in charge of the soldiers, he shouted at the adults to shut up. And then he said, "This is for Dimitar Petrovic. He is the enemy of my people." And then he waved to the soldiers on the other side of the meadow. "My men are telling your children to run to Mummy," he told them. And that's just what the children began to do. A couple of the older ones picked up the toddlers and ran with them.

Stumbling through the snow, desperate to get back to their mothers.' His voice cracked. The two women sat like stones, scarcely breathing.

'Then the soldiers opened fire. They used the children's heads for target practice. Scarlet on white. Explosions of blood on the snow.' Tears were leaking from the corners of his eyes. 'They were good shots. The children's bodies were mostly untouched. Perfect. Their heads – that was a different story. Pray you never see a child's head after it's been hit by a rifle bullet.'

There was a long silence. Then the priest spoke again. 'That's where Paskal and Poldo are. In that meadow, with their twelve friends.'

Karen wanted to smash something. Or worse. 'What happened to Jablanka?'

Begovic ran a hand over his face, as if he was washing it. 'The soldiers made everyone stay in the truck then drove them back to the village. They stood around laughing at the sight of everyone screaming and running down the road to the meadow.

'I'd left Belgrade by then, but I was visiting a colleague in Lipovac. I got a call late that night and I came straight here. I've never seen grief like it. People were falling apart. Most people had lost a relative but what the whole village had lost was its future. Jablanka was taking the weight of it all on her shoulders. She kept saying it was her fault for marrying Mitja, that she should have let him go free when he went to

Zagreb, then none of this would have happened. I sat with her for a while. Talking and praying. And she seemed calmer when I left.'

His shoulders slumped. 'In the morning, her sister found her dead. She'd hanged herself from the roof with two leather belts belonging to her sons.'

No wonder he never talked about his past. Karen had heard some harrowing stories in her time, but nothing as bad as this. 'How come this story never got out? I know you said not all of the massacres made it into the press, but this would have been front-page news. Like Srebrenica.'

'We didn't talk about it,' the priest said. 'Not to outsiders.'

'You didn't talk about it?' Karen was incredulous. How could you let an atrocity like that go past unmarked? How could you not shout it from the rooftops? Buttonhole every journalist in the Western world?

'We didn't have to,' he said. 'Not after what Mitja did.'

351

And so I was banished. That's what it felt like, anyway. An overcrowded fishing boat up the coast to Trieste then a long cramped train journey back to the UK. It was only when I set foot on Italian soil that I understood how stressed I'd been for the past three months. Tiredness hit me like a wall and, although I was convinced I was so sad I would never sleep again, I think I was virtually unconscious from Trieste to London.

I got back to Oxford late on a cold, foggy January afternoon. I don't know quite what I was expecting, but what I got was mostly a blank indifference. A war? How quaint. Now, about your teaching supervisions ... Melissa was fascinated, of course, but I realised that was more to do with getting her name on my subsequent publications as a joint author. I understood properly for the first time how very insular academics can become. I made my mind up that I was never going to let that happen to me. It's the main reason why I make sure I cram as much travel as possible into my working life and why I fight for research projects that give me a proper window into other people's worlds.

However, I didn't have time to brood back then over the lack of interest at Schollie's High Table in my Dubrovnik adventure, as one of the more senior fellows described it. I had DPhil supervision meetings to conduct and a first-year class to run on Imagining Geopolitics; I had papers to propose and, I thought, a book to write about the relationship between the fall of communism and the expansion of geopolitical thinking; I had to raise awareness and funds to help my friends back in Dubrovnik; and every night, I had to write to Mitja.

It's hard to imagine now, but in 1992 email coverage was patchy, slow and unpredictable. So I wrote him old-fashioned letters. He'd told me where to send them – 'They can always find me,' he'd said. 'I'm not allowed to be out of touch for more than a few hours, not ever.' I numbered them in the top left-hand corner of the envelope so he could read them in the correct order, but also so that he could be sure none had gone missing. Neither of us really trusted the authorities to allow us completely free communication.

His letters to me arrived sporadically. I'd go for a whole agonised week without a word, then five or six would arrive together, sometimes showing signs of having been ill-treated at the very least. Sometimes the envelope would contain only a few scribbled sentences at an angle on the page, a clear sign of late nights and poor light. Other times, there would be half a dozen sheets of tight script, giving a detailed account of the aftermath of some atrocity or a description of a particular landscape or a plan for us to have a day out in the mountains when the Balkans stopped tearing themselves to pieces.

I cherished the letters equally. What they represented was the totality of our relationship. We were more than just sex; we were laughter, we were intellectual curiosity, we were political opinions, we were engagement with the landscape. We were the future, not the past. I held those thoughts and feelings close to me. They were my only comfort when being without him became too hard to bear.

Which was most days, if I'm honest. His absence was like the enervating thrum of machinery just on the threshold of hearing, a vibration that wears down your resistance till you understand you would commit an act of violence to make it stop. I slept badly and I suspect I wasn't the world's best thesis supervisor. My mind, like my heart, was elsewhere.

By now, news was filtering out of the shocking extent of the massacres that had been happening with a numbing regularity since the JNA had started their full-scale war against Croatia. It seemed that not a week had gone by without another bloodbath in some small community or town. I'd heard a little of this from Mitja, but I don't think even he grasped at the time the full extent of the carnage that had been carried out against his fellow countrymen.

I knew from his letters that hospitals and clinics were desperate for supplies. So I decided that as soon as term was over, I was going to drive an ambulance loaded to the roof with medical necessities to Croatia. This wasn't just about my love life, it was about my humanity. I managed to track down an ambulance that was being taken out of service in the West Country, so Tessa and I caught a bus down to Plymouth and drove back in the rickety old vehicle. Tessa knew a mechanic who agreed to restore the engine, and I set about filling it.

We went round every Oxford college, talking to Junior Common Room meetings, to college fellows drinking port after dinner, to sports societies and dining clubs. Anyone who'd listen, really. I contacted pharmaceutical companies and persuaded those of my colleagues who taught medics to pump their contacts for anything they could get their hands on. By the time the Easter vac began, we had an ambulance crammed with medicines, dressings and all the paraphernalia that went with them. We were like a hospital pharmacy on wheels. Tessa's friend had persuaded one of his mates to repaint the ambulance with giant red crosses on every panel, just to drive home the point that we were on a mission of mercy.

I didn't tell Mitja what we'd done. He knew I was coming, knew Tessa and I were arriving by road. We'd arranged to meet in Pula, in the north, near the Slovenian border, almost as far away from the war zone as it was possible to be. He gave us directions to a little restaurant on the edge of the strip down by the port. 'It's easy to find,' he wrote. 'And they have space for car parking beside it.'

We'd had one or two sticky moments on the way with border officials wondering what we were up to. But nothing we couldn't bluff our way through. And finally, we were driving down the coast to Pula, singing at the tops of our voices.

Mitja was right, it was easy to find the restaurant. And my heart jumped when I spotted him sitting at a pavement table. He glanced up when he saw the ambulance then looked away. Then looked again, realising it was a right-hand drive with British plates. And then he understood what he was seeing. He jumped to his feet and ran across the street towards us, his face split open in a grin of pure delight.

That's how I'll remember him. Running towards me, arms wide, hair blowing back from his forehead, laughing like he hadn't a care in the world. Everyone should carry a memory like that.

Sometimes it's the only thing that keeps us going.

34

Macanespie rubbed his smarting eyes and blinked hard. He'd been staring into his computer screen for so long his very brain felt pixelated. He'd repeatedly watched the footage from the two cameras going back seven days and he was no longer sure whether he could trust himself. One thing was certain, though. He trusted himself more than he trusted Theo Proctor, whose resentment levels had risen in tandem with Macanespie's enthusiasm.

While the Scot had been scanning the footage with infinitesimal care, his colleague had been sending emails and making phone calls to the officers investigating the other murders in their putative sequence. First he had to explain the reason for his interest – the half-truth that new information had come to light connecting that particular killing with other similar cases. Then he had to find a detective who had worked the case and could remember anything about it. Then he had to persuade them to unearth any relevant CCTV footage from the evidence lockers and forward those images to Macanespie and Proctor. It was a task that demanded diplomacy and patience, which was normally Proctor's forte. But it was obvious that he was growing weary of playing the supplicant. There would be an explosion eventually, Macanespie knew.

Until then, he'd keep his head down. Every so often he would spot something that merited a second look. He'd put together a folder of images that he planned to return to when he finished his slow crawl through the footage. Which he reckoned would be any minute now. The last jerky frames passed across his screen, and he was done.

He went back to the shots he'd selected and clicked through them, checking whether what he thought he'd seen was real or illusory. On the first pass he discarded a couple. On the second pass, he discounted another. That left him with half a dozen screen grabs. He sent them to the colour printer down the hall, which gave him an excuse to go walkabout. He picked up the printed sheets and headed for the cafeteria, where he settled in at a corner table with a can of Coke and a packet of chocolate buttons. He spread the printouts across the table and ruminated as he popped the buttons one after the other into his mouth.

When he finished the chocolates, Macanespie shuffled the papers together and marched back to his office. 'Look at this,' he said as soon as he crossed the threshold. Proctor glared at him and gestured pointedly at the phone held to his ear. Unabashed, Macanespie laid the screenshots out across his desk and waited.

'I'll look forward to seeing that,' Proctor said. 'Yes, thank you.' He dropped the phone back into its cradle. 'Couldn't you see I was on the phone?' he grumbled. But still he got to his feet and came over to look at Macanespie's desk. 'What am I looking at?'

The Scot pointed to the first three shots. 'Wednesday evening. I focused on the woman, but in each of those shots, Simunovic has just gone past. The next three are Thursday evening. Same thing. What do you think?'

Proctor peered hard at the pictures. 'Wednesday she's got a floppy hat and sunglasses. Thursday she's got a different big hat and different sunglasses and a scarf round her neck. Every time she's wearing baggy clothes so you can't see what size or shape she is. If it's the same woman, she doesn't want to be recognised.'

'My thoughts exactly,' Macanespie said triumphantly. 'A heavily disguised woman on three consecutive nights, following a man who gets murdered on the third night. That's hard to swallow as a coincidence.'

'If it's the same woman,' Proctor said. He looked more closely. 'If it's a woman at all, Alan. Like you said before, it could easily be a bloke under all that.'

Macanespie grunted. 'He'd have to be pretty slim.'

'Yes, well, we're not all built like you. But seriously, under all that floaty material it could be.'

Macanespie nodded. 'It's an outside possibility, I suppose. But if it's a woman, it's more likely she's the spotter, not the killer.'

'So what are you going to do about it?'

Macanespie gathered the pages together again. 'I'm going to print out some stills from the first lot of film, then I'm going to see Cagney. Apparently he's in the building. He needs to see there's some proper work going on here.' He leaned across his desk and summoned up the stills from the footage they'd first seen in Crete then sent them to the printer. He made for the door and seemed surprised to find Proctor at his heels. 'Don't you have phone calls to make?' he said.

'You're not leaving me out in the cold on this,' Proctor said. 'We're in it together. Don't be an arse.'

Macanespie shook his head but made no further effort to shake off his colleague. He hustled down the hallways and up the escalator to the meeting room where Cagney set up temporary camp when he visited. There was no gatekeeper; Macanespie simply knocked and was invited to enter.

Cagney sat alone at the meeting table, his suit jacket draped over an empty chair. His cuffs were rolled back and his laptop was open in front of him. 'A delegation,' he said with an ironic raise of his eyebrows.

'We think we might have something,' Macanespie said without preamble. He spread the pages out on the table in front of himself, forcing Cagney to get up and join them.

'And this is?' he said, casting an eye over the photos.

'We think it's the same person on three consecutive nights. She – or possibly he – is about five or six yards behind Miroslav Simunovic every time. That close looks like a tail. Nobody else fits the bill. If that's not the killer, it's the spotter, I'd say.' Macanespie took a step backwards and gestured expansively at his work.

'Interesting,' Cagney said. He glanced at Macanespie, his lips twisted in what might have been a smile. 'But not exactly an image we can put out on *Crimewatch*. What's your next angle of approach?'

'We're gathering other CCTV footage. We'll be checking it very carefully to see whether the same person reappears. And eventually we'll get lucky,' Macanespie said confidently.

'I prefer not to rely on luck.' Cagney stepped away from the table and returned to his seat. 'But we're not without resources. No reason why you should be up to speed with the cutting edge of digital forensics, but I think there are ways to improve on what you've got here. There are programs that can amalgamate images such as these and actually offer predictive suggestions of what the undisguised face might look like. They can figure out height, certainly, and maybe give us a definitive assessment on gender.' He nodded slowly. 'I didn't think you had it in you. So carry on proving me wrong. Find me some more images that we can feed into the program. Email me everything you have.' And then he turned back to his screen.

Out in the hallway, they grinned at each other and high-fived. 'We're back,' Proctor crowed.

Macanespie punched him on the shoulder. 'Aye, and this time, it's personal. Come on, Theo. Time to *cherchez la femme*.'

'Or *l'homme*. Don't forget, it might be a skinny little guy.'

'Whatever. It's time to *cherchez*.'

35

Maggie could hardly bring herself to ask the question. But she couldn't bear ignorance either. 'What did Mitja do?' she whispered.

'What we always do round here.' The priest's voice was strong and bitter. He banged his stick on the ground.

'Revenge,' Karen said. 'An eye for an eye.'

He nodded. 'We like the jealous God of the Old Testament here.'

'So what did Mitja actually do?' Karen prompted him when it seemed he had no plans to continue.

'He arrived two days later, distraught. Nobody blamed him for what had happened. Nobody but himself. He was ashamed that he had been so wrapped up in himself that he hadn't thought about sending Jablanka and the boys to a safer place. He was angry that he hadn't arranged protection for his village when he knew he was a thorn in the side of his enemies. And he was guilty because he'd fallen in love with you, Professor. As if that had somehow kept him from taking care of his family. He spoke of never seeing you again, of taking that as a punishment. I sat up with him all night, persuading him that to give up love would be to give the victory to the evil men who had done this. In the end, I convinced him. Obviously.'

'Thank you,' Maggie said, her voice shaky.

Begovic inclined his head in acknowledgement. 'He stayed for a day or two and then he went back to his unit. He was burning with rage. I knew he could not let it pass.'

'You can't exactly blame him,' Karen said.

'I don't blame him. I pity him his pain and his shame,' Begovic said. 'But I know I could not have stopped him.'

'What happened?' Karen asked.

'He was in intelligence. He knew how to find out who was responsible for what happened here. He was also a popular officer. There were men who would follow him to hell and back and never stop to ask why. When he was certain he knew who led the raiding party here, he waited until the man's family were celebrating a wedding. With a dozen of his most loyal men, he came to the church. They barricaded the doors and threw burning torches and petrol bombs through the windows. Anyone who tried to escape through the windows was shot. They killed forty-seven people that day.'

'Oh my God,' Karen groaned. 'That's hellish.'

'Yes. But the next time I saw him, he said, "It ends here. There's nobody left alive to carry it on." And I thought he was right. He lived through the rest of the war unharmed. He went to live with you in Oxford, Professor. He would not have risked your life if he'd thought someone would be coming after him for vengeance. He's had years of living without looking over his shoulder. But now, at last, his past has caught up with him.'

'Not exactly,' Karen said.

Begovic frowned. 'But why else are you here, officer? The professor said Mitja had been murdered.'

'He has indeed been murdered,' Karen said. 'But it wasn't recent. His body has only just come to light. He actually died about eight years ago.'

The priest frowned. 'I don't understand.' He turned to Maggie. 'You did nothing about this? Had he left you? Was your marriage over?'

Maggie shook her head. 'I spent eight years thinking that's what had happened. But he didn't leave me. He was taken from me. Murdered. By someone he knew back in the Balkans. I didn't know that, though. I thought he'd abandoned me because he couldn't bear to be without the past he'd given up for me. I was so, so wrong.'

'And all that time he was lying dead.' The priest shook his head in weary resignation. 'Well, whoever killed him, it must have been one of the Serbs. Perhaps someone who was a young child and grew up with a heart full of hatred. So, still it goes on—'

His homily was interrupted by the ringing of Karen's phone. 'I'm sorry, I have to take this,' she said, getting to her feet and walking away down the nave. When she was out of earshot, she said, 'OK, Jason. What have you got for me?'

'We found the hotel,' he said.

'What? Tamsin what's-her-name came up with the goods?'

'No, boss. Good old-fashioned coppering. It was your Phil that suggested it. I ran into him in the canteen in Kirkcaldy nick. I got a photo of the key-card and made a list of hotels and guest houses. I started with the ones nearest the John Drummond and spread out from there. I phoned round to eliminate the ones that didn't have red key-cards and then I went on the knocker. Bingo.'

Karen was impressed in spite of herself. The Mint wasn't quite smart enough to claim credit for himself – or maybe he was just smart enough to realise Phil would likely tell her what he'd recommended. Either way, it was a step in the right direction. 'What have you got?' she asked.

'It's a guest house near Murrayfield. The room was registered in his name, Dimitar Petrovic. He booked in for two nights and he paid in cash. There were sixteen other rooms occupied that night. Some of them paid by cash. It's not that dear.'

'Have you got a printout of the names and addresses of all the other punters?'

She could almost hear the beaming smile. 'I've got copies of all of it,' the Mint said proudly.

'Well done. Do me a favour and email it to me. I'll take a look at it as soon as I can. Maybe see if Professor Blake recognises any of the names.'

'Right you are, boss. Because, after all, somebody on that list is likely a murderer, right? And we are so going to nail him.'

36

The priest's story shocked Maggie so much she could barely take it in. Her first response had been on automatic pilot, answering questions that seemed to have shrivelled to insignificance in the face of the enormity that had just been revealed. The ringing of Karen's phone shattered her brittle surface and her emotions started to engage.

'I don't believe it,' she said feverishly. 'He's been blamed for something somebody else did.' It was unthinkable. The man she had known, the man she had loved for more than twenty years . . . that man could never have done what this crazy old priest was accusing him of.

Father Begovic gave her a pitying look. 'My child, I understand why you want to believe that. But there's no escape from the truth. Mitja was responsible for those deaths. He was mad with grief. You must have seen the change in him yourself when you returned in the spring.'

Maggie's head came up, her eyes defiant. 'Yes, I saw a change in him. He was under huge strain. He hardly slept. He hardly ate. He was enduring the pain of seeing his country under attack, his people being massacred and turned into refugees in their own land. He was suffering. But he hadn't turned into the kind of monster who would orchestrate mass murder at somebody's wedding. You're wrong, Father. There's been a mistake.'

'No mistake, Professor. I am profoundly sorry for your pain. But we all have to face dark truths sometimes. And the dark truth about Mitja is that under the veneer he got from his education and his time with you in Oxford, he was as savage, brutal and full of revenge as all the generations of his ancestors.'

'No,' Maggie said desperately, her voice rising. 'I won't believe it. He was a gentle man. He was always sensitive to what other people needed. Open-minded. Open-hearted. Not the monster you're talking about. Where's your proof? How could a man like him, with his high profile in the Croatian Army, with NATO, with the UN – how could he get away with something like this with no comeback? It doesn't make sense. The Serbs were always so sensitive about being por-trayed as the bad guys, they'd have been all over an incident like this, making propaganda while the sun shines. A Croatian general leading a massacre? It would have been a gift-wrapped sensation for them.'

'I don't know. Perhaps because it was personal, and that

was something they understood? Perhaps because they couldn't complain about what Mitja did without admitting what they did first? Or perhaps because there was no evidence and, like you, nobody would have been willing to believe that the educated, civilised General Petrovic could do such a thing.' There was a sting in Begovic's voice and Maggie realised that he too was hurting at the thought that the man he'd helped to create had been capable of so terrible an act.

'Still, it's hard to believe nobody talked.'

The priest frowned. 'But they did. Not at the time, true, but a few years ago. A man and a woman came here. They were following up a report of the massacre from the Serbian end.'

'What? Were they journalists?'

He shook his head. 'No, some kind of investigators. I think they had something to do with the war crimes tribunal. I didn't inquire too closely. I thought it was best to seem indifferent. As if there was nothing around here that could possibly interest them.'

'Didn't they notice the memorial? Surely that would have been a bloody big clue that something very bad happened here?' Maggie's pain was starting to manifest itself as anger, but she didn't care. She wanted answers more than she wanted this old man's good opinion of her.

'The memorial was not there. We erected it only two years ago, to mark twenty years since the deaths. We talked about it for a long time, but we were not ready before. So when

370

they came, there was nothing to see.' Again, he rubbed his hand over his face as if washing it. 'We carried our hurt on the inside.'

'These people, did they have names? A nationality?'

He shook his head, defeated. 'I don't remember the names. It's a long time ago and we were deliberately trying not to talk. As to nationality – I think she was British. She spoke English as if it was her native tongue. But definitely not an American or a Canadian. He was some kind of Scandinavian. But it doesn't matter. Nothing came of it. It was little more than a rumour, he admitted as much to me. They didn't have any eyewitnesses and they didn't have any specific accusations against any individuals.'

'So why did they come here, if there were no specific accusations? This is a tiny village in the middle of nowhere. What brought them to your door?'

'The rumour said that the killers came from this village. Well, it was obvious to them when they saw the place that we didn't have enough men for a raiding party. That this was not some armed outpost of the Croatian guerrilla movement. And they didn't ask about Mitja by name. They interviewed me, and a few other villagers. None of us mentioned Mitja and they went away none the wiser. So by the time anybody said anything, it was ancient history and nothing came of it.'

'Something came of it,' Maggie said angrily. 'Because Mitja's dead.' And if all this was true, a small voice inside her said, she might just be relieved.

There are few places as beautiful as the Balkans in spring. Fruit trees in blossom, meadows carpeted with wild flowers, trees in leaf a hundred shades of green. Back in the early nineties, it was still common to see carts drawn by horses. Men with rolled-up shirtsleeves drove tractors that had the antique look of children's toys, and I can remember occasionally even seeing oxen pulling ploughs. Women worked the fields, heads covered in bright scarves. Civil war was raging throughout Croatia, but depending on where you were, you could go for days without noticing. So it was that first time Tessa and I returned.

When people think about war, they imagine whole countries consumed by conflict. The truth is that the battle lines are drawn patchily. Strategic targets are chosen and focused on. Particular towns are bombed and besieged while just a few miles down the road, life stumbles on in an approximation of normality. What else are you supposed to do if they're not actually shooting at you, after all? We have an astonishing capacity for keeping our heads down and just getting on with things.

Of course, beneath the surface, life was far from normal. Everyone was living in a state of anxiety. Would their town be next? Would some JNA commander decide their menfolk were too dangerous to remain alive? Was this the time to make a break for it and head for those distant cousins in Slovenia or Albania?

Those were the conversations I wanted to be part of. When his military responsibilities claimed Mitja, which was more often than not, I spent my days finding people I could interview. I didn't have a clear idea what I would ultimately write about the region, not least because I had no idea how bloody and brutal the next few years would become. But I knew I wanted to record as much front-line testimony as I could so that, when I did come to write, I would have a thorough spread of research materials.

It wasn't always easy to conduct these interviews. The first problem was the language barrier. Even after three months in Dubrovnik, my Serbo-Croat wasn't really good enough for discussing abstract concepts. I could comfortably hold conversations about the day-to-day, so without an interpreter, I was limited in terms of what I could ask. Paradoxically, I think now that this turned out to be a positive thing. The work I ended up doing on the region and its wars is completely underpinned by the experiences of the local populations; it is rooted, as human geography should be, in an embodiment of the conflict.

The second problem I had was persuading people to talk to me. I grew up in a country with a small population – there are just over five million Scots – so I understand what a friend of mine calls 'half a degree of separation'. Everybody appears to be connected to each other. In Croatia, with its four million, that phenomenon is even more pronounced. It seemed as if everyone knew who Mitja was, and my relationship to him. That made some people eager to talk to me; but for others, it was a very good reason to avoid any kind of communication. But I knew I had to persuade the unwilling. If I didn't cover the spectrum of experience and opinion, I couldn't hope to produce work of any value.

It was a challenge and I was glad of that because it meant I wasn't spending my time pining for Mitja's company. I knew he had an important job to do, even if he couldn't tell me what it was most of the time, and I didn't want to be the kind of pathetic camp follower who sits at home twiddling her thumbs. When we could be together, it was all the richer because my work meant at least one of us could talk about what we'd been doing all day. God knows he needed something to take his mind off the constant jockeying for power on both sides of the battle lines. When I look back at that period, I have no idea how anyone kept track of the shifting sands of power and loyalties on either side. Somehow, Mitja held all that in his head.

All that and more. Not only did he have to stay on top of what was happening. He also had to develop the intel to help his commanders create a strategy for survival for their country. He couldn't go anywhere without bodyguards. We met in hotel rooms then, and whenever he came to me, there were always men with submachine guns on guard at either end of the corridor. If it had been up to them, they'd have been stationed on the threshold of the room. But that was where I put my foot down. Even generals are entitled to some privacy.

Later, he wrote me a letter explaining that those moments snatched with me were what kept him sane. 'I could see the guys around me starting to lose their grip. They'd been removed from any kind of normality for so long they'd forgotten the reality of what we were fighting for. All they had to cling to was the ideology. And that way you lose your humanity. You become the beast you're fighting. You saved me from that. And because you saved me, I learned what would preserve and protect my guys. Although they didn't want to leave the front, I made them take time away from the war. I sent them back to their families whenever I could. I think that's part of the reason we were able to hang on against the overwhelming odds.'

I'm proud of that now. At the time, I sometimes felt guilty that I was taking him away from what he should be doing. But not guilty enough to give him up. I remember one magical day in particular. Tessa and I were due to leave for Oxford the next morning, and somehow Mitja had managed to squeeze a whole afternoon away. We'd come down from Zagreb to Stari Grad a few days before and he surprised us by turning up in a Land Rover. His bodyguards kept a discreet distance while we drove to the Velika Paklenica canyon nearby. 'We're going up the Anika Kuk,' he told us. 'It has the hardest climbing routes in all of Croatia.' He must have seen the horror on my face for he burst out laughing.

'Don't worry,' he said. 'We're not doing the rock climb. I know you don't climb. There's a walkers' path to the summit, we're going up that way.'

'Some other time,' Tessa said. 'We'll come back when the war is over, Mitja, and you can take me up the rock.'

'That's a deal,' he said. 'But all we're doing today is enjoying the scenery.'

It was the perfect day for it. Clear and sunny, but cool and crisp too. We started up the canyon, towering cliffs looming over us. Sometimes looking up at the overhangs was almost as vertiginous as looking down from a summit. We climbed steadily upwards, the wide path cutting up the steep mountainside in a series of zigzags. When we came to tumultuous streams tumbling over rocks and boulders, there were bridges to take us safely across. Although the scenery was wild, the terrain had been tamed for us.

Or so I thought till we reached the final section, a steep scramble over broken cliffs and promontories. By the time we struggled to the summit I was exhausted, my thighs trembling with the effort. Mitja and Tessa both burst out laughing when I collapsed on my back, groaning, too knackered to appreciate the stunning views down the mountain and across to the coast. I was saved by the contents of the rucksack Mitja had been carrying – water, salami, cheese, bread, olives and apples. Water never tasted so good.

After we'd eaten, Tessa set off ahead of us on the descent. Mitja and I sat on a chunk of rock, leaning into each other, talking about a future together. A future we imagined would arrive a lot sooner than it did.

37

Karen replaced her phone in her pocket and checked out Maggie and the priest. It looked like the conversation had gone downhill after she'd butted out. Maggie was on her feet now, edging into the aisle and away from Father Begovic. Karen took a few steps towards them, but Maggie met her halfway. 'We're done here,' she said. 'Whoever killed Mitja, the answer isn't here.'

Karen was inclined to agree with her. The conversation with the priest had recast everything in a new light. Petrovic as avenging angel, as war criminal – that was a very different picture from the patriotic hero and supporter of the peace-keeping NATO and UN forces that she'd been fed previously. And it was equally clear that it was as much a surprise to his widow as it was to Karen herself. How would that feel, she wondered. To discover that the man you loved, the man whose memory you cherished, was soaked in the blood of innocent people? How did you even start to integrate those contradictions?

'Did he have anything else to say?' Karen asked. 'Like evidence? Like how this whole thing stayed buried all these years?' She had to speed up to keep pace with Maggie.

They were at the car before Maggie replied. She fastened her seat belt and said, 'It stayed under the radar because it was personal. In the twisted calculus of death they use here, you don't have to report a war crime if it arose from family circumstances rather than the furtherance of war.'

The perversity of human illogic never ceased to amaze Karen. 'Tell me you just made that up.'

'I wish.' She buried her face in her hands. Karen waited, understanding that it would be a bad move to start the engine and drive off. She didn't think Maggie was actually crying, so thankfully she wasn't going to have to go into compassionate mode when what she really wanted to do was to interrogate the professor.

At length, Maggie raised her head and sighed. 'Apparently word seeped out about eight years ago. A rumour from the Serb side. An investigator turned up and started asking questions. She didn't know Mitja's name and of course nobody told her. She could see this wasn't exactly an armoured compound of highly trained and heavily armed guerrilla fighters so she accepted there had been a mistake and left.'

Karen snorted. 'Not much of an investigator, then. Did she not notice the graveyard on the way up the hill?'

'The priest says that was only built a couple of years ago.'

'Eight years ago, you said? So she was here before Mitja was killed?'

'Yes.'

Karen could feel the pieces falling into place in her head. 'So somebody was talking.' She started the engine and turned the car around. Again, people materialised as if by magic, watching them leave as stony-faced as they'd watched them arrive. 'Somebody was saying the words "massacre" and "Podruvec" in the same sentence.'

'For all the difference it made. If Father Begovic is right, what happened is that one of the children of the victims grew old enough to carry on the feud to the next generation.'

Karen pondered that for a moment. 'I don't think so,' she said. They rounded the bend and confronted the graves again. 'Because—'

'Please, pull over,' Maggie said urgently.

Karen drew alongside the grass verge and killed the engine. 'I want to see his boys,' Maggie said. She got out and walked across to the memorial, head bowed. Karen followed a few steps behind.

At the plinth, Maggie scrutinised the photographs more closely than she had before. About halfway round, two photographs sat next to each other. Two boys, barely distinguishable one from the other. Cheeky grins, laughing eyes, a matching rumple of black hair. They had a sparkiness that reminded Karen of Phil's nephew and made her think they'd have been a handful.

'They look like him,' Maggie said, her voice cracking. 'He never wanted kids. Which suited me, because I didn't either. Stupid woman that I am, I thought our reasons were the same. That we were sufficient for each other. That we had plans enough for ourselves, just the two of us. Not this. Not that he didn't want kids because he couldn't face the prospect of that much pain a second time.'

Karen couldn't think of a single thing to say that wasn't banal. So she took another step forward and put an arm round Maggie's tight shoulders.

'How did he bear it?' Maggie said softly. 'How did he manage to carry that burden alone? Worse, how did I not notice? What kind of partner was I, not to see his pain?'

'He chose not to let you see it, Maggie. And from the sounds of it, he was a man who knew his own mind. If you hadn't been such a rock for him, he probably wouldn't have got through it as well as he did.' It wasn't much of a consolation but it was better than nothing, Karen reckoned. Years of death knocks had made her proficient at 'better than nothing'.

'I can't take it in,' Maggie said. She patted Karen's hand then slipped away from her, taking a last look around before she walked back to the car.

They set off in silence. A few kilometres down the road, Maggie said, 'What were you going to say when I asked you to stop? You said you didn't think Mitja was killed by a member of the family he killed. Why?'

'For one thing, Begovic was quite clear that Mitja said there would be no survivors to carry it on. And it was a wedding. You take babies and little kids to weddings as a matter of course. To believe his theory, you'd have to believe that there was a kid who survived somehow and that whoever brought the kid up also knew enough about the massacre to provoke the kid into taking revenge. Now, if they cared that much, why wait all that time? Why not just deal with it long before?'

'Because it would be the kid's vendetta, not yours. That matters, believe it or not. And because this is a region that invented the notion that revenge is a dish best eaten cold. There's a school of thought that says the whole 1991 Croatian war kicked off because the Serbs saw their chance to take revenge for what the Croats did to them fifty years before. Round here, they still argue about whether they were better off under the Austro-Hungarian empire or the Ottomans. Trust me, waiting sixteen years to get your own back is a blink of an eye for this lot.' Maggie's bitterness was evident; Karen couldn't help thinking she was enjoying a freedom of speech that being away from the university allowed her.

'OK. I'll bow to your superior knowledge. But there's something else that suggests to me that the general's murder wasn't a straightforward vendetta.'

'What's that?'

'I had a visit earlier this week from a couple of government officials. The kind that don't feel the need to explain exactly what they do or which department they really work for. Frankly, the kind you'd never tire of slapping. They showed up because my criminal records search for Dimitar Petrovic was flagged up on their system as being of interest.' Karen flashed a quick look at Maggie to see how she was taking this unexpected turn in the conversation.

'That's not really surprising. He was attached to NATO and the UN during the nineties. He briefed Foreign Office officials on occasion. The security services obviously kept a watching brief,' she said wearily.

'That wasn't why they were interested.'

'What do you mean?'

Karen pulled a face. 'I don't know how to say this without making you furious. But I'm going to tell you anyway because I need all the help I can get to find the person who killed your man.'

'I'm past fury, Karen. I haven't got anything left today. My tank is empty.'

'OK. The reason they wanted to know why I was interested in Mitja was that they thought he'd spent the last eight years operating as a kind of vigilante, hunting down war criminals and assassinating them.'

Maggie made a strange choking noise. Karen swiftly turned to check out that she was all right and was bewildered to see the professor was laughing.

'Oh, Jesus Christ,' Maggie spluttered. 'You have no idea how funny . . . ' She laughed again, almost a howl this time. There was nothing Karen could do but wait it out.

After a couple of minutes, Maggie recovered herself. 'I'm sorry,' she said. 'You must think I'm a madwoman. It just cracked me up, you coming out with that line so portentously. There's no way you could know this, but Tessa's been convinced of the very same thing for years now.'

'Tessa? Your lawyer Tessa?'

'Yes. She does a lot of work at The Hague for the international criminal court. She's worked on Rwanda, Kosovo . . . And other stuff. Anyway, according to her, after Mitja went missing, people started gossiping that he was behind this vigilante justice thing. I never believed it because I didn't think the man I knew was capable of such cold-blooded murder. But she said I was just being sentimental. What an irony.' She laughed again, but this time it was harsh and bitter. 'God, I wish she'd been right. Then at least he'd have still been alive.'

Karen sighed. 'I'm sorry. Anyway, they were taken aback when I told them the reason I was looking for info on Mitja. But in the light of what we learned today, it seems likely to me that he was a victim of this vigilante killer. Maybe even the first victim.'

'Oh God,' Maggie groaned. 'Today just goes on getting worse and worse. And presumably this killer was somebody he knew and trusted. Or else he'd never have gone climbing with them. I can't imagine what his last thoughts must have been like. The sickening betrayal of it. Everything he'd done, everything he'd been, reduced to that terrible moment.'

Karen forbore from mentioning the last moments of the Serbian clan at their family wedding. In the light of that, it was hard to have much sympathy for Mitja Petrovic. The single act that now defined him in her head didn't come into any category Karen recognised as heroism. But still, that didn't mean his killer got a free pass. The status of the victim wasn't supposed to have an impact on the hunt for their killer, in spite of the tendency of the media and even some cops to create a hierarchy of victimhood. It was a propensity that Karen deeply disapproved of. To her, the dead were equal when it came to dispensing justice. 'I'm going to catch him,' she said. 'The person who did this. I'm going to make him stand trial.'

'Won't you have to hand it over to the spooks?'

Karen shook her head. 'My house, my rules. He was killed in Scotland. It's my case.' She saw a roadside inn up ahead and pulled into the car park. 'We need to eat. And I have something I want you to look at.'

The interior was plain – wooden tables, padded stools and benches; a long zinc counter with a couple of beer taps and a boxy coffee machine that might have been state-of-the-art in the seventies. It smelled of pipe tobacco, thanks to the two elderly men playing backgammon and smoking fiercely by the empty fireplace. They barely glanced up as the two women entered and looked uncertainly about them. A short woman with hair pulled back in a tight ponytail appeared behind the bar like a jack in the box. She said something Karen didn't understand. Maggie replied and within a few sentences they were chatting like old friends. The exchange ended in smiles and nods and Maggie led Karen over to a table in the corner.

'We're having a bottle of the local Riesling, which is drier and fruitier than you'd expect. And a stew from whatever the landlord killed at the weekend. Probably rabbit and an assortment of game birds. With potatoes and bread,' Maggie said. 'There wasn't a lot of choice.'

'That's fine by me.'

'So what's this thing you wanted to show me?'

Karen took out her phone and opened the list of names that Jason had sent her. 'We've managed to track down the hotel Mitja had booked into in Edinburgh. We thought his climbing partner might be staying in the same place so we got hold of the list of fellow guests. None of them has an obviously foreign name.' She sighed. 'It's never that straight-forward. So we think either his companion was somebody he knew back then but wasn't necessarily from there, or else they were using an alias. Obviously, if it's an alias, chances are you're not going to recognise that. But if it is someone else from back then – a Brit or an American or a Canadian – you might just spot them.'

Maggie looked sceptical. 'It's a long shot, don't you think?'

'It's the only shot I've got right now.' She offered the phone to Maggie. 'You want to take a look?'

Maggie shrugged. 'After today, what else have I got to lose?' She reached for the phone and started to read the names. Her face was without expression as she scrolled down, shaking her head as she went. There was a moment where she blinked a few times in quick succession but she continued to shake her head. When she came to the end, she handed the phone back. 'I'm sorry. None of those names mean anything to me.'

Karen had seen some good liars in her time. At that precise moment she'd have put Professor Maggie Blake in the top three.

38

Four days of hustling and checking out grainy CCTV footage had left Alan Macanespie with a vicious pain behind his right eye and a mouth coated in the residue of endless cups of sour coffee. What kept him going was his newly awakened determination to show Wilson Cagney he wasn't a washed-up failure. He wasn't quite sure how his new boss had got under his skin. But he had.

His enthusiasm for the task hadn't rubbed off on Proctor, who seemed to be in the process of transferring his resentment against Cagney to his partner. Macanespie pinged a new set of stills across to the Welshman, who immediately grumbled.

'I'm going to need new glasses by the end of this job,' Proctor complained. 'What's this lot?'

'Number four. Tenerife. That's the last, I think. Unless there's more to come from your last round of hustling?'

'I've shot my bolt. There are several countries where I can no longer go on holiday for fear of being arrested at passport control.' It was a weak joke but at least it was an attempt at the humour that had formerly characterised many of their exchanges. Proctor stared at the screen. 'That's definitely a woman. You can see where the wind catches her top.' He pointed to slim shoulders and the definite outline of breasts and hip.

'I agree. I was pretty sure after Madeira, but I don't think there's any room for doubt.'

'Have you fed these through to the digital reconstruction woman?'

Macanespie nodded. 'I told her this was the last bit of data she was likely to have from us, so she can get cracking on an e-fit. Hopefully the twenty-three pics we've sent won't throw up too many contradictions.'

'Yes, because if those images are the spotter rather than the killer, they might not all be the same person.'

'See, when you die and go to heaven, you'll be spending all your time telling St Peter how they could improve the place. You're like a one-man weather system. Black clouds overhead.' Macanespie shook his head in disgust. 'I think it'll be interesting to see what she comes up with. I've never seen one of these predictive e-fits before. Wouldn't it be amazing if the printer spat out something and we all went, "Oh, it's her"?'

Proctor snorted. 'More likely we'll go, "Looks like Picasso

drew that one". Or, "Who knew Hillary Clinton was a serial killer?"'

Macanespie was saved from having to reply by the arrival of an email. 'Well, well, well, there's a turn-up for the books.'

'What?'

'An email from the lovely DCI Pirie. I wonder what she's got to say for herself?'

'If you open it, you'll save yourself from an early death from suspense.'

'Christ, you're a walking exemplar of Welsh humour,' Macanespie muttered, opening the email. As he read Karen's message, his expression grew increasingly incredulous. 'For fuck's sake,' he said. 'How the fuck did we not know this?'

'What?'

'Listen to this: "Dear Mr Macanespie, I'm just back from a trip to Croatia where I uncovered some information that I suspect you may not be privy to. In early 1992, a Serb detachment raided Dimitar Petrovic's home village, Podruvec. In an alleged reprisal attack for the effectiveness of General Petrovic's work, they massacred the children of the village, including General Petrovic's two sons. His wife subsequently hanged herself. You can confirm this with the village priest, Uros Begovic. Some time later, Petrovic identified the leader of the Serbs. He assembled a small but loyal group of soldiers and they carried out a revenge attack that wiped out the commander and forty-six members of his family." Forty-six? Christ, he didn't do things by halves, did he? "Rumours of this massacre were circulating about eight years ago. It seems possible therefore that Petrovic not only falls into the definition of 'war criminal' and may indeed have been a victim of vigilante justice and in spite of the disparity in murder methods, might be an early victim of the killer you're looking for. In which respect, had it occurred to you that the reason for the change in MO might be something as simple as the killer not having ready access to ammunition for his gun? I look forward to sharing the fruits of your investigation and suggest we meet again to discuss collaboration moving forward. Yours respectfully, blah blah." For fuck's sake. "Respectfully"? She's something else, that one.'

Proctor had the look of a man bemused. 'Petrovic led a massacre?'

'That's what she's saying. How in the name of God does one wee fat lassie nip across to Croatia for five minutes and dig up something the whole war crimes tribunal missed for years? Do you have any idea how Cagney is going to flay our arses for this?' Macanespie sunk his head in his hands, his shoulders slumped.

'This is not our responsibility,' Proctor insisted like a reflex. 'We can only investigate what's brought to our attention. You and me, we were never responsible for teasing out reports on the ground.'

Macanespie looked up, bleary-eyed. 'It's a bloody big one

to miss, considering we're supposed to have had Petrovic in our sights.'

'Yeah, but that wasn't exactly an active, current search, was it? I mean, yes, people were looking eight years ago when he dropped off the radar, but let's be honest, nobody'd given him a thought for years until Pirie ran her CRO check.'

Macanespie sighed. 'So, is this a game changer, or what? Do we add him to the list of victims and set up a meeting?'

'I think we just get on with our own inquiries and ignore Pirie.'

Macanespie was too tired to argue. But he had a sneaky feeling Karen Pirie wasn't going to be that easy to ignore.

I'm done with this.

I had such big ideas of what this was going to be. I was ready to write about Bosnia, about Kosovo, about my growing understanding of the history and politics of the region from a lived perspective.

It turns out that my life has actually been lived on the wrong side of the looking glass. I have nothing to write worth reading, nothing to say worth listening to. And that's a very bad place for an academic to find herself.

I'm done with this.

39

By the time Karen had arrived home from Croatia, she'd been exhausted. The combination of the travelling and the stress of what she'd uncovered had left her drained. Phil had taken one look at her and prescribed a bath, a large gin-and-tonic and bed. 'You never admit to yourself how much these investigations take out of you,' he scolded her as he poured relaxing bath oil into the cascade of steaming water.

'By comparison with the families and the friends of the victims, I've got nothing to complain about,' she said, dumping her travel-weary clothes in the laundry basket.

'OK, you've only got one bag of shit compared to their half a dozen. It's still shit, though. You need to be kinder to yourself. You're not indestructible.' He rumpled her hair as she climbed into the bath.

'Oh no? Want to bet?' Karen groaned in pleasure, feeling

the heat soothe her weary muscles. 'Tell me about your day, take my mind off murdered children and vendettas.'

Phil sighed. 'To be honest, I don't think anything in my day would cheer you up. Tell you what, I'll bring in my iPad and we can watch *Celebrity Masterchef* from last night. That's a different sort of crime, but I guarantee you'll have a laugh.'

She almost felt guilty for letting go the burden of what she'd uncovered in the Balkans. But she told herself the trade-off would be that next morning, she'd be ready to roll with some fresh ideas.

As she walked in with her giant cup of coffee the following morning, Karen knew she'd been half right. She was ready to roll. But she had nothing new to roll with. She turned on her computer and summoned up the smiling head-shot of Mitja Petrovic that Tessa Minogue had sent her. She knew she was probably projecting what she knew on to the image, but she did think she detected a certain steeliness in his eyes. He was attractive, no denying that. But he wasn't some tailor's dummy. There was a spark in his expression, a devil-may-care quality to his grin. And behind it, that uncompromising look. She wouldn't have enjoyed taking him on in a fight.

Karen sipped her coffee and stared at the screen, her mind ticking off all the things they'd done and what might possibly still be left that could lead them in the direction of Petrovic's killer. She was sure Maggie Blake had reacted to one of the names on that list of sixteen. However, there was no way of knowing which. Karen wished she'd thought of reading them aloud one by one. But it had never occurred to her that Maggie would have any reason not to blurt out any name she recognised.

So what might that reason be? To whom could Maggie owe silence that would trump her dead husband? Did she have a new lover who had decided to take Petrovic out of the game so he could have a clear run at Maggie? Was this nothing to do with the Balkan wars and everything to do with old-fashioned jealousy?

Karen leaned back in her chair, linking her hands behind her head. Was it likely? There had been no trace of a partner in Maggie's life. She hadn't mentioned anyone. Karen reckoned that if there had been someone new, it would have moderated the terms in which Maggie spoke about Petrovic. She wouldn't have been nearly so keen to perpetuate the idea that he was still alive in Croatia; she'd have wanted him written off so she could enjoy her new life.

And nobody else had mentioned a new lover. Neither Dorothea Simpson nor Tessa Minogue had so much as hinted in passing that there was anybody else in Maggie's life. But that didn't necessarily mean Karen was chasing the wrong motive. Petrovic might have been taken out of the running by someone who then failed to talk his way into Maggie's bed. But if that was the case, why had Maggie not admitted it? Could it be she felt guilty about her rejection?

So guilty she'd protect the man from the consequences of murder?

'Only if she thought she'd led him on,' she said out loud, punching the air. Of course, that was the moment when Jason walked into the office. Mildly embarrassed, Karen mumbled a greeting. 'I was just thinking of an alternative scenario,' she said, clocking his wary look.

'An alternative to what?'

'What if Petrovic's activities in the Balkans had nothing to do with his death? What if it was all much more mundane than that?'

Jason frowned. 'How?'

She was moving too fast for the Mint, Karen thought. 'Imagine some other guy was in love with Maggie Blake. Really besotted with her. Somebody who thought that if that annoying war hero General Petrovic was out of the way, Maggie would be his for the asking.' She paused.

Jason nodded. 'I get it. And he wouldn't know that the general was actually her husband so if she moaned about him like people do when they're married, he might have thought she was kind of suggesting she'd be up for somebody who treated her better, right?'

Karen managed to follow the mangled prose to a reasonable conclusion. 'Exactly. So the mystery man goes off buildering with the general and takes the chance to murder him.'

'How has he got a gun?' Jason interrupted.

'I don't know. How does anybody get a gun in this country? Considering they're supposed to be banned, they're bloody everywhere. Let's just say for the sake of argument that he got a gun and shot the general. So he comes back to Oxford and when it looks like Petrovic has done a runner, he moves in on Maggie. Who says no, she really wasn't coming on to him. Because she wasn't. She was just being polite, or not wanting to hurt his feelings or whatever. And she had the general to hide behind.'

'So he's done a murder for nothing. That'd piss on your chips.' Jason took a Coke out of his desk drawer and popped the top.

'That's the understatement of the morning. But time goes by and there's no comeback. And then one day, Fraser Jardine finds a body on the roof of the John Drummond and it all kicks off. And Maggie sees the man's name on a list of potential suspects and she's hit between the eyes with a terrible moment of guilt. It's all her fault.'

'Aye, like Adam and Eve and that. The woman made him do it.'

Who'd have thought that the Mint knew the Bible? Or that he could draw meaningful comparisons from it? 'You are full of surprises today, Jason. But you're right. In that moment, she realises that the general's death is squarely at her door. So she hasn't got the right to dob in the actual killer.' Karen gave a wry smile. 'It all makes a horrible kind of sense, doesn't it? So we'd better start working our way through every name on that list until we find the mystery man.'

'I printed the full list out while you were away. Names and addresses and that. Some of them have got car registrations as well, so we can double check that.' He raked around in his desk drawer and produced two sheets of paper.

As Karen held out a hand to take it, her phone rang. The caller ID was blocked, but that wasn't uncommon with calls from police phones so she took it. DCI Pirie,' she said chirpily.

'Karen? It's Jimmy Hutton. DCI Hutton.' She should have recognised the voice of Phil's DCI. They'd been out in a foursome with Hutton and his wife a few times. But he sounded stressed, his pitch higher than usual. Her heart rate rose, the sense of panic in her gut familiar to anyone who loves a cop. But she tried to stay calm.

'Aye, Jimmy. How can I help you?' As if it was just a routine call between two officers of equal rank.

'Karen, I've got some bad news.'

There was only one kind of bad news. 'Jimmy? Tell me he's alive.' She was aware of the Mint getting to his feet and moving uncertainly towards her. Her mouth was suddenly dry, a sharp metallic taste on her tongue.

'He's been run over. He's on his way to hospital.'

'The Vic?' Karen was on her feet now too, grabbing coat and shoulder bag. 'I'm on my way, Jimmy. Hang on, would you?' She held her phone to her chest and took a deep, shuddering breath. 'Jason, I need you to drive me. Phil's been in an accident. The Vic. Blues and twos.'

They ran out of the building, Karen with her phone to her ear, still talking to Hutton. 'How bad is it?'

'I'm not a doctor, Karen. He was conscious when they loaded him into the ambulance, that's got to be a good thing.'

'The Vic, yeah?'

'The Vic. I'm heading there now.'

Into her car, flashing blue Noddy light clamped to the roof. Jason pulling out into the traffic like a madman, careering through the clogged streets, dodging in and out of bus lanes. Running red lights, jinking between cars and buses.

'What happened?'

Hutton breaking up, then back again loud and clear. 'So we were waiting for him when he gets back from the airport.'

'This is the money-laundering bastard, right?'

'Right. And he reverses into his drive. Big ugly fuck-off white BMW SUV, just what you need in Cramond. And we front up and he panics. Phil's standing in front of the Beemer. Stab vest and everything, "police" on the front in big letters. Arms out, couldn't be clearer. Fucking stay put, dickhead.' Hutton abruptly running out of steam.

'Only he doesn't, right?'

'Right. He stood on the gas and hit Phil full on. Didn't fucking stop.' Hutton's voice cracking, like he's on the edge of tears. Karen's ears ringing, like someone slapped her on both sides of her head at once.

Hammering down Queensferry Road towards the dual carriageway and the road bridge over the Forth. Heart hammering too, like the Runrig song. Why is she thinking about Runrig now, for fuck's sake? 'He's going to be OK, though. He's tough as old boots, my Phil.'

'Just get here, Karen. Just get here. He needs you.'

The line went dead. She didn't think it was a black hole. She thought it was just that Jimmy Hutton couldn't speak any longer. She couldn't work out why she wasn't crying. Why she wasn't feeling anything except a terrible urge to get to Phil's side.

'You all right, boss?' Jason said without taking his eyes off the road. Just as well since he was doing over a ton, horn blaring and light clearing people from their path.

'Bastard ran him over. Went right over the top of him.'

'What? In the street, like?'

'No, it was a take-down. Guy rapes his wife then gives her to his pals. That's his speciality. But they're doing him for money-laundering. And he just drove straight into Phil.'

'Fuck.' Jason pressed his lips tight together. She realised he was close to tears.

'He'll be OK. He'll be fine, Jason.' She kept telling herself that all the way across the bridge and down the motorway and along the dual carriageway and into the emergency bay at the Victoria Hospital in Kirkcaldy. Karen leapt out of the car almost before it had stopped. 'I'll see you inside,' she said, running as fast as she could into the A&E department.

When police officers are brought injured to hospital, everything changes direction to focus on their needs. The emergency services cleave to each other in times of crisis and nothing stands between an injured officer and the care he or she needs. So as soon as Karen identified herself she was hustled through to a tiny waiting room where she found Jimmy Hutton and a couple of guys she vaguely recognised. They were all huddled on chairs, hunched up as if making themselves appear smaller would somehow help Phil.

Jimmy struggled to his feet like an old man and drew her into an embrace she didn't want. All she could hear was a mumble of apologies and other well-meant pointlessness. 'What are they saying?' she demanded as soon as she could disentangle herself.

He couldn't meet her eyes. 'It's not good. He's unconscious. They think he's got internal injuries as well as broken bones. Both legs, his pelvis, ribs.'

Her heart seemed to tighten. She couldn't draw in enough air to keep dizziness at bay. 'Where is he?'

'They're prepping him for surgery. The good news, Karen, there is some good news ... The good news is, no head injuries.'

'I need to see him.'

'I'll get a nurse,' one of the other guys said.

As he left, Jason came in, looking as young and frightened as she'd ever seen him. 'Any news?' he asked.

'They've got to open him up and find where he's injured,' Karen said. A thought struck her like an electrical charge of rage burning along her veins. 'You have arrested him, Jimmy? The bastard who did this? You do have him in custody?'

Hutton ran a hand over his bald head. 'We were stunned, Karen. He was gone before we could do anything to stop him. There's a nationwide alert out for him and his vehicle. He'll not get anywhere, not with the ANPR cameras. They can search the data in real time. They'll get him.'

She didn't know what to do with herself. Literally. Sit down, stand up, walk around, bang her head against the wall. They were all equally possible, equally ridiculous. If Phil was here, he'd tell her to get a grip.

Her immediate problem was solved by the arrival of a middle-aged Asian woman in blue scrubs. 'I'm Aryana Patel,' she said. 'I'm going to be operating on Mr Parhatka.'

'I'm his partner,' Karen said. 'His bidie-in.' To clarify what kind of partner.

Ms Patel nodded. 'I have to tell you he's quite poorly but we're reasonably confident that with the right intervention, he's going to make it.'

'"Reasonably confident" – what does that mean?' It was Jason, his fear transposed into aggression.

'It means they're not making promises they can't be sure

of keeping,' Karen said, laying a hand on his arm. She faced Ms Patel. 'Can I see him before he goes into surgery?'

'He's unconscious. He won't know you're there. And . . .' She made a face. 'He's not been cleaned up yet.'

'I'm a cop. I've seen the human body fucked up in even more ways than you have, Doc. He might not know that I'm there right now, but I need to be able to say to him at some point down the line, "I was there. I held your hand. I kissed you."'

The doctor nodded. 'I understand. Come with me.'

Nothing Karen had witnessed before had prepared her for the wave of shock and pain that hit when she saw Phil. His clothes had been cut free from his body but they still lay under and around him like the shed skin of a lizard. His legs were all unnatural angles. Bone pierced the skin in at least three places. His face was paler than she'd ever seen it; he looked, bizarrely, as if he'd shed pounds since she'd left him that morning tucking into a bowl of grapefruit and pineapple. She wanted to throw herself on him, to protect his broken flesh from more damage. But the stolid, sensible Karen was still in charge. She stepped to his side and took his limp hand in hers. She raised it to her mouth and kissed his fingers, noticing his knuckles were scraped and raw. 'I love you,' she said. 'You know you're my hero, Phil. You give my life a meaning I never expected it to have. So you better get a grip and get back to me. You hear me? I love you.'

She kissed his hand again then backed out of the room. She let herself cry then, soundless sobs and fat unstoppable tears, forehead against the wall, shoulders heaving. Nobody bothered her. Nobody tried to offer pointless comfort. The staff just bustled around her and let her be.

And then she got a grip.

40

It was clear that Jimmy Hutton and his team intended to keep vigil until Phil emerged from surgery. The thought of being trapped in that tiny room full of big men who didn't know what to say was enough to make Karen want to lock herself in the cleaners' cupboard. To her surprise, she realised the only person whose company she could tolerate was the Mint.

'I'm going for some fresh air,' she announced to the room. 'Jason, with me.'

Startled, he jumped to his feet, eyes swivelling round the assembled guys like a panicking wild horse. 'OK, boss.'

Once the door closed behind them, he said, 'We're not really going for fresh air, right? You hate fresh air.'

It was a line he'd learned from Phil, she suspected. 'There's a Costa Coffee down in the atrium of the new bit,' she said. 'That's where we're going to set up base camp. I already sorted out with Ms Patel to give me a bell as soon as Phil's out of the theatre.'

Armed with lattes and muffins the size of a baby's head, they annexed a table as far from the main thoroughfare as possible. 'Are you all right, boss?' Jason reached for the packets of sugar he'd snagged on his way and tipped four into his cup.

'To quote our national Makar on the occasion of her widowhood, "Hellish, but thanks for asking." I'm scared and I'm worried and I don't know what to do with myself except the one thing I know I'm good at.' Seeing his frown, she added gently, 'That would be coppering, Jason. And it's the thing about me Phil was proudest of. So he'd be bloody furious if he thought that him being on the operating table meant me ignoring my work.'

'So we're going to work?' He looked as dubious as he sounded.

'We are. We're going to drink our coffee and eat our muffins and we're going to think very hard about where we're up to and how we move forward. And if we can't come up with any better ideas, we're going down the road to our house and we're going to hammer the phones and the Internet until we find every one of those hotel guests and either eliminate them or nail them to the wall. You with me? Or do you want to go back and hang out with the boys? I won't think any less of you if you do. We all deal with crap like this in our own way.'

Jason shook his head. 'I'll stay with you, boss. We're a team, right? And Phil, he's still kind of part of our team. So it's like, you and me.'

Karen nodded. She wasn't sure whether she'd be able to concentrate but she had to try. Surges of black rage and hot fear ran through her at unpredictable intervals; she wondered if this was how Maggie Blake had felt when her general had disappeared without a word. She worked her way slowly down the coffee and the muffin, letting the caffeine and sugar do their thing. She worried at the problem of Petrovic's death so she didn't have to think about Phil being carved open by Aryana Patel. But nothing shifted, nothing suggested itself.

And so they ended up back at the house where she and Phil had built their life together. Having Jason there was a blessing; being there alone would have been unbearable. They sat in the study, Karen on the landline and the laptop, Jason on his mobile and Phil's iPad, working their way down the list. Late in the afternoon, five hours after they'd left the hospital, they agreed there was nothing more they could do. They'd eliminated nine of the sixteen for a variety of reasons ranging from a prosthetic leg to having only set foot outside the Isle of Eigg once in a lifetime ahead of this trip. Of the remaining seven, three had given addresses that had no correspondence in reality. They could have been having an illicit affair; they could have simply lied on the principle that they didn't want junk mail; or one of them could have been a killer. Either way, there was nothing more that Karen and Jason could do.

Karen had gone through to the kitchen to make another cup of coffee when the idea hit her. If Maggie had recognised a name, there was a chance that Dorothea Simpson or Tessa Minogue might know it too. They needed to run those names past the two women. And this time, she wouldn't make the same mistake. She'd ask them face to face, going through the names one by one.

Excited by the idea, she hustled back to the study to tell Jason. But halfway down the hall, the phone rang. Aryana Patel sounded as knackered as Karen felt. 'He's out of surgery,' she said. 'He's had a very bad time. We've had to remove his spleen and part of his liver. We had to take out a section of his large intestine and setting the bones of his legs and pelvis has been a real challenge. But he's holding his own.'

'When will I be able to see him?'

'You can come any time you like. But he's in intensive care and we've put him in a medically induced coma to give his body a chance to get over its initial trauma. So for the next three days, he's going to be deeply unconscious. Some people like to keep a bedside vigil, reading and talking and playing music. Others prefer to stay away because they struggle with seeing the people they love like that. It's not like someone being in a coma as a result of injury where you want stimulus to rouse them. With a medically induced coma, the aim is to keep the patient stable and pain-free. So I would say it's entirely up to you, Karen.'

She thought for a moment. Surely the best get-well-soon present she could give Phil would be a solution to the problem of the mysterious skeleton on the roof. She and Jason could go back to Oxford and pursue her latest idea and still be back long before Phil awoke. 'I think I'll keep myself busy at work,' Karen said slowly. 'But only if you promise me you'll call me at once if there's any change in his condition.'

'I'll make sure there's a note to that effect at the nurses' station. And his parents are already here. I'm sure they'll be straight on the phone if you're needed.'

Another good reason for going to Oxford. Karen ended the call and carried on into the study. 'Phil's out of surgery and he's doing OK. But they've kept him in a coma so he can heal better. It'll be three days before he's awake. So we've got a window of opportunity to do something that'll totally impress him when he wakes up. It's brainwave time, Jason. Let's get going.'

'Going where, boss?'

'Oxford, Jason. Where else?'

41

The trouble with dramatic revelations was that the world didn't stop turning. Sitting at her desk, looking out at the view of rooftops and distant spires, Maggie couldn't quite believe that everything on the skyline was still the same. Her convictions about her life had been altered beyond recognition, but nobody else knew. Nobody except a Scottish cop, and she didn't know the half of it. Now Maggie was back in Oxford, everything felt unreal and trivial.

The way she thought about her place in the world had shifted. She wasn't the woman scorned any more. She knew she'd been an object of pity and of ridicule when Mitja had disappeared. Both reactions had been equally insulting. Now she would have the upper hand over those who had enjoyed her misery and their idea of her as the abandoned partner, but she'd be prey to a whole new kind of pity for her bereavement. The pain was bad enough; the reactions of others would only make it worse. Just the thought of it made her want to go back to bed and pull the covers over her head.

She wondered how long it would be before the official identification of Mitja would seep out into the public domain. She'd checked online and seen that the discovery of the mysterious skeleton had made headlines in the Scottish media but barely a mention in the national news outlets. Once the media realised whose remains they were, it would be a different story. The dramatic murder of a Croatian general on British soil would provoke news stories and features. Some enterprising journalist might even venture into Mitja's past and uncover the dark secrets Maggie and Karen had learned. The very thought of that made her feel physically sick. Not because she had a vested interest in whitewashing his past but because she knew he was more than that single appalling incident and deserved not to be defined by it.

Acknowledging that thought was difficult enough. Like most people, she'd despised the politicians and generals around the world who had resorted to genocides and ethnic cleansing in pursuit of their ambitions. She'd condemned them as war criminals and applauded the setting up of the international criminal court. She'd sat round other people's dinner tables and criticised the US for its refusal to participate at The Hague. It had appeared to be one of the few issues where there was only one acceptable side for a civilised person to stand. And now, because of what Mitja had done, she was having to concede that sometimes the world was more complex than it was comfortable to admit.

Some people would have swept such considerations under the carpet and simply got on with their lives. But all Maggie's academic training militated against that. When the facts were in conflict with her world view, then she had to adjust that world view to accommodate her new knowledge. How she carried on, knowing what she knew now, was the burning question. Because knowledge always brought responsibility in its wake.

She gave herself a mental shake and stood up. Time to take the day in hand and make something of it. She had a student whose DPhil thesis concerned the geography of bodies in Oxford-based crime fiction and Maggie had promised to see whether she could arrange a trip to the balustraded rooftop of the Radcliffe Camera, where Lord Peter Wimsey and Harriet Vane had enjoyed a crucial conversation at the end of *Gaudy Night*. According to her student, Dorothy L. Sayers' description of the view of Oxford from the topmost gallery of the eighteenth-century circular library provided her with a key anchor for her thesis. Maggie thought it was more about making a sentimental journey, but it gave her an excuse to experience one of Oxford's landmark buildings from a new angle.

The Camera was part of the Bodleian Libraries, the vast complex of book storage at the heart of the university. Cheryl Stevenson, its Head of Technical Services, was an alumna of St Scholastica's and a frequent guest at High Table for dinner. She and Maggie had become friends, most recently linked by their membership of the same book group. Over the years, Maggie had been allowed behind the scenes at the library for such historic moments as the closing down of the Lamson pneumatic tube system for transmitting book requests, finally superseded by a digital version as late as 2009.

Now, she texted Cheryl and suggested a drink after work. Within minutes, Cheryl had responded, suggesting the King's Arms which, although always busy, served Young's Double Chocolate Stout, her favourite beer. With that agreed, Maggie returned to her desk and forced herself to consider the entries she was due to contribute to the forthcoming edition of the *Dictionary of Human Geography*.

Maggie arrived at the pub in good time, intent on snagging a table. The pub, being the oldest in the city and set in the very heart of the tourist zone, was always thronged, but by judiciously staking out a trio of American tourists who didn't look as if they were set for a long session, Maggie managed to achieve her goal with five minutes to spare. When Cheryl arrived, hot and flustered and seven minutes late, she was gratified to see an empty stool and a full bottle waiting for her.

'Madhouse in there today,' she said, straightening her glasses and slipping out of her coat. 'With all the rebuilding, I seem to spend every day arguing with architects and builders and, frankly, idiots about the simplest of things.' Cheryl was from Glasgow, equipped with an accent that could make the most generous of compliments sound like a threat. Maggie suspected she gave as good as she got.

It felt strange to be having a catch-up conversation with a friend that was defined more by what she couldn't say than what she could. Maggie spoke of things that no longer mattered much and tried to remember how she acted when she was interested in another person's concerns. At last, they worked their way round to Maggie's reason for the meeting. 'I've got a DPhil student who's desperate to get on to the roof of the Camera. Any chance I could borrow a key and take her up there? She's adamant that it would make all the difference to her thesis to see the view that wowed Dorothy L. Sayers. Because *Gaudy Night* is such a love letter to Oxford. And her thesis is all about how crime writers use the cityscape in their work.'

'I can't see why not. I think I can trust you not to hold a wild party up there. I could take you both up, if you'd rather?'

'I don't want to put you out,' Maggie said. 'And I'm not sure what her timetable is.'

Cheryl drained her glass. 'Since we're here, come back with me now and we'll pick up a set of keys for the upper-storey doors.'

Half an hour later, Maggie was back in her rooms. In the centre of her desk was a plain ring of keys labelled 'Upper

Camera roof.' Her admission to a high place where she could look out over the city that had shaped her life. A place where she could make a decision about her future. 'Lead us not into temptation,' she muttered ironically.

If she was to set herself back on an even keel, she had to try to reboot her life. What would she normally do if she'd been handed the gift of a set of keys for one of the most spectacular viewpoints in the city? A privileged access that few people ever had the chance to share? She'd share it. That's the sort of woman she'd always been.

She picked up her phone and texted her best friend, the woman she'd always turned to ever since they'd first bonded back in Dubrovnik.

> Tess, I've got keys for roof terrace of RadCam! Come and see the view with me. xxx

The answer arrived in a few minutes. Maggie was still staring at the keys, her face solemn.

> Love to. When? x

> Tomorrow morning? Meet you on steps at 10?xxx

> OK. See you then. You OK?x

> Yes. Tell you all about it when I see you.xxx

Amazed at herself for maintaining so normal a front, Maggie abruptly put the keys out of sight in a drawer. Tomorrow she'd contact her student.

Or not, depending on what she ended up doing.

42

By the time Karen and the Mint arrived in Oxford, it was too late to go knocking on the doors of elderly women. They checked into a budget motel on the outskirts of the city; Jason looked as if he could barely stand as he said goodnight. Karen knew she should be feeling the same but her brain wouldn't stop tick, tick, ticking like the timer on a Hollywood bomb.

The minute she arrived in her room, she called the intensive care unit at the Vic. The duty nurse knew her voice by now; she'd been calling every hour since they'd left Kirkcaldy. 'No change,' she said sympathetically. 'He's very peaceful. His vital signs are giving no cause for concern. Mrs Patel said to tell you she'll be in first thing in the morning and she'll speak to you then.'

'Thanks,' Karen said. She realised that she'd been so relieved that Phil was still alive that she'd asked Aryana Patel nothing about the long-term prognosis. How long would he be in hospital? What were the implications of his internal injuries? Would he walk properly again? Would he still be a cop at the end of his convalescence? All questions she needed the answer to. Her life was going to change, no two ways about it. And Karen, who didn't much like surprises, wanted to be as prepared as possible for what was coming at her down the road.

She'd still be with Phil. That went without saying. Whatever had happened to his body, his heart and his head would still be Phil. She knew that life-changing events like this sometimes destroyed relationships, but that wasn't going to happen to them. She wouldn't let it. Simple as that.

Karen stripped off her clothes and threw them over a chair. The world had been a different place when she'd put them on that morning. What had happened to Phil had drawn a line through her life. Now events would be characterised as being 'before Phil was attacked' and 'after Phil was attacked'.

Karen pulled on a T-shirt and got into bed, pulling the covers up to her chin like an obedient child. She closed her eyes but nothing changed. Her head was still busy. Her heart still raged. And then her phone vibrated on the night table. She leapt into action, grabbing it and jamming it to her ear without checking who was calling.

'Karen? It's River. I just heard about Phil.'

Until River's voice filled her head, it hadn't occurred to

Karen how much she needed a friend. 'I should have called you,' she said.

'Never mind that. How are you doing?'

'Shite.'

'Do you want me to come over?'

'Don't be daft. It's gone eleven. And besides, I'm not at home.'

'Where are you?'

'He's in a medically induced coma. I'd go mad sitting by his bedside playing his Elbow CDs to him. So I'm in Oxford.'

'The general?'

'Yeah. We were going nowhere, then I had an idea.'

'And of course it wouldn't wait.' River's voice was affectionate; not a trace of criticism for actions that most people would have struggled to understand.

'When he comes out of that coma, he's going to need to know that life goes on. And me solving a big old mystery like Dimitar Petrovic's murder will be like a tonic to him.'

'You're probably right. Did you take the Mint with you?'

'Aye. He's pretty upset about Phil. I thought he'd be better with me rather than having to stop his lip trembling in front of the big boys.'

River chuckled. 'You don't fool me. I'm glad you're not by yourself. Listen, there's nothing I can say that'll make any of this better. But if you want to talk, any time of the day or night, I'm here. OK?'

'Aye. Thanks.'

She'd have been hard pressed to say why, but after River's call, Karen felt less panicky. She snuggled down, cuddling one of the pillows to her like a giant teddy bear. In spite of her conviction that she'd never sleep, reaction to the day's events overtook her within minutes. When she surfaced, to her amazement, it was after eight.

Groggy with sleep, she raced through the morning rituals – phone call to check on Phil ('no change'); shower (bloody awful trickle); hair and clothes (drier hotter than hell) then down to the self-service breakfast. The Mint was already there, eating Coco Pops and drinking orange juice. Judging by the debris around him, neither was his first.

Karen armed herself with a cup of coffee and two boxes of Fruit and Fibre, persuading herself that this was a healthy breakfast.

The Mint looked up expectantly. 'Any news?'

'No change.' She tipped cereal into a too-small bowl.

'That's good, then. Better than a turn for the worse.'

'You always this cheerful in the morning?' Karen added milk and dug a spoon into the cereal. The Mint looked wounded but at least he kept his mouth shut while she jacked her caffeine and sugar up to manageable levels. Once she'd finished shovelling her food down with the determination of someone who doesn't want to think about anything else, she took a deep breath and said, 'Sorry.' She got out her notebook and checked Dorothea Simpson's mobile number. 'Give her a call and say you'd like to have a word with her.'

'Why me?' Panic flared in his eyes.

'Because I'm the boss and I don't want to forewarn her that this word is an important one. As far as she's concerned, you're just the oily rag. So she's not going to be on her guard.'

'OK.' He dialled the number. With a face as informative as his, there was no need for a speakerphone. Karen could tell when the call connected and when it was eventually answered. 'Aye, hello, Dr Simpson, it's Detective Constable Murray from Edinburgh. We met the other day at your house ... Uh huh. Well, I could do with another wee word with you, just to clear up a couple of details? ... Well, I'm in Oxford, so this morning would be ... You're not?' His look of dismay made Karen want to cry. 'Well, we could come to you ... you are? Brilliant. Where will we find you? ... Excellent. We'll see you very soon.' He ended the call, pink with achievement.

'That sounded successful,' Karen said.

'She's not at home,' he said. 'So I said we could come to her. And it turns out she's at St Scholastica's. She goes in for breakfast a couple of times a week. She's going to be in the SCR, whatever that is.'

Karen beamed at him. Was she finally turning him into a cop? 'Well done. So what are we waiting for?'

On the way to the college, Jason said, 'What's an SCR?'

'It's the Senior Common Room. It's like the staff room for the college tutors.'

He shook his head. 'It's like a secret code, all these fancy names. A way of keeping the likes of us out in the cold.'

'You're not far off the mark, Jason.' And then, just to put the icing on the cake, Jimmy Hutton called to say they'd picked up the driver of the white BMW tractor.

'Stupid twat was trying to drive it on to the Rotterdam ferry at Newcastle,' Hutton told her. 'Like somehow because he was in England they wouldn't be looking for him.'

Already Karen felt the day was going to be a lot better than the one before.

They found Dorothea Simpson alone in a long drawing room with views of the river. It was furnished in the style of an English country cottage, with comfy-looking sofas and armchairs scattered around a series of low tables. A pair of deep bay windows were lined with cushioned window seats and a refectory table held a collection of newspapers and magazines. Dorothea led them back to the table, where she had clearly been reading a copy of the *London Review of Books*. 'I can't afford all the periodicals these days,' she said. 'So I come in for breakfast two or three times a week and catch up with my reading afterwards.' She lowered herself into a padded captain's chair and sighed. 'I wasn't expecting to see you, Chief Inspector.'

'Who could resist a trip to Oxford?' Karen said.

'Who, indeed,' said Dorothea without a trace of irony.

Karen took the crumpled list of names from her bag. 'We're anxious to track down the person General Petrovic went to Edinburgh with. We think it must have been one of his climbing associates, but so far we've drawn a blank. But we do have a list of names from the hotel register of a trip we know he made to go buildering. You know, climbing the outside of buildings for fun. Anyway, I thought it might be helpful to ask people he knew if they recognised any of the names from the hotel register.'

Karen would have sworn that Dorothea's nose twitched. 'You think this might be his killer?'

Karen forced a light laugh. 'I've no reason to suspect them. There's nobody on the list with a foreign name. No, I'm hoping they might be able to remember the general talking about someone he used to go buildering with back in Croatia.'

'Have you shown this list to Maggie?'

'She's not around this morning,' Karen said. It wasn't an answer to Dorothea's question but she hoped the other woman wouldn't notice that.

'No, she's gone off to the Radcliffe Camera,' Dorothea said. 'She's borrowed a set of keys to get up on the roof. It's a special favour for one of her DPhil students.'

Happy that Dorothea had been diverted from inquiring too closely about the list, Karen unfolded the paper. 'I thought I could go through the list and you could tell me when any name rings a bell.'

Dorothea nodded doubtfully. 'I'll do my best. But my memory is not as sharp as it once was.'

'Never mind. The first name on the list is Christopher Greenfield.' She paused while Dorothy repeated the name, shaking her head. And so it went on. Nine names and no reaction. Then Karen said, 'Ellen Ripley.'

Dorothea perked up. 'Did you say, "Ellen Ripley"?'

'Yes. Do you know her?'

Dorothea chuckled. 'Don't you know who Ellen Ripley is?'

Karen shook her head. 'Should I?'

'Oh, Chief Inspector! "In space, no one can hear you scream." Surely you're not too young to remember Ripley?'

Karen felt stupid. Now it was pointed out to her, of course she remembered Sigourney Weaver's iconic portrayal of the heroic Ripley. What was even more interesting was that Ellen Ripley was one of the trio of names they'd been unable to trace. 'I guess I never think of her as having a first name.'

'I suppose not,' Dorothea said. 'And in fairness, I suppose I might not either were it not for the fact that Mitja used to tease Tessa about being our Ellen Ripley. Taking on the alien monsters like Milosevic and Mladic.'

'The general called Tessa Minogue Ellen Ripley?' Karen said, trying not to show the sudden buzz of excitement in her stomach. 'And did they go buildering together?'

'I honestly don't know about that. I believe she went walking in the Highlands and Snowdonia with Maggie and

425

Mitja and their friends. But why don't you ask her yourself? Maggie's taking her up on to the roof of the Radcliffe Camera this morning as a special treat. The view is supposed to be phenomenal.' Dorothea peered at the grandfather clock standing against the wall. 'They were meeting at ten. They'll be on their way up right now.'

43

Their feet clattered on the iron staircase leading to the very top level of the majestic Radcliffe Camera. Maggie glanced down, taking in the baroque details of the interior, wondering exactly how far it was to the ground. Behind her, Tessa was beginning to breathe heavily. 'Bloody hell, Maggie,' she complained. 'I can't believe you're fitter than me these days.'

'You spend too much time working and not enough time in the hills,' Maggie said. 'Not enough mountains to climb in The Hague.'

'This is amazing, though,' Tessa said. 'It looks entirely different from this height. You look around at all this elaborate decoration that was hardly ever going to be seen by anybody and you just wonder at it. To go to that much trouble, to create all that detail and to have it appreciated by so few. That's a real love of craft for craft's sake.'

'It's sad that hardly any of us have the skills these days to make something this beautiful. I was thinking that only the other day, looking out of the train window. So much of what we've built, what we've made is unnecessarily ugly. Why is function divorced from aesthetics? Why is it so hard for us to grasp that a warehouse doesn't have to be bloody ugly?'

'I guess it costs more,' Tessa said between breaths.

'I don't think cost always enters into it. It can't be that simple. I think it's that we just don't care enough.'

'There's always been plenty of ugly, Maggie. But mostly the ugly doesn't survive. It gets knocked down and replaced by something equally unattractive. Or if we're lucky, something beautiful. I mean, what was here before the Camera? I bet it wasn't anything special.'

They reached the door at the top of the stairs. Maggie unlocked it and stood back to let Tessa go on ahead of her. 'Houses. That's what was here. Undistinguished housing belonging to different colleges. Probably similar to the style of buildings on Longwall. So you're right. The ugly was always there, it just doesn't survive.' She locked the door behind them. 'Better make sure some adventurous undergraduate doesn't come sneaking out while we're not looking. Cheryl would have my guts for garters.'

Tessa was already drinking in the panorama, hands leaning on the stone balustrade. 'Wow. This is some view, Maggie. Thanks for bringing me up here.'

'Did you and your buildering cronies never come up the outside?' Maggie asked, casual as she could manage.

'Not my scene, buildering,' Tessa said, equally casually. 'You'd never get up here, though, it's far too public. And spotlit at night.'

'Dorothy L. Sayers has a very vivid description of the view from up here. I should have brought it with me. Something about the twin towers of All Souls being like a house of cards surrounding the grass oval in the quad like an emerald in a ring. New College with dark wings wheeling around the bell tower. Magdalen like a lily, tall and slender.' Maggie waved an arm at the scene, walking round the parapet to take in the rest of the sights. 'Schools, Univ, Merton, St Mary the Virgin, Christ Church Cathedral and Tom Tower, Carfax. It's all there, all Oxford.'

'Do you suppose this is how Jesus felt when the Devil took him up to a high place and offered him all the temptations of the world?' Tessa laughed. 'Listen to me. The curse of a Catholic schooling. The nuns have me branded for life.'

With the battlements of the Bodleian Library behind her, Maggie turned to face Tessa. 'Is that where you came by your sense of justice? The nuns?'

Tessa looked at her askance, as if she'd caught some nuance in Maggie's voice that didn't quite fit their light-hearted excursion. 'I suppose,' she said.

'It's all a bit Old Testament, though, isn't it? More retribution than rehabilitation.'

'My idea of justice? I hadn't thought about it in those terms. I think people shouldn't dodge the consequences of their actions, that's all.' She forced a light laugh. 'This is a bit serious, Mags. I thought we were having a nice wee outing to cheer us up after the crap we've had to face this past week.'

Maggie was glad Tessa had been first to raise the subject. 'I think it'll take more than a pretty view to wipe out what I've discovered. You haven't asked me about Croatia.'

Tessa shrugged and leaned against the balustrade, her back to the view. 'I reckoned you'd tell me in your own time. I didn't want to push. I know this is hard for you.'

'I see. I wondered whether it was because you already knew what I might uncover.' Maggie's chin tilted up, her expression as challenging as her words.

Tessa frowned. 'I'm not sure I know what you mean.'

'Really? So why did you kill him, if it wasn't because of the wedding massacre?'

Tessa's bewilderment was so convincing that Maggie momentarily doubted herself. But then she remembered the list Karen Pirie had shown her. Ellen Ripley. The teasing nickname Mitja had given Tessa. The fact that Tessa had been out of town when Mitja had gone missing. Tessa's insistence that Mitja was the serial assassin of Balkan war criminals, that improbable accusation from anyone who understood his fundamental humanity, that very humanity he'd betrayed by his single act of vengeance.

'I really have no fucking idea what you're on about. What wedding massacre? Who am I supposed to have killed? Are you talking about Mitja? Why in the name of God would I kill Mitja?' She sounded outraged, bemused, insulted.

'I remember nights when the three of us – and sometimes other people too – would sit up late, raging about the impotence of the international criminal justice system. How outrageous it was that Milosevic was being held in comfort in The Hague while the monstrous crimes of his regime still reverberated in ordinary people's lives on a daily basis. How offensive it was that so many of the war criminals who'd presided over massacres and rape camps and appalling desecrations of people's lives were walking about free as birds.'

'All of which you agreed with, I seem to remember?' Tessa had adopted a look of puzzlement, accompanied by the kind of soothing voice people use with drunks who might turn violent at any moment.

'And I particularly remember when you heard what had happened to Dagmar.'

Now the shutters came down. Dagmar and Tessa had been lovers on and off for about nine months after the Croatian war. Then Dagmar had been caught up in the siege of Sarajevo, trapped like so many others in the kind of nightmare nobody expected to happen at the tail end of the century when Europe was supposed to have learned its lesson when it came to war. They ended up on the wrong side of the lines one night, Dagmar and her current lover.

They were identified as lesbians and systematically gang-raped by more soldiers than either of them could count. And then they were thrown into the street in the January snow in the middle of the night. Dagmar died from internal bleeding two days later. Her girlfriend killed herself a week after that. When the news came back via a Red Cross contact, Tessa had been wild with a toxic mix of grief and rage. Maggie had been convinced that if those soldiers had been within reach, Tessa would have torn the flesh from their bones. As it was, they were never identified, never brought anywhere near justice. And Tessa never spoke of it again.

Tessa looked away. 'I'm sorry, Maggie. I have no idea what's going on here. I don't know why you're dragging Dagmar into this conversation. I don't need to be reminded about what happened to her to understand how much Mitja's murder is hurting you.'

'That's not the point I'm making. The point is, we all spoke with one voice. It wasn't long after you heard what had happened to Dagmar that you started working with the Yugoslavian war crimes investigators, was it?'

Tessa shook her head. 'You know that, Maggie. We talked about it at the time. You know I wanted to feel like she hadn't died for nothing.'

'I know. And I was totally behind you.'

Tessa put a hand out and touched Maggie's arm. It was all Maggie could do not to flinch. 'I know you were. I loved you for the passion of your support.'

'And that took you back to the Balkans to investigate reports of war crimes. And I'm guessing that you hadn't been there that long when you heard the rumours about the wedding massacre.'

Tessa spread her hands in a gesture of bafflement. 'I don't know anything about a wedding massacre. I told you. I've no idea what you're talking about.'

Maggie shook her head. 'Don't fuck with me, Tessa,' she said, her voice hard and precise. 'It wasn't commonplace to hear about Serbs being butchered by Croats. It's not something you'd have let slip by you. It would have been interesting if only for its curiosity value. And when you tried to nail it down, all you could get was the name of a Croatian village near the border. It meant nothing to you then. The irony is that it would have meant nothing to me back then either.'

'This is a very weird fantasy.' Tessa tried to move away but Maggie gripped her wrist.

'Stick around, Ripley. There's more to come. So you and your Scandie sidekick turn up in this village where you've heard the raiding party came from. Podruvec, in case you've forgotten the name. It's not that kind of place, though. It doesn't feel like a guerrilla stronghold. But you're persistent. You've always been persistent, Tessa, haven't you? Thorough, dedicated, tenacious.' Maggie spat the words like insults.

'I don't understand what you're talking about, Maggie.

Who's been feeding you this strange story? Has that cop been winding you up? Trying to provoke you into some sort of reaction? Are you OK?'

Tessa's expression of concern simply stoked Maggie's anger. She wasn't going to be that easily diverted. 'So you asked around. At some point, somebody said something they weren't supposed to and you learned that Podruvec had been the scene of a massacre of its own. And somewhere down the line, you found the missing pieces of the jigsaw puzzle. The man behind the wedding massacre was your best friend. The heroic General Petrovic.' Maggie's voice faltered momentarily. 'I know how shocking that must have been. Because last week, it left me feeling like the foundations of my life had been stripped out from under me.'

'This a fantasy. I don't know why you're turning on me like this, Maggie. We love each other, remember?'

'Remember? How could I forget? How sick is that? You shoot my husband in the head then take me to bed to comfort me?'

Tessa recoiled as if Maggie had slapped her. 'You think I killed Mitja? What? Because I was jealous of him? Because I wanted you? That's fucking sick, Maggie.'

Maggie shook her head. 'Not because of me. I don't think the world revolves round me. No. I think you killed him because somebody had to pay for what happened to Dagmar. You were burning up with revenge and self-righteousness. You were grieving for someone you'd loved and you were enraged that the official route wasn't giving justice fast enough. And then you found out about Mitja and something inside you snapped. One of your closest friends wasn't just a hypocrite. He was a war criminal who was escaping justice. You created this warped, twisted version of moral equivalence between the animals who violated Dagmar and a man who overreacted against the people who murdered his children.'

Tessa's eyes widened and her lips curled in a snarl. Finally Maggie had pushed the right button. 'Is that what you think he was? A poor wounded animal who "overreacted"? He killed nearly fifty people, for fuck's sake. The overwhelming majority of whom had taken absolutely no part in anything remotely approaching a war crime. He was as much a butcher as the bastards he stirred us up against.'

For a moment, all there was between them was the sound of the city; the murmur of traffic, the rise and fall of voices, a distant siren. Then Maggie spoke. 'And that's why you killed him.'

Tessa straightened up. 'He had a lovely life. You gave him a beautiful life. He was loved. He had a roof over his head and food on the table. He held forth to adoring audiences who thought he was a hero. How can you think that was appropriate? You, who saw the damage at first hand. The Balkans wasn't just a report on the news to you. You saw it. You lost friends, I know you did. In Sarajevo. In the summer offensive in ninety-two. How was it right that he walked among us pretending to be a good man? How was that right, Maggie?'

'And who made you judge and jury and Lord High Executioner? Because it didn't stop with Mitja, did it? You got on your high horse because he made a terrible, terrible mistake, but you liked the view from up there. You realised you could right all the fucking wrongs. Punish the guilty. And with Mitja on the missing list, you could make him the scapegoat for your vigilante campaign.'

'I'm sorry I laid the credit at his door. But you can sneer all you like, it doesn't change the fact that justice should be swift if it's to be truly just. Not bogged down in legal hair-splitting and endless procedural delays. And what I delivered was just.'

'And was it just to let me go on hoping the man I loved with all my heart was still alive? Was it just to make love to me knowing his blood was on your hands? Christ, you've turned my life into one of those Jacobean revenge tragedy melodramas, and all without me knowing a bloody thing about it. How could you do that, Tess? How could you live with yourself?'

For a moment, she caught a glimpse of the Tessa Minogue she'd thought she knew. A flicker of tenderness, of compassion. 'Who he really was, that was the worst insult to both of us. His whole life was a lie. All I was trying to do was help you heal. Truly, Maggie.'

'Help me heal? You caused the injury in the first place. I

was happy in my ignorance. And even now I know, I'd still take him back in my arms. Because that single misguided evil act does not define him. But what you did – a whole series of evil acts – Tess, that was cold-blooded. None of your victims did you any personal harm. You had no stake in their deaths except self-righteousness. You probably tell yourself you did it for Dagmar. But that's just an insult to her memory. You did it because it made you feel good.'

Tessa shook her head and spoke slowly, as if to a small child. 'That's not true. I did it because nobody else could deliver what felt like justice to those people back in the Balkans. Do you think anyone mourned Miroslav Simunovic or any of the others? They were dancing in the bloody streets. I'm not sorry for what I did, Maggie. I'm sorry for your pain, but that's all. So now let's get off this bloody roof and get on with our lives.'

'You think that's it?' Maggie couldn't believe Tessa's insouciance.

Tessa gave her a pitying smile. 'Well, what else? There's no evidence. A name on a hotel register? Anyone who knew my nickname could have done that. A bullet from a gun that's rusted away to nothing on the bottom of some river somewhere? Take it from me, Maggie. I've been careful. And you can't say I haven't left the world a better place than I found it.' She took a step sideways, intending to pass Maggie and make for the door.

But she wasn't quite fast enough.

44

As soon as she understood the import of Dorothea's words, Karen was on her feet and running for the door. 'Jason,' she shouted over her shoulder as she went. The Mint stumbled to his feet and ran after his boss, catching her as she reached the car. 'Drive,' she yelled at him.

He did as he was told. As they hurtled through the college gates, Karen clamped the Noddy light on the car roof and wrestled her phone out of her pocket. At the third attempt she managed to type 'Radcliffe Camera' into her GPS. 'Left,' she shouted as they approached the end of the street. 'And keep going straight till I tell you.'

'What are we doing?'

'Trying to stop something very bad happening. The Radcliffe Camera's a big high building, Jason. And I reckon Maggie Blake recognised the same name Dorothea Simpson did off that hotel residents' list, since the person she's up there with is Tessa Minogue. Left up ahead. Kind of half-left, not hard left.'

Jason hammered onwards, blasting the horn at any car foolish enough not to move. They arrived at a set of traffic lights where they were forbidden to drive straight on towards the New Bodleian and the Sheldonian Theatre. 'Just go,' Karen shouted at him. 'We're the fucking police, we can go wherever we need to, Jason.'

'Is she going to push her off?'

'What do you think?' As soon as they passed through the next traffic lights, leaving chaos in their wake, Karen turned off the light and said, 'Pull over, now.'

The car had barely stopped when she was out and running down the pale yellow stone corridor of Catte Street, the Bodleian to one side and Hertford College to the other. She burst into Radcliffe Square, almost turning her ankle on the rounded cobbles, craning her head back to look at the balustraded parapet beneath the lead-covered dome.

What she hoped to see was two figures leaning on the parapet taking in the view. What she saw the moment she raised her eyes was the figure of a woman tumbling head first past the three windowed stages of the building, ripping the air with a screech that set the hairs on Karen's neck on end. Then the dull crump as she hit the ground. Karen skidded to a halt, horrified.

But Jason carried on running, straight for the body that was now a misshapen black heap. Karen pulled out her phone and called the emergency number as she regained the power of movement. But she didn't head for where Jason was hunkered down by the body, trying to keep the growing knot of onlookers at a distance.

Karen had long since steeled herself to be the one who would run towards the sound of the guns. So she strode purposefully towards the shallow flight of stairs that was the only entrance and exit for the library. Whoever came down from that roof, she'd be meeting them halfway.

45

Alan Macanespie's enthusiasm was starting to wear a little thin. It was hard to maintain momentum when there was so little progress to latch on to. After the excitement of spotting something that appeared to be significant, he and Proctor were in limbo, waiting for the geeks to work their magic on the material he'd sent them.

All that remained for them was to plough through reports and statements from the investigating officers on the murders they'd tentatively identified as part of their series. Much of the information was in languages other than English; they'd had to fall back on running all the digital versions through online translation programs and marking up anything that seemed of interest so it could be reappraised by officers with the appropriate language skills. It was mind-numbing work and left Macanespie with a low undercurrent of anxiety that there was definitely material that was getting lost in translation. But until Wilson Cagney put his head above the parapet and gave them the high-profile resources they deserved, they'd just have to make the best of it.

And to be honest, over the past few days he'd developed a degree of sympathy for his clothes-horse boss. It was all well and good to throw conspicuous volumes of assets at a problem you had a high probability of solving in a satisfactory manner. When it came to a challenge where success looked uncomfortably like failure – a mole in the system, an assassin fuelled by info from their office – there were definitely strong arguments for keeping things low-key. And it didn't come much lower profile than Macanespie and Proctor, the dead-end kids.

Late morning and Macanespie was on his fourth cup of coffee. At times like this, he wished he still smoked. He'd quit when they'd banned it in the office, mostly because he couldn't be arsed going all the way outside to stand in a huddle of sad fuckers a dozen times a day. But sometimes he yearned for a valid excuse to go and stand outside the office and look at the sky. Anything other than Proctor's miserable gob.

For the dozenth time that morning he checked his Twitter feed. Nothing new of any interest except a link to a voucher for a free cappuccino at his local coffee shop. What was the point of a plastic loyalty card that you had to swipe every time if it didn't register the fact that you only ever drank

Americano with milk? While he was busy doing nothing, he thought he might as well check his email. Again.

But this time there was something new in his inbox. A message from an unfamiliar name but a domain name he recognised. He clicked it open and read, 'Hi Alan. I'm the sucker who agreed to let my software take a look at your girl. Interesting job, thanks for putting it my way. First off, it's definitely a woman. Secondly, it's the same woman. And thirdly, the range of options the software came up with was surprisingly narrow, which suggests to me we might actually have a decent likeness. I've attached the range of five esti-mates. Let me know how it turns out. We're always trying to justify increased funding for the work ... '

Macanespie swallowed hard. He almost didn't want to open the attachment. It was a Schrödinger's Cat moment; until he opened it, it could be a solution or it could be a fresh conundrum. Either result posed its own problems. But he couldn't sit staring at it indefinitely. He had to go for it.

And so he opened the file. At first glance, he thought there must be some mistake. That some real photographs had been mixed in with the e-fit somehow. Three of the five were similar to the person in the other two, but not so sim-ilar that you'd mistake them for each other.

As far as the other two were concerned, there was no doubt in Alan Macanespie's mind. He knew that face. He'd known that face for years. She hadn't made the final cut for a possible mole for two reasons; firstly, she wasn't staff, only working on an ad hoc basis; and secondly, she'd been working on other projects at least some of the time. He licked his suddenly dry lips and looked across at Theo Proctor. 'It's Tessa Minogue.'

Proctor frowned. 'What? Tessa's sent you an email? Why? What's she got to say for herself?'

'No, you're not getting it. I've not got an email from her. I've got the analysis of the CCTV stills back. Come and see for yourself. It's Tessa Minogue. No mistaking her.'

Proctor's chair shot out behind him as he rushed round the desk to check it out. When he saw the screen, he gasped. 'Oh. My. God.' He clapped his hand to his mouth. 'Tessa Minogue. Bang to rights.' And then he turned to Macanespie and grinned. 'Are we heroes, or what?'

46

Karen ran up the stairs to the entrance then had a moment of confusion, made worse by entering a dim interior from bright sunlight. She glanced around hastily, then spotted a curved staircase leading upwards. She hurried up the stairs, dodging past the occasional student. When she emerged in the spectacular space of the Upper Reading Room, she had no eyes for its splendour. All her senses were tuned towards spotting either Maggie Blake or Tessa Minogue trying to make a getaway.

She ran along the gallery, checking every one of the rows of desks aligned like spokes on a wheel from the central hub where the library staff looked at her in appalled astonishment. Before anyone could accost her, Karen started on the next flight of steps. All at once, Maggie Blake practically ran into her arms. She jerked backwards at the sight of Karen, shock apparent on her face. 'There's been a terrible accident,' she blurted out. 'Tessa—'

Karen put a hand out to steady her. 'I know. We need to talk.' She glanced down the stairs, where a librarian was making his determined way towards them. She flashed her ID at him, and said, 'Police business, sir. If you could make sure nobody goes up on the roof?' Then she took Maggie firmly by the arm and led her downstairs.

'I don't understand. What are you doing here? Why are you in Oxford at all, never mind here?'

'All in good time.' Karen kept up their brisk progress till they were back out in the sunshine of Radcliffe Square. Without letting go of Maggie's arm, she walked round the side of the building opposite the crumpled body. A police car was already at the scene. It would soon be time to hand Maggie Blake over to the local officers investigating Tessa's death. But Karen wanted her chance first.

'I can't believe it,' Maggie kept saying. 'One minute we were admiring the view, the next . . .'

Karen could see some café tables and chairs outside the big church at the far end of the square and she steered Maggie towards them. She waited till Maggie was seated and sent Jason a quick text. **Over by church w Prof Blake.** Then she sat opposite her, placing her phone on the table between them. She was about to speak when she had a moment of panic. She knew exactly what to say when she was about to interview someone under caution back home, but what was the English caution? She'd have to rely on her memories of TV crime dramas, which was almost laughable. She cleared her throat and set her phone to record. 'I'm going to record this conversation,' she said. 'It's what's called an interview under caution.' She mentally crossed her fingers and went for it. 'You do not have to say anything. But it may harm your defence if you do not mention when questioned something which you later rely on in court. Anything you do say may be given in evidence. Do you understand that?'

Maggie frowned. 'I understand the words, obviously. But I don't understand why you're saying them. I've just seen my best friend have the most terrible accident and you're talking to me as if I'm a criminal. I don't even know how she is, for God's sake.'

'That is the first expression of concern I've heard from you, Professor Blake. We've come all the way from the upper floor of the library down here to the café terrace at the church and it's taken you till now to ask after your friend.' Karen's tone was dry and crisp.

'I'm in a state of shock, for crying out loud. Like I said, I've just witnessed the most horrible accident. And my best friend could be lying there dead and you won't let me go to her.' The catch in her voice sounded genuine. It would certainly play well in front of a jury, if this ever got that far.

'What were you doing up there with Ms Minogue?'

'How did you know where we were? Why are you here?'

'I know it's a terrible cliché, but right now, I'm asking the

447

questions. Why were you and Ms Minogue on top of the building?'

Maggie tutted and made an impatient gesture with one hand. 'I have a DPhil student who wanted to see the skyline as part of her research. I managed to borrow a key and I thought I'd give Tess the chance to see one of the most spectacular and private views the city has to offer. We went to look at the view, Karen. Why the hell else would we be up there?'

'Because it's a high building with a relatively low parapet. The perfect place for a murder that looks like an accident. Especially when it's payback for a murder that happened on top of a high building with a relatively low parapet.'

Maggie gasped. Karen thought she was laying it on for effect. She considered that the professor's first involuntary response to her words had been a quick flicker of wariness. 'That's a vile thing to say.'

'It's a pretty vile thing to do,' Karen said coolly. She noticed over Maggie's shoulder that an ambulance had arrived along with two more police vehicles. She hoped Jason was holding his own. 'You asked how I knew you were here. I've just come from talking to Dr Simpson. She had some very interesting things to say.'

'Dorothea? Why on earth have you been talking to Dorothea again? What has she got to do with this?'

'Do you remember a few days ago in Croatia when I showed you a list of names? They were the people who were registered in the same wee hotel in Edinburgh as your late husband on the night we presume he was murdered. You remember?'

'Of course I remember.' Maggie's face had assumed a guarded expression, as if she knew it was time to stop hiding behind the appearance of grief and shock. 'And I told you then I didn't recognise any of the names on it.'

'And I didn't believe you. I thought you reacted at one point. I just didn't know whose name had provoked the reaction. So I thought I'd try the list on somebody who knew you and the general pretty well. Somebody whose house you were tenants in. Presumably Dr Simpson was well placed to know who your friends were, who came to the house. That sort of thing. So I ran through the list with her. Can you guess what she told me?'

This time, the shock was real. 'I have no idea,' Maggie said, definitely wary now.

'She told me that your husband's nickname for Tessa Minogue was Ripley, after Ellen Ripley, the character Sigourney Weaver plays in the *Alien* movies. Apparently he called her Ripley because she was so implacable in her fight against war criminals. And the Ellen Ripley on our list gave a fake address. Nostromo Court. *Nostromo*'s the name of the ship in *Alien*, unless I've misremembered.'

Maggie shook her head. 'I never heard him call her that. Dorothea's made a mistake. She's old. She gets things confused. You can't rely on anything she says.'

'Really? I thought she was pretty sharp. And I liked it because it made sense of the bits and pieces of information I've been tripping over in the past few days. The strange woman who turned up in Podruvec because she'd been tipped off about a massacre. The fact that whoever killed those other war criminals – and so, probably the general – had access to information from the tribunal in The Hague. The climbing aspect – I'd already heard that the three of you went hillwalking together. And she kept you very close. So close you'd never have suspected her till I handed you Ellen Ripley. And you knew nobody would ever be able to prove what she'd done. So you became her. You took her to a high place and threw her off.'

Maggie shook her head again. 'You're making it up as you go along. You haven't a shred of evidence for anything you've said. And shall I tell you why you don't have a shred of evidence? Because it didn't happen. Because people like me don't resolve our problems by throwing our friends off tall buildings.'

'You're nothing special, Maggie. You're just like the rest of us when it comes down to basic human instinct. And you'd be amazed what turns up in the way of evidence once we start looking. Take a look around you, Maggie. This place is hoatching with tourists. Every one of them has a camera phone at the very least. What do you think are the chances of you not being caught on somebody's camera?'

Maggie gave her a scornful look. 'I'm a smart woman,

Karen. You think if I had done something as disgusting as you're suggesting that I wouldn't have made sure there were no cameras pointing at me? This is a fantasy. You're stuck with a cold case you can't solve and you're making something up just so you can close the file. Well, that's fine. Close your file. Blame my friend Tessa for killing my husband if that keeps your track record nice and neat. Do what you like. But don't try taking me on. I won't be your scapegoat.'

'You did it, Maggie. It doesn't end here.'

Maggie sighed and pushed her hair back from her face. 'Even if any of it was true, in a moral universe, how could you possibly justify prosecuting me? There's no moral equivalence in any of this sorry story, is there? It reads like a terrible chain letter written in blood and tears. I'm sorry if that sounds melodramatic, but that's how it feels. The sort of cautionary myth we invent to try and persuade people to behave better. But we never do.'

Karen looked past her to the crime scene. Except it wouldn't be a crime scene, she suspected. Maggie would be convincing. There would be nothing to gainsay her account except possibly the curious insistence by an elderly woman on a dead lawyer's nickname. It wasn't the stuff of successful prosecutions. Maggie Blake was going to get away with it. And as she herself had indicated, who was to say that was a bad thing? Karen stood up, suddenly weary, and gestured with her head towards the bustle of emergency service personnel doing their jobs. 'It's not my call anyway. You need to come with me and give the locals your version of events.' She picked up her phone and ostentatiously switched off recording mode.

As she ushered Maggie ahead of her out of the café terrace, she leaned in close and said quietly, 'You never get away with murder. Now you'll find out what Mitja lived with every day of your life together. Welcome to hell, Professor.'

Maggie gave her a startled look. 'You say that like I had a choice,' she said, her voice bitter and cold.

They walked across the square in the incongruous sunshine, two clever women who might have been friends in a different set of circumstances. Karen saw Jason detach himself from the knot of figures inside the crime-scene tape, phone to his ear. He looked around frantically, clearly trying to spot her. She waved to catch his attention. He was hunched oddly over his phone. Then he staggered, as if he'd lost his footing on the cobbles. Easy done, she thought. She'd slipped herself earlier.

Now they were closer and his eyes were fixed on her, pleading. His face was stretched in a grimace. And now he was crying, sobbing like a bereft child. With half her mind, Karen was processing what she was seeing. The other half already knew what it meant. She stopped a couple of feet away from him, oblivious to everything around her. 'He's dead,' she said, knowing it with utter certainty.

Jason gulped. 'He took – he took a heart attack,' he howled.

His words came at her from a distance, a gulf she couldn't cross. She turned away, the centre of a kaleidoscope of colour and a wash of noise. In that moment of catastrophic loss, she comprehended everything. Mitja, Tessa, Maggie. The things we do for love. The things we lose in the process. The foolishness of thinking we can keep the darkness at bay.

With her eyes fixed on the blue sky and the golden stone, Karen Pirie turned her back on all of it and started walking.

Acknowledgements

This book has its roots in the achievements of two very different but equally remarkable and genuinely iconoclastic women – the late Dr Kathy Wilkes, Philosophy Fellow at St Hilda's College, Oxford, and Professor Sue Black, head of the Centre for Anatomy and Human Identification at the University of Dundee.

Kathy was a passionate exponent of the clandestine teaching of philosophy behind the Iron Curtain in the dying years of the Soviet regime. She was caught up in the siege of Dubrovnik and her tireless work on behalf of the city and its inhabitants was recognised with honours from the city and the state of Croatia. There is a square in Dubrovnik that now bears her name. What I have written about the siege and the city relies heavily on Kathy's own writings and our late-night conversations in the aftermath of the 1991–92 Croatian War. She was an extraordinary woman – an inspirational teacher, a challenging intellect and a generous friend.

Sue was the lead forensic anthropologist to the British Forensic Team in Kosovo, deployed by the Foreign and Commonwealth Office on behalf of the United Nations to shine a light on the atrocities committed during the conflict in the 1990s. The integrity and humanity of her leadership is remarkable, and I owe a great deal to the searing honesty of her accounts of her time in Kosovo. I also remain profoundly grateful for her friendship.

Their stories were the starting point for mine – which is entirely fictitious – and I had more help from many other sources. I owe a huge debt to the generosity of Linda McDowell, Professor of Geography at Oxford University; Dr Janet Howarth, Dr Anita Avramides, Maria Croghan and Bronwyn Travers of St Hilda's College, Oxford; Dr Olivia Stevenson of Glasgow University; Angus Marshall, Consultant in Digital Forensics; Mary Miller of Dundee Women's Aid; and Jo Sharp, Professor of Geography at Glasgow, who told me interesting things, fed me delicious meals, continued the quest for the perfect cup of coffee, made me laugh and, along with the indefatigable Leslie Hills, kept the renovation squad at bay. Thanks also to my back-room crew who provide endless support and never let me feel the fear – David Shelley and the Little, Brown team; Anne O'Brien, Jedi copy-editor; Jane Gregory and her girls (and Terry!); Liz Sich and Rachael Young, for making sure the train runs on time; and most of all, the Kid and the Bidie-in.